When The Night Swallowed The Moon

A Standalone Vampire & Werewolf Fantasy Romance

Ophelia Wells Langley

Contents

When The Night Swallowed The Moon by Ophelia Wells Langley

Published by O.W.L. Publications, LLC

www.opheliawlangley.com

Cover by JV Arts

Developmental Edits by Jo Thompson at Unread Story Editing

Copy and Line edits by Shawna Hampton at Magic Words Editing

Formatting by OWL Publications, LLC

ISBN: 979-8-9862973-8-5

Trigger & Content Warnings

This book contains scenes that may depict, mention, or discuss: animal death, anxiety, assault, attempted murder, blood, bones, branding, death, decapitation, depression, emotional abuse, fire, hallucinations, kidnapping, murder, physical abuse, PTSD, adult scenes with sexually explicit material, suicidal ideation, torture, war flashbacks.

If you or someone you know needs help, you can find a list of resources for organizations here: https://beacons.ai/owlish/moreinfo

Dedication

To those who feel like they will never heal, fated to always carry the burden of their trauma...
You deserve to find a love that stays with you through the journey of healing.

SHE WOULD BE HIS DOWNFALL
HE WOULD BE HER SAVING GRACE

Prologue

Once upon a time, in a world full of magic and secrets, there was a beautiful but lonely princess with hair as dark as the night, eyes as bright as the noontime sky, and skin as light as the moon. It was said that she was magical, that she was descended from an ancient fairy people. Rumors swirled that she could talk with the heavens and that flowers sprouted wherever she walked.

But she wasn't always lonely, and she wasn't always a princess. She lived with her widowed mother and her sister on the edge of a small farming village. She loved her sister dearly, and though they shared the same dark hair and ivory-colored skin, her sister's eyes were the shade of emeralds by day and rubies by night—a most peculiar effect that the townspeople scorned. As the sisters grew, so, too, did rumors of the young girls' strangeness. To keep their innocence for as long as she could, their mother moved them into an old, abandoned mill on the outskirts of town.

The widow worked long hours in the fields, harvesting flaxseed to sell the grain at the market; all the while, the girls spent their days building homes for the forest fairies among the standing stones, picking wild berries, and weaving golden crowns from the fields of drying flax. The princess would read to her sister stories full of romances, of noble knights who saved damsels and their passionate declarations of love. Sheltered from the town gossip, the two were none the wiser to their unconventional upbringing.

One day, they found a book in their mother's belongings. The spine was tattered, with lettering that had long since faded away. Inside were stories about standing stones of reverence and power, places where magic waited patiently in the shadows, vast lands filled with humans who could change into any creature they wanted, and demigods who walked the earth. The sisters stayed up late into the night, reciting magical spells, dreaming of handsome princes and brave knights, while their lips and fingers turned purple from the wild berries they ate.

Blissful childhood days turned into months, the months into years, until one day, the princess was no longer a girl. Word spread quickly throughout the towns and villages that she had blossomed into an agreeable young woman. Soon, men from kingdoms near and far were knocking on the wooden door of the mill, asking for her hand in marriage. It wasn't long until a handsome prince swept in and promised she could have whatever her heart desired, so long as he had her hand in marriage. She agreed on the conditions that she could visit her sister and mother, and that a handsome dowry would be left for them in her stead. But no dowry would ever reach her family, and the princess didn't know of the jealous nature of the prince she was to marry.

The prince and princess's wedding was the talk of the year, and no expense was spared for the prince's beautiful new bride. Exotic flowers were imported, and there was food the likes of which the new princess had never heard. Nobles far and wide attended the event, and they complimented the prince on choosing such an exquisite wife. Presents and jewels, dresses and cloaks, and priceless heirlooms spilled out of the rooms set aside for the new couple to live in after the wedding.

When it was over, the new princess asked to visit her family, but the prince had become so besotted with her beauty that jealousy coursed through his veins. He refused to let his new wife out of his sight. Despite her pleading, he would always reply, "It would be unseemly for my wife to visit such a hovel."

The jealous prince forbade her from leaving the castle and traveling to her childhood home, and he placed guards at every corner of the castle to watch her. Despair soon filled her days, and the prince, vowing to cheer up his new bride, showered her with gold, priceless jewels, and hand-stitched dresses that shone like the stars in the sky. And though she looked like the fairy princesses she had read about, she knew no tales would be written of her.

Months passed with still no heir or love born between the newlyweds. All the princess wanted was to see her mother and sister once more, but she was a prisoner in her new home, held against her will, dreaming of life outside of the castle. Slowly, her dreams faded, and the joy she had once felt in a heart that was all too eager for love dried up.

Soon, too, the land shriveled, much as her heart had. A terrible blight swept across it, sickening the crops and spreading disease throughout the kingdom. Once bustling, vibrant trade routes turned quiet and solemn, and markets that had been full of life now whistled as the winds swept through empty stalls. The lucky few left alive packed their things to move on to greener pastures, happily forgetting the pain they left behind.

Soon, the affliction leached up from the land and into the souls of those who had stayed behind. The sickness escaped no one, and eventually, the royal family fell ill. As the bells rang to notify the land that the castle had succumbed to a lifeless fate, lightning lit the sky in veins of silver.

And so it was that night the princess fled on the back of a horse.

While the people mourned the loss of their prince, a strange evil brewed in the darkness beyond the castle walls. It stalked the nights on a horse with eyes as red as smoldering coal and a mane as black as tar. The Ominous One sought out those close to death, offering them a reprieve from their pain in exchange for part of their soul.

The dead and dying lay in the bones of old homes while the princess pushed her horse farther and faster under lightning that webbed across pitch-black skies. All was darkness in these forgotten towns. No fires burned in the fireplaces, no lights shone in windows, no one stirred inside. Only the Ominous One moved within the ghostly halls, seeking, searching, yearning. But, time and again, the Ominous One would leave a town feeling hollow and unsatisfied—the souls too far gone for his saving. And, time and again, his anger—and his appetite—would grow.

The princess rode past the devastated fields of crops, past the derelict houses, and past the decaying bodies, driven by her only desire: to make it home. And as she passed the last house on the outskirts of the town she used to call home, her horses' hooves thundering against the cobblestone road, the Ominous One stepped from underneath the eaves.

Inside the old mill, with its leaky roof and creaking stairs, herbs drying from the rafters, and broken shutters barely able to constrain the storm to the outside, the mother cradled the sister, bedridden and delirious from a fever that had lasted for weeks.

'I have tried everything,' the mother whispered, tears streaming down her face. 'But she is so weak.'

The princess fell to her knees at the foot of her sister's bed, cursing the stars above and the hellfire below for not being brave enough to leave the castle sooner. As her curses turned to tears, the princess knew she would do anything to keep her sister alive. She climbed into the bed, refusing the siren call of sleep until, at last, she could no longer keep her eyes open.

Soon, the house grew quiet, every living creature within its crumbling walls tucking in for the night. All that was left awake was the shifting wind, beating on the shutters, ushering in a new era of despair as the Ominous One closed in on the tiny, run-down old mill.

The Ominous One, eager for the living creatures that

were so close, kept watch from the edge of the dying forest. It wasn't until the sun crested the mountains in the distance that the Ominous One knocked on the door with a request and a black bag jingling with coins.

'You will not enter, you will never own us,' the mother said, refusing to take what the Ominous One offered. Her bleary-eyed stare was firm as the sigils on the wood of the door glimmered with defiance.

The Ominous One hissed, unused to meeting such resistance. 'You have until the sun sets. I will return for her then.'

The tar-black horse whinnied as the Ominous One mounted, and it turned the horse toward the protection of the trees. They blended into the long shadows that formed before daylight struck.

'Come,' the mother whispered, waking the sleeping princess carefully. 'We must talk.'

And so they did.

That morning, as the rain fell from the sky, so, too, did words from the widow's mouth. She told her daughter that the fairy stories the princess had read as a child had all been real, lessons and incantations and spells crafted carefully by their own mother, and her mother before her, and her mother before her, should a time like this one come to pass.

So the mother and the princess gathered dried herbs into a satchel, along with a lantern and a blade, and carried the sister with the emerald eyes down the stairs and to the stone clearing.

Sheets of rain poured forth from the sky, but the

standing stones shone in the distance, giants guarding a deeper secret from the mortals in this world.

The Ominous One stood at the old mill's doorstep, while the princess laid her sister down in the center of the stone ring.

The princess drew the blade across her palm, while the sigils on the old mill's door singed the exposed skin of the Ominous One.

The Ominous One assaulted the windows and the doors of the old mill, trying to get past the protective sigils, while the princess called upon the old magic with her mother's careful incantations.

The princess screamed as she ripped open the sky before her and pulled forth the damp earth from an unknown land beyond, while the Ominous One roared into the downpour, unwilling to accept defeat.

The Ominous One yanked on the reins of the black steed, while the princess hefted her sister's arm over her shoulder.

The princess squeezed the emerald-eyed sister and pressed a final kiss on her cheek before shoving her through the rift, while the Ominous One kicked the red-eyed horse into a gallop so their souls could finally be his.

The world snapped shut. Thunder roared overhead. Wind wailed through the dead trees. The standing stones shook. The princess fell to her knees, and the mother looked on as hundreds of small white flowers sprouted wherever the princess's tears fell, the purity of her pain transmuting the soaked soil. The old magic had returned, and the Ominous One had seen it all.

And as the Ominous One crested the hill, having shuffled through the shifting sludge, the whipping winds, and the lethal lightning strikes, the magic within the circle broke. The rain never ceased, even when the land rumbled in agony as the stones began to shatter.

The mother would not lose another child. So as rocks flew in the air, she dragged the princess from the circle. One rock struck the mother in the back of the head, and she tumbled down the hill, taking the princess with her.

The princess slipped from her mother's grasp and slid down the muddy embankment, landing at the base of an ancient willow tree. Its roots curled around her, protecting the princess from the flying debris as the old magic of the earth finished wiggling its way into the princess's grief-stricken heart.

The storm cleared, and the forest was still. The aftermath of the stones' self-destruction was not yet known when the Ominous One knelt beside the princess.

It is said that after the dead of winter, white snowdrops are the princess's tears, and the keening sound you hear in the middle of the night before a storm strikes is the princess mourning the fate of her beloved sister.

And so it was that the lonely princess, who had once known the amber warmth of a mother's love, who had once known the honeyed laughter of a sister while they played in the golden flax fields, became one with the darkness.

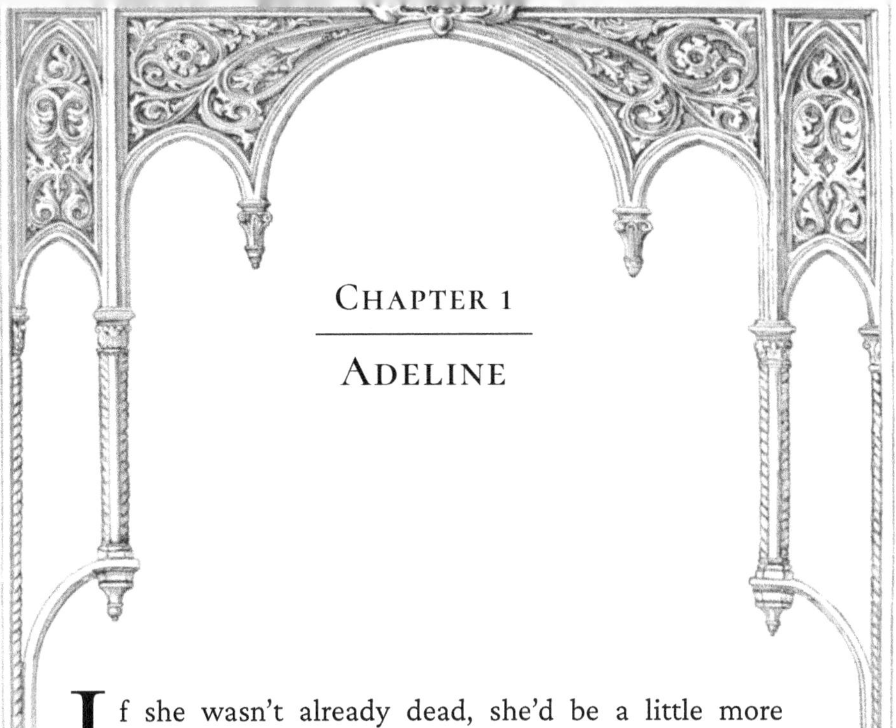

Chapter 1

Adeline

If she wasn't already dead, she'd be a little more worried about her fingers turning blue. Or that she couldn't feel anything from her knees down, or that her face was so cold it felt frozen in place. Since when did snow always fall at such an alarming rate, anyway?

What a preposterous question, Adeline. You know the weather always acts differently up here.

It was useless looking for a dead man, but even though it had been a hundred years, she knew she would find him. It was just a matter of when. It was all she had ever wanted: to know what happened, why he had disappeared, if he was still alive. Under the guise of hunting for were-shifters, Adeline had also been able to track down enough information to find him. Hunting for were-shifters was her way of eliminating her maker's threat to rule, and the only thing she could think of to keep her search alive.

She shook the snow from her shoulders and tucked her hands under her arms. Flakes of white swirled in front of her, clinging to her lashes and blotting out the rest of the world. The earth tilted precipitously on its axis, and she stumbled several times, landing on her knees. Hardly anything made Adeline feel sick anymore, but this was almost too much. The wind blew viciously, and if she hadn't covered her face from the nose down mere minutes ago, she would probably have felt like she was suffocating from icy fingers clawing down her throat.

Was she walking downhill, or up? East, or west? Either way, her skin tingled. And not from the cold, either. The sun was rising, and if she didn't find a food source and somewhere to rest, it wouldn't matter where she ended up because she'd be too weak to fend anyone off.

Her steps faltered, and she slowed her movements to a crawl, almost resigned to meeting her fate. But she hadn't come this far to give up now. This storm wouldn't best her, of that she was determined. She fumbled at the pouch at her waist, her frozen fingers grappling at the glass bottles inside. Finally, she withdrew one; the substance it contained had long dried out. Never once had she needed to resort to the concoction within it. But when she popped the cork and held it up to her nose, a vile scent emanated from the tiny container. She chucked it into the snowstorm, happy to be rid of whatever it held. Her free hand reached into the pouch and fondled the remainder of the bottles with the same dried-out, dark ruddy-brown color.

Useless. It was all useless. The world tilted once more, a violent spin on its axis as the sky dumped even more snow around her, and she scrambled to stay upright. Bile crept up her throat, but if she stopped now, there was no way she would get back up.

Gods damnit, she had to be close. Her research had led her this far, even with the impossible weather. And she had to find the creature before anyone else did, if only so she could understand what kind of a mess she had gotten herself into.

There came an ever-so-brief break in the storm, and suddenly, before her stood an enormous forest. Within the depths of the ancient trees, there was the faintest yellow glimmer of a lantern in a window. Her heart soared as the swirling white flakes picked back up. She locked her eyes on the faint light ahead, determined to meet her fate there instead of out in the wilds.

Could this be the place she had spent decades searching for? Hope soared in her chest, but she willed it to be quiet, unused to fate ever acting in her favor. The final linchpin in her plans for freedom, and she was worried that it would slip right through her frozen fingers. The hunt for this were-shifter had taken her all over the country. She had been tracking this specific creature for so long that the serendipity of the moment was not lost on her. Once she killed the final shifter, she would be free of her maker, free to continue her heart's search of the last century—Colin.

She was almost certain that this was the creature's home—all of the pieces she'd put together across her journey had led her to these mountains. This forest. And if it wasn't? Well, whoever was inside was in for quite a treat.

Though her boots were soaked, her pants coated with ice, and her woolen cloak practically useless, Adeline trudged forward. Just the thought of someone inside that tiny little cabin kept her moving. Perhaps whoever was there would provide her with willing sustenance. Adeline took a few tentative steps up the porch; the wind whipped her cloak around her legs, and it snagged on a beam. She tugged at it, tearing a hole in the material as she made her way to the front door. She raised her fist and knocked, weakly at first, and then somehow, she summoned up the strength to knock louder.

Perhaps no one was home. But then why would they leave a lantern in the window? She would never understand these mountain folk. They all seemed so backward to her, living in some of the harshest environments to do what, trap animals and skin them for money, or cut down centuries-old trees?

She tried the handle. It wasn't locked, but the door did feel a little stuck. Leaning her shoulder against the wood, she shoved—hard. It swung open, and the cold air propelled her into the tiny log cabin. Adeline spun around and shoved her body weight against the back of the door, and tiny though she might have been, she was one of the strongest vampires in her coven. Finally, with a groan and a creak, the door shut, leaving her standing inside the quiet, empty cabin.

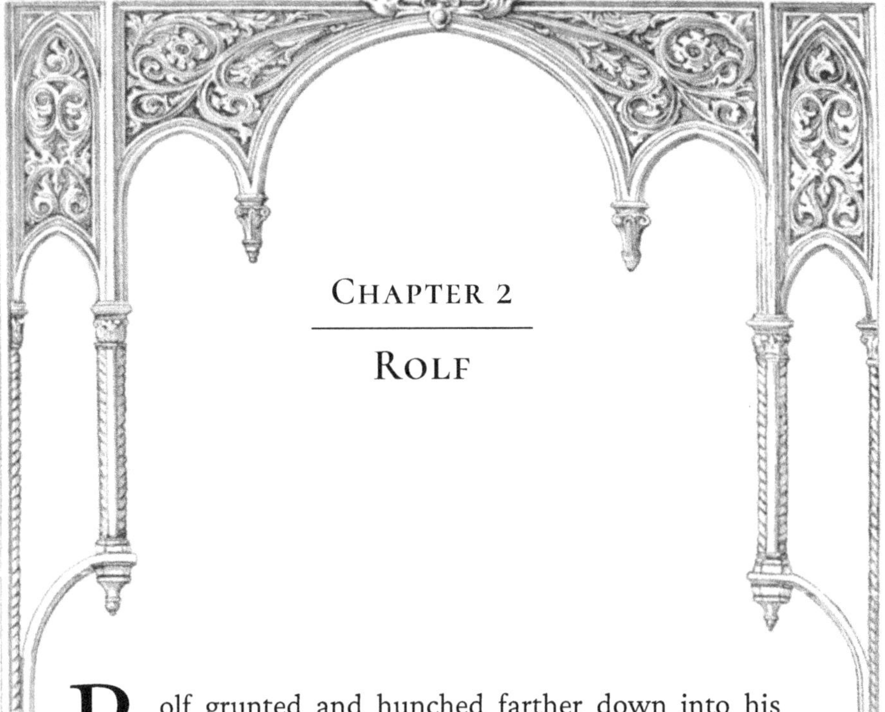

Chapter 2

Rolf

Rolf grunted and hunched farther down into his thick wool overcoat. After living here for decades, he knew better than to move during a whiteout in these mountains. The ground could shift so quickly that he'd be taken downhill within moments, another victim of an avalanche.

From the rock outcropping, he watched as a tiny black speck moved slowly toward his cabin. Stumbling and falling, but still, they made their way ever closer to his home. Their scent carried on the wind, and he knew whoever it was wasn't human. But what were they doing this far north, and in these conditions?

Nestled in a valley among large conifers in an ancient evergreen forest, and well out of the path of an avalanche, the cabin had withstood all kinds of weather. He had known not to be too careless when finding a place to settle down. When he first arrived in these woods, he had known many men who had died in these mountains.

Avalanches would often sweep away large swaths of land, taking anything in its path down into the valley below. Perfectly preserved bodies turned up once the snow melted. Their faces locked in a perpetual scream of terror, the scream they made as the white waves swallowed them whole and stole their last breaths.

How unusual. To have a storm this forceful at this time of year.

Shivering, he pulled his arms closer to his body. The speck entered the tree line and was lost to the shadows beneath the boughs, and he knew they would find his cabin. He lifted his nose to the sky, smelling the precipitation riding on the next wave of the storm. Once there was a break, he'd have to move quickly, make it down the mountainside, and back home before it picked back up again.

The snow slowed briefly at the same time the wind did, and he launched forward. With his axe held tightly in one hand, he bolted downhill on his wooden ski shoes. Fellow loggers had shown him the invention some years back, and he loved how the shoes allowed him to float on top of the thickest snowfalls. He figured it was the closest he would ever feel to flying, and each time he soared downhill, he couldn't help smiling like the biggest fool as the biting wind cut into his skin.

His cabin nearing, Rolf slowed to a gentle crawl and then to a stop at the almost-buried woodshed. He unbuckled his shoes as quietly as he could and slid softly into the calf-deep snow so his feet wouldn't crunch. Frozen mud and shuffling tracks led up to his door, and the scent of a woman was almost lost completely in the wind, but not quite. Gooseflesh crawled along the back of his neck in warning as his eyes dashed around the small deck on the front of the house. Some of her clothing had snagged on a splinter of a post, leaving behind a few tendrils of cloth. He noted that the deck's supports needed to be sanded down and stained again before the posts were buried in the snow. Rolf had hoped he would have another month until a snow like this one would fall, but alas, it seemed true winter had set in.

He plucked the threads from the splintered wood and held them up to his nose. He inhaled, and images flashed before his eyes—summer by the river, wildflowers in bloom, the tang of copper as rain pattered on smooth cobblestone roads. A tinge of magic floated around him, and it was as he'd thought: she was not human. Rolf's jaw dropped open, and he inhaled once more. This time, he picked up hints of something else, but it was too faint. Within moments, the images were gone, replaced instead by a sinking feeling in his stomach. He tightened his grip on his axe. With his free hand, he reached toward the handle.

Snowflakes swirled at his back as the door flew open, smacking into the wall with a bang. Ushered in by the gusts of cold air, Rolf had steeled himself to meet the stranger in his dwelling when his breath caught in his lungs.

Silhouetted by the warm glow of embers in the fireplace, a short, curvy woman stood in the center of his cabin. He couldn't see her face, but his nose confirmed she was not human. If she were fae, there were only two kinds that she could be, and neither of them he wanted in his cabin. Or his woods.

"Good evening," he shouted over the roar of the wind.

He had survived this long in these mountains by keeping his wits about him and would continue to do so. No stranger would catch him off guard, especially not this close to the changing. He grappled for the handle and slammed the door closed, and the walls of his cabin shook with the force. Rolf dropped the axe, but kept it within reach.

She turned away from the fire and faced him. Her bright blue eyes sliced right through him, and it took everything he had to look unfazed at the lethality that rolled off her in waves. She was dangerous, but gods, she was gorgeous.

Her leather boots, once a light brown, were now almost black from trudging through the snow. She wore a riding habit with trousers—the cut and quality of the fabric indicated she came from nobility.

But hunting? Out here? It was out of place for the wealthy women who lived in the larger cities to wear such a garment unless they were on a hunt. The hunter's moon neared, and usually excursions had ended by then. And even though it snowed often in the mountains, the intensity of this storm was unusual this time of year.

Her woolen cloak hung off her shoulders, and thawing ice dripped into puddles on his wooden floor. The wet fabric stuck to her body, clinging in places that showed off her curves. With thicker thighs and calves, she stood like she was used to being in charge. In charge of what, he didn't want to entertain, but with the finery she wore, she was someone who would be missed.

Whoever she was and wherever she came from, Rolf didn't want to find out. This was his cabin, in his woods, in his part of the mountains. It had been decades since he had anyone even close to his home, and her presence now rankled him. He liked his solitary life.

But the mountains had a way of forcing your hand. He hadn't spent years out here alone without learning that this place would always find a way to teach what you most needed to know. Still, he couldn't take any risks, not this week. He would make sure she was warmed up and fed and then sent on her way.

Quickly.

His voice sounded gruffer than he remembered when he finally asked, "Whom do I have the pleasure of hosting?"

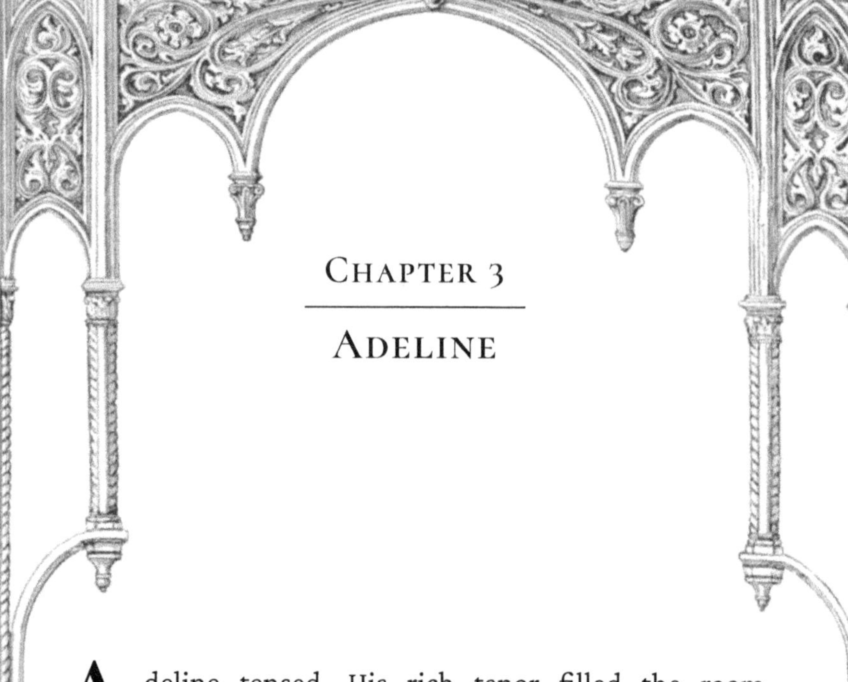

Chapter 3

Adeline

Adeline tensed. His rich tenor filled the room, igniting something primal deep inside her chest.

She shook her head, drops of water sprinkling onto the floor. Flexing her fingers at her side, she felt the prickling of her nerves as the feeling returned to her hands.

His body heat radiated across the space, and her skin prickled with anticipation. After centuries of needing to be an expert at reading rooms and situations, she cursed herself for her weakness in this moment. Would he turn her back out into the cold? She could withstand it, of course, but it wouldn't be pleasant, and the gods only knew what would happen if she had to go back out there in this state.

Maybe he'll take pity on me.

There had been a few times in her immortal life when she had used her feminine wiles against the weaker sex. Men tended to fall for her traps of seduction and helplessness far easier than women. But this time, she couldn't leave anything up to chance. If she was going to lie to him, she needed to believe it so fully that no part of her would give away the lie, because his eyes scrutinized every little movement she made.

Broad-shouldered and brooding, he was easily a foot taller than she was. Even leaning casually against the door, his posture was stiff, as if he were readying himself for a fight. His face was half-covered by a bushy black beard, and his expression remained passive, though his eyes were dark amber orbs that watched her every move. Longer, shaggy hair fell around his face, curling at the ends, snow melting from it.

Adeline's eyes flicked to the vein at his neck as he swallowed. Pressing her lips together, she fought against the urge to lunge and bite the man's neck. Because, though any other woman should be afraid to be alone in a cabin in the woods during a snowstorm with a strange man, she felt a little thrill knowing she could easily overpower him despite his size and bulk.

"I apologize for intruding," she said, her voice demure. The man crossed his arms over his chest, his forearms flexing underneath his jacket. Her mouth watered as the tips of her fangs came in. She swallowed a few times before continuing, hoping the pause added to her ruse of distress and would also hide her growing lisp as her fangs fought to emerge fully. "I had already been walking for days when the storm hit."

If she played her cards right, not only would this man let her weather the storm, but she might even be able to feed off him and get her strength back. And then, only then, would she continue her hunt. It would be no use hunting the vampire's enemy if she couldn't even keep her eyes open.

She looked the man up and down once more. He had a vaguely familiar face, but she couldn't quite place it.

The likelihood that he was the were-shifter seemed small, at best. After all, her research had told her to find ancient dwarf caves along the eastern face of these mountains. She was too far north, still, and this was merely a convenient—and necessary—stop along the way. Three days out from the full moon meant that her time was limited, but she was certain she would find the were-shifter after she was able to rest for a bit.

She just needed to keep her guise up long enough, even if she couldn't stop the thrill of the hunt that itched in her veins. That annoying, tempting, delectable pulsing of his hot blood threatened to expose her too early. With a final, forceful swallow, despite her mouth being as dry as the desert lands in the south, her fangs finally receded.

Tread carefully.

Adeline shivered as the rest of her body started to warm back up. She kept her arms loose at her sides despite the desire to reach up and touch her neck as she eyed the axe resting against his leg. It glinted in the soft glow, the steel edge sharp enough to make her wary.

The man dropped his arms, tucking his hands into his pockets. The shuffling of fabric brought her back into the moment.

I am so *tired.* Her eyelids fluttered, and her stomach rumbled.

His gruff voice raked down her spine. "Walking for days?"

"Yes." Adeline turned away from him, drawn toward the warmth of the fire. She held out her icy hands and hummed as the flames eased away the purpling color in her fingertips, but her ears were tuned to every minuscule movement behind her. She wouldn't be a renowned killer if she let her defenses down. "We were crossing into the lower mountains when our carriage was attacked by some highwaymen."

That was not entirely the truth, but it was for the best that she did not elaborate. The simpler the lie, the easier it was to believe. And, besides, he didn't need to know every little detail. At least, not yet. Not until she got a better read on him.

"You're quite far from the pass." The floorboards creaked underneath his shifting weight. She kept her body relaxed—she wouldn't attack unless it was necessary. He added, "It's been decades since there have been problems with rogues attacking."

Slowly, she turned and met his eyes. He was tight-lipped and looked unconcerned. As he shifted his weight, he favored his left side. Her eyes flicked to where the axe now hung loosely from his grip, then she found his amber-colored eyes once more. They bored into her with quiet indifference, but Adeline knew something else brewed underneath his calm exterior.

"I wouldn't know." She tried to sound unconcerned about the holes he was poking in her defense. Adeline refused to let her nerves get the best of her, especially since her glamour wouldn't work in her weakened state. "I have never been this far north before."

"Hmm." He nodded. The man pushed off the door,

then walked to the fireplace. He grabbed a few logs and squatted in front of the embers. First, he stacked the wood in the center of the grate, and the corded muscles in his forearms flexed as he next tucked some kindling in the middle of the stack. He inhaled, and she was transfixed by his wide shoulders while he blew a few times until the flames caught.

Adeline held her breath, knowing that the next few minutes would decide her fate. This forest was the last place on the continent that she hadn't hunted. She hadn't come this far and come so close to catching her prey to bungle things up. The thought of his life source filling her sent her stomach into a wild churning. If she acted carelessly now, it would ruin her chances of besting her maker once and for all. She went through her mental list once more: kill the were-shifters, earn her freedom, find Colin.

Simple.

The world tilted, and her vision blurred as the seconds stretched into minutes. If she didn't find a safe haven soon, she would have to tear into his neck. And she certainly wasn't about to drain her only life source while the storm raged on outside, for gods knew how long.

Fuck. Her fangs elongated despite her best efforts to keep them at bay. She hated relying on man's cantankerous nature.

Chapter 4

Rolf

Rolf blew on the embers, and the fire roared to life with each breath. The flames crackled and leaped in front of his face, and he sniffled a few times as his nose thawed.

The woman was lying. Never had he ever met a worse liar. Not even the highwaymen were this transparent.

The only part he knew to be true was that she had walked for days. Why she was walking, he'd ask her later. But until then, where else was she supposed to go? She would freeze lest he provide her some reprieve. Besides, if what she said had any inkling of truth and the vagrants were back, despite how hard he'd worked to keep them away from his woods—yes, *his* woods—then he didn't want anyone out there in this storm with a chance of running into them. But something told him the highwaymen should be the ones afraid of running into her.

And she should be afraid of me.

She emanated a wariness that his baser senses felt, and as the storm raged outside, he knew the chances of her getting out of here, down the mountains, and to the village before the snow got too thick for anyone to move lessened by the hour. It was one of the reasons he had ended up here, in these mountains, in these woods. He'd fled into the most unforgiving part of the country, where ancient fae used to roam, wishing he could fade into the folklore instead of being hunted down wherever he went.

Fuck.

He didn't want anyone here; it was the whole reason why he chose to live here in the first place. But if she was going to be stuck here, he figured he should know who he was sharing his shelter with.

The woman cleared her throat, and it shook him from his thoughts.

"I thought, perhaps, that I could weather the storm here?" she asked, impatiently tapping her foot. The floor creaked beneath her shifting weight, and he wondered how long he could draw this out. Would she break down and tell him what he needed to hear if he pretended not to listen to her?

Rolf shoved another log onto the fire, watching as the bark sparked and the flames licked the wood's crevices, and then stood up slowly. Grunting, he turned to the beautiful stranger.

"I don't see that there's much of a choice." He jerked his chin toward the window. Despite the sun rising on the horizon, the storm clouds kept the world blanketed within their depths.

She nodded, swaying slightly. Her eyes fluttered, trying to close despite her efforts to focus on him. Rolf stepped forward and grabbed her arms to help her balance. Her hair came undone with the jerky motions of her body, and the scent of amber and petrichor enveloped him. A part growl, part hum started deep in his chest as he inhaled her scent once more. Her eyes snapped up to meet his, and then he was lost within the icy blue of her stare, tumbling deep into the cool depths of her gaze.

Danger! Danger! the voice in the back of his head screamed. He wanted to ignore it and stare at her for the rest of the evening. When was the last time he had met a woman so captivating and dangerous and secretive and...

She flipped her hair over her shoulder, and that's when he finally saw the tops of her ears.

His breath hitched, and the hair on the back of his neck rose. *Vampire.*

He had been right; she wasn't human, but the lack of sharp points at the tips of her ears indicated she was a subset of the fae. One of the powerful undead who fed off others' blood. The sun would rise soon, and she was still standing, albeit almost delirious, and perhaps that was why she needed a place to rest so desperately.

"You're freezing," he rasped, hoping his shock at the revelation of what she was would stay hidden. How in the hell did a vampire find his cabin? He steeled his emotions, locking them up tight. The last thing he needed was a vampire asking him questions—about anything. "Here."

Ever the gentleman, Rolf guided her to a small chair, placed it near the fire, and helped her sit in it. His code of honor told him that, even though he had a vampire under his roof, she was still a woman in need of shelter, and who was he to force her back outside in these conditions?

"You may stay the night," he said, reluctance weighing on his shoulders like a bad decision. "But after you are rested, you must leave."

"Thank you," she sighed. She sagged into the seat, her eyelids heavy with exhaustion. Her hands fumbled with the laces of her shoes, but her fingers were stiff. "Do you mind?"

Rolf nodded and knelt to help her untie the boots. He swallowed nervously and tried to calm his heart so she could not tell he was worried about being so near her.

This was the closest he had gotten to one of her kind since he had beheaded two of them with his axe over a decade ago. He had found the pair slowly draining a helpless halfling fae. It had been easy to behead them as they were distracted; otherwise, he would have been dead within moments. Vampires were unnaturally fast and strong, able to use a magic that other fae did not have. He had been so blind with rage, so intent on making sure their heads were wholly separated from their bodies, that he forgot to see where the halfling had gone and if it needed any medical attention. It took him the rest of the day to track down the poor fellow, and by the time he got there, the halfling's wounds had been so severe that he eventually succumbed to death.

The woman's fingers grazed his, and her skin was so cold to the touch that he worked even faster to get her feet free. With a tug, the boots slid off, and he placed them near the fire to dry. As he turned around, he saw the woman had slumped against the back of the chair, asleep. Or unconscious. Either way, he was relieved she wasn't awake anymore.

Mumbling under his breath to the sleeping figure, he said, "I hope you don't mind, miss. I'm not about to let you freeze. But I can't let a killer such as yourself be in my home without some form of protection."

She slumped forward onto his shoulder with a sigh as he scooped her into his arms. He strode to the back corner of his cabin, where a curtain hung from the ceiling. Pushing it aside, he laid her on his bed. Her outer garments were soaked, so he carefully removed her riding pants and jacket, taking care to keep his gaze on the more modest parts of her body.

After all, he was a gentleman, and certain things would not be proper. Even if she were a deadly creature, and could sink her teeth into his neck.

He stood up, and his hand wrapped around his throat as he wondered if the bite of a vampire was painful.

She moaned and curled in on herself, her toes purple. A few thick woolen blankets were hanging off the edge of the bed, so he tucked them around the rest of her body, making sure the thin cotton shift and half corset she still wore weren't as wet as the other items.

As he stood there, watching her relax under the weight of the blankets, he wondered how long vampires needed to sleep to get their strength back up. And when she woke, would she be strong enough to overtake him? He was unsure how long a vampire needed to sleep, and he had no idea how strong she would be. She was short, to be sure, but the way she had held herself, even delirious and hypothermic, gave him pause.

She's used to being in charge. He ran his hands through his hair and pulled, wishing he could shake the feeling of regret that he had made the wrong decision. He should have thrown her back out into the snow like the trash her kind was.

Rolf had a few silver chains stashed away under his bed. Quietly, he got down on his knees and swept his arm underneath until he felt the burlap sack graze his fingers. Dragging it out slowly, careful not to make the chains clink, he unwound them and wrapped one strand around the base of the bed and then her ankles. Each time he lifted her foot or the chains clanged, he cringed and froze, watching to see if she woke. But she slept soundly.

Like the dead. He chuckled to himself darkly, but he was relieved that it appeared she was such a sound sleeper.

He slid the remaining chain over her midsection, slipping the fire poker between two links to connect them, and hoped it would hold so he could get some sleep.

Then Rolf pulled the curtain back, grabbed his axe and the large bear fur from the wall, and settled in near the hearth.

He woke every hour to keep the fire roaring with fresh wood. Each time the vampire sighed in her sleep, he would sit up, his heart pounding in his chest, his hand instinctively reaching for his axe.

After he had settled down on this mountain, he spent decades chasing out the vampires who entered these sacred woods. After a while, they stopped coming, and his life was one of relative peace. It was yet another reason in his long list why he chose to stay here. He was unbothered and enjoyed being alone—no one to hurt, no way to be found.

The muted midday sun cast an otherworldly glow through the storm that raged outside. It still hadn't stopped, and he guessed there was easily two feet of snow on the ground now. His stomach rumbled, and he chided himself for not filling up his pantry before yesterday. He glanced at his kitchen, curious about what kind of food the woman would eat.

But then his hand drifted to the back of his neck.

Of course.

He would need to get provisions before the door to the root cellar was completely buried. Besides, having a vampire within these walls meant he would need to keep up his strength. He checked the links of the chain around her one last time before he slipped outside.

The root cellar was in an old mine shaft, leftover from when the dwarves ruled these mountains. Toward the end of the tunnel, it had caved in, and the fallen rock shone with remnants of ancient pick strikes. The dwarves were rumored to have been extinct for centuries, but occasionally, when he had a long day in the forest and was trudging home, exhaustion filling his bones, he would see shadows out of the corners of his eye. Rolf liked to think that they fled farther into the mountains, happy to be reclusive and to fade into history as part of the folklore.

He brushed off several feet of snow and yanked the cellar door open, the scent of earth assaulting his nose. His stomach grumbled again, and he eagerly filled a sack with some dried garlic greens, potatoes, carrots, onions, a heel of hard cheese, a handful of dried fruit, and some cured sausage. Stepping back out into the swirling white, he saw that several more inches of snow had almost covered his tracks.

An old rabbit skittered by, his back leg broken. The animal struggled to leap in the snow drifts, seeming almost resigned to its fate. His fur was coated in balls of snow, and he could barely keep his blue eyes open. The snow hare gave one long, lingering look at Rolf, as if begging for mercy.

Just like another blue-eyed creature had, hours before. Rolf took a few lumbering steps and scooped up the exhausted creature, tucking it under his arm.

Rolf reached his cabin and pressed his ear to the door, hoping she was still asleep. He knew going back inside would be futile if she was awake and the restraints had failed. When he was satisfied that she was still asleep, he pushed the door open. The vampire still slept, the chains held, and he breathed a sigh of relief.

After assessing the break in its leg, he put the old rabbit into a makeshift cage and went to work chopping the vegetables. The rabbit thumped and whimpered a few times but calmed as soon as Rolf put a few scraps of food in the cage. Then he proceeded to make a quick pot of stew over the fire. He sliced off some sausage and cheese, careful not to eat it all yet, because only the gods knew how long they would be trapped here.

The woman mewled in her sleep, shaking Rolf from his thoughts. Slowly, he undid the chains and tucked them back under his bed. Then he dragged his chair over to where she slept, wondering what troubled her to make her sleep so restlessly while he whittled a shaft of wood into a sharp point.

Chapter 5

Adeline

Blurred faces and watered-down images plagued her unconscious mind, which was odd since she hadn't dreamt much of anything since she had turned.

Part of her loathed it, the languidness with which memories, feelings, and desires blended in her mind. There was a reason she had enjoyed the dreamless sleep that came with being a vampire. It made everything slightly more tolerable when you were immortal if your sleep was a void—a calm numbness instead of wrought with the pendulum of human emotions. It certainly made what she did for her coven endurable.

The hazy pictures played out in her head, as if she watched her countless past lives from a distance. Memories hovered just out of reach—reminders of what it meant to pass as a mortal century after century and remain unchanging.

Then it was a warm summer evening, and she was walking arm in arm with a faceless person who smelled like... smelled like what? She couldn't tell, but she knew it was familiar, comfortable. Each time she turned her head to see who it was, the face would blur and the details would blend, like an artist swiping away at their canvas. The faceless person disappeared, replaced with the muted sounds of crowds chanting as soldiers returned home. But none of them had the face she searched for. None of them was the human she longed for.

Even while asleep, frustration built up inside her chest like a pebble in her shoe, uncomfortable and unwilling to be shaken out. She tossed and turned, her body refusing to relax until the sun went down. Even then, she could not wake until well into the evening hours from sheer exhaustion and lack of sustenance. The calm, distant beat of a heart finally roused her from her repose. A tiny voice whispered in the back of her head that there was warm blood within her reach, and she could easily feed for days off the hulking mass of the woodsman's muscle.

Her ears prickled with the other sounds that filtered through her haze. A shuffling in a chair. The soft *chhh-chhh-chhh* of a knife scraping against wood. The crackling of logs on a fire, the deep, even breathing of the strange man from the night before.

Her eyes flew open. She was staring at a rough-hewn log, thin shavings of the bark still clinging to the surface. Her eyes traced the crisscross pattern of wooden logs stacked one upon the other, up to where the ceiling met the wall.

"Good evening, vampire."

She froze. How did he...?

"I trust you slept well." His voice cascaded down her

back, crawling along her spine. It spread warmth down her toes.

Adeline rolled over, letting some of the blankets fall surreptitiously from her chest. Well practiced in the art of seduction, she would have him wrapped around her finger in no time. And then maybe she would get some answers. But the man's eyes stayed firmly on the piece of wood as he whittled away, unbothered by her movements. Either he was extremely daft to be so careless in front of her, or...

"I did, thank you," she finally replied. Her throat was sore, and she swallowed a few times to remove the raspiness beneath her tone. She opened her mouth to speak again, but he cut her off.

"You're thirsty." It was a statement, a gruff one at that. And still, his eyes did not meet hers. "You need blood."

He had already called her out for what she was. Who was she to evade the truth? Well, part of it anyway.

"Yes," she answered. She sat up and looked around the room. Her clothes hung from a rack attached to the ceiling, freshly washed and dried. Her boots had been cleaned and polished and rested near the fireplace. The man had changed from his thick wool outer clothing to plain cotton trousers and a relaxed linen shirt. She ran her tongue along the edges of her teeth, eager to sink them into some flesh. Her eyes flicked to his neck and then his forearms. He flexed, and the veins in his arms pulsed, tempting her to lose the very fine hold she had on her control. "I will not ask you to offer any. You've been far too kind as it is."

He snorted. His dark honey-colored eyes flashed with some unknown emotion that warmbloods feel. And even though her heart typically beat slowly, she felt it thump against her chest a little more rapidly.

"I was not going to offer it, vampire."

She nodded. "Understood."

Adeline swung her legs over the side of the bed, and her feet touched the cool floor. She shivered, despite her best efforts to appear reserved, and wrapped her arms around her middle. Outside, the snow piled ever higher. Perhaps it was her imagination, but the wall of snow that fell from the sky made it feel like she was being crushed to death.

Her borrowed time was running out. She had used every last resource she could to find the were-shifter before the sanguine full moon, but had ended up here instead. She almost cursed out loud at the ridiculousness of it all.

An intense snowstorm was enough to get her off track? With mere days left before her bargain ended, Adeline could have sworn the gods were working against her. Again.

The thought of her coven—or even her maker—being concerned almost had her running out the door without any form of sustenance. They were used to not hearing from her for weeks or months, but this time around? Yes, they would be looking, especially since she was supposed to come back with the prized were-shifter.

Her eyes skirted the room, and it wasn't until she saw a tiny cage in the back of the cabin, with a cloth draped over the top, that she picked up on the faintest pulsing of a tiny heart.

A rabbit?

"A rabbit," he said at the same time the image danced in her head.

Don't be a fool.

He wasn't reading her mind.

Adeline frowned and looked at him skeptically. He wouldn't offer his blood, but he would offer up a helpless creature?

"An old one," he continued. "With a broken leg. Certainly not long for this world. He would not make it home in the storm that is currently raging outside."

She tilted her head, her brow still creased in disbelief. "For me?"

"For you." He nodded his head over his shoulder at the cage.

She didn't know why, but her stomach flipped at the thought of him providing her fresh blood. Though it was only a rabbit, and nothing close to what she could have if she just. Bit. His. Neck. She was, oddly, grateful and figured she could at least tell him so.

But then she eyed the wooden spear and wondered if he planned to use it on her.

He can try...

She smirked inwardly. An ancient one such as herself didn't need much to get her strength up. All she needed was enough for her vampiric magic to filter in, and then if he tried anything, at all, the man would be dead before he blinked an eye.

"Before you feast..." His voice had a low timbre that shot straight down to the center of her belly. "You should know that he may have eaten something not so agreeable to your kind."

Adeline stopped at the man's back and turned. The vein in his neck pulsed, but his heart rate didn't increase. It took great fortitude to remain unbothered by a vampire like her. This man was either much more daft than she initially thought, or he was exceedingly clever. She crossed her arms, glaring at the back of his head, and opted for the fact that he was clever. "Oh?"

The ends of his black hair curled around his ears, and she could tell he hadn't shaved in a while, for the shadow of a beard around his jawline made his profile look far more severe than before. "Yes, I believe he may have been fed a little bit of garlic greens."

Garlic greens. She chuckled. Yes, he was clever, but the greens would only slow her cognition. "That old wives' tale? You think—"

The stranger shrugged. "He is dizzy and weak and close to death, hence why he is in the cage, waiting for you to help him on his way. It does not matter to me whether you take from him now, or after he has passed."

She looked at the cage again, and her teeth elongated with the promise of blood. This time, she listened more intently with her immortal ears.

There.

The heartbeat *was* getting fainter. Soon, the creature would pass, and though the blood would still satiate her, it would not give her the strength she needed to feel completely revived.

With a sigh, she stalked over to the cage. Reaching her hand into the contraption, she grabbed the poor creature around the scruff of its neck and pulled it from its enclosure. As she did before she bit into any life source, she thanked it. Though she was a killer, she never took her food for granted. It was the willingness with which her food let her drink that kept her grounded. Her maker had always scoffed, and so had the other vampires, but this was one part of her humanity that had stayed with her after she had been turned.

When she was a young vampire, it hadn't been so easy. The first few kills had been impulsive, filled with craving — something Erik told her was called *bloodlust*. But as she grew into her vampiric talents, it was easier and easier to control her urges. Still, the guilt consumed her, so she made a concentrated effort to always thank her food for its willingness to feed a creature of death, like her.

It was the one thing that she felt made her an excellent assassin. Her control. She had a strict moral code when it came to killing, too. Erik had made her kill time and time again for him, and she worried she would become numb to the feeling. She recoiled at most human emotion, she maintained that they all had something redeemable. And if not, well, then she didn't mind too much when their flesh met her blade, and they screamed in terror.

Before she was able to eat the creature, he said, "You should know this comes with a caveat."

"A caveat," she repeated, hunger gnawing on her stomach. She was in no position to bargain.

"You feed, then you leave." He gestured from the rabbit to the door with the wooden spear in his hand. She looked out the window, unable to see anything beyond the blanket of white outside. He must have sensed her hesitation because he added, "You can take whatever supplies you need to get to the villages below, but I will not have a vampire under this roof for any longer than necessary."

As much as it pained Adeline to agree to this, she was left without any options. She was tempted to glamour him into submission, but she still needed sustenance in order to overtake unsuspecting prey. She was far too weak to even try.

Even still, she needed her answers, and so far, this man was the closest thing she had to getting them. The were-shifter should be close by, according to the last map she had consulted before she headed this way. Maybe since the man was eager to get rid of her, he could point her in the right direction.

"Deal," she said, knowing how quickly time could waste away. The full moon crept ever closer, and she was determined to get her prey.

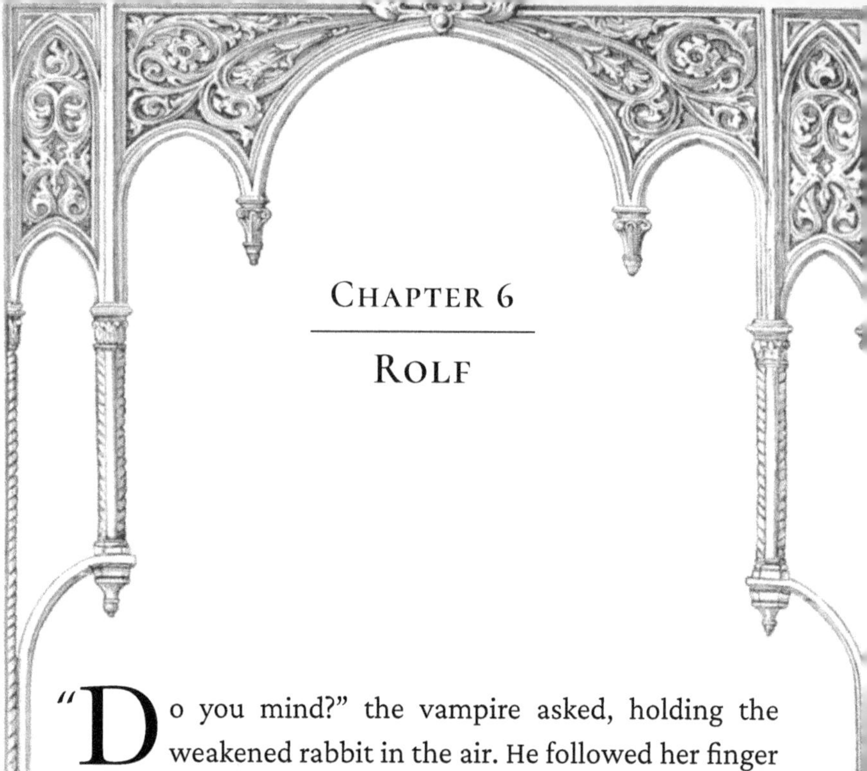

Chapter 6

Rolf

"Do you mind?" the vampire asked, holding the weakened rabbit in the air. He followed her finger as she pointed to the sink.

"By all means. I hate cleaning blood off my floors." And he didn't like cleaning up unnecessary spills. He turned to the fire, giving her his back, even though each time he did so, he could feel her glacial stare driving into him. It took every ounce of willpower he had to keep his heart steady when he felt so vulnerable.

Rolf shaped the end of the stick into a needle-thin point. He turned it in his hands, finally satisfied that it was as sharp as he could get it, and set it down on the floor next to his chair. It was an old habit, constantly finding and making weapons out of whatever he had nearby:—a sharp stick, his axe, a heavy rock—even his bare hands had worked on more than one occasion.

His skills were varied, but they all centered around one thing: survival.

The fire popped as the wood split and fell into the ash. To save himself the agony of hearing his guest bite into the poor dying creature, he grabbed a few logs and threw them into the flames. Sparks flew every which way as the green wood fought against the flame. Smoke filled part of the cabin, so he stalked to the nearest window and cracked it. Snow poured in and melted upon contact with the warm window ledge.

He stood there for a few moments, breathing in the fresh air so he wouldn't have to smell the coppery tang of fresh blood. It was a scent that repulsed him, and the vampire could barely contain her noises as she ate. It took all he had not to react to the abrasiveness of the sound of the squishy, twitching rabbit in her mouth. If he had hackles, they'd be raised. It was the most unforgiving sound he had heard in a while.

The vampire was not going to leave. He knew this as he stared out the window, the snow piling higher and higher against the side of his home. A storm of this magnitude was at least a month early, and given the volume of snow falling, it would be late in the spring before it melted again. He was thankful he at least had the wherewithal to replenish his woodpile the other week. But food? Rations? He hadn't had a chance to harvest the rest of his garden. All of those root vegetables and squashes are now buried underneath at least three feet of snow.

And if he were to have an unwanted guest for a few more days, how on earth would he be able to keep her from his neck? The rabbit was the only source of blood he had, besides his own. And the gods themselves would have to come hold him down before he offered himself up.

He had a plan, and all he needed was for the rabbit blood to work its way through her system. He shuddered and rotated the spear in his hands.

"I'm finished," she said. "You can turn now. Don't worry, I am a clean eater."

Doubtful, he thought as his stomach swirled. As slowly and casually as he could manage, he closed the window and pivoted to focus on her face. She had managed to keep everything clean. Not even the stain of fresh blood marred her porcelain skin—

Her vampire skin, he silently corrected himself.

Rolf watched as her fingers lingered on the corner of her rose-colored mouth. Though he had originally tried his best not to look the night before as he undressed her from her wet clothing, now, in the light of the cabin and the roaring fire, he had to peel his eyes off her curves. He closed his eyes and breathed deeply, centering himself again.

She had to be influencing him. He had heard about the Vampire doing this, rumors that swirled in the seedy underbellies of the cities he had passed through. But all this time, he thought that's what they were—rumors.

But now? His eyes snapped open, and her icy glare met him, along with a question.

"How did you know?" she asked. Her hands moved deftly in her hair, taking out countless pins and shaking out the tresses.

Her amber-and-vanilla scent filled the room, and images of cobblestones wet with rain mingled with the blossoming of late-summer flowers. He watched entranced as she smoothed her hair and twisted it into a knot at the top of her head, and her fingers wove the pins back in. They disappeared seamlessly into the dark depths of her curls, and he wondered why she didn't leave her hair down.

"You have a slow heartbeat." Rolf leaned back against the windowsill. "And with how cold and wet you were, you should have been dead hours ago. And yet..."

He gestured to her clothing and then, finally, to her.

She crossed her arms in front of her chest, humming in agreement. "And yet, here I stand."

"And here you stand." Rolf squinted, unwilling to let her read him.

Her eyes fluttered down and back up, then quickly looked away. He almost smirked when her gaze flicked back to his arms.

"So, vampire." He almost growled the words. He couldn't help it. He loathed her kind with every fiber of his being. Not only did he hate them, but he had also practically driven them out of his woods over the years single-handedly. It wasn't something he ever set out to do. It was just in his nature. "Tell me, why are you here? In my woods, armed to the teeth? What had you 'walking for hours' so close to daylight?"

"Adeline," she snapped back. "The name is Adeline. I might be a vampire, but I do have a name. I'd prefer you to use it."

The corner of his mouth curved into a sardonic smile. Her name rolled around in his head for a moment. It was a pretty name, simple, but as with all mythical creatures who resided in the human world, names held much meaning. "Adeline. That's an interesting name. 'Nobility' in the old language, correct?"

A subtle dip of her chin gave it away.

"Choosing to be tight-lipped now, hmm?" he asked, pushing away from the window and stepping closer to her.

Adeline held her ground and straightened her back. He stepped even closer, and still, she didn't shrink away. Which meant she hadn't figured him out yet, either. That was good. It could work in his favor.

"Adeline, of noble birth. Vampire huntress. How are you able to be awake in the daylight?" He narrowed his eyes as he looked down at her. They were almost chest-to-chest. Rather, he was a good twelve inches taller, so he was chest-to-her-head. Her eyes stared at the pulsing vein in his neck.

He stepped even closer, and her face betrayed nothing, but her breath hitched. Her eyes were unwavering as they met his scrutinizing gaze, and he could have sworn she was immune to the electricity between them as her body swayed closer to his. She looked like such a delicate creature, her curves begging to be free of the countless layers of cotton undergarments. And gods, how he loved a woman with a body he could really sink into. The thought caused his blood to rush to his ears, and he cursed inwardly, wondering if this was because his loneliness had finally gotten the better of him or if she was playing with his emotions. He always knew it would be hard to live alone, but he hadn't realized how hungry his own body would be for touch.

And now, of course, his flesh threatened to betray him. But he wouldn't give in. Not yet.

Push her to the edge, he thought. *See how easily she snaps.*

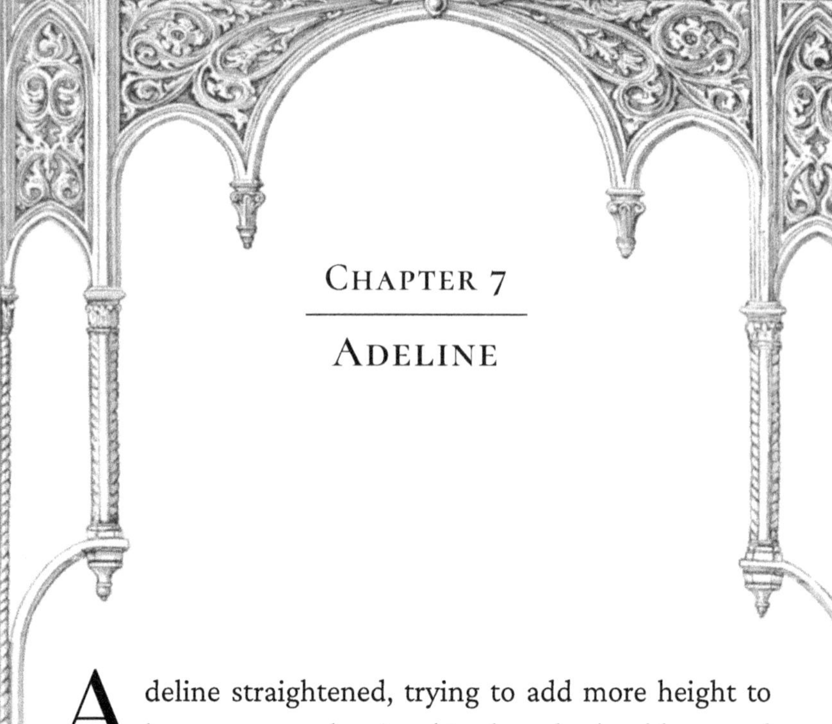

Chapter 7

Adeline

Adeline straightened, trying to add more height to her stature, despite his broad shoulders and towering presence filling the room. Short she may be, she was still strong and had centuries of killing woven deep into her muscles. She clenched her hands at her sides so tightly that the tips of her fingers turned numb. His eyes flicked to her fists, and his lips quirked into a lopsided smile.

He leaned back and crossed his arms, but he was still too close, and his scent clouded her mind. Fresh-cut wood mixed with leather and tobacco floated between them, wrapping around Adeline, wanting to pull her closer to this stranger. She almost swayed forward, so drawn was she into this peculiar feeling. There was something else there, too, but her senses weren't as heightened as usual, and she cursed the lack of healthy blood again.

If she'd had a proper feeding and not the measly little morsel of rabbit, there was a chance she could have killed him quickly. Yes, the garlic-laced blood *did* make her feel a little lethargic, but it wasn't going to kill her like the fables of old said. That alone wasn't enough to concern her.

It was the fact that he had called her a *huntress*, and that now he knew she could walk in the daylight when other vampires struggled. She should kill him. Letting him live to run his mouth at the tavern in the towns below would destroy all the work she had done to keep her identity a secret. And yet, she hesitated.

She relaxed her fists, and the feeling slowly returned to her fingers and hands. No, she shouldn't kill him until the effects of the garlic had worn off.

"Why *do* most vampires have a hard time walking in the daylight?" His voice turned gravelly. She refused to be sucked into the sexiness of it. "But you do not?"

"I don't have to tell you anything," she said, dodging his question. How was he so calm confronting her? He was hiding something, and she was in no shape to get into an altercation with him. But she would *love* to sink her teeth into his neck and feel him struggle underneath her. "Besides, in a few days, if I am not returned safely, there will be hell to pay."

"It's not like I can tell anyone your secret, anyway," he whispered, leaning close to her.

But given the chance, would you?

His amber eyes locked onto hers, and she had to peel her gaze away. She feigned disinterest, but her mind whirled. If he knew she was one of the Originals, he would not be pressing her this way. Besides, what did he stand to gain from knowing even *more* about her kind?

The sunlight couldn't kill vampires, as the fables all

said—fables she had started centuries ago to keep suspicions at bay. The vampires were just more sluggish, as if drunk and stumbling home from the pub. Their reactions lagged, their speech slurred, and they were far easier to kill. Adeline had been desperate to please her maker so much that, one night, she had planted a tiny seed of doubt in some impressionable young courtier's head.

This was why Adeline was the assassin no one had heard of. Starting the rumors about the vampires only coming out at night was one of her greatest accomplishments. She prided herself on it each time she heard them. As her maker's right hand, she was responsible for orchestrating so many political maneuvers through the centuries. Did an elemental king die under unusual circumstances? Did a human refuse to marry, take a female lover to bed, and was that lover rumored to control every possible political move? It was most likely Adeline.

Adeline was the biggest asset to Erik the Grey, her maker, and his quest for power since she was one of the rare few who could move about in the daylight, unaffected. It was her ability to blend into both the shadows and the light that made her his prized possession. But it kept her chained to him. For the last century, however, she had finally been able to taste freedom.

Adeline was so tired of that kind of immortality. Her entire vampire existence had been in service to males around her. Rage itched underneath her calm demeanor. She clenched her fists tighter, refusing to give in to the feelings, and breathed deeply to calm her nerves.

The world swayed slightly, and his scent tugged at something deep within her psyche. Her hold on reality was slipping, and she closed her eyes tightly, trying to regain her wits.

She was *not* going to go mad in front of this man.

When the cabin stopped spinning, he had taken a full step back from her. The air went cold without him so close, and she shivered despite her best efforts to control her body and the fact that a fire raged in the hearth. Adeline took another deep breath, and the aroma of pine now mingled with a crisp fruit scent. It opened up the floodgate of memories that swam in front of her eyes. Were they hers, or did they belong to the rabbit?

A dark, ancient forest, misty and shrouded in magic...

Hers.

Damn it all.

"What makes you think I'll tell you anything else?"

Was her speech slurring?

"Call it a hunch," he said, and it sounded like his voice was in three places at once.

"You fed the rabbit something else?" Her tongue felt sluggish in her mouth, as if a weight had been placed on it, and she couldn't seem to get the words out. She rolled her tongue along her teeth. The man tilted his head, regarding her thoughtfully. He was chewing something, and when he exhaled, a perfumed breath escaped his lips.

Dried berries on the ground, littering the pathway home...

Was this the rabbit? *No.*

"Mm-hmm," his deep voice flowed through her like water, caressing her while it pulled her under.

"Clever boy." Her hand reached behind her, and she grabbed the lip of the sink. Adeline leaned back, letting it support her weight. The numbness had moved from her fingers to her wrists and now her forearms.

"I have dealt with your kind before," he countered.

"You should be ready," she slurred. Her coven would come. And then it would all be over, and her hard work would slip through her fingers once more. And then what would become of her? "The juniper won't kill me, you know."

She fell to the forest floor, screaming out for anyone to help her...

He chuckled, the sound vibrating down her spine. "Oh, I know."

The man reached into a little leather purse tied to his belt, withdrew a handful of something, and placed it in his mouth. He chewed far too loudly for her sensitive hearing. Her knees shook, and she spat out a curse as she landed on the floor.

Her cloak fell around her. The stones behind her exploded and knocked her to the ground. She crawled down the hill and underneath a willow tree, her heart breaking, her sister gone forever.

"It won't kill you, but it will at least keep you incapacitated until I figure out what to do with you."

Boots squelched on the ground.

"What should I do with you?" the voice whispered in her ear. The nasal voice was lethal, but she couldn't move; something had hit her spine. What had she said?

Then...

Pain and bliss and terror swirled together as she clawed at the mud.

A shadow fluttered across her vision, and the man

knelt in front of her, close enough to peer into his rich gold-and-amber eyes. Her body shook with fear, a reminder of the last time she had been so weak and at a stranger's mercy. Surely, this man wouldn't kill her? Adeline tried to shake her head to clear her mind of the thoughts that shouted warnings at her, but her neck was numb.

He wouldn't, especially since he had polished her boots. Right?

His pained expression focused only on her as her entire body became immobile and her eyes lost their focus.

"Please just let me live..."

Chapter 8

Rolf

Rolf let out a sigh, watching her muscles twitch. Adeline went lax as her body sank to the ground and her eyes rolled into the back of her head. Damn if she wasn't a fighter. The creature of the night mumbled something incoherent, still fighting to get upright, though her body was no longer under her command.

He kept a fair bit of distance between them, observing her for signs that she was faking it. But as the herbs flooded her system, little by little, he noticed how hard it was for her to have the barest of movements.

A twinge of guilt wrapped itself around his ribs and squeezed, and though he had sworn he wouldn't talk to her any more than necessary, he found himself saying, "I can't have you in my cabin for long, especially when your coven might be looking for you. You're going to be so mad at me when you wake up."

He withdrew another handful of dried fruit and shoved it into his mouth.

"Ba—" she stuttered. And though she couldn't open her eyes, she took a deep breath and slurred the rest: "Basssstard."

"I know," he said, his heart breaking at how weak she looked. Gentlemen never treated their guests this way, but he didn't have a choice. Not if he wanted to find a way to live. "But I don't see another way around this. Trust me, you won't want to be here in a few days, either."

"Who—" she started. Rolf exhaled and wiped his forehead, thankful he had the foresight to give the rabbit more dried juniper berries. Her lips barely moved, but she managed to whisper, "Wha're you?"

"Not something you want to mess with, I assure you," he whispered, tucking some of her hair behind her ear. If she could move, she would have recoiled—should have recoiled—from his touch. "I promise you, though, that I won't hurt you."

Yet, he thought to himself. He wouldn't hurt her yet.

Her head lolled on her chest, and delicately, he scooped her up. Once more, he placed her in his bed and covered her with furs.

He skinned the rabbit carcass and tossed the meat into the stew. His stomach growled again, and he was quietly relieved that the juniper and garlic worked so well, because at least he could let his guard down for a few more hours. He debated, briefly, chaining her up in case she woke too soon, but he didn't have it in him to make her even *angrier.*

And with the snow piling higher, they were going to be stuck here, together, for a while. Maybe, by the time she'd had proper rest and the blood had a chance to nourish her enough, they could be civil, he could outfit her for the trek down the mountain, and he would never see her again. Adeline was someone important, and her coven was sure to come after her. Covens usually did when one of their own went missing. The faster he could get out of this mess, the better.

Adeline cried out, her body paralyzed and the words still muffled, but despite his head screaming that he shouldn't get close, he pulled his chair over to the edge of the bed and wove his fingers through hers. Almost instantly, she calmed. Though he knew he should let go of it, he stroked her hand with his thumb. She looked so helpless in his bed, the strength having left her body when the juniper berries took hold.

He ate his stew with his free hand and watched as her dreams played out across her face. Another violent nightmare tore through her, and she sobbed, tears pouring down her cheeks. Carefully, he put down his bowl and brushed a strand of her hair from her face. The guilt flooded him, and he almost wanted to wake her, but he let his hand cup her cheek until she settled. He was shocked that she was warm to the touch. He thought she would have still been ice cold; she was, for all intents and purposes, dead.

What kinds of terrors wove through her dreams to make her cry out in such a way?

Another tear rolled down her cheek. It settled in his palm, and he had this strange feeling that he had done this once before. But he couldn't recall anything in great detail, as if he were looking through a linen sheet hung to dry in the heat of the summer. Occasionally, the wind would blow and share a glimpse of what was behind it, but then it would settle, and only long shadows would play against the canvas.

He shook his head, wondering if he was trying to recall a memory or if his loneliness was merely playing tricks on him. She cried out again, and he stroked her cheek, wiping away any evidence of her pain. Adeline sighed contentedly and rolled over. Slowly, he pulled away and tucked her hands under the furs.

Soft orange firelight danced along her back, silhouetting her shadow onto the wall. He traced the lines of her body, his hand hovering in the air above her figure, moving in time with her deep breaths. She sighed again, and the furs slipped from her shoulders. Several marks peeked out from underneath her corset.

He jolted in his chair, anger coursing through him at the thought of anyone laying a hand on her. Which was foolish since he had only talked with her for a few hours. But he already felt protective of her. He shook his head, trying to free his thoughts.

Bad idea. She will kill you. Even if she doesn't realize it yet.

Rolf leaned back in his chair, folding his arms tightly across his chest, forcing his body to give her a wide berth. But how was he supposed to get space when the snow piled higher and higher every minute?

He groaned and ran his hands over his face. His scraggly beard caught in his fingertips, and he scratched at the skin underneath, his mind whirling with ways to keep himself at a distance.

The snow touched the base of the window, and if it kept falling at this rate, they would be completely snowed in by the morning. He bent down to retrieve his stew, and her scent filled his nose again, weaving its way deep into his subconscious. He cursed and tossed the bowl into the sink with a clatter, not even bothering to see if she stirred from the sound. Then he yanked his chair back by the fire, resolved to put as much physical space between them as he possibly could. If only he knew it would work.

"Adeline, Adeline," he exhaled, and he paced the room.

She cried out again, and he forced his feet to stay planted by the front door. The room darkened as her crying intensified, and he wondered, for a moment, if the shadows in the cabin could sense her distress. His hands flexed at his sides, and he knew that he couldn't drug her again. Already, he felt like he had broken some sort of gentleman's code.

But he was no gentleman.

The next time she woke, she would be furious. He would take her wrath, because he always did what he had to for survival.

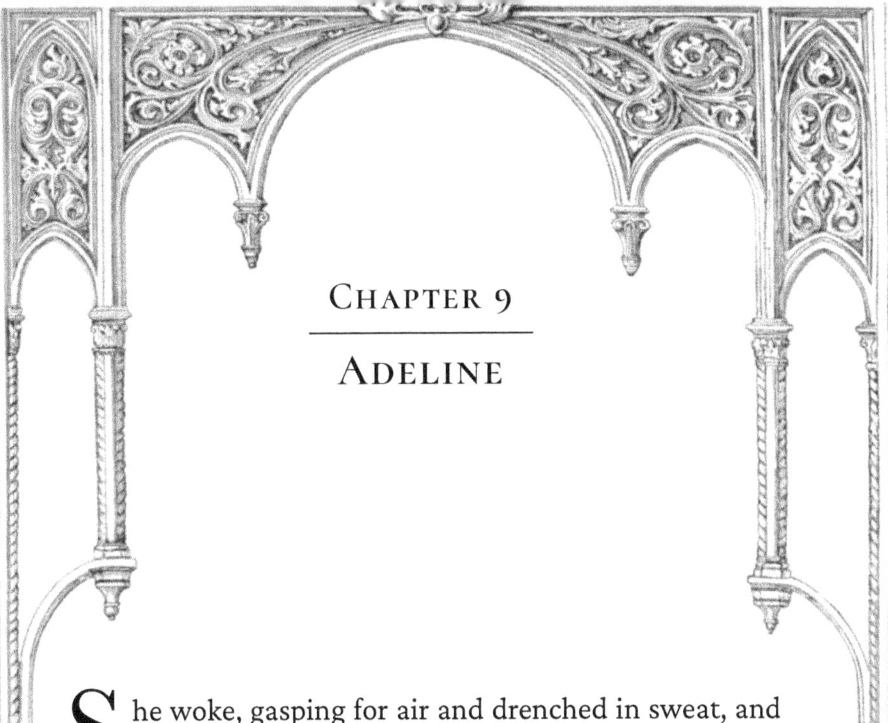

Chapter 9

Adeline

She woke, gasping for air and drenched in sweat, and her hands flew to her face. But as she gingerly felt the skin underneath her eyes, her fingertips came away dry. Thankful that her weaknesses were still locked up tight, she felt her shoulders relax.

Adeline hadn't dreamed of her mother and sister in ages, but, oddly enough, it was the same old dream from when she had been turned: The face her sister had when she shoved her away. The tingling feeling in her arms and legs as she sank into the mud in the center of the stone circle, and how odd the world looked. The hooded figure who followed them to the stones. The sound of rock blasting apart. The sound of her mother screaming her name.

Her hand drifted to her neck, to a phantom throbbing where sharp teeth had punctured her skin for the first time. She took a deep breath, willing the emotions back down until she finally remembered where she was.

Awash in the warm glow of the fire, the cabin felt almost peaceful, and languid shadows filled the nooks and crannies. A thin curtain separated her from the rest of the room, allowing her a modest amount of privacy. The furs scratched at her skin, and she inhaled, the scent of woodsmoke and juniper filling her lungs. She stretched, wishing the ache in her limbs would leave. It felt like it took an eternity for the food to work its way through her system. Her stomach rumbled, and she yearned to feel the warmth of untainted blood running down her throat. But she was in no hurry to repeat the effects from the night before.

The crackle and pop of a log aflame snapped her back into the present. Her head swiveled to the bastard sitting on the chair by the fire. He whittled away at a new piece of wood.

"You," she snarled and pointed her finger at him. Her nails elongated into sharp, black claws. It took every bit of her willpower not to lunge at him and tear into his neck. She would still be too weak, but damn if it wouldn't feel good to have him at her mercy. Return the favor, so to speak.

"Good evening," he said, as calm as ever. It boiled her blood. Gods, she was so tired of being at the behest of *males*.

Adeline threw the sheets off and swung her legs over the side of the bed. "You put juniper into that rabbit's food. For that, I should..."

"Should what?" he asked and tilted his head, exposing the length of his neck. "Bite me?"

Adeline narrowed her eyes. The vein in his neck

pulsed, and a shiver coursed down her spine. She may be weak, but not so much that she would do something stupid. What would his blood taste like as she drained the life out of him? Would he fight her? Would he scream? Would his eyes roll in the back of his head from the pleasure or the pain?

He'd had the foresight to feed himself juniper as well as that rabbit. Which meant that he would have eaten more potent quantities, too, no doubt. If she acted on her anger now and sank her teeth into his soft neck, who knows what would happen if she were unable to finish the job?

Damned either way and dependent entirely upon his hospitality, she didn't move. Adeline curled her fingers into fists, her nails digging into her palms. A drop of blood landed on her calf and trailed down her leg.

His eyes flicked to the red liquid that crept toward her ankle. And then his gaze traveled back up her legs, catching on the hem of her chemise, the laces of her corset, finally tearing his eyes away before it got to her bust. She stifled a self-satisfied smile.

He pointed at her with his whittling knife. "You're going to stain my floor."

The blood stopped a hairsbreadth from the wood beneath her feet. Adeline stared daggers at him, refusing to move.

"Apologies," she hissed. "But I'm not feeling very obedient at the moment."

He simply pointed at the blood trailing down her leg.

She rolled her eyes and unfurled her fingers to reveal completely healed palms. Adeline stuck her finger in her mouth and wet it. She swiped at the droplet of blood—leaving a deep red stain down her leg. Fully aware of the man's eyes on her, she straightened. "Better?"

"Thank you. Yes," he said and focused his eyes back on the stick in his hands. She wanted to reach over there and slap the wood out of his grip, feeling even saltier since he hadn't answered her question.

"Of course. I wouldn't want to ruin your palatial estate," she muttered and looked around the simplistic cabin. She took in all of the tiny details she had missed when she was awake. Though sparsely furnished, she had to admit it was fairly comfortable.

What kind of a man would choose to live out here alone? Especially a man that looked like *him*.

The bed was of high quality, and the bed frame looked hand-carved, as did everything else in his home. She scoffed internally. If she was going to spend most of her time asleep in this man's presence, she might as well be comfortable. A few herbs were drying above the fire. Ski shoes and woven wicker snowshoes hung on the wall near the front door, to the left of the fireplace, the accompanying poles crossing in the center. A thin rug splayed across the center of the room. It had a few burn holes near the fire from where sparks had landed on it. The fabric was stretched out and lumpy, unraveling in certain areas. It almost reminded her of her home growing up.

Her eyes then traveled back to the enigma of a man in the center of the cabin. The stranger's mouth quirked into a lopsided smile. Even underneath the thick beard, she could make out a dimple on his left cheek. He had said that she would regret being here in a few days. Who was he to feel like he had to drug her and also warn her?

"Palatial estate? This is one of the nicer places I've ever lived," he said. "Small and humble—nothing like the grandiose castles of vampires and courtiers. But, then again, it's not like I need much."

"I think I prefer a place small and humble," she said, partially to herself.

He gave her an odd look.

"What?" she asked. "I tire of the extravagance. The pomp."

He grunted in response as if he didn't believe a single word coming out of her mouth.

Other vampires would have laughed in her face, but the truth was, she loathed high society. The restrictive clothing, the rules, the careful way she had to form her sentences, and even the way she had to stand. Erik had loved it, craved it, wanted to be a part of that world forever. But she never felt like she fit in. Sure, she could hold her own and put on the greatest act, as if she were born and bred from noble blood herself. But she wasn't, and the only time she had ever felt like she belonged was when she was with Colin.

Her heart stuttered in her chest.

She blinked and was in the past, in a dingy room filled with the dawn's soft, dappled light. The smell of freshly baked bread filtered through the open windows, as did the shouting of the vendors opening their shops and cafés in the street below. Sheets tangled in their limbs, and Colin's large hand resting on the dip of her waist. They smelled of sex, and she languished in the strong curve of the body enveloping her before she fell asleep with the sunrise.

Adeline shook her head, pushing the flood of memories away. She didn't need the distraction of Colin right now, she needed to find the were-shifter and get the hell out of here. She walked to where her leather boots rested by the wardrobe. They shone from the care he had taken to clean them while she slept. Adeline's clothing lay folded in the open wardrobe with militaristic precision. Her hands fondled the clean wool and the creases in the fabric. What kind of person would clean a vampire's clothing after drugging them?

"Thank you for...your hospitality?" she said, surprised at how genuine her gratitude sounded. The anger in her chest grew smaller as she looked over her shoulder at the man more intently. What a curious person he was. Feeding her contaminated blood but then polishing her boots and cleaning her clothing while she slept.

"It's not in my nature to deny anyone, no matter their story, a safe place to rest, to the best of my ability." The chair squeaked as he shifted to give her privacy to dress. "But I couldn't let a ravenous vampire into my home without taking certain precautions."

Adeline nodded, turning back to the wardrobe. If that was the closest she would get to an apology, she'd take it. She tugged the riding pants up her thick thighs, and the wool chafed her skin. As warm as these were, nothing would compare to being properly fueled. She would need a good supply of blood, and soon, if she was to make it down the mountain without succumbing to the elements. Vampires, though notoriously hard to kill, had to be careful about putting themselves in vulnerable positions; freezing like she did before was one of them. She wouldn't make the same mistake twice.

"Probably for the best," she muttered as she buttoned up her trousers. But her hands stalled as she tried to unravel how many days she had lost trapped in the cabin with this woodsman.

"Two nights, three days," he said over his shoulder. "And the snow hasn't let up yet. We're under about five feet already."

It's almost as if he can—

"And, no, I can't read your mind, but I figured you'd want to know, seeing as how you threatened having an entire entourage concerned about your whereabouts."

She tried her hardest not to balk at the man. He certainly read body language well. This was the second time he knew what she was going to say before the words had even formed in her head. There was certainly more to him than he let on, and she still didn't even know his name.

If she offered up a little morsel more, would he bite?

"Thank you," Adeline said, reaching for her blouse. She threaded her arms through it and added, "They're quite used to me being gone. I would be surprised if they came searching at all."

"Is that so?" he asked, his back still turned toward her. She couldn't see his face, but something in his tone, the tiny inflection at the end of his question, implied he was nervous.

"Mm," she hummed. Her fingers buttoned up her collar, fingering the lace at her neck. It was crisp, as if he had starched it, too. Countless questions gnawed away at her resolve, and she found the words leaving her lips before she could stop them. "If you are so afraid of what I am, why go to the trouble to clean my clothes?"

She knew she would pay the price for being so forthright. But instead of a biting remark, her question earned her a chuckle.

And what a sound. Rich and deep, like melted chocolate. It washed over the room and knocked into her chest. She rocked backward on her heels from the shock because she hadn't said anything particularly amusing.

And still...

She wanted to hear it again. The way the sound caressed her spine, turning her stomach with a flutter—when was the last time she had heard someone laugh like that?

It had been a century ago, back in the small room she had rented, with *his* arms around her. Her head rested on his shoulder. She had mentioned something offhand, sardonic, but he had laughed like she was the cleverest creature he had ever been with. He even said as much. She knew right then that she would love him until the end of his mortal days, and it broke her heart.

Later that evening, when she woke, he was gone. And her life had never been the same since.

It can't be, she thought.

Adeline took a few steps, fingering her shirt cuffs, and leaned forward. The closer she got to him, the more her pulse quickened. She inhaled his scent again. It was muskier now but still there, hidden beneath layers of fresh-cut pine and woodsmoke.

Oud and tobacco, worn leather and parchment. It was a combination she would never forget, and it was woven into the furthest cavity of her cold, dead heart. The one time she had genuinely thought she could leave her past behind, turn over a new leaf, and live among mortals had been because of her love for a human.

Colin.

The scent of him was locked so deep within the sealed-off parts of her soul that even thinking his name made her hands tremble.

Can it be?

As if moved by a specter, her hand reached out and touched the stranger on his shoulder. Before she could get the words out of her mouth, he had her pinned against the wall by her neck. She grappled with his large wrists, but something kept her from fighting back. Though she should have been scared, his astonishing deftness did the exact opposite. As did his show of strength. Her feet weren't touching the ground, but he held her aloft as if she were as light as a feather.

His face mere inches from hers, he growled at her, "What're you doing, vampire?"

"I—" she choked out, and his hand relaxed slightly. Though she was still weak, she knew she could get free if she wanted to. She also knew that he would most likely dismember her before she had the chance to do any real harm. Because he was something more than just human. It was in the way his eyes pierced her soul. But she had to know. She watched his face closely for any signs as she asked in a raspy whisper, "Colin?"

A flicker of a shadow crossed his face, so subtle, so fast

that she could have dreamt it. But then his forearm twitched.

Perhaps it was the lack of blood going to her head, so she asked it once more.

"Colin?" She refused to look away, hope soaring in her blood for the first time in centuries.

He loosened his grip, but her hands were still latched onto his forearm, and though they were cold, her palms felt like they were burning wherever she touched him.

"My name is Rolf," he replied. "I know no man by the name of Colin."

Her entire body sagged, and he let her go. She slid to the floor, her head slumping onto her knees.

"I'm so sorry," she said, her voice barely a whisper. Adeline waved her hands limply around the cabin. "You reminded me so much of someone I used to know."

He sat down across from her, but there was no flicker of recognition in his eyes. How long had she been searching for answers, following dead ends, only to end up here in this cabin, drowning under the snow and the pressure of being trapped here with this alluring and frustrating stranger?

"That juniper must have been stronger than I realized," he said, grimacing.

At first, she practically kicked herself for thinking he was Colin. There *was* something so familiar about him, and if her body had been better fueled and rested, maybe she could pinpoint what it was that confused her so.

But she knew, deep down, that no matter how well-fed she was or how rested, she had thought he was Colin because her heart had felt empty for so long. She had longed to find him, and here was someone who vaguely reminded her of the lover she had a century ago. But that would be impossible. Colin was human, and he would have died some twenty or thirty years ago.

No, he was long gone. And she had to be okay with it.

After a century of hope and pushing off the inevitable, she had to let the fantasy of Colin go. The invisible thread that had tried to sew up the gaping wound in her heart began to tug, and Adeline didn't fight it this time, each stitch feeding into her resolve that not only had she not found Colin, she had not found the were-shifter, either.

Her fate was now entirely out of her hands, and she almost sagged with the relief. Soon, she would no longer feel the ache of missing someone so much that she had to cut him out of her heart to survive the next day.

Now, with her fate in her maker's hands, maybe she could finally give in to everything she had fought so hard to keep alive for so long. Maybe, given time, what she had with Colin would seem like a fever dream. Just like the memories of her sister, Leda, and her mother, from before she was turned, his face would also become a fuzzy image that she could transpose onto anyone when she felt nostalgic.

The thread snagged, and in her head, she tried to pull the needle through, desperate to put an end to her folly, but it stuck on a familiar emotion—a tiny spark of hope that refused to be snuffed out. Her hand moved to her chest as she tried to rub the ache away. She should have accepted his disappearance long ago.

Instead, she had offered to hunt the were-shifters as a

ploy for her to find out what had happened to Colin. And now, what did she have to show for it?

Nothing, you foolhardy ninny.

Her head fell back against the wall, and she groaned, the needle refusing to budge as the urge to talk about him overcame her.

"I have been searching for answers to his disappearance for over a century. He and I had...We had defied all odds just to be together. After the war, we spent a few blissful years together in Salonen. He was injured where I was interning as a nurse—"

Rolf towered over her, his arms crossed on his chest. He raised a brow and scoffed, cutting her off.

Adeline frowned up at him, not liking the interruption. "It's not like I was hungry and looking for a constant supply source. I was trying to learn the ways of more modern medicine."

"And what did you learn? Bloodletting with leeches?" Rolf asked. "You could have just offered up your teeth instead."

She bared those teeth at him and glared. He quirked a tight smile and held his hands up in surrender.

"I jest," he said. Rolf squatted in front of her, his eyes lingering on the curve of her neck. They trailed a path along her collarbone, and she watched his face intently. His tone was softer when he said, "Please, continue."

"I met him as he recovered from his wounds." Adeline stared into the distance, keenly aware that his gaze was locked on her. "He had this scar that always resembled a spiderweb to me, the way it had knit together as it healed."

"He was a soldier?" Rolf's eyes flickered to the wardrobe to her right, staring at the bottom drawers.

Adeline nodded. It didn't matter to her who or what he was, just that he was hers and she was his. Foolishly, as one does in new love, she thought they could withstand the restraints of immortality, that she would be able to leave all of her killing behind and start over.

What a fool I still am.

Adeline knew better than to so willingly divulge precious information—especially information that could be used against her. Something about this man's eyes, though, pulled everything out of her. The way his face so openly watched her.

If she didn't get this out, didn't share the last of her memories about Colin, the thread would sew her heart up for good. Maybe that's why she was being so open with Rolf. She was the keeper of Colin, the last one to know him, to cherish him.

"The stairs used to be so painful for him, and despite my size, I am uncannily strong." She laughed despite the unshed tears that welled in her eyes. Who would remember him once she was gone? She didn't want Colin's memory to fade into the ether when her coven came to return her to Erik. "He would insist that he could climb them himself, and so I'd let him, knowing that he'd make it up the first three and then get frustrated. He would pretend he had forgotten something back in the infirmary and turn around. All so he wouldn't be seen as weak before me."

"He sounds stubborn," Rolf said quietly.

Adeline nodded. "That was one of the things I loved

about him. We would bicker about the smallest things, inconsequential tidbits that ultimately meant nothing, but he knew how to bait me."

The vein in Rolf's neck pulsed at double time, and a few beads of sweat lined his forehead. His fingers fiddled with his skin under the collar, and his face had gone pale.

"Are you well?" she asked, reaching for him.

She touched his forearm, and his eyes locked on hers. He swallowed a few times, the muscles in his neck flexing as his throat bobbed up and down, up and down. She stared at the vein, willing herself to stop being so weak. That rabbit he fed her wouldn't last for much longer. Eventually, she would be forced to go for his neck. And, consequences be damned, she'd have to stomach the effects of the juniper, too.

"Yes," Rolf rasped. He swallowed thickly and stood abruptly—his face ashen, as if he had seen a specter. "I think I just need some fresh air."

A rush of cold air blew the hair from her face when he opened the door and stepped through. It carried that unmistakable scent—she closed her eyes and inhaled, but her senses were still so muddled from the rabbit she could barely make out that there was something underneath Rolf's woodsy sweat and *oud*. Something else she couldn't put her finger on.

This is no ordinary man.

He stepped onto the porch, and Adeline's jaw dropped at the wall of white stacked up outside. Only a few inches left between the bottom of the roof and the top of the falling snow—closer to seven feet had fallen in three days, and still more fell from the sky.

She knew from her searches in libraries across the continent that storms like this were rare, sometimes only occurring every five hundred years. It was unheard of, however, for them to happen at such an alarming rate.

Unheard of, but not impossible.

Immortality was never without its surprises, and there wasn't much left to shock her anymore.

Except for what had transpired over the last few days.

The coincidences were too uncanny for her liking: her horse dying on the pass as she made her way to the last known location of a were-shifter. The only shelter she had found was with a stranger who lived alone. He also knew the secret lore of her kind.

And then there was her coven.

Adeline knew that even if the snow was deeper than a full-grown man outside, they would still come. Erik would do whatever was within his ability to make sure she paid for her insolence and upheld her end of the bargain. And as the time of the hunter's moon came closer, her time was running out.

The walls felt like they were closing in. It was all a bit too much, even for her. It was becoming clearer with each log that burned down in the fireplace that the longer she was stuck here, the worse her situation—and Rolf's—would become.

She closed her eyes, fighting against the urge to pounce on him and tear into his pulsing veins as soon as he walked through that door.

I'm getting desperate.

Even after his so-called hospitality, she couldn't bring herself to do it. A small part of her wanted to leave his cabin peacefully and not add another dead body to her never-ending list.

Get a grip, Adeline.

Resolved to quench her thirst without him, she stood to look for some wine. It was the only thing she could even stand to drink besides blood, and might help clear out the rest of the juniper and garlic she had consumed. She opened the few cupboards near the sink, but there were only dry goods and some root vegetables. The cabin was so sparsely furnished that there was only one other place for her to look.

Her eyes flicked to the wardrobe, then the door, then back to the wardrobe. Maybe he stored wine in there and kept it hidden from her, wanting her to be weak and under his control. After all, he had fed her tainted blood and immobilized her.

He had given her the juniper and garlic-infused blood. But he had cleaned her clothing and polished her boots. He put her paralyzed body in his bed. But he hadn't tried anything.

Everything he had done was out of a sense of self-preservation, and she admired that. But something was off.

Her eyes flicked to the door Rolf had exited through again, and she licked her lips once more. The wine would only hold her cravings off for a short while. And then she would need blood. Because whether she wanted them to or not, her coven would show up. The deepening snow wouldn't stop them. Neither could Rolf. Besides, he didn't deserve to be wrapped up in vampire politics. Even if she tried to convince them he wasn't worth it, they would delight in spilling his blood. Slowly. Most likely in front of her.

Her stomach twisted at the thought. Why was this man any different?

She stood in front of the wardrobe, intent on the two drawers that Rolf had briefly looked at during their conversation. Instead, she withdrew one of his clean, folded shirts and inhaled the scent at the collar. Her eyes grew wide, and her fangs came in as she drifted down to the drawers he had glanced at earlier. Her hands touched the brass handle, fingernails elongating to trace the burnished filigree.

He's hiding something and you know it...

And she was determined to find out what.

Chapter 10

Rolf

Rolf paced back and forth, his hands threaded through his hair, and breathed the cold air deep into his lungs.

He was swimming in dangerous waters, but something about her kept pulling him back into her undertow. Her eyes haunted him, needling their way deep into the caverns of his psyche. Looking at her, he could almost remember what had happened to him that night, long ago, when he had woken up covered in blood that wasn't his.

And here she was, this strange, immortal creature, weaving stories about how her coven wouldn't come looking for her, that she had been attacked by rogues on the road? No, he didn't believe it. But then, when she had started telling him about this *Colin*, he had leaned in.

Her bright blue eyes had shone with an emotion he thought her kind incapable of feeling. It seized his heart.

She needed comfort, and he wanted to give it. And

when he had shut her down and run out here because he couldn't breathe? The light in her eyes had faded so fast, he couldn't help but feel pulled under by her disappointment.

Hope.

That look in her eyes had been hope.

He shouldn't care, though, because her very presence was the antithesis of everything he had fought to achieve. He hadn't survived these past few decades by being an idiot. He had finally found a place he could call home, settle down, and live out his life. No more running or waking up fearful of events he couldn't remember.

She needed to leave. She threatened everything he held dear.

Though the snow swirled and his entire porch was almost buried, the air around him was suddenly too tight, too hot for him to breathe. His heart thrashed inside his chest, trying to claw its way out. There was something oddly touching about her story, the way her voice became wistful and dreamy when she talked about her lover.

His hand found its way back to his collar, and his fingers dipped below the fabric to touch the scars on his shoulder. He laughed to himself, trying to brush off the seemingly small coincidences.

Surely, this vampire was messing with his head. They had certain powers, did they not? Perhaps she was inside his mind, reading his thoughts. And if she was, could she tell him what had happened all those years ago?

He perked up at the sound of a drawer closing.

Rolf pressed his ear against the door. Another drawer slid open, and Rolf stormed inside.

"What do you think you're doing?" Rolf barked, fury laced behind each punctuated syllable.

Adeline blanched like he was going to strike her, and he stopped advancing. What had happened to her to make her act like this? His rage flickered, but she recovered quickly, and her spine straightened. Her face turned to stone, and her eyes were clear—a sure sign that the juniper and garlic were moving through her body much quicker than he had anticipated.

She's strong. And stubborn.

His eyes caught on a sleeve that was covered in brown stains as she pulled it from the drawer, and his fury bubbled inside his chest.

What right did she have?

She lifted her chin, holding up the arm of the coat, and said, "I was looking for wine. But found this instead."

"You won't find any wine in there," he snapped.

Rolf strode across the room and grabbed Adeline's wrist, yanking her upright and to the side. With his other hand, he slammed the drawers of the wardrobe closed. The wardrobe rocked backward from the force, and the doors crashed back into place.

Her eyes widened as he gripped her wrist harder.

Good, let her fear me. It'll be easier for her to leave, then.

He pulled her close enough that their noses almost touched.

Rolf growled down at her, punctuating each word: "Leave. My. Things. Alone."

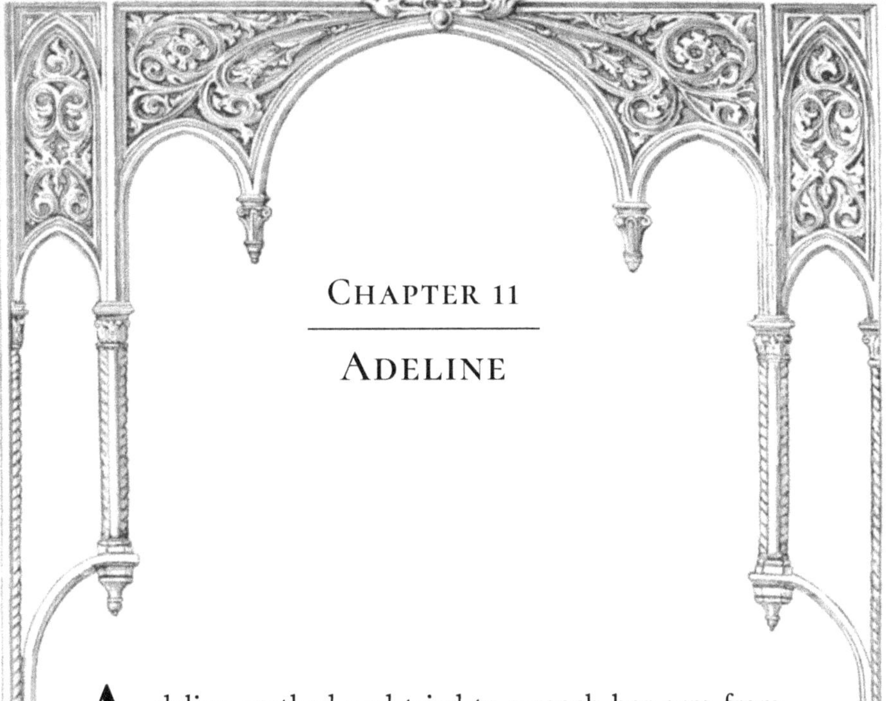

Chapter 11

Adeline

Adeline seethed and tried to wrench her arm from his grasp, but he only tightened his grip. Her weakened body was easy for him to move, but her nails lengthened into sharp points as her anger reared its ugly head again.

And gods damnit, she would drink some of his blood —even if it was laced with juniper and garlic—because she hated being tossed around like a rag doll.

When she had pulled out the coat, it was stiff with dried blood.

Three different scents littered its threads—human, vampire blood, and...

"What are—"

Rolf's growl cut her off. "I said, 'Leave my things alone.'"

She narrowed her eyes and tried to step away despite the ripple of sensation that walked up her spine at the primal sound of his anger. He refused to let her go, pulling her closer and looming over her in an attempt to intimidate her. Had she been in her right mind, she would have pushed back. But her legs wobbled, reminding her she was in no position to fight him.

Yet.

"As you wish," she sneered, clicking her nails together.

Calm down, Adeline. You need him willing.

"I didn't think it needed to be said out loud," Rolf countered. He finally dropped her hand and asked, "Did you find anything interesting?"

"Don't patronize me. And don't try to downplay this," she hissed again, pointing to the closed drawer. This was not how she had planned for things to go. It was time for her to claim her freedom. She had been too caught up in the possibility of the improbable that she had let her guard down. This was *not* her. Everything about this situation had been so unusual.

"Downplay what? My privacy?" Rolf scoffed.

"That you've been lying."

"Lying," he replied mockingly.

Gods, he is infuriating!

She needed to hit something. Some*one*.

Adeline raised her palm to strike him, but Rolf's hand caught her arm in midair. Her obstinacy was hard-earned and a source of centuries of pride, so she fought against his resistance. Her arm shook with the effort to break free of his grip and have her nails meet his face. The longer he stood there, holding her shaking arm, the angrier she got.

"I'm not the only one who has been lying, Adeline. What are you *really* doing here?"

"I am an assassin," she spat back. No need to tell him

everything, not yet. She still needed sustenance, and telling him all of her secrets was not the way to get it.

Rolf raised a solitary eyebrow at her. “What are you doing *here*, Adeline?”

“Hunting,” she spat.

“Hmm,” Rolf hummed. The sound reverberated low in his chest; she wanted to put her hands against him and feel his taut muscles beneath her palms.

Stop it.

He stood his ground in front of her. As angry as she was at him for grabbing her so roughly, for keeping her from lashing out, she found herself leaning into his body heat. She could hear his heart thumping, and then her eyes wandered again to the veins in his neck. They pulsed in time with the pounding of his heart, and they looked so tempting. Her teeth sharpened, and she flashed him a wicked smile.

But then...

Rolf dropped her arm and brought his hands up to the curve of her jaw. His calloused hands scraped her skin, sending sparks of lightning down her spine. He threaded his fingers through the hair at the base of her neck, and his intense glare softened, drifting from her eyes down to her lips. He tugged her closer, and she braced her hands against his chest to keep from falling into him.

Oh.

Her heart leaped into her throat, and she swallowed thickly. The sharp points of her nails pressed into his skin. He hissed as she pushed in a little farther, every bone in her body screaming for her to—

Stop it, stop it, stop it, stop it. Stop. It.

His broad shoulders filled her vision as her body instinctively molded to his. His heart beat rapidly beneath her palm.

She opened her mouth to object, but Rolf cut her off.

"You have to know," his voice was a heady whisper that brushed against the darkest corners of her soul. "I cannot—should not—be doing this. But, by the gods, I can think of nothing else I want to do more."

Stop it.

He bent his head, his lips hovering above hers as he waited. His eyes locked onto hers, and his whole body was a plea to give him an answer.

"You—" she started, but her throat felt too tight to speak.

Rolf nodded as if he could read her mind. He tightened his grip on her hair and tugged her head backward. His pupils dilated as she licked her lips. Heat pooled in her center, and she could find no excuse to say no. If she played these next few minutes right, she might be able to drink some of his blood and get her strength back.

His hands slid down to her waist, and he pulled her even closer, if that was at all possible, pressing her against him. She could feel how eager he was and raised an eyebrow at the sensation of him straining between them. Her nipples hardened against the fabric of her chemise.

Adeline shook her head, confused at what her body wanted to do. She flattened her hands against this broad chest and leaned back to stare at Rolf. She asked, "You want me, even though you know what I am?"

Chapter 12

Rolf

B*ecause you have no idea what stands in front of you,* he almost said, but instead, he whispered against her lips, "Even knowing what you are."

The silence yawned between them as he waited nervously for her reply. Was it seconds? Minutes? He studied her face carefully, noting the tiny speckling of freckles across her nose. They had faded to a light brown, but he imagined what she would have looked like back when she was human, her skin sun-kissed and ruddy from being outside. Her eyes, an intense glacial blue, had tiny flecks of gray swirling around the pupils, which dilated each time she turned her gaze on him.

He wanted to devour her. Every part of her. And never let her go. But she said nothing, just stared up at him, her brows knit together in confusion. Whatever demons she was battling, he wanted to slay them for her.

When he could not stand the silence any longer, his grip loosened on her back.

"But you paralyzed me," she whispered. And then she said louder, "And you've been lying to me."

Rolf bristled at the irony. This whole time, she had been in his cabin under a ruse, and she dared to think she was the one who deserved answers. So maybe he had incapacitated her, but damn if it wasn't out of his need to be cautious. An immortal bloodsucker in his home? No, he did what he had to and would not feel guilty.

"I'm not the only liar here," he said, his voice carrying a warning.

Adeline's eyes hardened, and she took a step backward. His arms instinctively wrapped around her, his fingers pressing against her lower back. Her lips curled into a sneer.

She wasn't going to sidestep this again, not if he could help it.

"So, you're hunting," he said.

She tried to step away, but he tightened his arms around her, secretly loving how her curves felt against him. One of his hands trailed up her back, and he cupped her jaw again. He placed his fingers against the pulse at her neck, holding her delicately so he could feel her heartbeat.

Her eyes were clear and bright blue like the noonday sky. "And you are not human."

Fuck.

For a split second, her pulse raced underneath his grip, and he gave her a sly smile. "Well—"

She cut him off by raising her arms and wrapping them around his neck. "Where is that coat from? Whose dried blood is it?"

With each question she threw at him, blurred-out images flashed in his head, but then they were gone.

He stuttered, "I...I do not know."

His grip around her loosened, and suddenly he was once again that frightened young man from decades ago when he woke up with no memory, in a strange red coat, covered in blood that wasn't his...

"You speak the truth," she whispered, her eyes scanning his face for any sign of trickery.

"Yes."

"Why?"

He shrugged, figuring it was better to say nothing.

That question held so much weight and had no simple answer. Neither of them spoke; they just stared. In moments like this, he wished someone could reach into his head and read his mind. It would make everything so much easier when words typically failed him.

The fireplace crackled, and his eyes jumped to the window. An orange glow pushed through the snowy haze, casting a soft yellow light over everything outside.

The golden hour nears, he thought as his skin crawled with anticipation. It was always this way, the final morning before the full moon took its place in the night sky. But her eyes were on him, on his neck, on his lips, constantly scanning his face.

"You lied to me about your coven, too."

It would be the only reason she kept staring at his veins with such intensity. She would need fresh blood, untainted, if she were going to leave, but he hadn't offered any of his. Though she tried to hide her worry now and again, he could see the panic behind her eyes.

She nodded once. "They near."

Fuck. So long as she could make it out of here before her coven arrived, everything could still be as before she showed up.

"When?" he growled.

The past few decades had been predictable. Easy. Just as he liked it. There were no blank spaces in his memory, there was no blinding terror when he woke up in strange places. But he had been so lonely on his own, in his cabin deep in the woods. And he had been so careful, living his life by as strict of a moral code as he could.

"The full moon," she said.

Fuck.

The look in her eyes told him she knew how close it was. She needed to leave, and soon, or it would be too late. A part of him hated knowing she was leaving because he *liked* being stuck inside with this beautiful, complicated, combative creature. She made his basest desires hungrier. Made him even more feral.

"You will leave tonight," he stated, his tongue feeling like sand. It was useless fighting his attraction to her. The very thought of her leaving his cabin, of never seeing her again, had his heart in his throat; at the same time, his mind kept telling him how unlikely this pairing would ever be. He took a deep breath and strengthened his resolve. "You can take a pair of my ski shoes, but you will leave tonight."

Her lips formed a tight line, and her face had gone ashen. How could she be a killer when he could read her so easily? She was afraid of something—the panicked look she kept trying to push away, as well as her increased heart rate, told him as much. She nodded in acquiescence. "I will, but..."

"But?" He stepped closer to her, tentatively raising a hand to cup her cheek. She hesitated at first, but then leaned in, her skin only slightly cool against his rough palm. It felt like his hand was alight with a thousand fires that traveled up his arm, settled in his chest, and flared to life.

A thousand fires that burned for her.

"You need sustenance," he said, knowing deep down that meant she had to feed from *him*. He dropped his hand from her face as his mind whirled with all of the things that could go wrong once she let him bite her. "And we don't have much time."

"But—" she started to say, her fangs already sharpening to fine points.

He cut her off with a kiss, his tongue diving deep into her mouth, playing with her sharp teeth. She moaned and pressed herself against him, weaving her hands through his hair. A trilling of danger swirled in his chest. It squeezed the air from his lungs and lined his forehead with a sheen of sweat. After he'd tracked down and hunted the Vampire from his forest for decades, now he was giving in?

No, this is so she can go and leave me in peace.

As it was, he knew it would take a miracle if he could pull this off—he was too enmeshed with his desire for her.

Finally, he pulled away. He eyed her fangs and asked, "Can you stop yourself?"

Adeline nodded her head. "Yes, I have perfect control over my needs."

"Then, do it," he rasped and swallowed a few times.

"Are you sure?" Her eyes flicked to his throat, back up to his lips, and finally, to his eyes.

He closed them for a second and nodded, almost resigned to the fact that she would know everything as soon as she took some of his blood. He knew there was no hiding from a vampire once they tasted your blood. Still, he had nothing else to feed her. Where would he find rabbits or squirrels under several feet of snow? And if her coven was coming, and she didn't leave in time, he was a dead man anyway. There was no way he could fend off more than one at a time right now.

Besides, if he was going to do this, willingly let a vampire take some of his blood, he might as well indulge this ridiculous desire to tear the clothes from her body. As if reading his mind, Adeline slid her hands up the front of his chest. His body hummed in response.

Her fingers curled into his pecs, and she licked up the side of his throat. He suppressed a growl.

Her lips fluttered against the vein that pulsed in his neck. She said, "Then let's have some fun."

It was the only confirmation he needed. He sighed as he tugged her against him. The delicate floral warmth of amber escaped from her hair and wrapped around him, warping reality and removing the last of his good sense. She threaded her arms around his neck, and he slid his hands down her back to cup her rear. He marveled at how they rested comfortably underneath her as he walked them over to the bed.

The deepest recesses of his mind knew he should not bed her, knew he should not imbibe. She was nothing like the fantasy he had concocted in his head. Even while he held her hand and watched her fight the dreams that haunted her sleep, he knew that she was much more dangerous than she let on.

But only a fool would pass on a moment like this.

And Rolf was not a fool.

He was simply toeing the line at losing complete control.

Chapter 13

Adeline

Adeline let him carry her, his large hands cradling her against the flat planes of his stomach. Her breath caught in her throat, her nose mere inches from his as she wrapped her legs around his waist. Hunger rolled off him in waves, and she wondered how long he had been here alone. There were no other signs of visitors—of any kind. No women's garments, no differently sized shoes. Only his set of clothing in the wardrobe and a few extra blankets. And that mysterious coat covered in vampire blood.

Sly fox, he will answer me about it.

But, since he insisted that she feed from him, perhaps she'd get her answers that way instead, and it would save her the trouble of having to hold him down when she was still weak. All she needed was a tiny pull to clear out the last feeding, and she would feel right again. And she needed to sooner rather than later because her coven was still coming.

It always felt the same, the way that everything seemed to slow right before she was called back. And now even the snow had ceased its onslaught in the last few minutes, as if nature parted the curtains to let the world know she was here.

She had always known her bargain had an expiration date, but only now had she let herself start to doubt what she was doing here. Throughout her centuries as an assassin, Erik had never led her astray. She always found her mark and got rid of it effectively. But all of her kills had been for him, for maintaining his power.

The world sharpened into focus, and she stilled in Rolf's arms. This hunt was entirely new territory, and she realized too late that Erik had been playing her all along.

Did the were-shifter even exist?

She doubted it. She had followed the evidence and still came up empty-handed.

"Always the dreamer." Her mother's and sister's words echoed in her head, reminding her that some things never change. Though she had hardened herself to the whims of Erik as a means to survive, there was always a tiny part of her that hoped she could make things work out in her favor. She was blindingly optimistic.

Perhaps that was why she was one of the Originals. Her optimism let her see the best in every possible outcome and helped her refuse to accept defeat. And besides, if her fate had already been decided by Erik, she supposed she could let go and have a little bit of fun with the stranger in the cabin.

For old times' sake.

Rolf set her down on the bed, and his fingers made

quick work of loosening her clothing. Her pants slid off with ease, and he tossed them on the floor. She started unbuttoning her shirt, and when their hands met on the middle button, he snatched her wrists and pinned them above her head.

Rolf covered her with his large body, pressing her down into the mattress. The bed frame creaked under their weight.

Adeline must have made a face because Rolf smirked. "Worried it won't hold?"

She shook her head, and his hands squeezed her wrists.

"Good. Because if it doesn't break by the time I'm done with you, it's worthless."

Words. She was at a loss for what to say. Had she ever been spoken to like that by a human lover?

No. They had all been weak and scared when she finally told them what she was.

Except one.

Colin had been reckless and daring. He stole kisses in the street, proudly flaunting her on his arm, but she had let him because they were in love. He knew the way to her heart and never felt threatened by who she was.

Rolf, though, was a different beast entirely. That self-assurance in his movements, the strength, the way her body hummed when he growled. That strange scent layered underneath the pine and juniper that she still couldn't place.

Could he be what she sought?

No, she thought.

Were-shifters almost always gave themselves away by

how quickly they angered, or even through the musky scent that seemed to linger on everything they touched. He was calm and measured. Practiced and almost indifferent. That is, until the tension between them finally broke.

Besides, he smelled lovely, a scent that triggered something deep in her core that filled her with longing.

If she could lean in, let herself go, and allow him to take control, then she knew it would be easier for her to feed from him when the timing was right. It would be simple, painless, and she promised herself she wouldn't take more than needed. At most, she would feed enough to have the energy to run or fight off her coven.

How many would come after her this time? Ten? Twenty? On a good day, with her full strength, she could quickly dispatch five, but she had been weak for far too long. And now she would pay dearly for it. She didn't want to drain Rolf—she didn't want her last moments of freedom to be spent killing the only one who had shown her a shred of kindness in a century.

"Is this where you bit your other lovers?" Rolf whispered in her ear, pulling her from her thoughts. He pressed against her, settling between her legs, planting kisses down the side of her neck. His tongue flicked against her vein, and she shuddered.

His heart was so loud she could feel it beating through his chest and into the palm of her hand. She clawed at his shirt, desperate to get it off so she could feel his skin against hers. But he chuckled as he nipped at her throat, and his hands continued their exploration, toying with the tops of her thighs.

"Yes," she replied and turned her head toward him.

She inhaled that scent again, letting it sink deep into her bones so she would never forget that this was her last night of freedom. Her fangs elongated at the thought of being at the mercy of his carnal need.

Rolf's hands moved fast, and in seconds, he had pulled out his whittling knife, poised to slice through the laces of her corset. He cocked his brow, and she nodded eagerly, wanting to feel his bare hands against her skin.

"What will it feel like?" he asked, his knife brushing against the stiff boning of the corset.

"What will—" Adeline asked, but then he sliced upward.

The sound of the laces shearing away and the sharp intake of his breath when she lay almost naked before him would be forever ingrained in her mind. There was nothing sexier than a lover ravenous for your body, and he looked at her like he was starved.

He trailed his fingers over the thin chemise. The unabashed hunger in his eyes melted any regrets she had. His thumbs grazed the hardened peaks of her nipples, and she moaned. He took his time, touching every part of her, delicate in a way she hadn't been treated in a long time. Her hands trailed down her chest, and she played with her nipples, watching his face change from hunger to reverence.

Why would he offer himself up to her?

She would worry about that later. For now, everywhere he touched made her feel like she would be burned alive. She needed him in ways that would once, long ago, have been considered unholy.

And I have holes. She snickered to herself.

Finally remembering he had asked her a question, she replied, "I can make it painless."

He pushed the corset aside and nodded. His throat bobbed, and she knew he must be nervous, but nothing in his composure gave him away.

She recalled her first moments when she was turned, the sensation of pain that she now knew could have been avoided. Just a simple swipe of vampire blood before the fangs punctured the skin.

"But when I feed, it might feel... odd. It might light you on fire and burn, a pain unlike anything you have ever felt. Or it could feel like a thousand hands giving you pleasure, until you reach completion, rolling in the waves of the aftermath."

"Oh," Rolf said. His hands had stopped roaming, and his thumbs rubbed small circles on the tops of her inner thighs. "And how do we make sure it's the latter?"

"We can try a few things." Adeline bit her lip coyly, arching her back so she fell open for him as his thumbs slid closer to her throbbing center.

He knelt on the floor in front of her and grabbed her legs, pulling her to the edge of the bed with a possessiveness that would have usually turned her off. The chemise gathered around her waist, and she sat up and pulled it the rest of the way off. The cool air caressed her nipples, and she shivered when Rolf leaned forward, his lips pressing tentative kisses to the tops of her breasts. Adeline moaned softly and twined her fingers in his hair. She arched her back, urging him to suckle at her breasts.

"No, no, my darkness. I'm going to take my time with you," he drawled.

Oh gods.

Her stomach clenched at the nickname. His *darkness. His* darkness. She rolled it around in her head. For tonight, she could pretend because, after all, how could it be that this felt so familiar and so foreign at the same time?

Rolf let out a deep chuckle as he settled before her. He trailed a path along the inside of her upper thigh with his finger. It crept closer and closer to her hot center, teasing her.

"Spread your legs," he commanded.

And she shocked herself when she did. When had she ever been this easy to command?

She could feel his breath between her legs, and in a moment of hesitancy, the weight of what she was about to let him do to her scared her. The last time she was *this* intimate with a man was a century ago, with Colin, and her heart had never fully recovered from being so vulnerable. She tried to pull back and clench her thighs, but his large hands held her legs firmly in place.

"No. Stay. Just like that." His eyes were glazed over and sent a shiver up her spine.

"Stay," Colin had whispered that night.

But she didn't. She needed blood, and so she left him in the midnight hour, when the drunks were stumbling home and easy targets. Languidly, she had slipped back into bed, into his arms, and they made a lazy sort of love before falling back asleep. He had kissed her head as the sun rose and told her he would be back. But he never returned.

He was the only human she had ever considered turning into a vampire, so their life could go on forever together. Her coven never even asked where she had been when she disappeared to go looking for him. They knew better than to pursue her while she was hunting, and that was what she had told them. She was hunting for the last few were-shifters, and she would return when she was successful. They didn't know that she was also looking for Colin.

Her throat closed up. Sometimes, she felt as if Colin only existed in her dreams. Their time together was so fleeting compared to the rest of her long life. But the ones of him had outlasted most of her memories. She shook her head, willing it to stay just that. A memory. She didn't need the interference of a long-lost lover invading the space she had tonight.

"You're perfect," he whispered in reverence.

His fingers played with her entrance as he stared almost lovingly at her. He dipped inside it, toyed with her. She bucked against him, her body begging him to go further, go deeper. But his lips quirked into a sly smile as he watched her reaction when he stuck his finger in his mouth and licked it clean.

"Please," she begged, and gods, how she hated begging. She was exposed and at his mercy.

But...I like it, Adeline admitted to herself.

It had been too long since she had been worshipped like this. Her body was the temple for an eager disciple who bowed before her, and she wanted more. She wanted him to wash away the centuries of pain, she wanted him to help her forget that after the full moon, she was no longer an agent of her own free will.

The coven would be here soon, and so what if she got

to enjoy the final few hours of her freedom? So she'd let herself succumb to his desires, and then she could feed, and then she would leave, hoping to be able to outrun them for at least a few more hours.

Rolf's hands gripped her waist and tugged her even farther off the edge of the bed. He kissed up her thighs while his hands massaged her backside, winding her up even more. A fire burned in her low belly, the anticipation adding to how wet she was already.

As if he could sense her nerves on high alert, Rolf took her legs and let them rest on his shoulders. His tongue flicked along her sex, and she melted into the bed.

Rolf licked and explored her depths with his tongue in a way that she had never experienced before. Perhaps it was the blessing of their being strangers that let him explore uninhibited. She moaned at the feeling of his face between her legs, and when he slid a finger inside her, she rocked against his hand. He stroked her deeper, finding the spot that made her legs twitch against her will.

"Gods!" she cried out. He stopped, hesitating. She rose slightly and threaded her fingers through his hair, almost shoving his face back down. Desperation leached out of her as she said, "No, no, keep going."

Rolf gave her a wicked grin and withdrew his finger. "I told you I'm going to take my time with you."

This was going to be a long day.

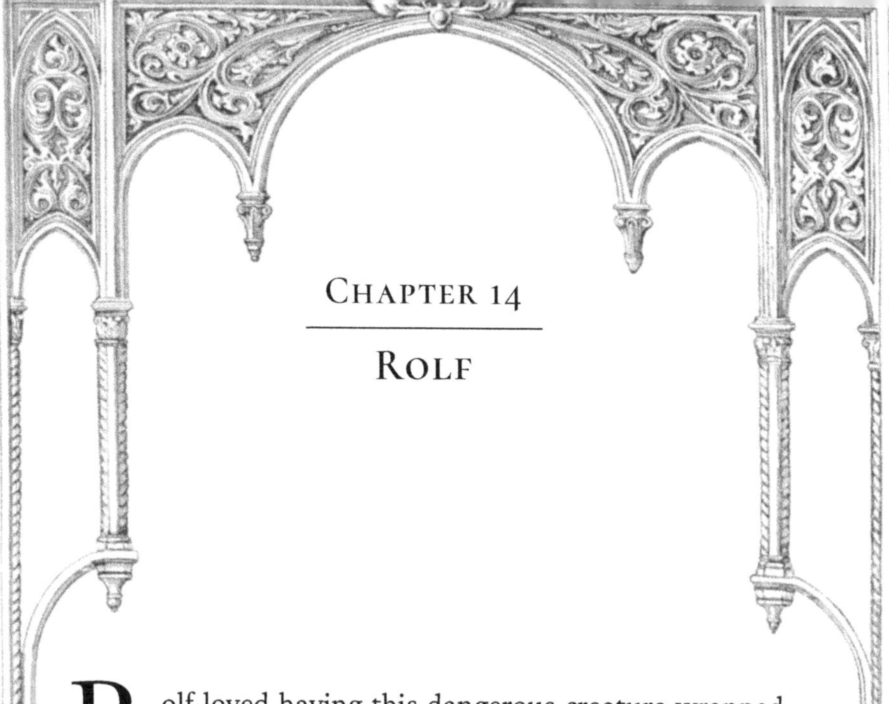

Chapter 14

Rolf

Rolf loved having this dangerous creature wrapped around his finger. He smiled into her sex, flicked his tongue over her clit again, and drove his finger back inside her. Adeline cried out, clenching around his finger, and she rolled her hips with the movements.

She was gorgeous when she squirmed like that, and he was overjoyed at being able to drive her to the edge of release. He could do this all night.

He withdrew his finger slightly and added in a second, sucking on her clit even harder. Her nails sharpened, digging into his scalp, and he groaned into her wetness. With his free hand, he stroked his cock through his trousers and realized, quite quickly, that he wasn't going to last long if he kept this up. Her legs started to shake, and he knew Adeline was on the verge of coming, too.

That won't do, he thought. So he slowed his movements and withdrew his fingers.

Adeline glowered at him. Even worked up and angry, she was so beautiful he wanted to stare at her forever.

"That's not fair," she panted, her eyes glassy. The frown that pulled at her eyebrows was cute, but then Rolf remembered that she was a vampire, and he just flashed her a smile.

"Patience, my darkness." He practically purred at his nickname for her.

What had gotten into him? Had he gone full animal for her?

Maybe.

He sat there on his knees, bowed before her, tasting her languidly to tease her release. What he couldn't understand was how he was so lucky, and also so cursed. Trapped under the snow with her, it was as if, for these last few hours together, the outside didn't matter. He wanted to stay within this tiny bubble of pleasure for as long as he could. Because everything about her was familiar. From the way she reacted to his ministrations, her scent, taste, the sounds she made. She was something he had been searching for so long.

She felt like home.

Home. The word shuddered through him as her legs started to shake again.

He slowed to a stop, and she cursed something he couldn't hear. All the noise around him sounded like he was underwater as his heartbeat filled his ears.

Home.

He closed his eyes, sitting back on his heels. The image was just out of reach, just within his grasp. But then it faded again.

"Gods damnit!" His fist slammed into the floor.

Adeline jumped and scrambled to sit up. A few splinters formed in the wood where his knuckles had landed. He always forgot how strong he was when he got upset.

"Rolf?" Adeline asked, eyeing the dent in the floor. She frowned, but not out of horror—it looked like genuine concern.

"I'm fine," he huffed.

But he wasn't, not really. He wanted this vampire assassin, and that worried him because he needed her *gone*. He needed the coven to follow her. He needed many things to return to the way they once were, before all of these confusing images and feelings had cluttered up his simple way of life.

His chest felt tight, but he longed to feel the same comfort from moments before.

Home, his heart sang. He closed his eyes tightly; more blurred images flittered behind them and then left. But what did home mean if he couldn't even remember where he came from?

"Clearly." Adeline snorted. "You think I haven't seen this before?"

"Seen what?" he mumbled, curious but not wanting to give in so easily.

"When men throw tantrums because emotions are too hard," Adeline replied. But there was no mockery in her tone. Instead, she slid to the edge of the bed and took his head between her hands. Her fingers wove into his hair, and she tilted his head up to meet her eyes.

His jaw dropped. Her eyes were dark blue, and her pupils were so big and black, looking into them was like staring into the night sky. He wanted to dive into their depths, let her swallow him up.

But then he saw his reflection peering back at him. Bedraggled hair, scruffy beard. He was wild and untamed, a right mess in the head. Why did he think he would be able to do this and go back to normal? Why he even thought he had a chance with her in the first place was folly.

Promise, I'll be a good boy. Just keep rubbing my head.

Her fingers moved in a soothing pattern, ruffling his hair and pressing into his scalp. Right now, she was a balm to the irritation under his skin. He could melt right there, into her lap. But emotions weren't the issue here, no. The issue was the fact that he was strongly attracted to the exact wrong woman.

This deadly creature is comforting me, he almost laughed.

Comfort. Home. No wonder his judgment was so clouded. He cleared his throat to speak, shoving the emotions as far down as he could. He would not fall for the vampire. He would not cave to her wiles and sex appeal. Nor would he cave to the fingers that were threaded in his hair. She was still a threat to the life he had made for himself.

A vampire like her would never be with someone like me. He knew it deep down in his bones. *Best to get this over with and send her on her way.*

He ran his hands up her legs, planting kisses on her soft skin. She hummed in response, and her hands stilled while she held her breath. He pushed her legs open and saw several scars peppering her thighs. The markings were so subtle he almost missed them, but the tip of one in particular peeked out at her hip. He recalled the smattering of scars on her back, and anger boiled underneath his surface—he grabbed her waist and turned her on her side.

There, on her upper thigh, was a brand. A crescent moon with a star burned into her skin so many times that the edges were mottled and twisted pink. His hands tightened on her legs. He had seen that brand before; some deeply buried memory tried its hardest to surface. His fingers traced the lines of the brand as Adeline went stiff under his touch.

Time for answers.

He exhaled. “What are you doing all the way out here, Adeline?”

It was exhausting having her here, feeling all these stupid feelings, knowing that an entire coven was going to come for her, that his home was at risk. He hated the idea of starting over. He hated the idea of more vampires invading his space and having to fight them off. He just wanted to be left in peace.

She was supposed to have gone once she had rested and the storm had stopped, but the snow kept falling. And falling. Unfortunately, he could not control the weather because his time was running out, and he figured she might as well know what he had been hiding all this time.

Because there was no place for her to run.

After a hundred years of fighting against his baser nature, he almost wanted the relief that would come when she took a blade to his heart.

Adeline tongued her fangs for a few seconds, as if hesitating to tell him the truth. He squeezed her hip once more, and her eyes flashed to his. She hung her head and sighed.

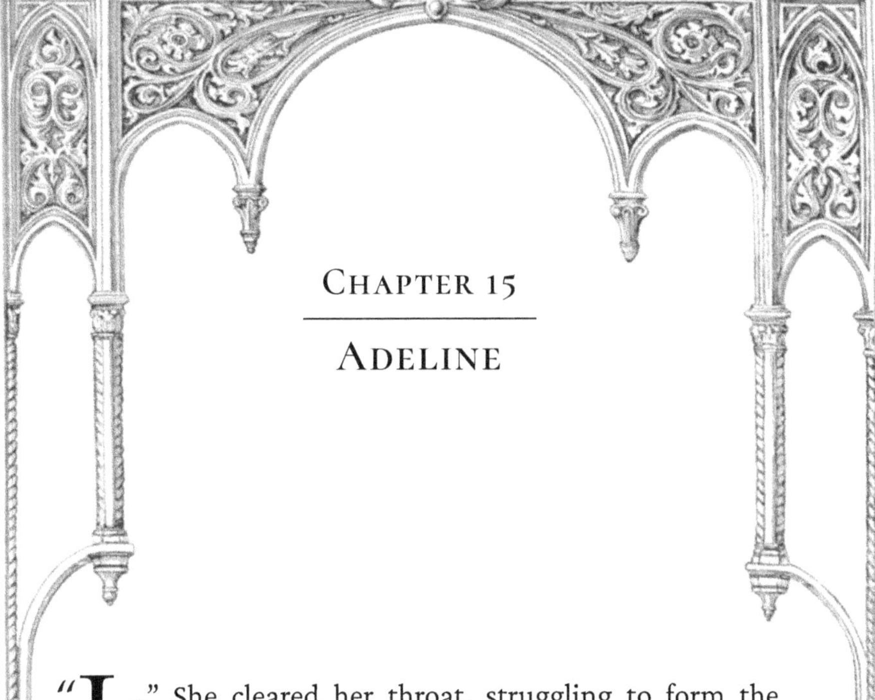

Chapter 15

Adeline

"I..." She cleared her throat, struggling to form the words. She averted her eyes, refusing to look at him while he kneeled between her legs.

"Why are you *here,* Adeline?" He pressed her again, his voice harsher than before.

"I made a deal with my maker. He let me roam freely while I hunted down the only creature who could kill us."

Because I thought I could finally be free. She longed for the promise of freedom. To do with her immortal life what she wished. But Erik had made it known that her life was his, that she would not be here without him, that she owed him for it. She was indebted to him, for as long as he deemed her necessary.

And for some reason, he thought she was always necessary. Adeline had tried to run away countless times, using her assignments as an assassin to give her time away. But she always gave in, in the end. Erik would torture her back into submission until her desire to be free overwhelmed her again. The final time she ran away, she had disguised herself as a novice healer and gone to work for some nuns in a hospital.

It was when she met Colin that everything changed. She finally dared to get out of the horrific arrangements Erik put on her.

She wasn't lying to Rolf when she said she wanted to learn modern ways of healing. Everything she had said tonight was truthful. And she had to wonder why. What was it about this stranger, in particular, that made her think he was Colin? That made her feel so comfortable that she could open her mouth and be honest?

He knew of no man. He said so himself.

Rolf dropped his hands and sat back on his heels, a frown plastered across his face. Though he looked shocked, she could hear how his heartbeat picked up and battered itself against its cage.

"A were-shifter," he deadpanned.

It wasn't a hard guess. Were-shifters were, after all, the only fae creature who could kill a vampire with one swipe of their deadly claws.

Though vampires were known to move quickly, heal fast, and have the strength of ten men, were-shifters had the stamina to keep up and claws so sharp could behead a vampire. In their human form, they were strong and could hold their own with any vampire in hand-to-hand fights. But as wolves? Large, ferocious, blood-thirsty creatures, the wolf shifters could take down several vampires at a time, easily dismembering them with a swipe of their sharp claws or a snap of their jaws.

If someone had the chance to injure a vampire enough,

they could bleed out. But if, at some point before they were able to die, all they needed was a drop of fresh blood, and there was a chance of survival. Cutting off their heads was the best way to keep them from regenerating.

Rolf's eyes had turned hard, but his hands rested on her knees, and his thumbs rubbed slow circles on the insides of her thighs.

Adeline shuddered at the intimate gesture. She longed for more, but why did that make her feel so guilty? "My freedom has run its course. If I don't find and kill a were-shifter by this full moon, then..."

She held her palms face up and shrugged. Already she had said too much. Rolf didn't need to know just *how* many were-shifters she had killed over the past century. She had killed one a year and always around the Hunter's Moon - her yearly deadline and the time of the year when the were shifters would find their mates, settle down for the winter, and bed. Erik's request had been to stop them from mating so that, soon, the vampires had no more immortal enemies left.

Erik wanted the vampires to be the top of the chain of command, and ending the were shifters was his way of ensuring all of the power remained in his hands.

But now? This was the first year that she would miss her deadline.

"Your coven will kill you." Another deadpan statement. And though it wasn't the entire truth, his guess was close enough. His hands gripped her knees, and he pulled her closer.

Adeline nodded, her mouth suddenly full of sand. The snow piled higher, still, but that would not keep them from coming to find her. And if they didn't come, she was convinced Erik would. He always had ways of finding her, no matter where she ended up.

"And here I've been keeping you from doing just that." Rolf ran his hands over his face and groaned.

"I think it was the snow, actually," she said, jutting her chin at the window.

It was the way he groaned that had her skin tingling. What she wanted to say was, *"Yes, now, let's get back to business."* If this was what was left of her freedom, she wanted to enjoy it. And what better way to do that than earth-shattering orgasms with a stranger during a snowstorm?

Rolf tilted his head to the right, exposing the side of his neck, and looked her in her eyes. "I'm ready."

Her heart stuttered.

She would be lying to herself if the thought of him worshipping her again didn't turn her on, but she could feel her veins itching with the need for fresh blood. He was a willing participant, and still she hesitated. Her eyes roamed the cabin, but she wouldn't find another rabbit. She would have to leave the cabin and search for some kind of animal outside. But with the snow so high, the full moon nigh, and her time running out...

Certainly, he didn't mean it...

"I mean it," he countered.

"Now?"

"If you need it, then take it, unless you won't be able to stop yourself. In which case..." Rolf shrugged. "I'll probably be dead by the end of the day tomorrow anyway."

"I have perfect control over my needs, thank you very

much," Adeline retorted. Her eyes flicked to the veins in his neck. She needed it, but she didn't want him to know how desperate she was. "However, I don't want to be comatose again, so I think I will pass."

"I haven't had any juniper or garlic since yesterday. Whatever is still in my system will be minimal," Rolf said. "I'm quite a bit larger than a rabbit."

She lifted an eyebrow, looking down at him, and back up. "Yes, you are."

He snorted but lifted onto his knees, rising to meet her eyes. When he tucked some of her hair behind her ear, she didn't flinch or pull away at the intimate gesture. She remained still as a statue despite wanting to lean into him because, if she was being honest, she was too shocked at her reaction to do much of anything.

"Fine," she conceded, kicking herself for giving in. "However, there is something you need to know first."

"Tell me," he whispered into her neck, kissing her earlobe.

"The feeling can sometimes be... addictive." She looked him in his eyes, all seduction gone. She wanted him to understand how serious this was because if she could feel his orgasm through her actions, then she would be unable to take only what she needed to get stronger. She'd want to take *more,* and she'd already told him she had perfect control over her needs. "You can't let yourself finish."

He frowned. "How hard could it be?"

"Please, try your best," she said, worried he wouldn't be able to contain himself. She didn't want the day to end before they had even had fun. And besides, there was a part of her that still believed she had a moral code.

"Understood." His lips curved into a seductive smile, and his hands found the undersides of her breasts. He cupped them, and his thumbs brushed against her peaks. They hardened in response.

I need more than his blood...

A shiver washed over her body, from her head to her toes, when his deep, gravely voice said, "Like I said, Darkness, I plan on taking my time with you."

Chapter 16

Rolf

Instead of letting his worry take over, he focused on her body, so close to his. He swallowed a few times as her eyes bore into him. He crawled over her, relishing the way her body was spread out before him. Gorgeous curves, thick black hair, eyes like the brightest stars in the sky.

My darkness.

Possessiveness overcame him for the briefest of moments. He wanted to claim her so no one else could touch her. His hand hovered around the ties of his pants as he debated baring his body to her. Then he stopped. Perhaps it was best that he remain clothed; her words still echoed in his head about not finishing. Something swirled low in his gut—fear? Desire? Right now, the two were so closely entwined he doubted he'd be able to tell them apart.

I wanted this, he reminded himself.

He had thrown caution to the wind, weighed the risks,

and had chosen this path. He planted kisses along the delicate skin of the underside of her breasts.

She hummed. "You know, I have never liked beards before now."

"What changed?" he asked and chuckled against her stomach, causing her to giggle in response.

She replied, a smile playing on her lips, "You did."

The look in her eyes hinted at mischievousness, and he wanted to pin her down and tickle her until she squealed. He moved his hands to grab her wrists, but she slithered out of his grasp easily.

"Don't," she laughed, glee dancing in her bright blue eyes. He didn't know vampires could laugh, but the sound was sweet and light and reminded him of that first glimpse of spring when the snow melted and the bulbs sprouted.

At that, he stilled and looked at her—really looked at her. Her pupils had dilated, and her nails and fangs had elongated. Normally, he assumed he should be afraid of this change in her, but her appearance hadn't changed out of anger.

Does she feel the same way? His heart jumped at the thought.

This entire time, he thought maybe he had been fooling himself. There was no way this vampire assassin would have feelings for *him*. And that revelation made him even more ravenous for the moans he wanted to elicit from her. If she were going to discover his darkest secrets, he would give her an experience she wouldn't forget. So when she eventually did kill him, at least he had given her something pleasant to remember him by.

He dipped his head then and kissed his way up her ribcage, stopping briefly to take each nipple into his mouth. Her fingers threaded through his hair, and she arched her back as if she wanted him to take all of her into his mouth.

Gladly, he thought and sucked on each of her breasts with fervor as he dipped a finger between her legs. Then he took one of her hardened peaks between his teeth and rolled it around, flicking it with his tongue. He lifted his eyes to watch her face as she gasped and groaned. Then he kissed his way up to the curve where her neck met her shoulder. He slid another finger inside her and nipped at her skin, biting a little harder when she sighed. He let go and smiled at the pink markings his teeth left.

"I need to feel you," she breathed.

He tilted his head, opening his mouth to say something, but her lips crashed onto his. He stroked her deeper and growled into her mouth, "You're soaked."

She whimpered in reply.

"How do you want me?" he asked, eager to let her take the lead. His fingers stilled, and he pulled back, searching her lust-filled eyes for a hint.

She smiled seductively and pushed his head down between her legs.

"Taste me."

It wasn't a request but a command, and gods did he want her to command him for the rest of their time together. He had always been in control, the one to call the shots, but he figured, for her, he could change things up a little. Right then, he swore that if either of them made it out of this predicament alive, he would gladly feast on her whenever she desired it.

She pushed herself against his face, and he groaned into her, driving his tongue deeper. Rolf swore he could do this for hours and never tire. Her exclamations drove him wild, and he desperately wanted to take her into another plane of existence. He slipped his finger out of her, sucking on it a few times, relishing her taste. She whined and tried to get his head back between her legs. Her clit was swollen, and he placed a simple kiss on it. He flicked his tongue over it again while his wet finger slid slightly lower, playing with her sensitive, puckered entrance.

He lifted his head in question, watching her body twitch and undulate as he probed her slowly with the tip of his finger. "Is this—?"

Adeline just nodded frantically and pulled hard at her nipples. With her consent, he sucked on her clit while his finger teased lower.

"Ohhhh, Rolf," Adeline breathed as his finger pushed into her. She clenched at first, but then relaxed, his finger working into her gently with slow circles. She moaned gutturally, *"Oh gods."*

He slid his tongue against her. She was divine, writhing under his ministrations, and he was starved for her pleasure. But her hands on his shoulder stilled him. Immediately, he stopped and pulled back.

"Come here," she whispered, trying to pull him up between her legs.

She threaded her arms around his neck and wrapped her legs around his waist. His free hand drifted to the tie at his pants, but he fumbled.

Oh.

He could smell blood before he knew what had happened. Her teeth clamped down on his neck, but he felt no pain, just an overwhelming tidal wave of extreme pleasure. His eyes rolled into the back of his head, and he groaned as he fought the pleasure that pulsed through his body and threatened to send him over the edge.

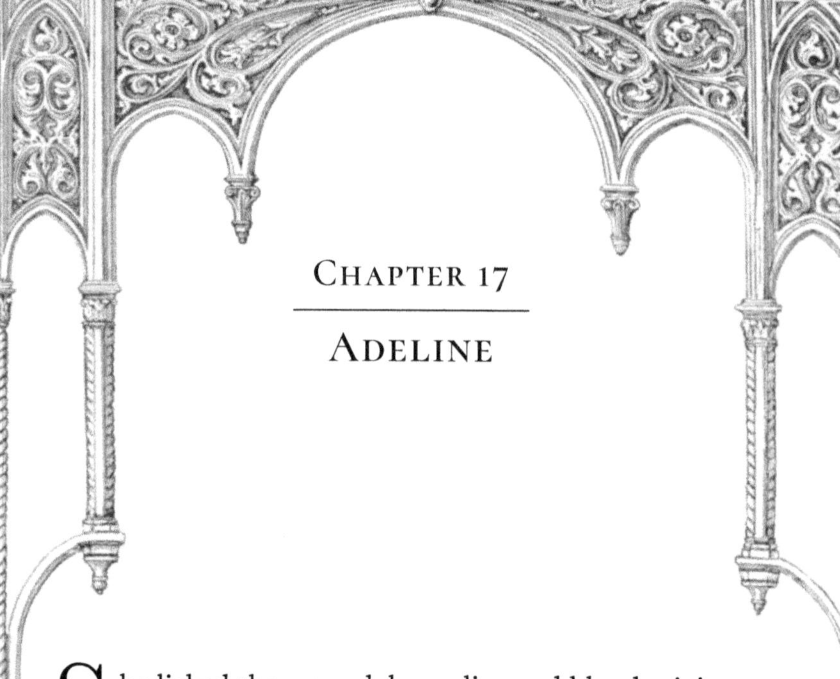

Chapter 17

Adeline

She licked the wound, her saliva and blood mixing to close up the punctures into tiny little marks that would be hard to notice if it wasn't for her vampire eyesight. She made sure to drink only what she needed to restore her energy, but even that left Rolf panting with desire, crazed while trying to catch his breath. He shuddered a few times and looked down at her with a look of mild surprise and...something else.

She tilted her head, opening her mouth to say something.

And then his memories flooded her vision.

Covered in blood, he woke up all alone and terrified. His head hurt tremendously, and his hands shook as he saw how much redness soaked his clothing. He patted himself down and breathed a sigh of relief when he realized it wasn't his.

But whose? No one else was near him.

Something silver glinted in the water at his feet.

A knife.

Adeline's eyes focused on Rolf, a question forming on her lips, and then she rocked back again with more memories.

A woman passed him on the street, pointed, and screamed, "Murderer!" He hid the knife in his boot and ran out of town. A wolf howled in the distance. Sweat broke across his brow, and his breathing turned labored as he ran into the mountainous forest at the edge of town. The bright light of the full moon cast thick shadows through the woods.

He rested against a large tree to catch his breath. His pockets were empty, and he couldn't even remember his name.

Fear clutched her chest as she relived these moments alongside him.

Despite the blood that still coated the inside of her mouth, her tongue went dry. It weighed in her mouth like iron. She dragged it along her teeth to scrape off what felt like layers of sand. Her stomach churned, but she couldn't stop the flood as the highlighted moments flitted in her vision.

He stumbled through the forest, the blood drying on his clothes, seeking answers for things he didn't do. The moonlight shimmered through the ancient boughs, and he suppressed a shudder. He wasn't afraid, merely confused and tired from running. Overhead, a falcon screeched and swooped down near his head. He ducked out of the way of its talons as it snatched a field mouse from the grass. The bird of prey flew high into the trees, and a feather floated down before him. Rolf turned to see where it had gone, but he tripped and stumbled into a small ring of moss-covered stones.

Adeline felt a sinking feeling as if she knew what would happen next. It felt familiar. She had done the same thing centuries ago with her sick sister in her arms. The stone circles were sacred places. Strange places. Where her mother had once told her, magic would sleep until called upon.

She started shaking.

Cold sweat crawled across her skin as her memories fought against Rolf's in her head. Rolf cupped her cheek, worry lining his face. He said something, but she couldn't hear over the roar of her heartbeat and his rushing blood through her veins. Adeline grunted and closed her eyes as another wave of images pulsed through her.

Magic filtered into his peripheral vision, the stones glowing with ancient wards. Then the shift happened. His hands changed. Fur sprouted from his ears. A low growl echoed against the rocks, and soon, his clothes were discarded, and he roared into the night.

"Adeline?" His voice sounded so far away as she swam in the whiplash of his memories.

His blood coursed through her veins. It thrummed inside her, giving her a renewed sense of strength and fury —fury at herself for letting her guard down and at him for keeping this from her.

She flipped him onto his back, her strong legs pinning him down. Shaking with rage, she grabbed him by the throat, and her sharp nails dug into the soft skin under his jaw. A droplet of his blood pooled where her claws pierced him. But he didn't fight back; he just watched her face, keeping his expression emotionless.

Her grip tightened, and she snarled in his face. This was the last were-shifter she had been hunting, and she found herself somehow in his cabin, with his naked and gorgeous body underneath her. Gods above, she was such an idiot. How could she have fallen for someone like him? "I should kill you right here. Right now."

He closed his eyes and exhaled as if he were saying a prayer to the Angel of Death that straddled him. "Do it. Please."

She was tempted. Oh gods, was she tempted. It would fix everything.

But the way he begged for her to take his life gave her pause.

Instead, she tilted her head and studied him. His eyes were closed, and he looked so peaceful. What demons haunted him so that he would want to meet his end? And if she did choose to take his life, which is what her coven would want, would she be bringing him mercy?

Through the centuries, Adeline had never known a were-shifter so willing to meet his death. Or have their blood taken by a vampire. Adeline looked around the cabin, noting how sparse the decorations were. Everything personal was tucked away, like that coat in the drawer, almost as if he was ashamed to take up space. To exist.

Her stomach roiled, and she hunched over with cramping. Her claws retracted, and she loosened her grasp on his neck. Rolf's hands slid up her thighs, her waist, and her arms until he finally cupped her face. She warmed to his touch, even though she was duty-bound to kill him on sight.

Another vision? No, just the remnants of the juniper and garlic in his blood. She shook her head against the swirling in her gut. Bending over, she rested her head against his shoulder. She inhaled, finding comfort in the scent of his skin, and...yes, there it was.

The faint musk that marked him as a were-shifter was now overpowering. She inhaled once more, and it was as if a veil had lifted; she now easily picked up the muskiness that the scent of pine and woodsmoke had masked.

She groaned internally.

How could she have missed it all this time? She was losing her edge. Desperation to find Colin had clouded her decisions once again. When would she finally wake up and realize that he was gone?

She stared down at Rolf, who didn't even try to fight back or get her off him.

Never in her immortal life had she ever felt so conflicted about a kill. It was obvious she had a connection with him, one that she had sworn she'd never feel with another after Colin. But her freedom was on the line, and she hated the idea of going back to the abuse and suffocating lifestyle under Erik.

Of course, he is the were-shifter. Why would any of this have been easy?

She figured she could refuse to hand him over. The worst her coven would do would be to lock her up again. Torture her with withdrawal. Let Erik warp her mind all over again. Retrain her like he'd had to do so many times before. She was always the obstinate one; why change their expectations now?

You weak-minded, licentious bloodsucker.

"I have been killing *your kind* for decades," she said without a hint of venom.

"I know."

Her hand tightened again on his throat, drawing a few more drops of blood. She spat out, “You are a deceptive, manipulative beast.”

“I know.” He sighed.

Did he not have any fight in him at all? She was used to heated battles against his kind, used to walking away with at least several broken bones, but she always came out victorious, carrying the head of the wolf shifter in her hand.

“Before you kill me,” he rasped, and she instantly released his throat, “can you help me figure out where I came from?”

She frowned. “What in the heavens do you mean, *where you came from*?”

He held up his hands in surrender, but she still flinched. Her muscles were wound tight, and she was ready to attack at the tiniest change in his behavior.

Rolf rubbed his forehead and lay his head back down. “I woke up with no memory. I don’t know if you could see that from the tiny bit of blood you took, but I have no idea who I was before the shifting happened.”

The world spun, and she trembled, trying to focus on the amber-colored eyes underneath all of the shaggy hair. It hit her like an avalanche. The coat. The dried blood that still smelled like vampire. The scent of *oud,* tobacco, and leather.

“I would need more blood,” she heard herself say.

You’ve lost your mind, Adeline. You’ve lost it, and for what? Some pathetic were-shifter?

If this were-shifter had been glamoured enough for him to lose all of his core memories, she would have to take quite a bit of blood to get past the magic that had held his mind captive for a hundred years. And she would have to take quite a bit *more* of it if she were to remove the glamour. But something nagged in the back of her head.

Why was he glamoured in the first place?

"Take what you need," Rolf said. "I do not fear death. Not anymore. Not after what I've done."

Adeline cocked her head. Were-shifters were known for violent rampages if they were untrained in their magic, but she had never known one to feel remorse for it.

"Would that we were all brave enough not to fear death," Adeline said. But she knew it wasn't true. She had drained enough mortals to know that their biggest fear was, most often, death. "How long have you lived without your memories?"

Rolf shrugged. "When you live alone for decades, not aging, time ceases to matter so much."

He hadn't known who he was for so long that he had lost track of the years? Adeline could relate. After a while, the centuries had all started to blend together, and she could no longer keep track of anything, let alone who she had killed or why. But then Colin happened, and it was as if her immortal clock only started when she had fallen in love with him.

"Do what you must," he said.

Her eyes snapped back into focus. She held up her hands, hoping she sounded sincere when she said, "I promise I won't take more than I need. But I can't promise it won't leave you a little woozy."

Rolf nodded his consent. "Either way, I will be dead when your coven shows up."

Adeline tilted her head, staring at him. He laughed, but it wasn't full of mirth. It was the sound someone makes when they know their fate, know their end is nigh, and there is nothing they can do about it.

How dare he be so endearing and vulnerable?

She quirked a smile at the absurdity, almost laughing with him. But she held back.

Foreplay was one thing, but a shared moment like this? No, that would be admitting too much, given that he was her target. She wouldn't let herself wonder what a life with him in these woods would look like. She wouldn't think about how he had knelt before her and worshipped her like a goddess.

Because no matter how many mental gymnastics she did, she couldn't figure out how any of this would work.

"Take it," he said, turning his head to expose the unmarked side of his neck. She shifted on top of him.

Adeline nodded and let her fingertip dip below the collar of his shirt. She wanted to peer underneath it, to see if there was a spiderweb of scars near his shoulder where a saber had pierced the skin. But Rolf held her hands in his and kissed her fingertips.

"If you do kill me," he whispered against her hands, "please know that this evening has been incredible. And, when you do, I want you to know that I do not fault you for any of it."

Her heart shattered into dust, like one of the ancient parchments she'd held in a library during her search.

"Stop it," she said gruffly, fighting back tears. This strange emotion threatened to bowl her over. He had to stop being so earnest, or it would ruin the last fragments of her resolve. She leaned over, letting her hair cover his face, and dragged her tongue up the side of his neck, pressing it into his pulse. Then she nipped at his lobe and whispered, "I won't kill you. Yet."

Rolf whispered back, "It wouldn't be a bad way to die."

He hardened underneath her, and despite her best intentions not to be turned on again, she couldn't help but wonder what it would be like to ride him and be in total control of what he experienced, his pleasure at her fingertips this time.

No, Adeline. Don't be a complete idiot.

The coven was coming, and she couldn't let herself get any more attached. Not when his life and her freedom hung in the balance. She had to untangle herself from this mess. Even if she could figure out how to lead her coven away from here, they would probably split up and send some vampire back to exterminate him anyway. And at least if she were the one doing the killing, it would be swift and painless.

It was the least she could do to repay him for his hospitality and *relative* kindness.

"I'll help you, just this once," she conceded, despite everything in her head screaming at her that once she did this, everything would change. "Under the condition that as soon as your memories come back, you will let me do what I have to. Whatever the cost."

"Agreed." He nodded.

Her fangs grew, and she sliced her tongue on their sharp ends, letting the blood fill her mouth. He lifted his arm to her, but she pushed it away and went for the flesh at the base of his neck again. Leaning down, she traced her tongue over his skin.

He sighed, but even though his breathing was slow, his heart beat wildly beneath her palm.

She numbed part of his flesh and inhaled his scent. Her core tightened despite her best efforts to bury the heat between them. The soft scent of his sweat swirled with the warmth of the woodsmoke, and she relaxed against him. Then she bit down hard, eager to get this over with.

He inhaled a sharp breath as her teeth punctured his skin. His fingers found her clit again, and he stroked her slowly as she drank.

Her head reeled with the hazy pieces of imagery that came through. His blood slid down her throat, filling her with heartache, desire, and loneliness. She wasn't as ravenous as before, so she let herself float along the current of his feelings, let them pass through her. When she had consumed enough, she stopped feeding and closed up the wounds from her teeth.

"Stay right here with me," she said, looking into his eyes to remove the glamour. Her hands grabbed his face, and her voice turned hypnotic. "You will remember everything from the time before you woke up. You will remember everything..."

As she talked, emotions pulsed through her, ebbing and flowing like a current. She inhaled the scent of his skin once more and let the effects of the blood take over.

The room fell away as she tried to undo the glamour that had been placed on him by the other vampire. She gasped. This glamour wasn't the work of some inexperienced vampire. No, it was done by one who was older than

Adeline, which would explain why it was so strong. She sank deeper into Rolf's body, fighting against the darker magic that had tried to rip away the very essence of him.

Specific memories blurred into each other, swirling together in an incoherent jumble of images. She could see his body changing after his first shift—from what had once been a youthful body into a formidable man's. The bone structure had slightly changed, his shoulders were wider, and his body hairier. His eyes had even shifted colors, to the deep amber she could lose herself in. Parts of his childhood morphed into dreamy, warbled images and emotions, cluttered with longing.

But the deeper history that she sought within his psyche still refused to untangle. The more blood she drank from Rolf, the stronger she got. He groaned underneath her, and she would have to stop lest she take too much and it take too long for him to heal.

There.

A solitary memory, buried so deep within him that it was no longer stored in his mind but etched into the walls of his heart. She withdrew, closing up his wounds, and sighed with relief. Her body trembled as new memories flooded her vision once more. She gasped and stared down at Rolf, focusing on how desperate and concerned he looked.

It can't be.

Chapter 18

Rolf

His hands rested on her hips, holding her steady while he waited for her to reveal something. *Anything*.

A century of not knowing what had happened before that ill-fated night. A century of guessing, of hoping that his memory would return one day. It made for a lonely existence.

When he woke in the alley, his head had ached as if he had been hit with a croquet mallet. He found no evidence of any injury. Based on the design and color of his coat, he figured he must have been a member of some regiment. But a member of what army and what country was a mystery since he could not find any identifying markings—even the buttons had been torn off.

Adeline gasped and crumpled into his arms. He shifted onto his side and pulled her into his chest, cradling her while she sobbed.

What could have been so bad that I cannot remember what happened?

When she finally came back down, her eyes were blown wide, and her eyebrows formed a soft frown.

She ripped open his shirt, pushing it down from his shoulders. Her fingers trailed along his right shoulder, down his pectoral, and stopped at the small spiderweb scar. She pressed in, and he hissed in response, the ache still very real despite the age of the mark. Her hand slid underneath his shoulder to his back, finding the opposite side of the scar that marked the exit wound.

"This," she breathed. Her eyes were rimmed with tears. "This shouldn't be here."

"Why not?" he asked, confusion coursing through his veins. What had she seen?

She sat up quickly and started to undo all of his buttons. He almost pulled her back, but her hands continued their frenzied exploration of his body. Tears fell from her eyes, and she dragged her hands down to his leg, where a jagged scar traveled from his mid-thigh to the top of his knee. The two scars she had found were the only ones that hadn't faded over time.

Finally, her hands stopped roaming, and she cursed under her breath. She swiped at her face quickly with the backs of her hands.

Rolf grabbed her face, pulling her back up to him. "What is it? What did you see?"

Her eyes were unfocused and cloudy. Slowly shaking her head, she whispered, "I don't want it to be possible."

"What do you mean, Adeline?"

Her breath hitched in her throat, and she finally

looked into his eyes. Her lower lip trembled as she murmured, "Say it again."

"What do you mean?"

"My name. Say it again," she implored. Her blue eyes were almost gray, and her entire body looked as if it was ready to collapse from the weight of whatever she had seen.

"Adeline," he said, wiping more of her tears away with his thumbs. He hated seeing her so tormented. Surely his life before turning couldn't have been that bad.

"Oh, gods," she wailed and then crumpled again into a heap in his arms. Her shoulders heaved as she sobbed against his chest.

"Shhh," he crooned into her hair, his arms wrapping around her tightly. Rolf turned to his side, taking her with him, and she curled into a tight ball. He rocked slowly back and forth, one hand rubbing her back as she cried. "It'll be okay. I can withstand whatever information you give me."

"I have been *such* a fool." Adeline's eyes went hard as she looked at the door to his cabin.

"Please tell me what you saw, Adeline."

Her eyes flicked back to him, and she pushed up to sit back on her heels. She brushed a few stray hairs out of her face and cleared her throat. He sat up with her and leaned in close, eager to understand what it was she had seen.

"Let me see if I can be more persuasive since I am stronger now." She sniffled, letting him wipe away the tears on her cheeks. She leaned into the touch for a moment, but then her eyes glazed over. "You will remember everything from the time before you woke up."

She chanted the last sentence like a prayer, and it washed over him in waves. They sat facing each other on his bed, holding hands. He was pulled into her glassy-eyed stare, and he had leaned forward to get closer when a low ringing filled his ears. Maybe it was his imagination, but he could have sworn the shadows in the corners of the cabin shifted into shapes.

Gooseflesh erupted over his skin.

Too late to turn back now. He swallowed thickly, the shadows growing in the corners of his vision.

A searing pain tore through his head, and he stifled a cry, closing his eyes tightly. Sweat beaded on his forehead, his heart was beating in double time, and he clung to her hand as he tried to stay grounded.

"Shh," Adeline said. And then, for the last time, she said, letting the sentence land softly, "You will remember everything from the time before you woke up."

The pain ceased, but he was too nervous to open his eyes.

Something sweet and thick, like rich honey, coated him from the top of his head to the tips of his toes. Adeline's amber scent floated over him. He closed his eyes and breathed her in as soft images floated in his mind: her laughter, her curves, her smile. He was swimming in the deepest waters, completely unafraid, and knew that deep down, he had only ever felt like that when she was around.

"I remember," he whispered. His eyes flew open, and he met her vibrant blue gaze with awe. "It was the first time I told you I loved you."

"Yes." Adeline nodded, holding back more tears.

His memories flooded his thoughts, and he fought against the onslaught as it threatened to overwhelm him.

How hard he had laughed, running around with his brothers in the garden, the squishing of their boots as they ran through the mud, all of them oblivious to the death of their parents and how it would tear their family apart.

But then he met Adeline, and everything changed.

His loneliness was replaced by hope and yearning. The sadness he carried slowly metamorphosed into a love so pure and deep that he could not picture a life without her. It didn't matter that she was a vampire, and she was sent here to kill him.

"There are so many memories..." He drifted off, savoring the gift Adeline had given him. She had brought him back from this numbing abyss, mere hours before she was supposed to end his life. But now, he didn't want to greet death so easily. He overflowed with gratitude to have these precious moments back.

And it was her. It was always her. The scent of her cloak, the tiny shred of fabric that had snagged on the post of his porch, had triggered all of this. It made sense now why he had felt so pulled to her from the beginning.

Adeline shifted, her watchful eyes taking him in. She rubbed her palm over the hair on his chest and down the hard planes of his stomach, but stopped before going any lower. "The memory was so hazy, I couldn't tell it was me. But it was the scents from that moment, the rain on the cobblestones, a hint of my amber perfume, and..."

"Your laugh, your smile," he breathed. And it was her giggle from mere moments ago that meshed with the scent of her cloak. Even if he didn't understand why, there was a bigger magic at work here that had brought them together and led them to this moment.

She nodded at his revelation, biting her lower lip. Her hands framed his face, and she bent down, kissing him delicately. "You changed so much when your magic came in."

"Magic?" he asked, confused.

Adeline nodded. "Yes, the stones. They amplified your shifter magic."

He stared at her. The stones amplified his magic? Which must have meant that he'd had some magic to begin with when he was still Colin.

"And what should I call you? Colin? Rolf?"

"Whatever your heart desires," he said, and he meant it. "Call me Frederick or Gertrude, I don't care. So long as you're the one calling me."

Adeline giggled again, a smile that split her face in two, and he felt like his heart would burst. "I will *not* call you Gertrude."

"You haven't changed at all," he said, breathless at the volatile beauty who sat next to him. It was his turn to get emotional, tears welling in his eyes. She brushed them from his face, and he captured her hand in his, stroking her hand with his thumb, never wanting to forget what it felt like to have her skin at his fingertips. "I have loved you every moment of my eternal life, Adeline. I never meant to forget you."

"It wasn't your fault," she said. Adeline stared into the distance, eyes boring a hole in the door opposite them. A slew of emotions passed over her face until all she wore was cold fury. It was at this moment that he saw the emotionless killer that she could be. "It was my maker. The glamour you were subjected to couldn't wipe away our love for each other."

Her maker. Of course.

And her coven would be here tomorrow at sundown. He rolled his shoulders back, imagining how his wolf would happily tear into each and every one of them if it meant that Adeline could be with him forever.

Rolf gathered her in his arms again, her head nestling against his shoulder with the scars. He tried his best to hide his sorrow as he said, "Well, this time, I'm not letting you go."

I'd rather die than live without you, he almost said out loud. But he didn't; he didn't want to think of either of them dying. Instead, he focused on how it would feel to tear apart the vampire who had caused so much destruction in their lives.

"You won't have to," she said, her voice hard as steel. A shiver crawled down his spine when she spoke again, her voice deadly. "I plan on never letting them near us again."

"And how do you propose to do that?" he asked, trying not to sound excited at the possibility of destroying the vampires who had a hand in keeping them apart.

"We'll kill them all," she said simply.

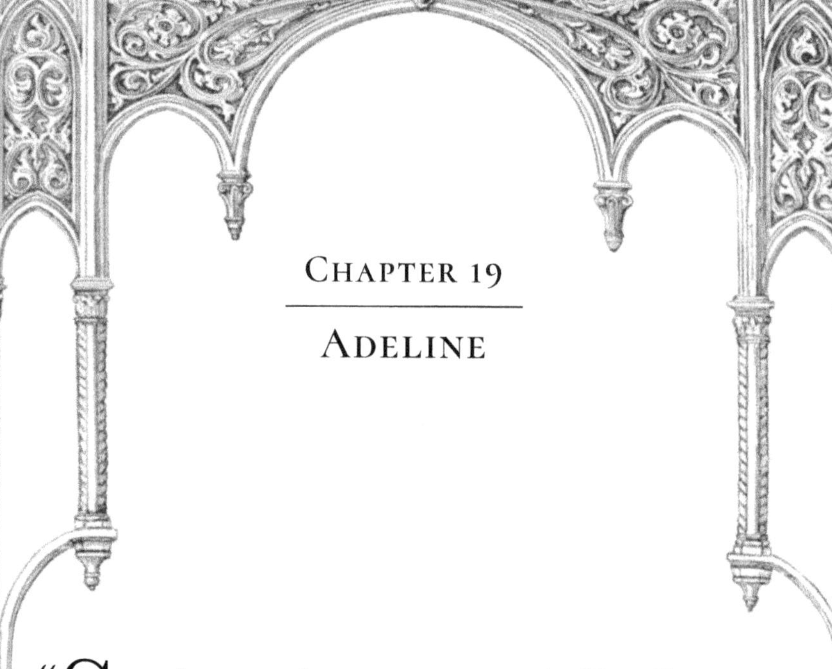

Chapter 19

Adeline

"So what, exactly, are you proposing?" Rolf asked, sitting down on the edge of the bed with his food.

"We fight them." She waved her hand in the air dismissively. Her nails clicked together, and Rolf raised his eyebrows at her. Rolf didn't need to know that she was *still* formulating a plan.

Adeline forced him to have some stew so he could keep his energy up, since she had taken so much of his blood. As she watched him eat, her heart filled with warmth at how casual things felt with him. How easy. Even after all those years of absence. Bitterness and betrayal wove through her thoughts at the many years she was forced to be without him.

Her maker was going to pay for everything he had done. Her nails elongated at the thought of sinking them into her maker's flesh and tearing out his heart.

Had Erik known this whole time who Rolf was? Is that why he had agreed to her bargain, knowing that she would most likely kill the were-shifter, never figuring out that it was Colin?

Insufferable insect! The first chance I get, I will gut him and watch his blood stain the bottoms of my feet.

Erik was more evil than she could have ever conceived if he had known who Rolf really was and still let her bargain for more time, for her freedom. As her maker, he had always been jealous when her attention went elsewhere.

Adeline had never been able to love freely under his watchful eyes. Even her time with Juliette had to be stolen. The two of them would sneak around the castle to be together. But eventually, that met a natural end when she realized Erik was catching on. That was the last time she escaped. A few years later, she met Colin.

Or...Rolf.

And now that she had found him, she was worried she'd have to give him up.

They'll have to get through me first.

Could she do it? When face-to-face with Erik and all that he had done to her, would she finally be able to bring him to justice?

Yes. He deserves nothing less than what I plan on giving him.

She had no idea how many vampires would come or who would be leading the group. But she had a willing form of sustenance, and she could feel her magic tingling, waiting.

Adeline paced around the room, looking for things she could make into weapons, because whether they wanted it or not—their time together was ending. Either she would end up killing Erik, or he would end up killing her, unless she could figure out a way to subdue him—and before her coven arrived.

As the hour of the full moon neared, she fought against the rising tide of panic. She needed a clear head to plan. Thankfully, since feeding from Rolf, her strength was coming back, and she was moving during the daylight hours; she needed to use that to their advantage. A few times, she looked over to Rolf and sensed the wolf getting restless under his skin. She could even sense the coven nearing, though she told herself that was just her imagination. There was one way for her to know, but it would take too much effort, and she needed to reserve her strength as the clock ticked closer to sundown.

If only she could freeze time, then she could bask in the fact that she had finally found him. That they were together, and nothing could harm either of them. As it was, Rolf didn't know what was waiting for him tonight. Adeline glanced outside at the midday sun; the storm outside had slowed, and the flurries were less frequent. She hoped to the gods above that the seven-foot drifts of snow had slowed them all down. If Rolf didn't shift in time before her coven arrived, they had no hope of getting out of this together.

Rolf took a bite of his stew, and she smiled wide when he caught her staring. She forced the thoughts of doom deep into her head and turned them into fuel for her anger.

He rolled his eyes and kept eating, but he turned away from her slightly.

"Don't get self-conscious," she said. She could stare at

him for hours, still amazed at the transformation his body went through when he had become a were-shifter. His shoulders had broadened, he got taller by at least another six inches, his eyes had changed, and the hair...

She shuddered, remembering his beard tickling her stomach and the way he looked at her from between her legs. He was a beast of a man, and the fact that he could be so delicate and attentive made her flush.

Does he know how to fight in his human form? Or does he not remember? Are his reflexes fast enough?

"I'm not self-conscious. You're just staring at me like I'm your next meal. It's a little unsettling to be humbled so effectively."

Adeline raised an eyebrow. "You *are* my next meal."

Rolf rubbed at where she had sucked on him earlier, and a flush crept up his neck.

"Did you know you were a were-shifter before you were glamoured?" Adeline asked, busying herself with sorting through the pile of wood and rusted weapons. She tossed the wooden spears that looked too flimsy into a pile by the fire and then snapped them into smaller pieces in several quick motions.

Rolf put his stew down. "No. My family became so fractured after the death of my parents that most of what I should have known was never discussed."

Ah, yes. She remembered now. The details were fuzzy, but he had told her that when he was younger, he had been sent away to a boarding school shortly after the funeral. Colin had been in his early thirties when they had met, close to her age, but even then, he had seemed decades older. She wondered if it was because he had to grow up on his own so young.

"I used to be so close to my brothers, but they all left when I was little. My oldest brother, Theodore, was twenty years my senior, but nothing like a father figure. Most of what I know, I had to teach myself."

"The weeks after you went missing, I visited your family home." Adeline held his axe, the weight slightly off since it was built for Rolf's grip. But it would do in a pinch.

She had traveled for days to the small village in the lowlands by the sea and discreetly watched his older brother, Theodore, before approaching. When she broke the news that she had been with him, Theodore looked ashen-faced and forlorn, but invited her to stay for a few days in hopes that Colin would show up back home. She met the selkie he had married, and the adorable children they had. Their life was so idyllic that Adeline left wondering if she would have been able to lead a somewhat normal life with Colin one day.

"You went to my childhood home?" he asked, his amber eyes shocked. "Why?"

"I never stopped looking for you." And she hadn't.

For the past century, whenever she hunted down a were-shifter, she was always looking for him. She sought him out in strangers' faces, yearning for his touch instead of the courtesans she slept with, always hoping that he would turn up, even after she knew he would be well into his old age.

And now, by some cruel twist of fate, or by Erik's marionette fingers, she had finally found him.

And Adeline didn't want to acknowledge the

inevitable. She wished they could stay here, in their bliss, insulated from their reality, forever. But she knew that no matter how hard she willed against it, Erik would ruin any shred of happiness she had. After all, it was what he did best—let her know who was really in charge.

But not any longer.

"I wish we had more time," Rolf said gruffly.

"But we don't," Adeline snapped, immediately regretting how harsh she sounded when Rolf's eyes met hers. She set the axe down and clicked her nails together impatiently. This was her last chance at freedom; she had delayed Erik for too long, constantly telling him she needed more time and more funds so she could exterminate the entirety of the were-shifters. "So we have to do this right."

The last time she had seen her maker was several decades ago, in a dust-filled library near a long-forgotten castle. She had been researching known locations of were-shifter packs when Erik appeared behind her, knife to her throat. In her haste, she made a bargain, one she had hoped would keep her out of his clutches for just a little longer. Adeline promised that each year, by the night of the full moon of the autumnal equinox, she would deliver the head of a were-shifter. Or she would live in his castle as his companion—forever.

Erik had spun her around, planted a sloppy kiss on her lips, and let her go. As he threw a sack of gold at her, he casually mentioned that the coven would be sent to ensure she followed through. They would come to collect the trophy and, if she failed, then they would come to collect her. So far, she had always followed through, dropping the head off at a pre-arranged location and leaving as soon as she could.

This time was different.

What she didn't know was that the were-shifter she had been hunting this whole time was Colin, post-glamour. And now that she had him, she would never let him go.

"Adeline." His voice was warm and silky as he called her back to reality. "Let me show you something."

Rolf walked over to the center of the cabin, nudging some of the weapons aside. He slid the chair by the fire out of the way and flipped over the corner of the rug, which hadn't been a stretched-out lump. It had been covering a door made entirely out of silver with a small, inset circular handle.

"A cellar?"

Rolf nodded as he unlocked and lifted the heavy door. Scratch marks lined the lid on the inside. The silver wasn't just on the door; it went down several feet into the tunnel, and two hooks made of silver protruded from the framing. "It leads down to a cave and a series of old dwarven tunnels. All of them sealed with solid silver doors or grates."

Adeline looked at him warily. He bustled about her as she turned to stare into the darkness below, wondering how far down the tunnel went. If he expected her to go down there, he had another thing coming.

Rolf grunted. Looking over her shoulder, she saw him heft a large bundle of rope in his arms. She raised an eyebrow and watched his muscles flex under the weight.

He bent down and placed two loops on the hooks, then kicked the bundle down the hole.

Next, he took a lantern, lit it, and hooked it onto a long wooden pole. As he lowered it down, she noticed deep gouges had been carved into the side of the rock.

Large enough that a were-shifter could have made them...

She angled her head, nails and fangs already elongating out of fear that this might be a trap. "You want me to go down there?"

"Well, yes, but I think we should dress first." He wore a goofy grin, like a kid ready to show off his favorite toy.

Chapter 20

Rolf

When he dug the tunnel, he made it too narrow and too tight for his wolf to squeeze through. He wanted it as uncomfortable as possible for his wolf to try and get out, so he lined the uppermost parts with molten silver and had a special door made that could only be opened by human hands. Pride swelled in his chest at how he had managed it, saving funds from fur trapping for several years, commissioning an old miner who could have easily been a descendant of a dwarf. He hadn't thought, however, that he'd ever be coming down here to show it off.

Rolf led the way, the lantern on a stick illuminating the musty tunnel a few feet ahead of them. They were both quiet, lost in their thoughts as they moved down the winding corridor. Adeline fit comfortably through the tunnel, but for Rolf, the ceiling wasn't nearly as tall as he needed it to be, so he walked awkwardly with his head tilted to the side. Water dripped down the walls of the tunnel, littering the ground with water, and he was glad he insisted they both wear shoes.

He swallowed a few times, trying to move the knot in his throat down, down, down into his stomach. He cursed as he stepped into a sizable puddle. He hadn't been down here in his fully human form in decades, always partially shifting as he opened the trapdoor. Showing this place to Adeline was like letting her in on some of his darkest hours, and though he knew she was the woman he had fallen in love with, there was a hundred-year gap that stood between them.

"What is this place?" Adeline whispered as the tunnel opened up into a small chamber.

Wooden beams framed the small space, and her hands drifted over deep claw marks slashed across the face of the cavern walls. Everywhere Adeline looked, there was evidence of his wolf. Deep gashes in the walls, tufts of hair caught in the joining of the beams. The animalistic fury of being trapped, unable to leave the underground jail. He was thankful the cave was dark, as shame flushed his cheeks a bright red.

"This is where I spend one night a month," he said. Even though it was a cavern, and his voice should have reverberated off the walls, the atmosphere pressed down around him, choking off the volume. He felt smothered being in the cavern in his unshifted form, knowing that he would be down here once the full moon crested the snowy peaks outside.

He swallowed tightly, wishing she would say something. *Anything* to quell the incessant chattering of insecurity in his head.

Adeline's hands touched the deep claw marks in the cave walls; her fingers were swallowed up by the depth of the gouges he had left behind. Was it awe that painted her features just now, or disgust? She turned before he could study her expression in the torchlight. He wouldn't be surprised if she had doubts—after all, one could say that he was a hopeless case.

"I have only ever known were-shifters as our enemies, the only creatures who can kill us with their claws. I never thought I'd be in love with one of them." Her voice swelled between them, filling the stifling quiet. He let her words wash over him.

Love? What on earth could possess her to love a creature like me?

Parts of his life had been so marred with memory loss that he had gotten used to the idea that he was a monster, that he had committed heinous acts of violence toward innocent people. Each time he had woken after the full moon, in his human form, covered in blood, he was reminded of how he had woken up the first time with no memory. He had always assumed that it was because he had shifted and killed someone the very first time.

What a cruel twist of fate for him to relive that feeling of dread every month. It was the driving force behind why he created this prison down here. He was tired of constantly wondering, waking up covered in sweat and blood, the fear that gripped his heart as he realized he never knew who or what he killed.

Adeline moved over to the beams and grabbed a tuft of werewolf fur, rolling it between her fingers. "Do you remember anything from your time during the full moon?"

There was one time he had woken up in a pasture, surrounded by dozens of carcasses of cattle. He fled as soon as he had his wits about him, but the screams of the woman who discovered the scene traveled on the wind. In one night, he had decimated her family's livelihood, almost certainly committing them to a life of poverty.

It hung heavy on his heart still eighty decades later.

She tucked the fur into an interior coat pocket and looked at him, a slight frown wrinkling her brow. What could he say so she wouldn't judge him for what he did—or didn't—do?

"No, but it's probably better that way." Rolf shook his head, toeing a link in one of the several large chains scattered on the floor. He swung his lantern over them, and they glinted in the soft golden light.

"Silver chains?" Adeline's voice sounded pained as she stepped up next to him. He couldn't bring himself to look at her for fear of the shame she would see written on his face and the pity he would see in her eyes. "Why, Rolf?"

"Because...I am a beast. A monster," he said simply. It was something he had finally come to terms with. After, of course, he had pieced together what he was when he went through the stones.

During the first years he spent roaming the woods, he picked up the odd transient jobs, living in makeshift shelters, and worried he would kill innocent people whenever he shifted. With no memory of his life from before, he picked up as many trade skills as possible. He was best at fur trapping since he inhabited places where the other wild creatures of the forests lived, and with the money he earned from it, he bought tools to learn the woodworking trades of the other humans in the area. He learned how to fell dead trees, chopping into the trunks like an artist sculpting marble. Rolf honed his skills quickly and soon became a master woodworker. And when winter blew in, he'd return to fur trapping to make ends meet during the colder months.

Only several years into his life as a were-shifter, he became terrified that he would keep waking up covered in blood. Rolf never knew if those he killed on his full-moon rampages were people who deserved it, or if they were innocent. The guilt of his blackout kills finally got the better of him. Which is when he decided to turn the abandoned cave he had been living in into his permanent jail.

Her hand cupped his cheek as if she knew the shame he held. He leaned into her palm, his free hand reaching up to cover hers.

"You are *not* a monster," she whispered. "I would know."

"My darkness," he whispered back.

Her pupils flared at the nickname he had chosen for her, and though he didn't want to say it out loud, for fear of pushing her away, she was his. Something blossomed in his chest, and he wondered what it meant.

Protectiveness.

A part of him knew that he would never love after her, that Adeline was all he would ever need. They were perfectly matched, as they had been back when he was Colin. And as foreign as that person felt to him now, he knew that from here and into eternity, there would be no one else for him. How he could feel this way toward her, so soon, still felt too good to be true. So he would cling to these small moments as much as he could—after tonight, he might not get another chance to feel this way.

She will be my downfall.

He would go down fighting for her. *With* her. Always.

He cupped her face and said, "You are not a monster to me. You never will be."

Adeline scoffed, almost as if she didn't believe she was lovable. How wrong she was.

"You have no idea the things I have done, Rolf," she said.

"You have no idea the things *I* have done, Adeline," Rolf replied, wishing he could convince her that she was worthy. But he knew what that felt like. The unworthiness, the shame. It didn't matter to him if she felt unlovable; his place on this earth was to make sure she knew his love, in any form, forever. Because to Rolf, they were the perfect pair—both broken, both monstrous, both finding a way to survive in a world that didn't want them. The vampires were hunted just as much as the were-shifters—if not by each other, then by humans who knew no different.

"I need to show you the rest of the tunnels." He took her hand, letting the subject drop. Once they survived tonight, he would make sure she knew how much she meant to him.

Once she saw what he was going to show her, perhaps they could make it out alive after all. He let himself fantasize about how many of the vampires he could kill once he was a wolf. One? Five? Twenty? And would the vampire who glamoured him be there tonight?

Gods, he hoped so. He smiled smugly to himself, a renewed sense of justice pushing out the fear he had of losing her.

He stopped when they arrived at the point where two tunnels connected, the darkness swallowing the light from the lantern as he pointed it to the left.

"This was the first cave I found while I was washing in the stream below. A white falcon kept swooping around a ledge, landing every so often to perch and scan the water for fish. It wasn't until I was drying on the opposite bank that I realized the bird was perched on the ledge of the cave entrance. It is small enough that I figured I could use it for shelter for the night. But while I was trying to find a way to get to it, I stumbled upon the cave to the right."

"A sign of good luck," Adeline mused.

He looked at her in confusion.

"White birds of prey are a sign from the goddess," Adeline said, her tone soft, almost reverent.

"Yes, I have often felt it was a sign of divine providence," Rolf replied.

He wanted to ask her more, but she squared her shoulders and pointed toward the tunnel on the right, asking, "Was this the other cave?"

Certain things felt fated to Rolf. Finding these caves was one of them. However, at first it never felt like it. He needed a place to sleep that night, there was a cave. But the more time he spent in these ancient woods, the more he realized certain things were out of his control. Nature had a way of forcing herself on you, and the best you could do was adapt. So that was what he did.

"Yes. I used to use it when I lived down here. It's easier for me to get in and out in human form without the possibility of falling to my death." Rolf swung the lantern light down the tunnel, memories returning from when he was a newly turned wolf. "It was full of old mining debris, and a small cave-in had blocked off access to this space. It wasn't until I started clearing it out that I realized the two tunnels were connected."

They walked down the tunnel to the right, their footfalls echoing in the small puddles. He held out his arm for her, and she took it, her hand resting comfortably in the crook of his elbow.

Adeline squeezed his arm. "You used to live down here?"

"Yes, when I was still trying to understand what was happening to me." In the months that followed his change, he had been so lonely and out of his depth. When he had stepped out of the stone circle, he shifted back into his human form almost instantly, still covered in blood. He fell to his knees, dripping with sweat, still coated in someone else's blood. He tore off the regiment coat and ran downhill until he came to a stream. The water was frigid, but he scrubbed himself raw with sand, eager to get all evidence of the last day behind him. He washed his clothes next, trying to get rid of the fact that he wore someone else's blood. That tiny detail would always confuse him. Why would they have covered him in someone else's blood?

The answer now hit him like a slap to the face. "I was never supposed to make it this far."

Adeline stiffened at his side, but she remained thoughtfully quiet as they reached the end of the tunnel.

Rolf stared at the snow beyond the gate. "It was all a part of their plan, wasn't it? Separate us, kill me, make it look like an accident."

"I think they had even more nefarious plans, Rolf," Adeline whispered, looking up at him, revenge burning in her eyes.

Chapter 21

Adeline

Adeline stared down the tunnel, the light of the early afternoon filling the end of it with a silvery light. Given the silence coming from Rolf, she wondered if his head was spinning as much as hers. The centuries-long plan that Erik had enacted to get back at her for wanting to leave kept unfolding before her.

He will never let me go...

Rolf was her punishment. For even conceiving of wanting to mate and settle down, and finally be happy. Someone knew he had shifter fae blood. And the only person who was always a step ahead of her was Erik.

"Why would Erik glamour me to get back at you?" Rolf asked. "Why wouldn't he just kill me?"

Realization dawned as she finally put the pieces together.

"Because I wanted to leave the coven. I was done with Erik. When you were Colin, I was ready to turn you into a vampire as soon as you asked. I considered myself already paired for the rest of your mortal life, even if you never wanted to be turned. We would have been mates in their eyes, and I wanted out."

"And you couldn't have that because...?" Rolf asked.

Vampire politics were one of a kind, especially when it involved the whims of Erik. But now that Adeline realized what her maker had wanted all along, everything made sense. She struggled to admit the full truth—Erik wanted her for himself for centuries. But she never made it easy on him. She resisted every chance she could get. She had the scars to prove it. "Erik never wanted me to mate. I am his most prized possession."

I am no one's possession, she seethed.

When she was turned, she was newly widowed due to the blight that had wormed its way into the land. But she wasn't heartbroken. Far from it. Her husband, a spoiled, selfish prince, had kept her from her family for years, claiming her beauty would drive men mad, and he knew she would run away with the most handsome suitor if she stepped out of her tower. She was a possession then, just as she was Erik's possession now.

It was never enough that she had become the deadliest weapon he used; he always wanted more. He had Adeline's body, he destroyed her mind. But he could never have her soul. By the time she had met Colin, it had been half a century since she let Erik have his way with her. As soon as she had dared to love, Erik had pulled on her reins.

If she was honest with herself, she hadn't been at the top of her game since Colin went missing—using every excuse she could to stay away from Erik and keep her search going, which is probably why she had missed that Erik had been leading her around on purpose.

He had laid this all out for her—the perfect trap to get her back. Forever.

We will be free, I will make sure of it.

"So he punished me." Rolf met her eyes, and she looked away quickly. "And now he's punishing you."

"Yes." Adeline shuddered, remembering how slimy she had felt when Erik had kissed her, how sticky his lips felt. How could she have once thought he ever had good intentions for her? "He's done all of this as punishment for me thinking I could leave. That I could be happy."

"So now we kill them," Rolf said, smiling. His eyes caught the light from the torch, but Adeline didn't dare let herself feel anything more than anger. She was afraid she would overlook the most minor details if she let even the tiniest sliver of hope weasel its way in. And right now, they couldn't afford for her to forget anything. One small misstep was a fatal mistake.

And she was determined to kill them all.

"We can be happy now, together," Rolf said, and Adeline knew he was saying it to make her feel better.

She shook her head. "Not until Erik is dead."

Her feet sloshed in the puddles of water as she walked to the end of the tunnel on the left. Rolf followed, the swinging lantern casting shadows on the wall. Her shadow walked steadily next to her, and for the first time in a long while, Adeline felt an emptiness as she thought about her mother and sister. When she opened the sky and sent her sister through the portal, she never knew where she had ended up, or if she still lived. The final look Leda had given her, a mixture of fear and hope, was mirrored in the last moments of every life she took. In the beginning, when she was still a newly turned vampire, she would see her sister's face in every kill.

The Angel of Death was always me.

"You said you were the monster? No, Rolf. *I* am the monster. I have harmed and killed countless innocents, all in the name of my maker. I have killed so many, I no longer remember their names."

"You used to know their names?"

Adeline nodded. "I felt like I owed it to myself to hold on to the last of who they were."

Guilt consumed her, thinking back to all of the killing she had done. She used to tell herself it was for her survival, and sometimes she even went as far as thinking she liked it. But when she finally started to undo the centuries of manipulation Erik had put her through, she realized he had been the one coaching her, convincing her that she was a ruthless killer.

Rolf didn't talk; he silently walked with her until they both stood at the end of the tunnel in a few inches of snow. The vines covered the silver grate, hiding most of the entrance with foliage.

If Rolf was to be her punishment, then Erik had gravely misunderstood how much she loved him. Perhaps he didn't account for her feelings because he could not feel anything beyond power and greed.

She continued. "I think Erik knew you by your fae blood. Perhaps, he even knew that you were a were-shifter. How, exactly, is something I still need to figure out.

But I know that he did this on purpose. As a way to put me in my place and remind me that he is still in charge."

"Because he's your maker?" Rolf asked.

"Because I was his possession." Adeline turned and stared down the dark tunnel, shuddering at the thought of Erik's hands on her body, how she would shut down every time she was alone with him.

Juliette had been her only saving grace for over a century, her only companion in a den full of creatures she couldn't stand. Her touch was gentle and warm and welcome, while Erik's was cold and slimy and distant. Her laugh was golden, reminding her of careless summers in the sun. Erik never laughed unless he was inflicting pain of some kind. Or collecting on his countless unwinnable bargains.

Her stomach swirled with disgust at herself. How could she have been so stupid to make a bargain with him?

"You don't have to tell me anything, but..." Rolf whispered as she fell into his chest. His arms wrapped around her carefully. "When we make it out of here alive, I will take as long as needed to replace every touch of his with mine."

She soaked in his warmth, wishing she could wipe her own memory clean from all the times she had acquiesced to Erik's cravings.

"*When* we make it out alive," she echoed, resolved to get them through this.

"So, Erik needs to die. Simple enough. What do you need me to do?" Rolf asked.

His hand slipped behind her neck, and she tilted her

head up to his. She needed to figure out a way to get both of them out of this situation so that they could finally spend an eternity together.

"Adeline." Rolf reached out and grabbed her arm, pulling her into him. "Tell me, I trust you."

Adeline closed her eyes and leaned into his chest, breathing him in. "First, we have to kill the entire coven. And Erik, if he's with them. And if we can't—"

Rolf let out a deep laugh, full of disbelief. "The two of us up against an entire coven of vampires? Do you know how many?"

She shrugged. *If he doesn't think we can do this, then we have nothing.*

It was as if she could finally see clearly. The full moon was only a few hours away, and he was the one creature here that could kill with minimal effort expended. She looked around at the tunnels surrounding them. Each entrance was coated in silver, and only Rolf could touch them in his human form unscathed.

Adeline's mind whirred with the threads of a plan she began to weave together. Vampires couldn't touch silver without their skin burning, but if they timed it right, and Rolf was able to shift back, then maybe they did have a chance at getting out of this predicament, not only alive but also with each other.

For the first time since she had consumed his blood, she let herself hope.

The fresh snow glinted a blinding white as the light of the full moon crested the mountain peaks. The storm had finally abated, and in the forest beyond, the night was still, clear, and crisp. The fireplace crackled, and embers swirled around the fresh wood, making it hiss and pop. She wanted the cabin to be hot so the vampires would think the blood would remain warm. It was the illusion she was after, that the blood was fresh and not something she collected hours ago. A keening howl from Rolf's wolf reverberated through the silver door in the floor. Chills spread across her skin, and she knew the night would be agonizing as she waited for the precise moment for him to turn back.

It all comes down to timing.

She stared at the jars of blood on the small table. Some of it was hers, but most of it was his. It took some convincing for Rolf to follow her plan, but in the end, they spent the last moments of their free time working out the details. At least six feet of snow surrounded the cabin. Rolf had gone out during the day to shovel most of it off the roof, to show that someone lived here, and to stomp around a bit as proof of life. He cleared off his snowshed and found a container of pitchwood and a small jar of tar tucked in the stacks of freshly cut pine. Adeline had nodded her approval and plastered him with kisses when he showed her.

Then Rolf and Adeline laid their trap.

Now, all she had to do was wait. The last few hours before dawn would be critical, so she could set the final scene for her coven when she greeted them. She knew they were on their way by the sounds of the forest outside. The owls and other creatures of the night had been kicking up a ruckus since the storm ended.

Her senses tingled. The roaring fire tossed dancing shadows along the walls that reminded her of spiderwebs. She rubbed her eyes and told herself she was seeing things. Besides, she had consumed enough of Rolf's blood to feel almost back to normal.

She glanced outside. The night sky was thick and peppered with stars that fought against the silvery glimmer of the moon. As it shifted higher in the sky, she knew the time was nigh.

Placing a final few logs on the fire, she watched the flames lick at the edges of the mantel. The smoke walked slowly up the chimney, and a few gray curls hovered in the air near the ceiling. It might not be enough to cover up the scent of arousal and sweat, but she hoped it would help mask her memories from the vampires as they took over this place.

One final look around the cabin, and she walked quietly over to the table. Picking up a few jars, she smashed them into the walls, then picked up a few more, and smashed them on the floor. She took her hands and dragged them through the shards of glass, mixing and smearing the blood they contained everywhere.

Adeline then continued to rampage through the rest of the cabin until it looked as if it had been part of a massacre. Blood splatter was everywhere, as was broken glass and overturned furniture. After she felt like Rolf's place was thoroughly destroyed, she picked the shards from her palms, drank a small vial of his blood, and lay down on the bed to wait.

With her eyes closed, she emptied her mind so she could focus on the sounds outside. If she focused hard enough, she could hear the pacing of Rolf's beast below. It growled but no longer bayed, the silver chains keeping the creature contained, unable to move around without searing pain.

The distant call of an owl sounded, but then the forest became eerily quiet. Dawn was but a mere hour away, the deep snow having kept the coven from reaching her any sooner. For that small miracle, she was thankful. She wondered if her maker would be with them, or if he had just sent his goons to do the dirty work.

She prayed it would be the former when there was a knock on the door.

Adeline swallowed, thankful that she had sucked on a juniper berry earlier in the evening so her heart rate would be slow when she confronted Juliette and her entourage.

By the sounds of the hearts beating outside, there were only six vampires in total.

She smiled to herself at the memory of dispatching three vampires when Colin had disappeared. They were younger than her, but only by a few decades. Thinking back on it now, that should have been her first clue that something was wrong—three of the Originals on her doorstep so soon after her lover had disappeared. It was no easy feat killing them, but she had done it. Alone and unarmed. If she had been able to do that when swallowed up by despair, then she could handle the ones here tonight.

She hoped.

Her hand grabbed the knob, and she opened the door, ready to meet her fate.

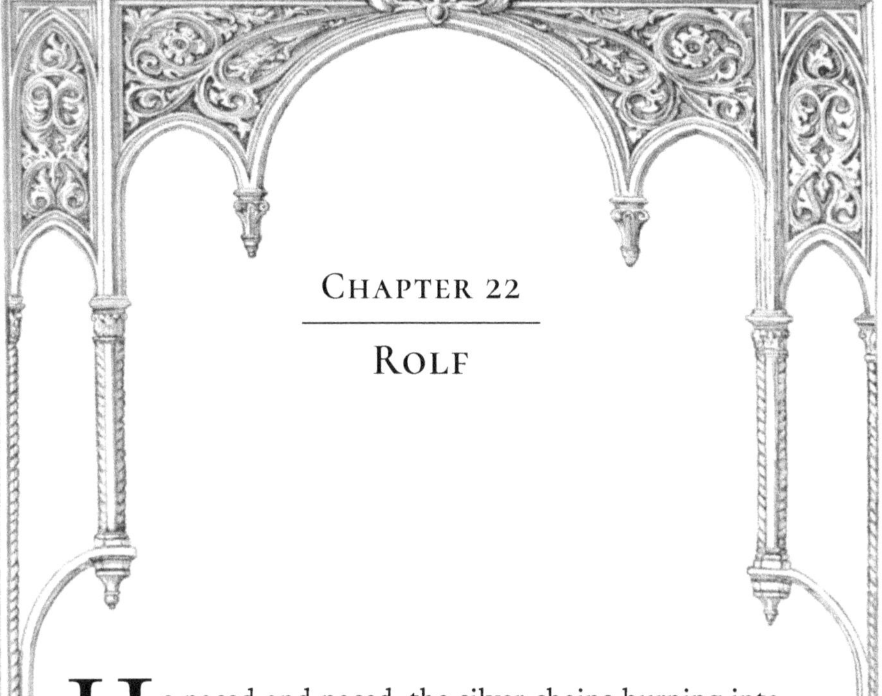

Chapter 22

Rolf

He paced and paced, the silver chains burning into his skin the more he walked. He let out a frustrated howl. He needed to hunt. He needed to chase. He needed to kill.

His ears twitched each time he heard an owl hoot or the floorboards creak. It felt like he had been down here hours, so much rage and pent-up emotion roiling underneath his fur.

But then, the forest grew still.

Vampires. He would know that feeling of creeping death anywhere.

His wolf growled low, ready to fight for the one thing that kept him going.

Adeline.

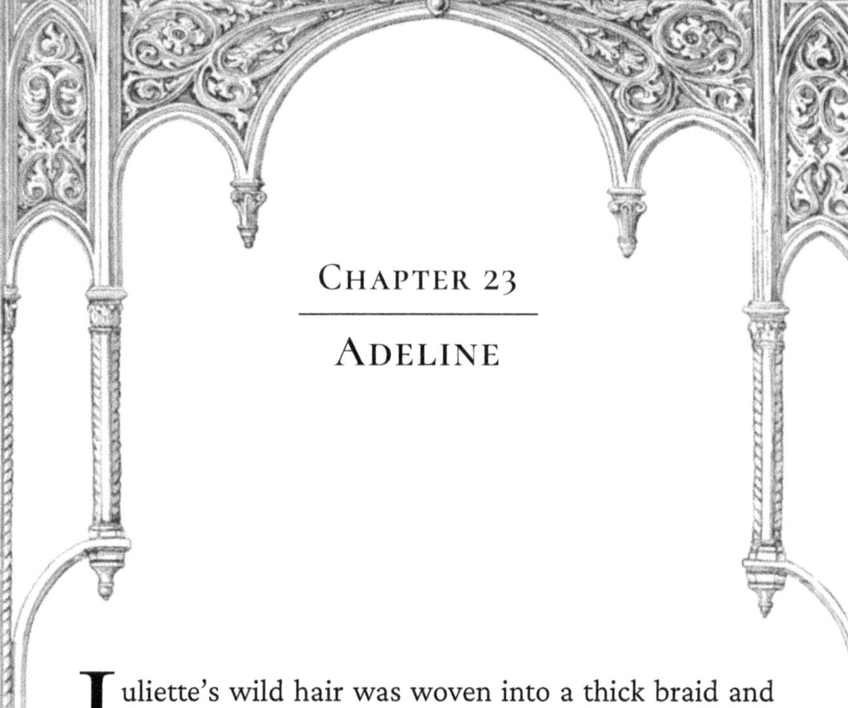

Chapter 23

Adeline

Juliette's wild hair was woven into a thick braid and tucked under a fur hat. Each member of the coven had ski shoes on their feet and looked wind-chapped. Juliette, though, appeared practically perfect with the flush of the cold winter wind on her cheeks. Adeline smiled to herself, remembering all of the love she once held for the blond fae.

But now? Juliette was as much of a killer as Adeline, and her moss-colored eyes skittered around the room, cataloging the scene laid out before them. Would she believe the story Adeline chose to tell for them?

Juliette's nostrils flared when the smell of fresh blood hit her nose.

"You've found him, then." Juliette tilted her head, eyes narrowed. "No head?"

"No Erik?" Adeline quipped back, refusing to move from the doorway.

What a fucking coward. Erik not being with them

meant he had bigger plans for Adeline. Just the very thought of it swirled her stomach, and she wanted to retch. His evil knew no bounds and she knew if she didn't succeed tonight that she—or Rolf—would be on the receiving end of gods knew what.

Underneath a mask of calm disinterest, she met the vampires' eyes, one by one, each looking away quickly. Only two held her stare: Juliette and a young vampire who stood with shoulders too straight and an eyebrow that quirked in a way that made him look cocky. These two would take the longest to kill, particularly because Adeline did not want to kill Juliette.

Some part of her still loved her ex, still felt connected to her, and she wished Erik had sent anyone else but Juliette. But that was never his way. He wanted to cause the maximum amount of harm with the least amount of effort.

Erik knew what he was doing. He was always two steps ahead.

"Are you going to let us in?" the young, cocky one asked.

Juliette didn't wait for an answer; instead, she stepped forward and pushed Adeline out of the way. Her ski shoes clattered on the wood floor, and Adeline cringed, hoping the wolf below stayed quiet.

"We traveled a long way to find you," Juliette said. She waved her hand around airily, as if Adeline should be apologizing for getting stuck here. As if this wasn't all a part of Erik's scheming.

You bitch, Adeline wanted to say while she clawed out those heartless eyes, but instead, she sighed and rubbed a bloody hand over her forehead, hoping Rolf's blood coated her skin enough. "Lucky for you, I've contained the were-shifter for your viewing pleasure."

Juliette raised an eyebrow. A century ago, Juliette had been able to read Adeline like a book. They had relied so much on each other underneath Erik's strong-armed rule of the vampires that it was more about survival than connection. At least, that's what Adeline had told herself when she left the coven the last time. But for Adeline, Juliette *had* meant something, and there had been a deeper connection there—only, it didn't last. And among the many things she regretted, leaving Juliette was the biggest. In a life that had felt so out of her control, once Adeline felt the confidence to regain it, she never looked back.

Now she realized that she should have. But it was too late. Adeline had made her choice, and others had suffered because of it. She only hoped that the space between them made it harder for Juliette to read her.

Because so much hinged on the next few moments.

Time to shine, Adeline. She stood a little straighter.

She had bested the conniving minds of courtesans, manipulated kings, and fought alongside countless armies to secure a political future for vampires. Surely, she could best this small hunting group so she could spend eternity with her wolf. "Come, I'll show you."

The coven members filtered into the small cabin, the tension pulling at the air around her. She discreetly licked some of Rolf's blood off her fingers, a renewed sense of energy and purpose settling in her stomach.

Juliette walked around to the bed and lifted the sheets

with a dramatic flourish. Adeline almost cringed, hoping her former lover didn't scent anything else.

"You *slept* here," she said, disgust dripping from her mouth. "With *him*?"

Jealous?

Adeline smirked and stood barefoot in a puddle of Rolf's blood. She wiggled her toes in the cooling liquid. "What was I supposed to do, sleep outside? Juliette, what kind of deviant do you think I am? Even *I* have standards."

One of the coven members had walked over to some blood splotches on the wall. He leaned in and inhaled. "That's wolf blood, all right."

"Of course it is, you git," Juliette said. Her green eyes turned to Adeline, flashing with an emotion Adeline hoped was jealousy. "The whole place stinks of wolf and sex and *your blood.*"

Ooh, jealousy looks good on her...

"And?" Adeline shrugged, needling Juliette more. She met the green-eyed stare straight on. "I've done far worse than fuck a wolf."

Juliette crossed the room to stand in front of Adeline, nose to nose. Adeline swallowed, trying her best to slow her heartbeat by thinking of something other than the fact that her trap might not work. It was a trick she had learned centuries ago when Erik had first sent her away to kill a king. Which king? She couldn't remember anymore. They all blurred together after a while. As a vampire, she had a slower-than-normal heartbeat, so anything that set her mind racing could trigger an increase in pulse. She couldn't have that.

Think of Erik. Think of how slimy his voice sounds in your head. Think of what might happen if you don't kill everyone tonight.

Juliette's eyes narrowed, as if she were cataloging every minuscule muscle twitch and movement on Adeline. Her pupils dilated slightly, and Adeline frowned. Voice lethal, she said, "You know, then."

I know so much more than she thinks. Adeline tilted her head and smiled at Juliette.

"Of course I know. I'm not as slow as you seem to think I am." Adeline turned and gestured to the cabin. "Why do you think I fucked him like I did?"

One of the vampires at her back huffed a laugh, and Juliette shot him a look.

Hoping against hope that this was why Erik had made them track her down, Adeline leveled a casual gaze at Juliette. "Do you want to bear witness as I kill the were-beast or not?"

Juliette waved her hand dismissively. "Why would we have gone to all this trouble to track you down if we didn't want you to show us your loyalty?"

Juliette twitched a finger, and a vampire stepped forward. Adeline tried to recall her name, but she hadn't bothered to learn the names of the newest members for a reason. She'd wanted nothing to do with them these past hundred years.

Adeline reached for one of the wooden weapons she had stacked on the counter. The entire room tensed, and Juliette tracked Adeline's hands. Adeline twirled it in the air, flipping her hand around the shaft before slamming the butt end of it on the roof of the trap door. She didn't know if Rolf's wolf would remember what they had discussed before he turned, but she hoped that the solitary thud was enough of a warning.

Here's hoping.

Juliette stepped forward, as did two other vampires, their bodies tense and waiting. Adeline laughed. "Apologies for the assumption, but did you think that I was going to kill the were-shifter with my bare hands?"

Juliette hesitated, thinking it over, but then nodded and gestured for Adeline to continue.

Adeline pressed her lips into a tight line. Then she bent down and lifted the rug from the floor.

Juliette's hand snatched at Adeline's shoulder. "If you try anything, I will quarter you alive and answer to Erik myself."

"Understood," Adeline said, looking over her shoulder to give Juliette the stare-down. Was she coming across as genuine enough? Adeline didn't care anymore; she just needed them down in the cave.

And then, almost imperceptibly, Juliette mouthed, "Addie."

Adeline kept her face blank, but Juliette's eyes flickered around the room.

What is she trying to tell me? Adeline's heart jolted.

A little over a century ago, when Juliette had first come to the castle, she was half-delirious with rage. Erik had tossed her limp body at Adeline, and it was expected that Adeline would train her, feed her, and show her how to glamour and use the small bit of darker magic vampires had when they were turned. Erik wanted Juliette to become Adeline's new apprentice. But Adeline had a soft spot for the new vampire. And soon they became inseparable. Adeline finally had a confidante and a friend, a friend who turned into a lover. Juliette was the balm to Adeline's isolated existence.

Adeline finished moving the rug, revealing the silver door beneath. A murmur traveled through the Vampire at the sight, and the entire room tensed when she grabbed an iron poker from the fireplace. She rolled her eyes and palmed it dramatically, flashing Juliette a sardonic smile.

Juliette huffed and crossed her arms, making Adeline chuckle under her breath.

Adeline threaded the steel through the handle, turning it to unlock the trapdoor. Moving as slowly as she dared, she grabbed the lantern from near the fireplace. A glance outside, and she knew she had less than thirty minutes until moonset and over an hour before sunrise if she had calculated her timing right.

Returning to the entrance of the tunnel, she held the lantern over the hole to double-check that the rope ladder was still secured to its hooks. Barefoot, Adeline climbed down the rope rungs, hoping she had covered herself in enough of Rolf's blood that she wouldn't trigger the wolf too soon.

Slow, slow, slow, she told herself over and over. A mantra she hoped wasn't useless.

The rope swung as one of the younger vampires followed Adeline down. And then another. And another. Adeline's feet touched the wet ground, and she took a moment to center herself. She wanted to reach up and palm the hidden whittling knife she had strapped to her skin, but thought better of it until the coven was farther into the cave.

Once all the vampires were on the ground, Adeline led them down the tunnel as slowly as she dared. She lifted her head a little higher, hoping Juliette would buy into her display of fake loyalty.

Her were-shifter huffed the echo down the tunnel, a shot to her heart. She hoped with all of her lifeless being that he wasn't in too much pain. When Rolf had suggested that he chain himself up, she had protested, not wanting him to be too injured in case he couldn't fight back. He had kissed her nose and told her not to worry, that he would be okay.

But she couldn't stop worrying about him the closer they got.

An enormous shape loomed in the dark, and the clink of chains sounded each time he took a breath. The space between them vibrated with tension, and Adeline gripped the shaft tightly, sending a prayer to whatever gods chose to listen tonight.

A solitary lantern hung down the tunnel on the right, the amber glow a beacon of hope.

Juliette was at Adeline's shoulder in the blink of an eye. She kept her voice low, but Adeline could feel the fear running through her as she asked, "How did you manage to chain the beast?"

Adeline turned to Juliette, held a finger up to her mouth, and shook her head slowly.

Juliette visibly swallowed, and Adeline would have laughed if she hadn't been so confused.

Of course, she's afraid, Adeline chided herself.

She had never let Juliette go with her on any of her missions, wanting to keep her from the depravity of Erik and the things he made her do. And maybe Adeline still felt protective.

After all, she had shared a connection with Juliette that she hadn't experienced in so long, and Adeline's loneliness had subsided when they became even closer. Precious stolen moments, when Adeline had Juliette all to herself and no one, not even Erik, knew. They snuck around and stole time with each other whenever he was gone. If Erik had caught wind of Adeline feeling even remotely intimate toward Juliette...Adeline shuddered. It would have ended in the worst possible way.

And now she's here.

A shot of guilt tore through Adeline, knowing it was because of her that Juliette now did Erik's dirty work. It was the one thing she had tried to shelter Juliette from. And she had failed.

What else had happened once Adeline left?

She shook her head. Thinking about such things now would only spell disaster. She had a plan and needed to stick to it before the sun came up.

Adeline stepped over to her wolf, noting that most of the chains holding him down were caked in mud, except the most visible one around his neck. That one glinted silver in the low light. Adeline shuffled her bloodied feet next to his snout. The warm breath caressed her skin and, when his eyes met hers, she swore there was a flicker of recognition behind the amber-colored orbs.

Here we go, she thought, and palmed the wooden spear.

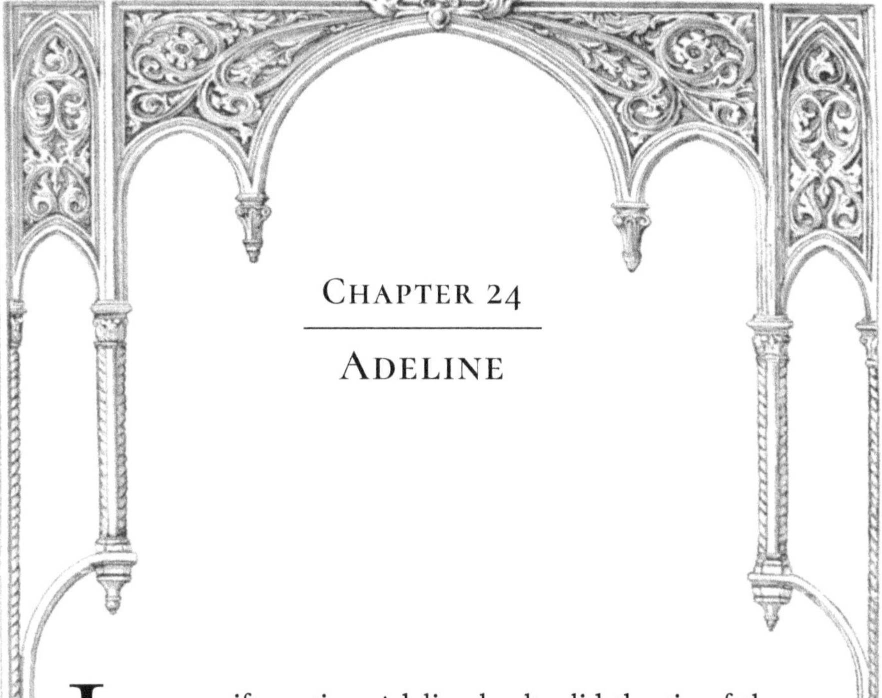

Chapter 24

Adeline

In one swift motion, Adeline knelt, slid the tip of the spear underneath the chain around the were-shifter's neck, and flung the metal toward the vampires.

Chaos erupted around her.

The chain pinned one of the younger vampires to the floor of the cave. The smell of skin burning filled her nose, and the shrieks of the vampire being singed alive enraged her wolf even more.

Her beast lunged toward another younger vampire at the mouth of the small tunnel, who was trying to scramble away. Juliette grabbed Adeline by the throat, forcing her back against the cavern wall, but not before Adeline got a silver-tipped swipe at her former lover's shoulder with the spear. It sliced through fabric and skin but got caught on the edge of Juliette's corset and snapped into two.

Juliette hissed as the silver burned a crescent-shaped wound into her skin. She pressed her sharpened nails into

Adeline's neck, drawing blood. Juliette's green eyes flared with anger, but Adeline held Juliette's wrist to keep the sharpened nails from driving into her tendons and veins. The snarl of the were-shifter and a bloodcurdling scream from a vampire distracted them both enough for Adeline to claw at Juliette's face with a free hand.

Juliette cursed and let go, clutching her face where deep gouges had been torn from her cheek.

Adeline rolled off to the side and darted around Juliette. She grabbed the lantern that was by a dismembered vampire and whistled a few times. Then she chucked the lantern up in the air, aiming for the exit back to the cabin. Its glass smashed into the wall. The pitch-coated wood ignited the cave walls, the flames swallowing the entire tunnel and blocking the way back to the cabin.

The were-shifter turned to approach Juliette and Adeline while two other vampires made a run for it down the tunnel that led to the cliff. The wolf lunged, and Adeline stepped in front of Juliette, meeting the wolf's eyes. For a brief moment, Adeline worried that he would charge at Juliette, but then one of the fleeing vampires stumbled in the tunnel and grunted. The wolf snapped his jaw and turned his attention to the vampire, because everyone knows that a wolf enjoys a good chase. He took off after the vampire, snarling.

Juliette's face was healing, which left Adeline with little time. A solitary dagger on the floor glinted in the light of the flames, and Adeline stepped forward to retrieve it. Juliette's eyes followed Adeline's gaze, and within seconds, Juliette grabbed it.

"Oh, Adeline," Juliette crowed above the roar of the

fire, stalking closer. "What on earth do you think you're accomplishing here?"

"You haven't figured it out yet?" Adeline taunted and stepped backward, heading down the tunnel to the right. How many were left alive now? "I'm going to kill you all."

"The hell you are," Juliette hissed, flipping the knife back and forth.

"And then I'm going after Erik," Adeline said, only loud enough for her words to reach Juliette's ears alone.

Juliette faltered, her brows furrowing for a moment, but she stayed fixated on Adeline's movements, unbothered by the destruction at her back.

The flames caught on more beams in the cave, and the fire crept down the other tunnel. Adeline immediately thought of Rolf returning to his human form. Would the moon slip down the horizon before he could kill the vampire he went after? Would she, too, succumb to poor timing?

She egged Juliette on. "Do you know what he did? Did you think I wouldn't figure it all out, Juliette?"

Juliette scoffed. "You think you're the only one who can have a happy ever after. That doesn't happen for creatures like us. Those are *fairy tales, Adeline*!" Juliette's scream rose above the sound of the roaring flames, her green eyes flaring bright in the dark.

She lunged and took a swipe at Adeline. Adeline's heart broke.

Juliette no longer believes in fairy tales? What did Erik do to her?

Juliette used to be a moon-eyed vampire, incapable of hurting even a fly. It was one of the reasons Adeline had been so drawn to her, at first. Because she reminded her of the sister she had pushed through a portal long ago. Juliette's kindness extended down to the servants in the castle. With Adeline's persuasion, Erik let Juliette manage the castle and the servants' quarters, effectively making Juliette the head housekeeper. Conditions improved for the servants, and the vampires were able to maintain a lower profile because they were able to keep their help for longer. Erik had been so satisfied that he even weakened the castle's defenses.

It still wasn't enough for Adeline to trust that Erik ever had their best intentions at heart, though.

"You know he's evil, Juliette. You know what twisted games he plays. With all of us." Adeline exhaled. She was worn down; Rolf's blood was already wearing off.

Juliette shrugged, stalking toward Adeline. They passed the decapitated head of a vampire, its face locked in an eternal scream. Adeline sidestepped it and continued down the tunnel. If she could keep Juliette talking, then maybe she could find a weakness in Erik's endgame.

"Did you help him?" Adeline asked, hoping against hope it hadn't been Juliette who glamoured Rolf. "Was it you who led Erik to where we were?"

"Where *who* was?" Juliette stopped in her tracks, but a howl resounded down the tunnel, cutting her off.

Adeline's heart skipped a beat. Her wolf had been successful.

Juliette snapped her mouth closed, gave Adeline a wry smile, and pressed forward, urgency in her movements.

"What, are you afraid?" Adeline sneered, emboldened by the triumph of her beast.

Juliette roared and lunged, driving Adeline backward. She didn't react fast enough, and Juliette now had her pinned between her legs. Adeline twisted, trying to throw Juliette off. Fighting against the strength of her former lover, Adeline cursed when she realized how far from the entrance to the tunnel they were. She needed to get through the gate before the moon went down.

Adeline thrashed and clawed, but Juliette grabbed her arm and held it aloft. With her other arm raised, Juliette slammed the blade down into Adeline's shoulder. She screamed out as the silver seared through her skin and muscles, rendering her right arm useless.

"I'm no more afraid than I am just pissed off," Juliette whispered in her ear. "Do you not understand that I am trying to *help* you?"

Adeline would have laughed if her shoulder wasn't screaming in agony. Help her? Help her *how*? By tearing her away from the man she loved? By reuniting her with her torturer? A lone pair of footsteps echoed in the tunnels behind them, and Juliette twisted the blade. Adeline fought back tears.

"What do you think will happen when Erik finds out what abhorrent things you've done?" Juliette whispered.

Adeline gritted her teeth. She didn't care about the other vampires, she didn't care about Erik. She just wanted to be free to live her life with Rolf. "I don't care."

Juliette cackled, throwing her head back. The flame crept closer, eating away at all of the wooden beams.

"I don't," Adeline said again. Her shoulder throbbed, and she felt like vomiting. But she pressed forward, knowing the sun would rise soon. "I just want to watch Erik die a slow and painful death."

A shadow fluttered behind Juliette, and for a brief moment, she thought it was Rolf coming to her aid. Instead, it was another vampire. The one who had fled down the tunnel after Rolf.

Where is Rolf? Fury and fear bubbled in her gut.

The vampire's face was half ripped off, and one of his arms hung limply at his side, broken bones protruding through his skin, which had tried to heal around the wound. He bled profusely from several punctures, but he was still standing. Adeline's heart sank when she realized that Rolf hadn't managed to take his head.

Juliette leaned forward, twisting the blade again. Adeline bit her tongue so hard she tasted blood. Her fangs immediately sharpened. At the sound of the vampire's strangled noises, Juliette turned and leaped off Adeline, rushing to his side. Whispering words of affection, she opened her wrist, allowing him to drink her blood to heal.

A new lover? It didn't matter. If he was precious to Juliette, he needed to go.

Juliette paid no attention to Adeline; instead, she focused on the injured vampire trying, but failing, to drink Juliette's blood.

"There, my child, eat," she cooed.

Let her feel what it's like to lose something, then.

With renewed purpose, Adeline grasped the handle of the blade embedded in her shoulder and pulled, grunting as it seared once more through her unhealed skin.

Rolf howled again, but it was cut short by a yelp.

No! Adeline's heart dropped to her stomach, and the

noise around her dulled to a thrum. She needed to get to Rolf before the sun rose, and he couldn't get away.

Kissing the handle of the blade for luck, Adeline grabbed the silver tip, wincing as the metal cut into her skin. She threw the knife at the half-dismembered vampire, and it landed with a *thunk* in his eye. He fell backward, sliding down the wall of the cave with the silver of the blade shining through the back of his head. Not fully dead, but beyond hope of ever healing, he was incapacitated enough to give Adeline time to run back and find Rolf.

"No!" Juliette screamed, but Adeline had already started running.

The heat of the fire pressed against Adeline's back as she headed toward the entrance. She didn't look back to see if Juliette was following her or not. The silver gate was in her sight when the breath was knocked from her lungs, and she tumbled forward. Sharp nails dug into her scalp as her head was yanked backward. She screamed, the echoes of it rushing past the grate as the flames roared above them.

Juliette dragged a claw across Adeline's exposed neck, and blood welled from the slice. "You headstrong fool!"

"Rol—" Adeline tried to scream, but her voice was too warbled. Her throat constricted against the blood loss. It poured from her neck, and she knew she would be so much easier to kill after losing this much. If only she could have seen him one last time.

The crackling of burning wood and his name on the wind were the last things Adeline heard as the world fell out from underneath her.

Chapter 25

Rolf

Rolf's heart stopped at the thick smoke coming from up the hill, and try as he might, his wolf wouldn't listen. The sight of the smoke only pushed his animal harder, even though the moon dipped and the sun climbed against the mountain peaks. Adeline told him what to expect, and he was still not prepared. A hundred years in hiding, fighting his baser instincts, had weakened him. The vampires were ruthless and some of the strongest adversaries he'd ever challenged, and he knew they would be since they came from the same maker as Adeline.

He screamed at his wolf to turn around and head back into the caves, but the craving for justice was so strong that he could not cut through the noise. His heart pulsed in his head like a deep bass drum in battle. He had never been this aware, watching his claws swipe through the Vampire with such ease and disgust.

The last vampire that had followed him out of the cave

lay completely dismembered at his feet. He snapped a vampire's arm in half, relishing the crunch of the bones in his maw as he thought of Adeline back in the caves fighting for their love.

And then he heard her scream.

Adeline.

His wolf crunched one final time, severing a head from a body, and tossed it into a ravine. He tilted his head to the east, knowing that his time as a were-shifter was running out, and bounded uphill in six feet of snow. He needed to make it as far as he could before the sun rose. He was mid-leap when the shift took over, and he roared. His frustration echoed down the small canyon at the base of the cave as his claws receded and his fur turned back into skin.

"Fuck!" he yelled, falling to his hands and knees. "No, no, no!"

His head swam, but he forced himself to stand and started running again.

Adeline screamed once more, his name traveling on the wind. It sounded like a goodbye, one last desperate way for her to sear herself into his consciousness.

When he reached the top of the mountain where the silver grate lay open, he was breathless but determined. Nothing would prevent him from getting to her.

Smoke filtered out of the cave, and he covered his mouth as he dipped inside. His eyes burned from the smoke and the heat; the scent of death and charred skin hung heavy in the air. He scanned the tunnel but could find no trace of Adeline or Juliette. A vampire was leaning against the tunnel wall, barely breathing, with a dagger in his eye. Rolf would have to come back and dispatch him properly after he searched for Adeline.

He turned and headed down the other tunnel, which was empty. The only creatures left were the dismembered vampire. As the sun filtered through the grate at the end, soft light filled the tunnels. A large puddle of blood shimmered toward the end of the cave. He knelt in the dirt and touched his finger to the liquid. Thick, but still warm. A recent spill. Adeline's scent lingered in the air, and his heart sank as he realized it was hers. Scuff marks showed knee imprints around the frame of a body. A few strands of hair around the scene told him everything he needed to know. Someone had pinned Adeline and slit her throat.

Rage pummeled him, and his wolf roared inside his head.

Where is she?

He scanned the rest of the tunnel. With Adeline bleeding so much, she would have to be dragged out of there. The gate was unlocked, but nothing indicated that she and her attacker had left that way. So he retraced his steps to the start of the fire near the cabin entrance. No one could have gotten Adeline through the flames or up that ladder without help.

Rolf walked back to the vampire with the blade through his eye. He wrapped his hand around the hilt and yanked backward. The vampire groaned, a garbled sound that was full of blood.

"Talk."

The vampire said nothing as he stared out of his one good eye. Blood trickled out of the corner of his mouth.

"How does it feel?" Rolf spat out. "Knowing you're at my mercy now?"

Silence.

"You must be in so much pain," Rolf whispered. He slit the back of his hand, watching the blood well up. The vampire's eyes widened, and his fangs grew; he started to salivate. "Would you like to feel a little better?"

The vampire was so focused on the fresh blood that he nodded.

"If I give you a little bit of my blood, will you tell me how they got out of here and where they went?"

The vampire only nodded, opening his mouth. Rolf squeezed his hand and let a few drops land on the vampire's tongue. He watched as the vampire's eyes rolled in the back of his head. A groan escaped his lips, and then he said, "I have never had wolf fae blood before."

"Consider it your first and only time. Now, talk."

"One more drop, please."

"That wasn't the deal. Talk." Rolf took his hand and squeezed a few more drops out of his cut. He held the blood just out of reach.

"Why, when you're just going to kill me anyway?"

Rolf smiled and squeezed his cut even more, letting the blood pool on the top of his hand. He had forgotten what it was like to talk with cunning killers. "True, but when I kill you, you can either go out feeling bliss, or I can make it as painful as possible for you."

After a moment of deliberation, the vampire said, "A portal."

He opened his mouth, waiting for the blood that didn't come. Rolf sat back on his heels, just out of reach.

A portal?

That was something he had only ever heard about in ancient fairy tales. He had grown up reading the stories in his family's library. But those powers belonged to ancient fae, who no longer roamed this earth. No one had that kind of magic anymore. At least, no one born in the last few centuries. Which meant that Erik was an older fae, if not the first vampire. And if Erik was that old, Adeline must be, too.

"You thought..." The vampire made a sound that he supposed was laughter. "You thought we walked here?" The vampire cackled so hard he started choking. Blood sputtered from his mouth, and he slumped forward in pain. But he didn't stop laughing.

Rolf said nothing, just watched curiously as the vampire tried to sit back up.

"You have no idea who you are dealing with," the vampire said through laughing fits.

The world swirled around him. He was up against some very old, very strong magic indeed.

Rolf hovered his hand over the vampire, letting a few drops of blood fall onto his lap. The vampire met Rolf's gaze with his one eye, and his nostrils flared as he snapped his teeth. "More."

Rolf shook his head. "Not until you tell me everything."

His head spun with the new information the vampire told him. There was a rumor in the coven that Adeline was one of the first vampires to be turned by Erik. And how Erik had ways of knowing things, controlling things, but this young vampire snapped his mouth shut at the final admission. Rolf pressed him for more, but was met with stubborn resistance.

Erik must have more magic than the other vampires, and if Adeline was as old as Erik, did she have magic, too? She had healed the puncture wounds from her teeth and removed the glamour from his memories. But Rolf had assumed this was something that all vampires could do.

She was a ruthless, exacting killer, and her strength was one of the most impressive things he had ever seen. When she killed the Vampire, armed with nothing but a shaft, his wolf had beamed, knowing that she was worthy of being his mate. His wolf wouldn't have settled for anyone less.

But magic? She had never exhibited any of that with him. Erik having portal magic meant that Rolf would need all of his cunning to get her back.

The vampire closed its one good eye and sighed.

"I will only ask you one more time how you wish to leave this mortal earth," Rolf said.

He squeezed the wound on the back of his hand and held it up in front of the vampire. And when the vampire said nothing, he closed his eyes and sighed. Rolf palmed the dagger, and in one fluid motion, he grabbed the vampire's hair and slit its throat.

Since he didn't have his axe down here, Rolf grabbed a few more pieces of wood from a pile tucked way back in the corner and stacked them high in the center of the room. Then, he dragged all the bodies onto the stack and stoked the fire.

Orange-and-red flames licked at the dismembered and mangled vampires, burning them into a pile of ash. The stench filled the cavern, and he shuffled his way to the ladder. He pushed the trapdoor open and fell into his cabin. His blood and Adeline's coated almost every surface, and he smiled wryly at the thought of Adeline strategically destroying his home. It looked like a tornado had torn through it, and the only evidence of them ever having a peaceful time together was the perfectly clean bedsheets. Almost as if Adeline hadn't wanted to taint the memories that the bed held.

He walked over to the sink and grabbed the pitcher of water, drinking it and letting the water run down his face. Then he grabbed his ski shoes, stuffed his leather pack full of supplies, and walked out the door to save the woman he loved.

Chapter 26
Adeline

The final howl echoed in her head, and she knew Rolf was gone. She was so weak she couldn't move, couldn't fight. Not yet. Her throat ached, and she was so thirsty. Her body jostled as if in a carriage, but someone held her tightly.

"Here," Juliette's voice said from somewhere nearby. Then something metal touched her lips, and the liquid inside was warm, full of life, but sickly sweet.

Adeline's eyes flew open, and she coughed, trying to spit the liquid out. She wasn't going to drink anything offered to her right now, no matter how weak and vulnerable she was.

"Damn the Gods, Addy! You need to heal. I know this isn't great, but it's all we're allowed to drink these days, and if you don't, Erik will..."

Juliette's voice faded in and out, but the only thing Adeline could focus on in her delirium was the nickname.

Addy? She hadn't been called that in ages. Juliette's

arms tightened around her, and as much as Adeline wanted to fight back and push her off, her arms were leaden. Besides, it was nice to be held by someone who cared for her. Like Rolf.

Where is Rolf?

"No," Adeline croaked. If Rolf hadn't made it, then why should she? Her heart ached without him. "Just kill me."

Juliette sighed. "Don't be so dramatic."

Adeline said nothing, her eyes clouding with tears. The carriage interior was lined with rich velvet and gilded accents. It smelled faintly of age-worn leather and dust. Which could only mean one thing: Erik. The blinds were drawn tightly, and they traveled at a fast pace, but she knew exactly where they were going, and she wished she had died back in the caves.

Juliette tried to feed her again, but Adeline turned her head, biting back a scream as the movement tore open the wound at her throat.

"Why are you always the difficult one?" Juliette mumbled.

Why are you trying to feed me? Adeline almost asked, but her throat was so dry and her tongue too thick to move. The more the coach jostled, the sicker she felt and the less she wanted to live, so why not refuse whatever it was that Juliette wanted her to drink?

Being helpless and at the whim of someone else was not what Adeline had ever wanted, which was why she had bargained with Erik. She had hoped that things would have turned out differently. But that was her first mistake —hope.

Gods, how could she have been so stupid?

She *knew* that a bargain with Erik would never end well. And, of course, Erik had been one step ahead the entire time, setting her up so she would fail, so she would have to hold up *her* end of the bargain, regardless of the outcome. It was the only thing that made sense. Why did he want her back when he could have anyone so easily in his grasp?

The carriage halted briefly, and she heard the sounds of a large gate creaking open. Through her haze and anger, Adeline could barely make out the shouts of vampire guards before she passed out.

Strong arms dragged her down a dark hallway. She didn't struggle, but she didn't help them, either. If she had any strength, she would have shaken them off and walked, because she would be damned if she was to face Erik in this state. Her wounds had healed for the most part, but some blood seeped through her clothes at her stomach, and her neck still felt tender.

The two vampires who carried her didn't say a word.

Where is Juliette?

But when she tried to turn her head, a searing pain tore at her throat. She bit back a cry, unwilling to look even weaker before Erik. It would already give him too much pleasure to see her suffering like this. She wouldn't allow him any more satisfaction, not if she could help it.

Her vision blurred with tears as she fought to get her emotions under control. The edges of her sight swam with shadows. Long ago, Erik had enchanted the castle against intruders, which made this place a vampire haven. Adeline had never figured out how he had done it, but since he was the oldest vampire in these lands, she always assumed the magic had been his before he was turned.

And now the shadows threatened to close in on her again. They clung to the edges, creeping along beside her, until she closed her eyes tightly, willing the darkness away.

When she opened them, the hallway was clear. Either the castle remembered her, or she was deemed not a threat.

A small win, Adeline thought, but didn't let her guard down quite yet.

A set of tall doors loomed before her, and she closed her eyes briefly, knowing whose glare waited for her. The doors creaked open, and suddenly, the room felt much larger than she remembered, despite the heat that pressed down around her and the dozens of vampires milling about.

Enormous chandeliers with hundreds of candles covered the ceiling, filling the place with smoke and the smell of burning fat. Large tables lined the walls, laden with decadent foods that went untouched—just another show of Erik's immense wealth and control. Since none of the vampires ate any of this food, it all went to waste or was sent back to the kitchens for the servants to eat once it went stale and moldy.

Erik was never one for a throne, claiming that the vampires were all equals. Instead, he sat at the head of an enormous table in a gilded and velvet armchair. But Adeline, and even the other Vampire, knew that they were no more equals than they were his pawns, his progeny. None of them mattered to Erik except for Adeline. And she had always struggled with why. Why had he singled her out? She could only guess since she had already given herself to him with her body and, once, her mind.

What was left for him to conquer?

The guards dropped Adeline to the floor before the table, and her knees slammed into the stone. Her matted, bloody hair fell into her face as she bowed low despite every part of her screaming against this. But she was the one who had made the bargain, she was the one who'd gotten herself into this horrible mess. If she hadn't been so headstrong, so damn confident that she could win her way out, Rolf would still be alive, living out his life in the cabin.

Why does everyone I love die?

"Tell me, Juliette, does the shifter live?" Erik asked, his voice cutting through the haze in her head.

She fought the bile that threatened to creep up her throat and forced her head to stay bowed.

"No," Juliette said behind Adeline. A swish of skirts, and she moved to block Adeline from Erik's view. "As soon as he was confirmed dead, I left. But he killed everyone in the process."

It wasn't just Rolf, Adeline thought. She had killed half the coven and she was damn proud of it. So why was Juliette lying? And why the kindness in the carriage?

Why is she protecting me?

Erik said nothing for a moment and then waved his hand. "I find it hard to believe that a were-shifter was skilled enough to take out my elite hunters."

Adeline wanted to speak but didn't know what game

Juliette was playing, so she kept her mouth shut and just watched the exchange.

"He had drugged Adeline and chained her upstairs," Juliette said, pausing for effect. The entire room had gone silent as all eyes focused on Adeline. "He had slit her neck as a way to lure us to him. She was delirious and weak when I set her free. The wolf was in a cave nearby and had already shifted when we went after him. It was a maze, and we didn't know we had taken the bait. It hunted us down one by one."

Erik raised his brows, the only tell that he was shocked. The rest of his body gave nothing away, and for a moment, Adeline thought Erik would not believe any of it. She cringed in anticipation of Juliette's head being ripped from her body in seconds.

"Adeline." Erik's eyes flicked to her neck. He *almost* sounded like a concerned parent when he asked, "How?"

Adeline swallowed and closed her eyes as if in shame. Instead, she was trying to see the scene Juliette recalled, because if *she* didn't believe her story, Erik wouldn't either, and it would all be for nothing. Every tiny detail, every moment spent in the cabin with Rolf, naked or otherwise, she shoved deep down into a hidden recess in her heart. In its place, an alternate history sprouted, one where she was the victim, where she didn't know that Rolf had been glamoured a hundred years ago by her coven. A separate timeline where her blissful moments with Rolf had unraveled differently. She could almost believe that all of this hadn't been her fault. That she was helpless and at Rolf's mercy—that she was still going to kill him.

Even *if,* by the slimmest chance, Rolf was still alive, he

should become a ghost or he would be killed. That, Adeline knew for certain. Erik did not like leaving loose ends.

"My horse died on the pass, so I walked the rest of the way down the mountain. A storm—unlike any I had ever seen—came out of nowhere and dumped inches of snow in mere minutes." Adeline's throat constricted as she swallowed against a fit of coughing that was sure to take over. Her hand went to her throat, the tender, fresh flesh pulsing with her slow heart.

Juliette nodded beside her. "We had to ski-shoe over six feet of snow—some places had drifts as high as twelve feet. We had never experienced a storm quite like it."

"I was exhausted by the time I finally found the were-shifter's cabin. It was in the mountains, where the last known sighting of an elusive were-shifter was living." As she talked, more details of the revised history unraveled before her, and she knew she could sell this lie. "As soon as I was inside, I collapsed. Only to wake up chained to his bed and being force-fed tainted rabbit blood. He kept me in paralysis until the full moon came, when he slit my throat and left me for dead. I could hear his howls when the shift happened, but I could do nothing."

She paused for effect, then whispered, "If Juliette hadn't shown up when she did, I—"

Juliette placed a hand on her shoulder and squeezed, but said nothing.

The entire room was quiet as Erik looked from Adeline to Juliette and back to Adeline. The corner of his mouth twitched. "You still didn't fulfill your end of the bargain."

Adeline's heart sank as she hung her head.

Of course, I didn't, you made sure I wouldn't. She bit her tongue. Hard.

"Which means you are mine. Forever." A slow smile spread across his face.

As she waited for her punishment, she let her mind drift briefly to the final few moments of bliss she'd had—the taste of Rolf on her tongue, the feel of him against her, the way his eyes lit up once he finally saw through the glamour placed on him.

Nothing would help her should Erik choose to torture her again, though.

Erik gestured with his hands, and the two vampires who had escorted her inside hauled her up to standing once more. The world tilted, and she wobbled. Their hands tightened on her arms.

"First, we will get you fed so you can heal—something Juliette should have done." Erik held up his glass and drank heartily, then waved it in the air. A servant stepped forward, a glamoured shifter fae wearing a mask, and poured a thick red liquid into his cup. It didn't look like fresh blood, but rather the same mixture Juliette had tried to feed her.

Erik whispered something to the servant, and they disappeared.

"You will sit beside me, Adeline, in your rightful place. As my mate. And wife."

Juliette stiffened, and Adeline's heart sank. His *what*? He had never taken a mate, let alone even expressed any sort of commitment to any creature in his long life besides himself. Erik's only interest was Erik.

Except...

My soul. It was the one thing he hadn't taken full control of, yet. But she wouldn't let him have it. It was hers to choose whom to give it to, and she was not in a giving mood.

But then it clicked. All of these years, ever since she had first tried to leave, he had been inescapable. Ruthless and conniving in his desire to keep her close, always forcing her back into his orbit.

Every time she refused, he would let her get far enough away, only to yank her back, chasing her like the day chased the night.

He may be the daylight, but she was not *his* darkness. She never was. But it didn't matter anymore. Rolf was gone, and before her was the best trap she had ever been caught in.

"Well?" Erik snapped, and Adeline's eyes flashed to his.

"Yes, sire," Adeline heard herself say, her voice wooden. Blood rushed to her ears, pulsing like the beat of a bass drum, filling her head with doom.

"Sit." Erik smiled threateningly. He gestured to the empty chair next to him.

Adeline took a steadying breath as the two fae released their hold. As if she were a puppet on a string, her body glided to the chair, and she sat. Her cup was filled with that same thick liquid, and she was aware that Erik's gaze was fastened to her movements.

"Drink," he said, and Adeline reached for the cup.

Had he put her in a thrall? No. No, this was just shock working its way through her body. She lifted the cup to her lips and took a small sip, stifling the reflex to gag and spit it out. It didn't taste like fresh blood, but it would have to do for now.

"Good girl," Erik cooed, and Adeline, once more, suppressed her body's desire to shiver and give away her true feelings. His finger trailed along the scab at her throat. He clicked his tongue and shook his head. "I will send you fresh food tonight. You will heal, and this awful scar will be no more. Then we will start the wedding preparations."

She took a deep breath, refusing to look at him lest her heartbeat give her away. "And when will we be married?"

Erik took a deep drink from his cup and smiled, his teeth coated in the blood mixture. "Three days, my little killer."

Adeline tried not to blanch as he trailed his fingernail down the side of her cheek. She had three days to figure out how to end her own life.

Chapter 27

Rolf

It wasn't so much a castle as a run-down palatial estate tucked against the side of a cliff. The sea crashed on the chalky white rocks, and the mist grabbed the stone foundation, white fingers clawing, trying to drag it out to sea.

Rolf perched in a tree, the rough bark snagging on his clothes, his hands covered in sap, and watched. His decades as a fur trapper meant he could sit up in this tree for hours, still as stone, and observe. He blended into his surroundings effortlessly since the ancient forest that surrounded the estate was dense with overgrown flora. Every so often, the wind carried the mist over the edge and doused him in cool brine. But he would not move.

Not until he was sure he had a plan. With only one way in and a few deadly ways out, the estate was easy to defend. But harder to infiltrate.

In his human form and alone, Rolf knew there was little he could do since the estate was full of deadly creatures. There was a time when something like this would have scared him, but with Adeline in their hands again, he would stop at nothing to get her back. He did, however, wish he had a militia to back him up.

Ours, his wolf growled.

Well, that's a first, Rolf thought. His wolf was communicating with him now, even after the full moon?

As the sun rose higher, the vampires stayed inside. There was no movement outside the castle, nothing to indicate it was even inhabited. Gray clouds filled the sky, and the scent of rain carried on the wind. Rolf shifted his position on the branch, trying to keep the feeling in his legs.

A tiny flicker of candlelight shone in a window in the uppermost tower, and Rolf perked up. He watched it move until it disappeared somewhere in the bowels of the structure. As he was trying to find the candlelight again, he saw a small wooden door the size of a large dog, nestled underneath the outer wall. It opened up to the precipice, where the waves just barely grazed the stone foundation a few yards below.

As he watched the door, exhaustion pulled on his body. He reached into his bag, grabbed a rope, and threw it around the tree trunk, tying himself against it lest he nod off and fall from the branch. He searched a few more times for the candle in any of the windows, but eventually his eyes grew heavy.

Adeline cried out, calling his name as flames roared behind her.

"You left me!" she screamed, pointing at him. Her neck split, blood poured forth, and the flames enveloped her.

"No!" He tried to run to her, but he was stuck, his arms straining to reach her.

A screech jolted him awake. The rope dug into his chest, and for a moment, he thought he was being held down, until he shook away his lethargy.

He tried to find the source of the noise, but only a Merlin falcon soared above him, hunting, its feathers blending into the late-afternoon sky. He rubbed his face, cursing at himself that he had fallen asleep, and scanned the forest, finally relaxing when he realized he was still hidden.

He untied the rope, stuffed it back into his bag, and readied for the climb down. He carried only a few weapons with him—his trusty axe, a few silver-tipped knives, some wooden stakes—and hoped they would be enough as he strapped a few holsters to his belt and into his boots.

Once sure that he had hidden the weapons well enough on his body, he stashed his bag underneath some bushes. Rolf kept to the shadows so he could slip easily behind a tree without being noticed. The closer he got to the castle, the more irritated he became. The thought of having Adeline so near, but still out of reach, sent his wolf into a frenzy inside his chest. It growled, grumbled, unable to be patient. But it would have to be, because he couldn't risk acting on impulse.

Rolf stayed low, crawling on his hands and knees underneath the ferns and shrubs at the cliff's edge until he was close enough to see the door from his vantage point without being spotted by anyone in the castle. He got down on his belly and looked over the edge. The craggy face had enough of a ledge that he could scale his way to the door—it looked to be only a hundred feet from where he lay. That is, if the tide didn't threaten to rip him out while he climbed. He tied one end of his rope to his axe and the other to the trunk of a scrub oak. And then, with a deep breath, he aimed for the center of the door and tossed the axe.

It landed with a *thunk*, the sound drowned out by the waves crashing on the rocks. He held his breath for a few moments, waiting to see if anyone would come running.

No one peered over the walls, no one opened the door. No one shouted. He exhaled.

Now or never.

And he rolled himself over the edge of the cliff, determined to get her back.

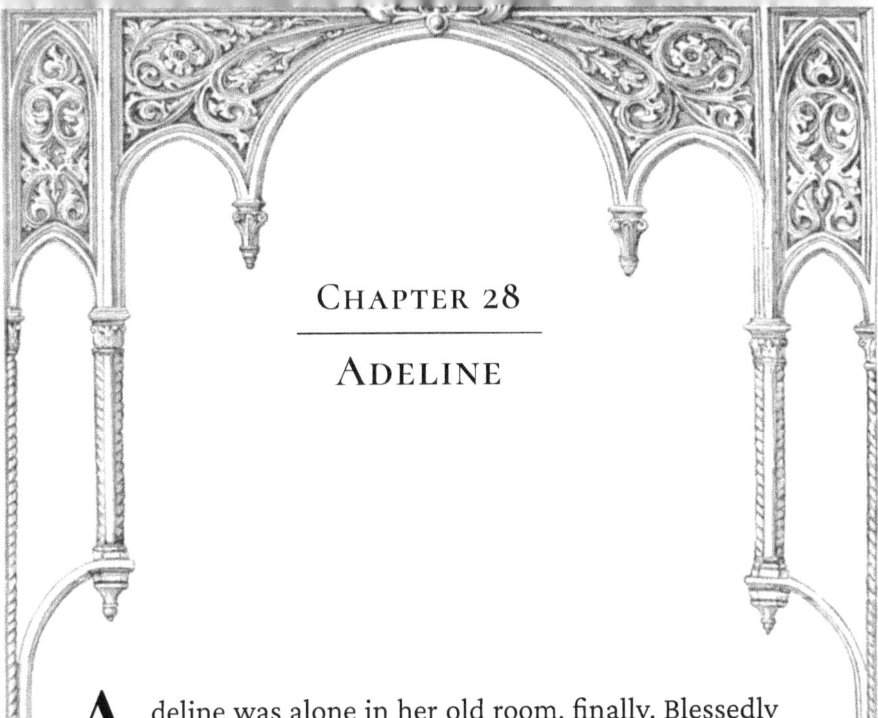

Chapter 28

Adeline

Adeline was alone in her old room, finally. Blessedly alone. She ran to the chamber pot and retched violently. Thick coagulated blood emptied into the bin, and she stared at the contents as waves of nausea rocked through her. Erik's caresses lingered on her exposed skin like a slimy sheath, and she ran her hands over herself, wanting to wipe them all away. Her skin turned red from the vigorous rubbing, and she clawed at her bloodied and muddy clothes, desperate to get everything he had touched off her body.

Then she grabbed a pillow from the bed and screamed into it, hoping to muffle the sounds of her agony. Erik's hold on everything within the castle walls was firm, and she did not want anyone to hear her agony and report back to him. If Erik knew she felt this way, it would mean he had won, and the last thing Adeline wanted was for Erik to realize he had finally conquered all of her.

His wife? His mate? No matter how loud she screamed, she couldn't shake the words that swirled in her head.

She wished she could at least hear Rolf's desperate howl once more. Death would be an easy release, knowing she would eventually be with Rolf again in the Forever Night. A creature like her, her spirit would easily find a home in the darkness beyond.

The sadness she fought to keep at bay finally broke through the dam, and she wept. She wept so long that the candles eventually burned down, and then, once she was finished, she tore the room apart.

She tossed pillows and overturned the mattress, she ripped down the curtains and tried her best to break the iron bed frame, but she was too weak. She even tried to destroy the vanity, but it had been bolted to the walls.

No matter what Adeline did, she could not find anything of use to make a weapon.

Unless...

Adeline dropped to her knees by the vanity. Though the bolts that kept it fastened to the wall sported a dwarven design, she still tried her best to unscrew them with only her fingers. She grunted and groaned, but they would not budge.

"Damn those dwarves and their metalworking!" She smacked her hand against the wall, her palm turning purple from the force. Adeline knew she wasn't thinking clearly, but never in her life had she felt so far out of her depth. Exhaling, she looked around the room at the mess.

"Come on, give me *some*thing!"

A knock on the door startled her, and Juliette's voice sounded on the other side.

Adeline held her breath.

The locks clanked, and then the door opened.

"Your dinner," Juliette said, her eyes roaming over Adeline's naked body, discarded clothes, destroyed room, and the vomit in the bowl.

Juliette barely twitched as she stepped inside Adeline's room; the wards that Adeline had once carved into the threshold were useless after sitting for over a century. She never knew if they ever really provided her protection, such was her limited experience working with them. But, still, she carved them into the shadows of the door just as her mother had taught her when she was a human.

"I will not drink whatever that is." Adeline tried her best to sound strong, but she was exhausted. The last meal she'd had was Rolf, and that was such a minimal amount of fuel. After losing so much blood, she needed fresh blood to get her full strength back. Besides, she had stupidly used up whatever strength she had left, destroying the room.

"You've been busy," Juliette said.

"Don't." Adeline didn't want to dive into small talk. She was exhausted and broken-hearted, and Juliette was keeping too many secrets for her to sit through endless pleasantries.

"You should try and eat something," Juliette said, pouring a glass of that thick red liquid. "You need strength."

"I will not." Despondency threatened to drag Adeline under into an unrelinquishing hug.

"Always the dramatic one." Juliette rolled her eyes, set the cup down, and turned to Adeline. She chided, "You need something in your stomach if you're going to go back out there."

"Why did you lie?" Adeline asked, standing. She toed a deflated pillow on the floor, the stitching undone, and down feathers spilling out of it from where she tore it open.

Juliette met Adeline's stare unflinchingly. "Why wouldn't I?"

Adeline couldn't stand the falseness that radiated off Juliette. She shook her head. "That's not an answer. Your anger was so convincing when you showed up to the cabin, but you didn't kill me."

"No." Juliette exhaled. Her shoulders dropped, and so did the carefully curated image of being put together. "Injured you enough to incapacitate you, yes. But kill? I could never."

"But—" Adeline stopped, her hazy memories from the fight in the caves flitting in and out. Was that why Juliette had helped the other vampire? To give Adeline time to get to Rolf?

There was something else, something Juliette was keeping close to her chest, and Adeline wasn't in the mood to play games. She wanted to be left alone to figure out how to fashion a weapon. Juliette's eyes flicked up and down Adeline's body, and suddenly she felt very exposed in front of her ex-lover like this.

A flush crept up Adeline's neck, the moments of intimacy between them flooding back into her memory. How hopeful Adeline had been to have a companion once more, and a gorgeous, curvy, and blond one, too. After being alive for several hundred years, Adeline found herself experimenting with all kinds of lovers—centuries of immortality could do that to someone.

But Erik would only permit her the occasional dalliance under the condition that he could watch. After all, Adeline *was* supposed to only be his. He would follow her lovers into the bedroom, ogling Adeline and how her lovers worshipped her. Erik would persuade Adeline to do what she wished and with whom, so long as she fed off them and promised her return to his bed once she 'had it out of her system.' It was the tiniest taste of freedom he afforded her because, according to him, she was always full of lust.

Full of lust, or was it the only time I felt a reprieve from him?

Juliette was different. Juliette was *hers*. And Erik had never found out.

"Addy, trust me," she pleaded. Juliette's voice was strained, and Adeline couldn't tell if it was due to deceit or earnestness. "The last thing I wanted to do was to bring you back here."

Adeline had to coach Juliette on how to use her vampire magic to glamour her next meal so they wouldn't feel so much pain. The first time Juliette tried, her glamour wore off halfway through feeding, and she panicked. The man ran away with blood spurting from his neck. Adeline had to chase him down, glamour him, and finish him off. It had taken Adeline years to build up Juliette's confidence enough to hunt by herself.

Juliette taking action on her own in the heat of the moment? Unlikely.

Adeline shivered, suddenly very exhausted and worn

down. Juliette clicked her tongue and tossed Adeline a clean chemise from the wardrobe. She caught it and slipped it on, tying the top with blue fingers.

"Do you think I'm angry at you, Jules?" Adeline asked, using the nickname she had given Juliette when they first met. Then she shrugged. "I made a bargain when I knew I shouldn't have. This is a fitting punishment."

"You haven't called me Jules in a long time," Juliette said.

"You haven't called me Addy in a long time," Adeline countered. She sat down on the edge of the bed, sinking into the soft mattress. The last time she had been on this bed was to feed from some unknowing soul, desperate to please Erik, who watched, bored, from the shadows in the corner.

"You called me Jules because you said my eyes reminded you of emeralds," Juliette said. She twisted her hands in front of her, then crossed the room to sit beside Adeline. Her voice was soft as she added, "We could have been so great together, Adeline."

"We could have. But Erik would never have let us have what we wanted." At some point, their hands had woven together, and Adeline clutched Juliette's in her own. "His jealousy knows no bounds."

And now Rolf is dead because of it.

"So you left, leaving me to fend for myself and take your place?" Juliette's eyes were rimmed with tears. "I loved you. I thought you felt the same."

Realization dawned on Adeline. Had Juliette brought her back as retribution for abandonment? She squeezed

Juliette's hand, saying softly, "I did. My heart was once yours—and only yours—for a long time."

"Then why did you leave?" Juliette asked, looking down at their intertwined hands.

"I snapped." It was the truth, and she had held on to it too long. Adeline had wanted to leave for centuries, but had never been able to get away. She was so numb—so broken—that she let Juliette take her place, not once feeling shame for her decision.

"I took your place, Adeline. In more ways than one. There were nights when—"

"You don't have to say anything else." Adeline knew what Juliette would say, and no good would come of it. Now, faced with the reality of her decisions, this was the first time she had ever felt genuine remorse for what she had done to someone.

And after all the lives she had destroyed, why would she think she was ever worthy of happiness? Of love?

I didn't deserve Colin. Adeline bit back the salty taste of remorse. *I never deserved Rolf.*

If she had ever cared for Juliette, she would have never left her lover here to fend for herself, exposed to Erik's twisted mind. The waves of guilt that she had once pushed away so easily now threatened to drown what was left of her.

"I couldn't stay here under his thumb, under his evilness. I didn't want to play his games anymore. I couldn't even love you without worrying about him twisting your mind like he did mine. It wasn't fair. It wasn't right, but I felt like I had no choice. And no matter what I say, I know it will never make up for the fact that I was only looking out for myself."

Juliette bit back a sob. Adeline leaned forward and kissed her tenderly on the cheek.

"Do you love him? The wolf?"

"I do—did," Adeline whispered back, staring into the eyes of her former lover, watching decades of memories play out between them.

"I kept waiting for you to come back, rescue me, and be here. It took me ages to get over you, Adeline. I was so angry for so long."

Adeline cringed as the words landed. She had been so careless, thinking only of her survival and her trauma. Gods, how could she have been so selfish? "I would be angry, too."

Juliette straightened. "All those years I spent pining after you. I went along with his horrible demands, thinking that one day I could do what you did. But I have been delusional because I am not as brave as you."

Again, shame swirled with the guilt that had settled in her gut. How could she tell Juliette that she planned to end her life? There were rumors of other vampires who had taken their own lives. They were only rumors, though. As far as she knew, it had never been done before.

"Brave, or foolish?" Adeline asked, partly to herself.

"Bravery doesn't always wield a sword, Adeline," her mother had said when the girls came home. She and Leda had been playing princesses, and Adeline was the brave knight with a sword who rescued the damsel in the tower. The stick had broken, and Adeline cried, worried that she couldn't save her sister. "Bravery can also mean finding hope when all else seems

lost, living your life with honor, and doing what's right for others."

Adeline sniffled, and her mother wrapped her up in her arms. The scent of her mother's skin and drying herbs filled her nose, and she instantly calmed within her mother's warm embrace. Her mother pulled away and cradled Adeline's sniveling face. "But most of all, bravery is getting back up and trying again, even after failure. And I know how stubborn you can be, dear girl. You are the bravest person I know."

Juliette shifted on the bed, and the memory faded. Adeline's shoulders sagged. She missed the peace her mother brought, the calm ways she handled her daughters' loud and intrusive feelings.

"You *have* been brave." Juliette looked at Adeline with deep emerald eyes filled with hope. "Especially when I saw the lengths you would go to protect that wolf shifter."

So she still doesn't know that it was Colin...

Adeline bit back tears."No, Juliette. You are far braver than I could have ever been. I ran, but you stayed."

Juliette gave her a wry smile. "I did want to kill you, you know. Seeing you made me angry all over again. Furious, actually."

Adeline felt the scar along her neck. She had been convinced Juliette was going to kill her. She wished it had come true. "What was your plan? If you had killed me?"

"Run away? Like you? Assume a new identity?" Juliette stood and started pacing, her arms waving erratically in the air. "But I didn't have a plan. I never do. I'm not a planner, like you."

Juliette was brave, but she wasn't stupid. She could easily play the games Erik made her take part in. Adeline had always been the one to resist. She was not as easily moldable. Each time Erik brought her back, she was forced to bend the knee, to heel, to tread carefully lest she anger him even more. But it was only a matter of time before her scheming took over and she tried to find a way to get out from under his clutches.

I just want to be free.

"I don't have a plan, Jules. Not this time," Adeline admitted, standing up. "Jules, I am so tired of constantly running. No matter what I do or where I go, Erik is there, always bringing me back into his orbit. I am helpless against his pull."

"You are not helpless."

"What else do I have to live for? I lost Rolf again, and I have to spend whatever hellish life Erik has planned for me. Gods, I was so stupid to make that bargain!" Adeline cradled her head in her hands and wanted to tear her hair out.

"No, I'm not going to let you give up." Juliette stood and started pacing the room. Feathers from the pillow floated up around her skirts each time she turned. "You can't give up. You're the bravest vampire I know."

Adeline almost laughed at the echoed words her mother once said. She was so far from brave. She just wished this conversation would end so she could figure out how to end her life. Her eyes flicked to the window; though it was narrow, she might be able to slip through and throw herself off the cliffs and into the sea.

"Adeline, I need you to pull yourself together." Juliette's tone shifted, pulling Adeline from her brooding. She stepped closer to Adeline and knelt before her. "If you have any remorse for what I've been through, then you have to help me."

Adeline blanched but said nothing. Of course, she felt remorseful. "Juliette, I—"

"I have a mate," she whispered. The words floated in the air between them. "I found her, and I...I have to be with her."

Adeline finally looked at Juliette clearly for the first time since she showed up at the cabin.

Perhaps this was the gods' way of shaking her world, because now she could see more pieces of the puzzle. This was why she was here: to set things right for Juliette and help her former lover move on, find a life of freedom. The desperation in Juliette's admission was her request for permission to move on. Juliette was able to find a mate; despite everything she had been put through, she had found happiness. Who was Adeline to keep her from that?

"I love her, and I can't mate with her, I can't touch her, I can't see her, because..." Juliette waved her hands in the air in apparent frustration.

"That must be torturous," Adeline said, understanding the pain that came with being unable to be with someone you were convinced was your mate. But Adeline knew it was probably worse for Juliette. Vampires had different rules than regular fae for mates. Once they were through the mating ritual, their scents would merge, the little magic they did have would get stronger, and they would be almost impossible to kill.

But can mate bonds be forced? She was unsure if that was the reason Erik wanted her to be his in three days.

Adeline briefly recalled something she had read while

she was researching the were shifters. It hadn't been about vampires or were shifters, specifically, but it had mentioned the lore of mating and how magic between non-humans increased after a mating rite.

"You aren't the only one tired of his twisted games," Juliette said. From deep within her pockets, she withdrew two bracelets. Adeline's heart dropped into her feet, her chest clinched with fear. "He told me you have to wear these."

"Enchanted cuffs?" Adeline could barely form the words. Her throat was tight. He wanted her to feel powerless.

"Dwarven made specifically for you," Juliette said, cringing. Her shoulders curled in, and her whole body seemed even smaller. "I need you to find a way to help me because I can't be in this Gods-forsaken castle any longer."

Tears lined Juliette's eyes as she clamped them around Adeline's wrists. Dwarven wards were engraved in a delicate scroll, and between the two bracelets was a thin silver chain. The last time she had worn cuffs and chains, she was strapped to a table in the dungeons, stripped naked, whipped within an inch of her immortal life, and forced to drink the blood of imprisoned humans until she finally bent to Erik's will.

"I'll try my best, Juliette." Adeline knew she couldn't make any promises. Not yet. Not when Erik wanted her to feel defeated. She stared at the dwarven chains keeping her wrists bound and wished with her entire being that she had a flicker of fire still burning deep within her.

"Try harder, please. I'm desperate, Adeline."

Chapter 29

Rolf

Wet earth and the musty scent of stale air assaulted Rolf's senses. Waves crashed outside, filling the tunnel with a deafening sound and shaking the door behind him. Only a sliver of light shone through a crack in the door where his axe had struck. In hindsight, it was probably for the best that the axe had lodged so deeply into the wood, because without that crack, he wouldn't be able to see a thing.

He slid his feet forward, hoping he wasn't walking toward a dead end. The mud clawed at his boots, squelching each time he shifted his weight. Though it was cool in the belly of the castle, sweat formed along his brow. Several feet in, the light disappeared. One of his hands drifted to his holsters, triple-checking he had everything in its rightful place once more, while the other braced against the stones as he felt his way forward. Pitch-black enveloped him, and instead of succumbing to the terror of feeling like the tunnel was closing in, he let his eyes drift shut and tried letting his wolf come forward. Maybe if he could give it the right nudge, he could use its heightened senses.

Ever since Adeline had fed from him, he had felt closer than ever to his wolf. On the journey, he had noticed a constant throbbing in his chest and an animalistic urge to destroy everything in his path that kept him from her. And now that he knew he was close, it was a battle reigning in the impatient beast. Which was vastly different than how it had been in the past century, when only the full moon would connect him to his animal.

Curious, he thought, and it almost felt like his wolf hummed in agreement.

His toe thudded against something, and his eyes snapped open when his hands braced against solid wood.

A door? His hands groped for a handle, but he found nothing. *Fuck!*

Rolf almost kicked the wooden slab, but stopped himself. There was no telling what or who was on the other side.

What do I do now? His wolf snarled as he turned around. A speck of light shone at the very end of the tunnel, roughly a dozen feet away. He debated for a moment whether he should head back the way he came. But when he turned around again, there was a door with a small circular window where the solid wooden slab had been.

"Huh," he said. His wolf had gone quiet; otherwise, he would have felt his hackles rise. "If that isn't interesting."

Are my eyes playing tricks on me?

He looked behind him again, staring at the wall where

the wooden door led to the sea. It was gone. Gooseflesh prickled his skin, but he faced forward once more. The new door remained. Through the window, he could see a torch flickering on the wall, casting long shadows into the tunnel. He rubbed his eyes, certain that his mind was playing tricks on him.

"Well, castle," he said, partly to himself to give him courage and partly to whatever trickery was afoot, "I suppose I don't have much of a choice."

For Adeline.

He took a deep breath, turned the handle, and pushed the door open.

An intricate grand staircase appeared before him, as if he had just walked through the front door of the castle. Which he knew he hadn't because he was far below the upper levels of the structure. He had expected at least a hallway or a dungeon with torches, but instead, the staircase's large wooden banisters, carved with intricate floral accents, curved upward, velvet runners covered several dozen wooden stairs, and chandeliers full of candles hung from above.

The space looked vaguely familiar, as if plucked from his memories as a child, but he couldn't quite place it, and each time he focused on a particular spot, his vision blurred slightly.

Magicked.

At the base of the staircase was a small table with a mirror and a candelabra. Rolf picked up the candelabra, glancing briefly at his image in the mirror. In the reflection, his hair had been shorn close, and his beard was gone. He was wearing an outfit similar to the ones his brothers used to wear.

Is this what I would have looked like?

With his free hand, he reached up and touched his cheek. His beard was gone, and his hair was shorn close, just like in the reflection. Leaning forward, Rolf wondered briefly what his life would be like now if he had not gone into the stone circle, or if he hadn't ever shifted, or if his wolf hadn't changed every part of himself. Even the eyes that stared back at him had changed, no longer the amber color he was used to.

Had his brothers' eyes ever changed? Not that he could remember.

A gentle breeze caressed the back of his neck, and his flesh prickled, nudging him out of his hazy memories. The door to the tunnel swung silently on its hinges until it closed. Awestruck, he watched as the lock turned on its own, as if moved by a specter.

With nowhere else to go, Rolf tightened his grip around the candelabra.

"Up the stairs, then," he said.

It was an easy decision. He would do whatever it took to get her back, even if it meant burning the castle to the ground from the inside. He would never be separated from her ever again.

Chapter 30

Adeline

Adeline's neck had healed—a thin scar trailed like a pink choker around her throat, the only evidence that it had been slit. Without fresh blood, though, her healing had taken longer than she wanted, and she still felt weaker than usual. Shadows played at the corners of her vision, and she was growing more familiar with the thought that her mental faculties were slipping. Sitting at the small vanity, she ran a brush through her clean hair, the scent of white amber and jasmine floating around her face with each stroke.

The delicate silver chain around her wrists clinked as she brushed a trail along the fresh tissue at the base of her neck. She hesitated, one of her fingers hovering at her collarbone, toying with opening it with her sharpened nail. She tongued her fangs, staring at the slow pulse in her neck.

If only it were that easy. Was she weak enough that a simple slice would open the fresh tissue up once more?

Perhaps. She had never known of a vampire to bleed themselves dry before. Besides, something nagged at the back of her mind as she recalled Juliette's plea from earlier.

Desperate, Juliette had said.

What does Juliette know of desperation?

She had looked at Adeline with such hope that, for a moment, Adeline had entertained helping. But then Juliette left, and she slipped back into the hopelessness. And now, in the quietness of the room, with a few candles flicking her shadow onto the wall, she wanted to end this nightmare. Just another game of Erik's, but with what payoff? Why did he want *her* so badly?

It wasn't like he couldn't *train* someone else to take her place.

She may be one of the oldest vampires, but right now, she was so tired and alone. She was that poor young woman she had been before she was turned. When she had married the prince, against her mother's wishes. When she had realized, too late, that he wasn't at all the savior she thought him to be. When she wished that she had been stronger to resist his charms and wiles. When all she wanted was to be back with her mother and sister, in the old mill, next to the forest.

All this time, she thought she had become smarter, stronger. But at what cost? She landed right back in the place she wanted to leave.

She swiped her hands along the top of the vanity table, cursing. Items clattered to the floor, but still, her reflection disgusted her. She wiped away a stray tear. Her mother would know what to do. Her mother always knew what to do.

Stop this pity party and just do it already!

Adeline sighed, her fingernail sharpening to a fine point. It dug into her skin, a blossom of red welling at the tip. But her hand shook. She cursed her image in the mirror and pushed away from it.

Pathetic, spineless fool.

She hung her head in her hands, the chain clinking against her cuffs, and groaned. Just because she couldn't be with the love of her life didn't mean that Juliette had to suffer. She had suffered enough on Adeline's behalf.

I've gone soft.

Or maybe she had been soft this whole time, but living under Erik's thumb, softness was never an option. Instead, she tucked away the gentleness. Buried it under layers of dissociation and ruthless killing as a way to numb her regret.

Maybe this was her chance to do something right after all these years. Adeline would help Juliette get free, no matter what. It would be her atonement.

Atonement. The word rolled around in her head, marinating in her thoughts of Rolf.

Could it be that she never truly deserved the love she always sought? As an assassin, she had never once questioned Erik's motives. The casualties were just poor souls who had been in the wrong place at the wrong time. But in the past century, out from underneath Erik's thumb, hunting down were-shifters on his behalf, a seed of discontent had been planted. At first, it was Colin who had shown her that there was more to her immortal life. After he disappeared, when she got a taste of freedom, that was when she realized that she wanted more than just doing the bidding of a power-hungry egomaniac.

And now, that seed of disquiet had grown and sprouted into something more.

The door handle clicked, and she was startled back to the present.

"I'm here to help you get dressed," Juliette said as she laid a few items down on the vanity and placed a dress on a chaise lounge. Then she grabbed the glass on the vanity and held it aloft. The liquid inside was even thicker, having sat out for a while, and Adeline's stomach twisted a few times. "Erik requested that you drink this."

Adeline pursed her lips, not wanting to vomit like she did earlier. "I can't."

"You *have* to, Adeline. He isn't going to send you a willing, fresh food source—you'd get better too fast." Worry lined Juliette's face.

Adeline shook her head, but took the goblet full of old blood. She needed to find a living source of food if she was going to be strong enough to get Juliette out of here. "Fine, but one sip. That's all."

She choked it down, gagging as it slid down her throat and landed in her stomach like lead.

Juliette gave her a pained smile and unwrapped a leather mat.

"What jewelry?" she asked and held up an elaborate diamond necklace.

Adeline's heart raced as she looked at what she was supposed to wear. The dress was a deep blue with a full skirt and a torturously low neckline. It had a full corset with delicate embroidery and pearl accents. On the dresser was an assortment of accessories—a fan, gloves, hairpins, necklaces, earrings.

"None." Adeline shook her head.

She would leave her neck bare tonight, on full display for everyone to see that she was not ashamed to bear all the marks on her body. Each was a badge of honor for the horrors she had faced, even the ones Erik had carved on her, and she was proud that she had made it through. Her hands skimmed the faded marks on her wrists, where Erik had repeatedly bound her during his many attempts to mold her into his perfect prodigy. At least the initials on her backside would be hidden. She would do what she could to prevent Erik from seeing that she had tried to burn off the other brands decades ago.

"You will look stunning, Adeline," Juliette assured her. "Erik will be captivated by you."

"He should be," Adeline said sourly. "He's won, after all."

"He hasn't won yet," Juliette said as she helped Adeline into the undergarments. "He just thinks he's won."

Adeline nodded solemnly. "And wearing this will convince him even more."

Juliette's hands stilled on the ties of the corset. Her breath was cool against Adeline's neck. "I really am sorry I slit your throat. It was one of my favorite places to..."

"To what? Kiss?" Adeline looked over her shoulder. Juliette's face was flushed. She forgot how endearing she could be sometimes. In all honesty, Adeline was happy for her. Glad, even. That she had something to look forward to beyond this hellscape. Adeline rubbed her neck, adding, "It's just flesh. It will heal."

Juliette cleared her throat and finished tying Adeline in. "Do you have a plan?"

Nope. "I've got a few I'm working on." Adeline spun around and slid her arms into the dress.

Juliette helped straighten the skirts. The satin swished under her quick movements, reminding Adeline of the beating of birds' wings. Her heart beat rapidly; her time to be with Erik was closing in, and she still hadn't figured anything out yet.

"So, you don't have a plan," Juliette chided. She grabbed the dangling chain and fit it back into the cuff, locking it into place.

Adeline straightened, trying her best to breathe in the stiff corset. "I am working on several angles, Juliette. You'll just have to trust me."

"But you won't share them with me," Juliette guessed. She grabbed Adeline's hands, and that pleading look returned to her eyes as she begged, "I'm your *ally* in this, Adeline. Please tell me what I need to do. I want us to be done with this awful business—I want us to be *free*."

Free. Would she ever be free? No, because Juliette had brought her back to this hellhole. And for what purpose? It had taken what felt like forever to free herself from her maker's manipulation. Not only did she think more clearly when she was out from under his thumb, but Erik had been twisting her reality to his advantage. It had all been a ploy to keep her dependent on him.

"We will be," Adeline reassured her. She needed Juliette to be on her side, since allies in this place were few and far between. But that didn't mean she trusted her completely, nor did it help with the immense guilt she felt at leaving Juliette behind.

Tears welled in the corner of Juliette's eyes, and Adeline squeezed her hands in return. If this had been anyone else, or if Adeline had been her usual assassin self, she would have scoffed at the flagrant display of emotion. Instead, she let Juliette lure her in as if it would help erase the guilt she still carried. "Let me see what he wants tonight and then..."

"Then?" Juliette's voice was barely a whisper.

Adeline smiled and grabbed the goblet of congealed liquid. Her stomach roiled, but she needed sustenance in some form, and she wouldn't dare ask Juliette to provide it. Adeline had never fed off one of her own since she was turned. And if Erik realized that Adeline had consumed something other than what was in the goblet, he would catch on to their scheming. She was meant to be under his control, and what better way to pretend it than with a little bit of nausea to add to her act? She had no choice tonight but to enter the lion's den—a tiny mouse ready to be caught in the claws of a predator.

"The countdown begins," Adeline whispered. Juliette met Adeline's gaze, and they both cringed. Adeline plugged her nose as she downed the cup in one swallow. She slammed the empty vessel on the table and nodded for Juliette to lead the way, fighting to keep the thickened liquid from coming back up.

Chapter 31

Rolf

The castle shifted and warped beneath his feet, changing its layout every time Rolf felt like he had figured out where he was going. It seemed like he had been walking for hours, trying to find his way out. Sweat beaded on his brow. Finally, fed up and frustrated, he stood still. An unsettled calm filled the air, as if the castle wrapped its cold fingers around him, taking his pulse, anticipating his next moves.

So he stopped playing. He closed his eyes and took a few deep breaths, listening for his shifter. His wolf, though, was eerily quiet—no pacing, no huffing, no agitation.

The castle must have severed my connection to him somehow. And if that were the case, Rolf would need to keep his wits about him. He opened his eyes. On the landing before him was his old library—at least a poor imitation of the one he remembered from his childhood. Though the shelves all looked familiar and the layout was the same, the edges of the image still blurred when he focused on it too hard. His eyes strained to get a glimpse of what lay beyond this illusion, without luck.

A sound echoed from somewhere behind him, and he looked over his shoulder. It was a singsong trill, like the one his mother used to make when she returned from her travels with his father. Her voice would fill the halls of the estate, and as a little boy, he would gleefully run all over trying to find her. When he finally did, he would fling himself at her skirts, burying his head against her legs as her laughter shook his whole body and her scent of sun-kissed lilacs filled his nose. But now, he could not recall what she looked like. Only disembodied pieces of her came to him now, like when she would kiss him good night, and her braid would fall over her shoulder, tickling his face. Or the sound of her kisses as she smothered him in hellos and goodbyes. Or the intense calm he felt when she wrapped him in her arms.

"Mother," he croaked, and he wiped away a tear.

Had she just returned from one of her trips with Father? Would she come peeking out from between the shelves to surprise him? He stared at the shelves once more, wondering if she was hiding from him. Was it his imagination, or did the books not have titles? He squinted his eyes once more, trying to make out the words on the spines, but his vision blurred.

The sound echoed once more, this time from behind him. He turned, seeking out the source. But no one was there. He cleared his throat, realization dawning on him slowly.

Not your mother, stay focused.

He shook his head, trying to clear the images from his head. How did the castle know these intimate moments from his life?

Slowly, Rolf slid his feet along the ground. It was cold beneath his shoes and didn't creak. This led him to think perhaps he was in the dungeons, where the floor would be stone instead of wooden. After sliding forward another few feet, he stilled.

The candles flickered toward his right shoulder, indicating a breeze coming from his left. And though the air around him felt suppressive, when he moved the candelabra to his right, the flames went still.

Curious.

He shuffled his feet to his left as subtly as he could so as not to alert the magicked castle to his movements. Inch by agonizing inch, he followed the breeze against the flames until, finally, his toes touched a wall, going through the bookshelves. They shook with transience each time he wiggled his feet.

To his left, the staircase kept climbing, leading to who knows where—the top didn't seem like it had an end. He figured he would have kept walking in place for hours, his brain tricked into thinking that he was headed somewhere until he collapsed from exhaustion.

Maybe this is how they get their prey, he thought. It was a clever entrapment: magick the castle with an illusion to entice you to follow until you are so worn out and weary that you are easy to capture.

It had almost been enough to trick Rolf. But his determination to get to Adeline before something terrible happened cut through any sort of trickery the castle tried to play.

I will get her back. He rubbed at the spot in the center of his chest that felt like a tiny flame lived inside. He reached forward with his free hand until he met the rough wood of a door. His fingers sought out a handle moving beneath the illusion of the books in front of him. Slowly, as if moving through thick mud, his hand slid over the surface until it connected with a rounded knob. Relief soared in his chest, and he grasped it tightly, afraid that if he let go, he would never find it again.

The edges of his vision warped once more, rippling as the staircase and bookshelves dissolved. The edges of a new scene unfolded around him. He didn't wait to see what the rest of the room looked like. Instead, he dropped the candelabra, letting it clatter to the ground. The fire snuffed out as he turned the handle.

It wouldn't give. He used both hands, grunting and twisting until it finally gave way.

The air pulled at his clothes, tugging on his lower legs as if to hold him back. Using all the strength he could muster, he yanked on the doorknob and threw the door open. The air tightened around him, tugging him backward, refusing to let go. His not-mother's voice echoing behind him, calling out to him.

He didn't hesitate, instead bracing himself against the threshold to then propel himself forward into a darkened hallway.

What's next?

He jumped when the door slammed shut behind him.

Silence enveloped him. Silence and pitch-black darkness. He could barely hear himself breathe.

The hair on the back of his neck prickled, sending shivers down his spine as anticipation coiled tight in his stomach. He was waiting. The whole space around him was waiting.

But for what?

He'd been in tense situations before on the battlefield. Now that his memories were returning after Adeline had removed the glamour, he felt thrust right back into the moments before combat.

The suspense in the moment before worlds collided. The sense of doom that filled your bones and weighed you down. The heightened awareness that pulled your head into the clouds as your soul separated from your body. The feeling of shame at liking how it felt to be so imminently close to your death that you would do anything to make it out alive. Seeking that high again and again, just to feel the intensity repeat.

Perhaps that was why he had been drawn to Adeline at first, as Colin. He was like a magnet drawn to the sense of danger she carried around her like a cloak. But when she told him what she was, he didn't believe her.

A vampire? He had laughed it off as if she were playing games. Until she showed him her fangs. And it felt like his heart had, once again, leaped from his chest. And he knew that there would never be anyone quite like her, for him, ever again.

Adeline, he reminded himself, as a cannon suddenly went off in the distance. He dropped to the floor, straight into mud.

Shouts of men filled his ears and echoed into the night. He was covered in mud and wearing his military clothing again—his shoulders adorned with medals. But where were his weapons?

Panicking, he patted himself down, realizing that he was unarmed and about to face the enemy on the battlefield once more. He closed his eyes tightly, knowing that this was just another illusion. All he needed was to find the end of this room, and he'd be even closer to freeing Adeline.

Chapter 32

Adeline

"If we're even seconds late…" Juliette began, wringing her hands at her side. She glanced back quickly at Adeline, cheeks flushed, eyes darting to Adeline's hair, which was coming undone with each step.

Adeline took a strained breath and tried to tuck a curl back in, but the damn chain between her hands made it almost impossible. "I know, Jules. It's hard to run and breathe in this thing."

Adeline's skirts swished around her legs as she tried to keep pace with Juliette. She had to bite her tongue to keep from tearing them off her body. It had been decades since she had worn skirts as full as these, and the damn things kept tangling around her ankles. Juliette turned again, taking Adeline toward the throne room at a pace wholly unwelcome for the amount of clothing she was wearing. This dress was painfully out of style, but she wasn't surprised. Erik clung to the idea that tradition was of the utmost importance, so why wouldn't they all dress like they belonged in another century?

Juliette stopped and grabbed Adeline's hand, half pulling her through another hallway.

Besides being fashionably out of fashion, Erik was also extremely punctual. She had always chalked it up to his lifespan—the older he got, the more of an asshole he became about counting the seconds. But now she knew it was because he had to have complete control. There had been times when the assassinations were delayed by circumstances far out of her control, and she had always felt his wrath because of it.

The way she loathed Erik. It was different this time, different than how she felt in the past. Now she knew he was pulling the strings on every single aspect of her life, as well as those in her life, too. She shouldn't have ever dragged Rolf into her mess. Her vengeance was hers alone, not his. She had been a fool to think that the two of them could both make it out of this game alive. Taking down Erik and the entire coven was *her* prerogative, and it had cost Rolf his life.

Shadows blurred the edges of her vision, a darkness pressing down around her the angrier she got. How she was going to do it, she still didn't know. As despondent as she felt, it only helped stoke the fire of rage that bubbled underneath her surface. She could feel the heat singing her bones, burning the marrow, incinerating what had been left of her heart, and she knew that as soon as she heard Erik's slimy, nasally voice, there was nothing to keep her from unleashing that rage and burning the whole place down to the ground.

"Hurry. Up." Juliette's sharp voice broke her from her thoughts.

Adeline snapped her head up, and the shadows evaporated, crawling back behind the curtains, into the cracks of the walls. She blinked a few times.

I must be weaker than I thought.

Perhaps tonight was not the night to try to kill Erik. No, she needed to be stronger. She picked up her pace once again, letting Juliette drag her along by her chains.

"I hope he's in a forgiving mood tonight." Something else must be worrying Juliette because the closer they got to the throne room, the more nervous she seemed.

"When is he ever?" Adeline quipped.

She would make her official appearance as Erik's potential mate and wife, but the mere thought of actually going through the mating ritual made her sick to her stomach.

Her free hand reached up to touch the curve of her neck where Rolf had nipped her. Quiet resolve settled on her shoulders.

There was no way she would willingly replace those feelings, or his touch, or the words he spoke to her. But as much as she wanted to cling to those precious last moments in the cabin and keep everything alive, she instead shoved them deep, deep down. Erik couldn't know that she had figured out his manipulations—he would have the upper hand all over again.

The thin scar at the base of her throat was on full display, and the neckline of the gown was low and wide; with each step, her breasts threatened to escape. With her hair pulled up, she felt even more exposed. She shivered against the thought of being so vulnerable in front of Erik again.

And for the briefest of moments, she wondered if he would be pleased with how she looked.

His displeasure was the one thing Adeline had feared above all else. She recalled, vividly, the times she had disappointed him, had refused to acquiesce to his demands. At first, he would deliver painful blows and then suddenly be so turned on seeing her in pain that his touch would turn into gentle caresses. His whispers were always desperate in their frenzied apologies, as if *he* were the one who should be afraid of *her*. Countless times, she would have to drink bottles of wine to forget what had happened.

Her stomach roiled, and the flames of anger again lit her chest up with a fiery vengeance. She'd rather die than succumb to feeling like she had to please him ever again. She refused to be afraid of him tonight.

Tonight is not the night to be caught in the past, Adeline.

No, tonight she would be the perfect future mate.

And then it hit her, her plan unfolding so beautifully. She knew exactly how she was going to get Juliette out.

Careful not to crush the crinoline fabric, Adeline picked up her skirts so she could match Juliette's speed. If this was another test of Erik's, she was determined to ace it. He wouldn't get the upper hand ever again.

Adeline almost slammed into Juliette's back as they came upon a large door. Juliette stood stock-still, breathing deeply, but her hands still shook. Adeline stood beside her and twined her fingers with Juliette's. She was careful not to say anything, but their eyes met, and centuries of pain and fear flickered between them.

"I have a plan," Adeline whispered, so quietly that she wondered if Juliette had even heard it. But then, as the door handles clicked, Juliette turned to her and gave her the tiniest nod. Adeline angled her hips toward Juliette, blocking the side where Juliette kept the ring of keys, should the doors open unannounced. "Put the key in my hair."

Juliette inhaled. "I can't."

"Yes, you can. Pretend you're fixing my hair. Erik won't like me looking so unkempt." Adeline tried her best to sound calm and assured, when in truth she had no idea what she was going to do.

Behind Adeline's shoulder, the keys jangled, and then Juliette's deft fingers wove something cold and small and metal into one of her plaits. The doors swung open, and Adeline hesitated to step forward until Juliette's fingers stopped fussing.

"There," Juliette exhaled. "Perfect."

Adeline lifted her chin, ready to pretend she was everything Erik wanted.

Chapter 33

Rolf

The battlefield was a bloody, muddy mess. Fallen comrades screamed for their mothers, for their lovers, as they lay dying while cannons exploded beyond them.

"Sir!" Rolf screamed, turning his head left and then right as he tried to find his superior. But he knew it was useless; the man was probably dead. The only thing Rolf could do was keep moving forward. He knew something lay beyond the field, something he was meant to get to. But the mud was so thick, the bodies were piled so high, and the enemy kept advancing, as if unaffected by the chaos of war around them.

This isn't right, he thought.

Smoke filled his vision, and he started to cough. Now and again, he thought he saw creatures bending over the dead, but each time he tried to get closer, they would vanish into thin air. He reached down to help a fellow soldier get out of range, but his hand grasped at thin air. Confused, he looked at his hand, and then back at the soldier, who had somehow moved another foot away.

Rolf shook his head, the world around him warbling uncertainly. He must have hit his head, but when he ran his hands through his hair, there was no wound and no blood. There was something on the other side of the field; he knew it with his soul. He had to reach it, but trudging through this mud was getting him nowhere. Another cannon went off, and he dropped back down into the mud. It covered him, swallowing up his limbs, weighing him down.

No. It wasn't like this. It had never been like this.

Another cannon exploded in the distance. He crawled forward agonizingly slowly. Another cannon, and then another.

"Attack!" Rolf yelled, trying to recall where his troops were, but it was hard to see anything for the smoke and debris that filled the air.

Nothing happened. There were no soldiers. He was the last one standing.

Where is everyone?

The mud kept getting thicker and thicker the further he crawled. Soon, he was clambering over bodies, still warm but covered in blood and with no hope for recovery from their wounds. Bile snuck up his throat as he pushed away a body without its upper half. This was worse than the old nightmares he used to have.

"This isn't how this is supposed to be!" Rolf screamed to no one in particular. As soon as the words left his mouth, however, the scene before him faltered and changed.

What the fuck?

Now, instead of a battlefield, he was in the hospital, surrounded by rows and rows of fallen soldiers. Pain seared up his leg, and he grunted as he tried to put weight on it. He braced himself against the bed frame and hoisted up onto his good leg. A discarded crutch lay on the floor, and he bent over and picked it up. It all felt vaguely familiar, and yet, something seemed off.

Adeline was missing.

This is when I met Adeline. Where is she?

He scanned the room, the dying and injured faces, and the nurses. Nothing. She wasn't here.

She won't be here.

Adeline *was* here when it happened the first time, though. But this was somewhere different, and he had already had his time in the hospital. He wasn't injured anymore. He wasn't healing from the battle.

He dropped the crutch on the ground. He put all of his weight on his bad leg. It didn't hurt. It *hadn't* hurt in decades. In a century. Since he went through the stones and shifted into a wolf.

"Okay," he said, out loud, if only so he could hear something he knew was real. "This isn't real."

The image before him warbled.

"This isn't real." His voice was louder. Whatever he was doing was working.

Where the hell is Adeline?

The edges of the room went blurry.

"This isn't real, and I'm here to get what's mine."

Adeline.

The room shook, and medicine bottles crashed to the floor, shattering.

"This isn't real, and I'm here to get what's mine."

Adeline. Mine.

There was a rumbling beginning deep inside his chest. A growl, a hunger for her. His wolf was trying to push through whatever kept them apart. Rolf growled with it, determined to make it to the end of the room. He took a step forward, and then another. The closer he got to the end of the room, the lighter he started to feel, his movement less of a trudge and more of a slow walk.

Mine. Adeline. Adeline. Adeline.

Her name was a mantra that propelled him forward. Nothing would keep him from her.

But he didn't dare say it out loud lest he attract a real threat. The vampires were still in the castle, after all, and he had to get out of this gods-forsaken trap. Surely, if he could make it to the other side of what *had* been a hallway moments—or maybe it was hours—before, the illusions would end?

"There is no threat here. It's some magical illusion to keep me trapped." He smiled when his toes touched the end of the room, even though the image before him seemed to go on forever. "This isn't real. I'm here to get what's mine."

Adeline.

He sighed with relief as his hands met stone and wood. Closing his eyes for a few moments, Rolf tried to call forth his wolf. They couldn't be separated forever, but perhaps now that Rolf knew these were illusions and not real life, his wolf would remember, too.

There. The slumbering beast stirred, filling his head with cunning and his chest with hunger.

Nothing will keep us from her, his wolf promised, growling. *Nothing.*

Nothing, he agreed. And he opened the next door.

Chapter 34

Adeline

The throne room was unseemly warm, and a droplet of sweat dripped between Adeline's breasts as she made her way confidently through the crowd of vampires. When she swiveled her head, the world swam before her, shadows flickering at the edges of the room. She needed to eat, and she needed it soon, but she would rather feel dizzy than drink whatever mixture Erik had wanted her to consume earlier.

She felt like a trapped bird, her heart beating wildly against her ribs. The other vampires laughed and drank from golden cups and kissed and fucked and danced while she walked by with her hands chained in front of her. How they could feel good drinking that stale blood while underneath Erik's watchful eye was beyond her; she preferred to have full control of her body, and right now, she fought against her urge to flee.

One foot in front of the other. He can't win this time.

Adeline straightened her shoulders as whispers

floated around her, their words weaving into her mind like snakes. The vampires' eyes flicked to her chains, but her mind was a fortress, and they were unable to break in. She could pretend for the next two nights that she willingly conceded her freedom. She had to if she was going to outmaneuver her maker and help Juliette be free.

Conversations dulled as she walked by, and the eyes of the others in the room never left her body or her hands. Or her neck. A few of the younger vampires stared, and Adeline suppressed a smile. Her choice to leave her neck exposed and on display was working. Whether they made way for her out of fear or respect, she didn't care. Her plan was working.

But then her eyes locked on a vampire whose stature and position to Erik marked him as second-in-command —Campbell. The closer she got to the front of the room, the more intense his glare became. The two of them had always been at odds. He was lethal, as most vampires tended to be when their place in the hierarchy was threatened. And Adeline becoming Erik's mate was the biggest threat of all. But his lethality wasn't the kind that would scare Adeline, because it came in the form of carelessness and privilege. Since he considered himself nobility when he was turned, it carried over into his immortal life in that annoying way privilege tends to do.

Don't let him get to you, Adeline.

If she could ignore Campbell and stick with her plan, then everything would be all right.

Sow discord among them. Get them to turn on each other. Wear down Erik's authority.

She stopped a few feet short of the table, and Erik

finally looked up from the servant he had been feeding off of. No one else in the room had a willing source. Erik used to bring in living sources all the time when she had been here last. What had changed?

Erik twirled his finger at her, and she spun carefully. He frowned slightly at her crumpled skirts and tousled hair, but his pupils were blown wide from his latest feed, and lust poured off him in waves.

Adeline almost sighed with relief. The first test was done. Erik had trained her to always be impeccable, and now, showing up just slightly rumpled, planted a seed of doubt. She was not as perfect as he wanted her to be, and she smiled up at him, knowing it would throw him off.

But Erik's eyes caught on something over her shoulder, and the room went still.

"Find something amusing?" Adeline refused to turn, but would know that voice anywhere.

Campbell.

He had a lack of interest in anyone lower than himself; he was known to always get what he wanted. From his brutal help in torturing Adeline when she had first tried to get away centuries ago, she knew his disdain for her came from a deep-seated jealousy. Adeline was far older than him, by at least several centuries, and her closeness to Erik caused her to have a lot of enemies—Campbell being the first in line.

He used to jump at the opportunity to put her back in her place, calling it his "game time."

Adeline wondered if Juliette had been privy to his twisted games, too.

When Adeline didn't take the bait, he asked again, "Do you find something amusing, Little Killer?"

If the room were alive, it would have gasped at hearing Erik's nickname for Adeline coming from Campbell's mouth. It was already an affront that he was speaking to her, Erik's future mate, without first consulting Erik. But using the nickname Erik had chosen for her?

He must hate *me right now. Good.* She tried not to smile.

That century of freedom had brought so much clarity to Adeline that she wouldn't buy into his intimidation so easily, not this time. She could dispatch him quickly. If he so much as laid a finger on her, he would lose his hand. But that wouldn't work for her plans, so she let it go and pushed her rage down, far enough so that no matter what Campbell said next, she would not be triggered. She needed to save it all for Erik.

"Yes," Adeline replied, still facing Erik. "I do."

"Please," Campbell drawled behind her shoulder. He swished the liquid in his cup and then drank what was left, slurping in her ear so loudly she cringed. "Enlighten us."

Erik was silent, viewing the exchange between them with quiet interest, and she knew he wanted to watch the game Campbell was trying to play.

Fine, she could volley. If she could keep up the ruse well enough, Campbell would unknowingly give her an advantage.

"No." Her voice was clear, strong. She wouldn't give in. She was counting on her resistance to Campbell to thrill Erik. If she could get him to react emotionally, then she could have the upper hand, for once.

Campbell scoffed and stepped closer; she could feel his breath on her exposed neck, the rustle of his silken fabric as he lifted his arm, the way his hand hovered over her shoulder. She could have easily snatched it and broken his fingers, but she let him touch her. She let him stroke the curve of her shoulder. Erik's nostrils flared, and his eyes turned stone cold.

Good, Adeline thought. *Let him get jealous.*

Adeline stood still as Campbell trailed his fingers down her décolletage, drifting closer and closer to the swells of her breasts. He wrapped his arm across her, his hand grabbing the chains that kept her bound, and pressed his nose into the curve of her neck. He inhaled, humming quietly, and pushed against her backside. His hardness pressed through her skirts.

Don't move.

It was moments like these that made Adeline a deft killer. Her thoughts would detach from her body, and she would breathe into the discomfort of a stranger touching her, groping her, covering her in their putrid scent. Then she would strike. Her nicknames in the courts of previous kings varied from Black Widow to The Asp. She was as deadly as she was cunning, which made her the perfect political ally between the humans and her kind. Her skills were the product of centuries upon centuries of training, mostly initiated by Erik but also by watching how humans interacted.

Males in power were simple creatures. If she played to their egos, played to their desire to conquer and bed, then she could mold them in her hands like clay. Females, on the other hand, were much more complex, and it was during her years spent as a courtesan while still a young vampire that she learned the most about the power of words and body language. Especially when it came to the cutthroat politics of being in court.

And now, Campbell thought she was playing the game with him, but really, she was baiting Erik. She wanted to see how far Campbell would take this silly little power-play move before Erik snapped. Gauging by how hard Erik gritted his teeth, Adeline figured Campbell would meet his end tonight.

She was *hoping* for it. Because the vampires needed a hierarchy, and if she could get someone as feared and slimy as Campbell beheaded by his maker, it would stir the coven into such a frenzy.

Campbell pulled her to him, and she let her eyelids flutter closed as his hand slid up her neck and tightened on it. She leaned into her pretense, letting out a small gasp as the fingers of his other hand walked down to the cleft of her breasts. He breathed into her ear, and she could smell the fruity, metallic tang of blood mixed with wine emanating from his mouth.

"What I would give to lick the sweat off your body," Campbell whispered into her ear, so low that only she could hear. She leaned back, her hand sliding between them. Her nails elongated, and she fought against her desire to slice into him. Instead, she stroked him, and he rocked forward into her. His hand tightened on her throat. "I would fuck you senseless. And while you lay there, with my seed spilling from you, I'd cut off your head."

The entire room had gone silent, and Adeline swore they could hear her heart thrashing against the cage of her chest as Campbell's hand slipped down the front of her body.

She silently egged him on. *Lower.*

"Enough," Erik whispered.

Even with her eyes closed, she could sense the rage pulsing from her maker. Adeline opened them, but Erik wasn't looking at her. He was staring at Campbell's hands, which hadn't stopped. Both of them groaned loudly when Adeline stroked Campbell through his pants. His hips thrust against her, but he held her steady with his grip around her throat.

His hand tightened, and she gasped for effect. He could easily tear her throat out, but she would withstand far worse if it meant Erik would snap. Campbell grunted in response, dipping his head to the crook of her neck.

"It should have been me," he said and traced his tongue along the newly knitted flesh of her fresh scar. His breath coated her, and she swallowed a gag; it had become even more putrid in the last few moments. She closed her eyes tightly against the onslaught of rotten eggs that wafted from him. Had he always smelled this awful? "I want to watch the blade slice through your precious skin, watch as you writhe under the tip."

Adeline closed her eyes again, willing herself to keep going despite the very real fear that Erik and Campbell would carve into her again. What if things didn't go to plan, and this was to be her life forever, constantly pleasing the next power-hungry male?

Not if I can help it, she swore. *I would rather die again.*

Fangs scraped against her skin, and her stomach sank at the thought of vampires feeding from each other without a mating bond. The implication had always been that it created a sickness of the brain. But as Campbell inhaled, pressing Adeline closer to him, she braced herself for the sharp prick of teeth and the feeling of being fed from—something she hadn't experienced since she had turned.

Being turned was a sensation she never wanted to endure ever again. She had felt a pain in her body as the blood left it—so excruciating that she wept and clawed at the stranger who drank from her neck. She had torn into his hair and clothing, trying to fight her way out of his grasp, until she slipped into a muted darkness. And then, instead of pain, her body had been alight with desire. She woke with her lips around someone's wound in their arm, moaning into him. Then she tore the clothes from her body and drove down on top of the strange creature whose hands roamed her curves with sick pleasure.

She could clearly remember the words he whispered: "I finally have one of you *dans la fôret*. And I will have all of you soon, too."

Adeline remembered when the burning desire had subsided—like the blindfold had come off, and she could finally see clearly. The scent of pine and wet earth filled her nose with a sharpness she had never known before. Varying shades of green took on more depth. Even the wind that caressed her naked body felt different. She was covered in their blood, and as her body came down from the high, she slowed her movements. That's when she realized she was staring into the eyes of the strange creature who had visited her family at the old mill. She had found it odd; his words suggested he had coveted her his whole life. But she had never even met him before. Her mother had told her only what he looked like.

Erik had kept his hands gripped to her waist, his eyes fused on the curves of her body and the way her breasts rose with each jagged inhale she took. He forced her to stay on top of him until he reached completion, leaving bruises on her hips in the shape of his hands that lasted for days. She had never felt more disgusted or confused.

As soon as he rested, she grabbed her clothes and ran, not realizing what she was, that she had died and now lived life as a vampire. That she was a threat to everything with a pulse. A few days later, she accidentally killed her first human by drinking too much of their life source. Unbeknownst to her, Erik watched her from the shadows the entire time, only stepping forward when she wept in the woods, holding her fresh kill.

Then he told her an elaborate story about what had happened.

She had been so close to death when he found her under the willow tree. He was her *savior,* he insisted over her tears as she clung to the innocent life she had taken. He had done it for *her own good,* of course. Her mother had promised her over to him; he had bought and paid for her. Her mother would live a life of riches, but Adeline could never see her again. It was the price to pay for immortality.

If only she had known then that nothing Erik ever told

her was true. It took her finally having the tiniest bit of freedom while she was hunting were-shifters for the spell to break.

I will bathe in his blood. I will kill him. I will kill him. I will kill him. She repeated it over and over in her head now, determination washing over her as Campbell's teeth pricked her skin.

He pulled back, clicking his tongue, then purred, "I want to consume you, and I *know* you would be so good."

Adeline shifted in Campbell's arms so that her lips were close to his ear. Her chains pulled tight, and she resisted the urge to wrap them around his neck. She whispered, "But I'm *not*."

"I can tame you," Campbell whispered into her hair. He spun her around, grabbed her throat, and stared into her eyes.

Tame me? She met his stare head-on, despite the worry coursing through her. But his gaze was locked onto her cleavage, and she knew, in that moment, that Erik would kill him for his lusting over her so openly.

Something brushed past her ear, and she stumbled forward as Campbell was yanked away, his nails gripping her arms, scratching her skin as he was lifted into the air. The key Juliette had tucked away slid down her scalp. Adeline reached up with her chained hands as subtly as she could to tuck the key back, but she fumbled and it fell into her palm.

Erik's hand was clamped around Campbell's throat.

Adeline brought her hands in front of her, gripping the key tightly.

He stared down at Erik, a sneer on his face.

"Do it," he choked out. "Kill me for touching her. We all know you can't stand to share the precious *Adeline.*"

Adeline stood as still as she dared, waiting to see if Erik was going to dismember Campbell in front of everyone or not.

No one spoke. No one moved.

Campbell looked Adeline up and down. Disgust pulled at his upper lip with a snarl, but then Erik's nails elongated and dug into Campbell's neck, choking him further. Blood leaked from the punctures.

"No one will have her," Erik snarled. "No one except me. She is *mine.*"

Adeline bit her cheek so hard it started to bleed, and she clenched her hand so tightly, the key dug into her palm. She was not property to be *owned*. She never was - not since she had been locked in a tower by the prince when she was human.

Looking back at her human life, she never wanted to belong to anyone in the world except her family. And then, as one does, she got older and the world around her looked different. What had once been a rosy, colorful life full of love and snuggles, age brought with it a different perspective. She saw that the magical soups that her mother often made were scraped together with last year's stale harvests, how her mother stayed up well after the girls had typically gone to bed so she could darn their stockings, how the pots that they used to make music eventually turned into pots used to catch the rain from the leaky roof.

She told herself that was why she had married the prince when she had turned twenty-two—that she could provide a life of ease for her mother and a life of health for her sister. She told herself that he loved her since he promised she could return home to see them. It was the lie that kept her going until one day, the truth came out.

"No one will have you," he'd told her on their wedding day. He was adamant that she remain in the castle, but later that week, she had gone down to the market with her maids. The prince lost his mind when he found out. He raged and ranted, worried his bride would be stolen from him.

"You are the most beautiful woman in the world, you are my wife, and the future mother of my heirs. I cannot risk you being taken and used against me. You will not leave this castle again."

He set guards outside their door, had them follow her wherever she went, and increased the number of maids and ladies-in-waiting to attend her. She felt smothered, she was never alone. The days turned into weeks, the weeks into months, months into years, and still she was not permitted to leave the castle, nor was she permitted to see her mother and sister.

"You promised when we got betrothed!" She hurled a vase at his head, furious. "It was the one thing I asked for!"

"I do not remember making such a commitment," he shrugged. She threw her hairbrush at his face. "You're a madwoman. Beautiful but barren, deceptive, and mad."

"Then let me be crazy with my family," she seethed.

"Never," he replied. "I paid for you, you're mine. And you're mine until you give me an heir."

"I will never! I'd rather die!" She screamed back.

He called in the guards, who shoved her into the northern-most tower. As the lock clicked into place, his voice carried through the door as he said, "If I can't have you, then no one will."

Trapped but finally alone, she longed to be saved by a knight in shining armor, like the stories she had read as a child. But, soon after, the prince and his whole family had died from the sickness that swept through the lands. The castle was in mourning, but that night, the lock at the bottom of the stairs was left open. She fled from the castle, heading homeward—the only place where she truly belonged.

After Erik turned her, he told her she was free to live her life as she wished. Until she tried to leave Erik's side.

Now, once again, she was coveted by powerful men.

"I will deal with you later," Erik said, his fingers gripping Campbell's neck until he gagged. He stared down at Erik with defeat, knowing he had been beaten. He let Campbell go with a flourish, and the vampire fell to the ground. Erik licked some of Campbell's blood from his fingers, humming with delight while he sucked. His eyes flared with rage, and he waved impatiently at Campbell on the floor. "Now, go."

Erik walked over to Adeline, his eyes scanning where Campbell had touched her. She tried not to let the disappointment that he had let Campbell go show in her face. It would have been the perfect way for her to sow seeds of discontent within the entire coven. She was sure Campbell was the perfect bait. She cursed internally at her stupidity, thinking she could get to Erik.

He was always twenty paces ahead.

"Come, Adeline," Erik said and held out his bloodied hand to his future mate. "We dine."

She refused to take his hand and gathered her skirts up, tucking the key into the folds while she did. Adeline had always thought that the immortality of a vampire's life meant that she was free of being beholden to men. But Erik was no man. He was a vampire, and she would always be his.

Chapter 35

Rolf

Rolf hovered in the doorway. He was tempted to look back, to see if the horrors of his past were still there, but for now, all was quiet. A curved stone staircase, lit sparsely by torches, rose before him. His skin itched as his wolf paced, impatient to get to Adeline.

Happy to have you back, he told it. *But, please, be quiet.*

The wolf grumbled deep in his chest, and Rolf's hand rubbed at his rib cage absently. He didn't realize how much he had missed the presence of his wolf until it had gone quiet earlier.

He felt a silent nudge from his animal as it settled within him, and then, suddenly, a tug started deep within his chest, near his sternum. It pulsed, but it wasn't in time with his heart. It was slower and felt strangely familiar.

Adeline. The tug shimmered when he recognized who it belonged to, sending shivers up his arms. There was no telling if she knew about the tug or if she could feel it back. But his wolf echoed in his head.

"Mate," it said.

Mate. Adeline was his mate. His wolf grumbled in his head again, and a sense of urgency pushed at him. He had no idea that were-shifters could mate with vampires. But if it was possible, as his wolf certainly seemed to believe, then he needed to find her before something worse happened.

He took a step forward and braced himself for more illusions to filter in again, but nothing happened. Maybe they only occurred in those two rooms, a failsafe that kept invaders at bay.

But he was going to do whatever it took to get to her.

In all the stories from his childhood, there had been one fable that stuck with him the most. About a beautiful but lonely princess who was destined to live her life alone in a castle tower. The jealous prince kept her hidden away, worried her beauty was too coveted and she would be stolen from him.

He couldn't remember how the story ended. In one version, the princess rescued herself, killing the prince with her own bare hands. And in the other, a wayward soldier fell in love with her, but the prince found out and plucked out his eyes.

If he had to have his eyes plucked from his skull to finally be with her, it would all be worth it.

He had to keep going. She deserved as much.

He tugged on the bond, wondering if Adeline could feel it, too, and hoping that maybe there was a chance she wouldn't do anything rash until he could get to her. A part of him wished he had never agreed to her crazy plan to take down the coven. He knew it was a risk, but at the time, he thought it would pay off—he hoped it would pay off. What did he expect, that they would ride off into the sunset like in tavern ballads?

What a lovesick fool, he thought and smiled.

Yes, he was lovesick, and he loved it.

His arms ached for her, and so did his mouth. He wanted to taste her again. He wanted to wrap his fingers in her long hair and inhale her earthy scents of petrichor and amber. His belly tingled with an insatiable desire to lick and nibble and kiss every inch of her body. His ears missed the rarity of her laughter.

Rolf's wolf paced in his chest, wanting to shift, wanting to ransack the entire castle so he could tear out the throats of every last one of them. But it wasn't the full moon. And he needed to be smart about this. He didn't know if unleashing his wolf was even possible without the power of the full moon, and he wasn't about to do something risky.

With each step he took, his stomach grumbled, and exhaustion pulled at his muscles. He had no idea how long he had been down there. It didn't matter because he was reaching the top of the stairs.

They opened up into a dingy, poorly lit hallway. The musty scent of the stairs collided with the stench of excrement and sweat. He hovered in the shadows of the stairwell, grateful there were no torches up here. Bodies milled about, mechanical in their movements as they carried things back and forth, disappearing behind multiple doors.

"The servants' quarters," he whispered out loud and then cringed, hoping no one had overheard him.

A servant walked down the hallway, their eyes staring into space. Distinctly marked by their pointed ears, the fae servant carried a tray piled high with food.

Glamoured, he realized, looking around. More servants milled about, their movements stiff and unnatural. All of them glamoured. If they were glamoured, then their chances of seeing and reporting him were minimal—not only that, but he could get around the castle with a lot more ease.

He breathed a sigh of relief. His chances of finding Adeline quickly climbed much higher if all he had to worry about were the vampires.

His wolf growled. His stomach rumbled. And it took him all of two seconds to snatch a small pastry from a passing servant. The tray wobbled slightly, but the servant continued down the hallway, unbothered. He bit into the delicate, buttery flakes and suppressed a moan as it melted in his mouth. With a glance down the hallway, finding the coast clear of vampires, he slid away from the door where the fae had gone.

Avoid the vampires, find Adeline. Then burn their whole nest to the ground.

He rounded a corner, following the scent of baking bread to the kitchens. Everyone inside moved so methodically that it made even his wolf shiver with unease.

"So unnatural," he whispered, unable to take his eyes off the silent, glamoured fae servants.

A servant crossed in front of him as he stood in the doorway, their eyes glazed over, staring into the room before them. Underneath their collar were dozens upon dozens of bite marks. Some of them had healed, but others were festering wounds, seeping with pus.

Prisoners. That's all they were. Forced to work and attend to the vampires in the levels above. How many years had they been stuck here?

He left the kitchen, following the curving hallway toward the scent of laundry. Steam billowed out of the large doors at the end of the hall; the scent of ironing and fresh linens hung in the air, competing with the smells of the kitchen. If it wasn't so silent and creepy, he would have found it smelled like home. How it used to feel running to the servants' quarters when he was a child.

But then he passed a door that was slightly ajar. It stopped him in his tracks. Curiosity got the better of him, and he pushed the door open wider.

Rows upon rows of doors lined a damp and moldy corridor. He grabbed a torch from a sconce on the wall and held his clothing up to his nose to prevent the smell of excrement and urine from clogging his throat. Muffled crying came from behind a few of the doors. The farther he walked down the hall, the worse the conditions got. Each door he passed was secured with thick chains and padlocks to keep the dozens of fae, and even several humans, imprisoned like they were in jailer's cells. He lifted one of the heavy padlocks, its face etched with fine markings.

Rolf had seen markings like this on shards of rocks in the tunnels under his cabin. He had figured it was an ancient dwarf miner who was bored and decided to carve into the stone. But now, he wondered if it had been wards. The swirls glowed as he jiggled the shackle.

Why would these locks have the same marks as the stones he had found?

Ward marks, his wolf snorted.

Rolf stilled but then asked his wolf, *And you know this because?*

There was no response.

"Figures," he whispered to himself.

According to Rolf's limited knowledge of the fae creatures, dwarves hadn't been seen in centuries. He had thought it was because they were gone. But now he wasn't so sure.

He peered inside one of the rooms through the tiny window at the top. Several fae were all crowded together, huddling by their only source of light—a solitary, tapered candle in the center of the room. None of them looked his way, their eyes still vacant as if the glamour had never been lifted.

Sickening, he thought, and shuddered. *His* glamour had been so strong that it had lasted a hundred years. How long had these fae been down here? Glamoured? Working for these foul bloodsuckers?

Anger burned his throat, and his hand trembled with restrained rage, the flame flickering with his jerky movement. All of the time he had wasted trying to remember who he was and what had happened to him, and it was because of Adeline's maker.

The vampires would pay. All of them. Because they were all complicit in this, and therefore they were all responsible.

His wolf snapped its jaws, and Rolf wished he were in

his shifter form so he could rip the vampires' heads from their bodies with a satisfying squelch.

This is despicable! he thought, and his wolf agreed.

It paced and snarled every time a fae cried out for their family.

What kind of monster would keep these magical creatures here against their will, away from their families and forests for gods knew how long, forcing them to work and eat and sleep in such conditions?

He spun on his heel, determination covering him in soothing waves. By the gods, he would figure out how to free these fae creatures, too. And then he would burn the castle, with the vampires trapped inside.

He was still stewing in anger, clutching the torch in a death grip, when a solitary humming reverberated down the hall. His heart beat loudly as he looked around, trying to find the source of the sound. Quickly, he placed the torch in a sconce on the wall, but there was no place to hide except the corridor and the laundry room. The laundry was too far away for him to reach without a guarantee that the doors were easy to open.

The humming grew louder, along with the sound of footsteps, and at the last moment, he ran back to the prisoners' quarters and slid behind the door, watching for whoever came down the hall through the crack.

A blond, curvy vampire rounded the corner, jingling a set of keys. She passed the corridor, humming to herself, but stopped, pausing for a moment to sniff the air, and then turned.

Just keep walking.

Sweat dripped down his forehead, and Rolf slid his

hand to the holster at his waist, wrapping his fingers around the hilt of one of his knives. His wolf paced in his chest, a low growl echoing in his head. He clenched his teeth together to keep the sound from escaping.

The female vampire did *not* keep walking.

Her floral scent filled the space between them as she entered the corridor, and Rolf inhaled, something piquing his memory. It was familiar, but he couldn't place where he had smelled it before. He reeked after his travels, but he hoped that the stench of stale urine and mold would overpower his own.

The keys jangled in her hands as she flipped through the set and walked to the end of the hallway. Rolf slunk back into the shadow behind the door, his large form barely fitting. The blond vampire stopped at one of the doors halfway down the hall, fit a key into the padlock, and turned. It glowed a bright blue before the mechanism clicked and the shaft unhooked.

She opened the heavy door with a grunt and ducked inside. Rolf took a steadying breath and slid out from behind the door.

Do I lock her inside?

He stepped forward quietly but hesitated too long.

A bell rang from within the room the vampire had entered. The quickening patter of feet echoed down the hall. He didn't want to find out if they were servants or vampires, so he melted back into the shadow of the hallway door. He cursed himself for not leaving when he had the chance, because now he was stuck.

He palmed one of his knives, a small assurance against the weight of fear that crushed his chest.

Chapter 36

Adeline

Adeline had little choice but to follow, especially now that Erik had a death grip on her hand. Her skirts trailed behind her, and she wished the floor would open up and she would be dragged down into the fiery underworld.

But no. Such was not her fate tonight.

Erik gestured for her to sit at his right, the spot reserved for his favorite conquest—her, always and forever.

Baiting Campbell didn't work, and now she was beginning to question everything. How was she supposed to win against someone this conniving?

He snapped his fingers, and a side door to the left opened. Adeline couldn't see who they brought in, but the clanking of chains told her it was most likely a food source. Her fangs came in since she hadn't had real blood in a few days, but she shoved them back, refusing to give in to the barbarity of feeding from a prisoner.

"No," Adeline whispered as an emaciated fae creature was brought forward. It was a test. Erik wanted her to fail, expected her to. The fae's eyes were glazed over and vacant.

"No?" Erik turned to her, his gaze filled with rage. "You will feed from her, Little Killer, if you know what's good for you. I will not be denied. Not now. Not anymore. Not ever."

I hate that nickname. Adeline swallowed, unable to even get her fangs to drop. She was not *his* little killer anymore. She shook her head, staring at him the whole time. "I will not."

He knew she hated being forced to eat because he was the one who used it to control her. It was one of his favorite ways to torture her after she had rebelled in some way. Tie her up, parade prisoners around the room, pick someone random, and then bleed them dry while he held open her mouth.

"Get a grip," Erik snapped, and Adeline's past tumbled into focus.

"Get a grip," Erik had snapped. His palm met her cheek with a slap, but she couldn't stop the tears. She was covered in blood, wishing she could go home, wondering where her mother was. Delirium set in, and she thought, for sure, she was back at the castle with her husband, the prince. The smarting of her cheek felt just like it had when he used to hit her, anyway.

But then the frenzy in her mind quieted. Erik told her that he came by the old mill where she had lived with her sister and mother, offering to take the sickest off the hands of the living. But when he returned to her home, she was gone. Eventually, he found Adeline weak and disoriented, resting under the boughs of a willow tree, close to death. He offered her eternal life, and she willingly agreed.

And that's how Erik had warped her mind for centuries. He told her the same story, over and over, until his lies transplanted into her memories and took root. The fabrications had faded once she met Colin and was finally, blessedly, out from under Erik's thumb. After Colin disappeared, something inside her unraveled, so much so that she could finally separate fact from fiction.

Erik bit into the creature's neck. It flinched only a little as his teeth pierced its flesh, but then the glamour kept it from thrashing about. Her stomach grumbled. Sure, she needed her strength, but in no way was she willing to compromise on the last thing that made her different from the other vampires.

"Such a shame you refuse to get stronger," Erik said, as if she bored him with her morality. He released the shackled fae. A trickle of blood trailed down his chin, but Erik didn't wipe it away. It dripped onto his collar.

He doesn't want me to be strong, though. She knew this in her core, some little voice that told her not to drink from the cup or the fae. That he was setting her up for a trap. There was always something else with Erik.

"I do, sire, but I crave fresher blood," she said, her words hanging in the air between them. She needed to take control of the conversation and make Erik believe that she would do what he wished with little pushback. After all, he still liked a challenge, and she wasn't quite ready to give him the satisfaction of breaking her completely. "This one is too weak."

Erik laughed, a sharp sound that pierced the back of

her head with images of torture. "My little killer is too good for this fae?" He gestured to the creature, whose blood ran down its neck.

Adeline fought against the tempting scent of the fae blood. Her fangs elongated, and her stomach rumbled. She wouldn't give in.

"Before you arrived tonight, I was reminiscing about the days of old. How eager you were to be here at my feet like a good little dog." Erik spat the last word, and she felt it land on her shoulder.

Adeline didn't flinch; she didn't even blink—she stared at the pulsing vein in his neck, fantasizing about what she could do to end his life. If she had a knife, she'd stab him in the neck and try to drag it down the front of his chest, yank out his heart, and light it on fire. Or maybe she would wait until he moved in to bite her neck and mate with her, then she would grab his jaw and rip it off.

The violent images soothed her, and she wondered if his blood would feel warm as it splashed over her.

He folded his hands underneath his chin. "You used to get me so hard, Adeline. No one has been able to do that quite like you."

Adeline swallowed down the disgust creeping up her throat. Erik must think she was a tiny mouse caught in the teeth of the lion—but she was done trying to play dead. Too often, it had brought her back here. If she couldn't figure out a way to throw him off his game and reveal what kind of cards he had, then she would have to try another way.

He smirked, liking her speechlessness. There was something else he wasn't telling her. The edges of the throne room rippled, and shadows played at the edges of her vision. She closed her eyes and shook her head, and when she opened them again, she shifted to meet Erik's gaze.

Erik raised an eyebrow, and a patronizing tone dripped from his tongue as he said, "I have learned so much since then. I hope you know that I never meant to hurt you. Everything I did, I did for your own good."

Your own good. He loved using that phrase on her so much that she knew he thought it would bring her to heel again. But he was wrong.

"My own good," Adeline echoed. A devilish thought crossed her mind, and she realized that she might have the opportunity to be done with him once and for all. She cocked her head, schooling her expression. If she was going to convince Erik that she was complicit in his plans, just so she could get close to him, she needed to believe she was compliant.

"Of course." Erik reached for her hand, and she forced herself to keep it there when he patted the top of it. He looked out at the room beyond, his features hardening. "And for the entire coven. Juliette included."

What could he possibly be inferring about Juliette? Adeline smiled at him and took a deep breath to keep her heart calm. She didn't want Erik to pick up on her worry.

He continued. "Our ranks are weakening; the vampires no longer outnumber the fae. We are a dying breed, and our union will make us stronger than ever."

Adeline stared at him more closely. At first glance, she didn't notice anything different. His hair was perfect, he had gained his composure after dealing with Campbell, and nothing in his tone gave way to his internal thoughts. But then she saw it—his index finger lightly tapping his leg.

He's worried.

She had been absent while she hunted the were-shifters, and the amount of interaction she'd had with other vampires had been minimal. The only vampires she had encountered had been at the drop-off locations for her shifter kills. At the time, she had thought it was because they were told to stay away from her, giving her a false sense of freedom. But now, she couldn't help but think there was another reason why.

If Erik was worried about his brood, he must think that being mated to her would offer an image of stability. But she wasn't going to heel; she was never going to roll over and finally take it. Because she *was* going to kill him. And she was going to enjoy every minute of it.

"Sire, if I may be so bold," she said before she changed her mind. "I think we should move the ceremony up."

The entire room went quiet. Erik twisted in his seat, his sharp features highlighted by the flickering candles above.

Adeline grabbed the goblet full of that coagulated, sugary blood mixture. As much as she wanted to gag, she held it to her lips and took a small sip. It was still as gross as the first few times she drank, but she swallowed it dutifully and then added, "Why not tomorrow?"

"I was hoping you'd say that," he crooned, a smile on his lips and blood still staining his teeth.

Chapter 37

Rolf

Through the crack in the door, Rolf watched glamoured servants carry out the body of a deceased fae on a stretcher, a white sheet pulled taut over the top. His wolf grumbled at the unfairness, and his hand tightened on the knife.

The blond vampire followed. Her clear voice directed the servants, and she used the same melodic technique Adeline had when she removed Rolf's glamour. The vampire's scent floated in the air behind her, stronger this time. It was a scent he had smelled before.

She was in the cave.

His wolf snarled in agreement. *Bite off her head!*

Rolf shook his head slowly. He couldn't kill the vampire now. Not when she held the keys to open these doors.

The group turned left down the hall, heading to the only room at the end, the laundry. He couldn't follow them unless he wanted to be spotted and risk even getting close to Adeline. As soon as their footsteps retreated, he slipped out from the shadows, walked to the open cell, and peered inside.

It reeked of iron, stale urine, and mold. He scrunched his nose, and even his wolf was revolted by the conditions.

"This is worse than the others," he whispered, shock shaking his voice. Tiny sprouted plants dotted the floor; roots were torn from their base, as if the creature within had tried to hold on to something as they were taken away.

Woodland fae, his wolf said reverently, sending him images of dozens of encounters his shifter had with them over the past century. Tiny, bark-covered creatures who lived among the trees of the ancient woods. Countless times, they would help guide his wolf to safety for the sunrise shift.

Tenderness blossomed in Rolf's chest.

"I had no idea," he whispered, holding back tears.

His wolf snorted in agreement. *That's what happens when you refuse to accept who you are.*

More determined than ever, Rolf knew he had to help get these creatures out. He turned to the lock where the vampire's keys still hung freely. They shone blue with the wards, magical lettering crisscrossing the face of the metal. At least ten different keys were hanging from the ring, all with wards reflecting on their handles.

He had two options: leave the keys there or take them.

He took them, wrapping his fingers around the cluster of keys so they didn't jingle. Putting the keys in his pocket, he whispered out loud to the room, "I will come back for all of you, I promise."

Then he ran back down the hall, giving the handles a test to see which ones were unlocked. He didn't have enough time to find the right keys, so as soon as a latch clicked open, he slipped through into the darkness beyond. Rickety wooden stairs in front of him wound several stories high, barely illuminated by the thin windows that circled the stairwell.

He started climbing, his mind whirling, dozens of different scenarios playing out. How was he going to get to Adeline *and* free all the fae servants? And how many vampires were actually in this building?

He pushed open the servants' door at the top of the stairs and crept down a hallway lined with even more doors.

"How big is this castle?" he whispered to himself. Was he standing in another enchanted room?

His wolf snorted in his head, *No, I'm here, aren't I?*

If he could hear his wolf, all was well. He sighed.

The hall was elegantly decorated and had only three doors. The one that led to the servants' stairs that Rolf had just exited, one to his left, and the other at the end to his right, which was at the top of another set of stairs, these well-lit and carpeted. Heavy curtains lined the walls, and a rug ran the length, which trapped the warmth inside the hall. He tugged at his collar, wishing he wasn't wearing wool pants. It smelled faintly of frankincense and citrus and was lit by only a few candelabras—it would not be a stretch to call it romantic, but, as with the rest of the castle, something was off.

Hushed noises filled the space, and his wolf went silent, trying to count how many voices it heard. A few women giggled in a room to Rolf's left, and a low-timbred voice followed. Gooseflesh prickled his arms, and immediately, he moved down the hall to put as much space between that room and himself as possible.

A door at the end of the hall had a light shining from underneath. Shadows flickered at the threshold as someone moved behind it. Drawn in like a moth to a flame, Rolf crept toward the door but stopped when a woman's voice echoed up the set of stairs in front of him.

He slipped behind some curtains to the right of the door and held his breath. Behind him was a set of glass doors and a small porch. He tested the handle, and it clicked open—an easy escape route if needed. He pushed the door outward, but he cringed when the hinges creaked and stopped at once.

Rolf's heartbeat pulsed in his ears, but he peered through a crack in the curtains.

There was a knock on the door and a jangling of keys.

"Enter," Adeline's muffled voice called from within.

His heart almost burst from his chest. It took everything he had not to launch himself from behind the curtains to get Adeline.

Patience, his wolf said, calmly. Rolf trembled, muscles wound tight, readying for anything.

His wolf growled a warning, and Rolf exhaled. He couldn't risk exposing his hiding spot, not now. He peered between the cracks in the curtains, and his jaw dropped when the blond vampire entered Adeline's room with a large box.

How did she get up here so fast?

The door clicked closed, and he dropped his hand from

the curtain. He tested the balcony door again, opening it more swiftly than the first time. The hinges didn't squeak, and he was able to slip outside.

The balcony was small, barely wide enough to fit two people, and though it was the pitch-black outside, the waning gibbous moon shone bright enough to highlight the sheer plunge to the sea below. Rolf leaned forward, bracing himself against the ledge as he peered inside, trying to get a view of Adeline from the shadows.

The solitary window was small, barely wider than his arm. Inside, her room was alight with candles, and he had to shift his position a few times to see everything. Adeline and the other vampire were hidden, but he did get a clear view of a small vanity, and now and then he could spot their hands gesturing. He shivered from the chill of the sea air as it pushed up against the stone, but he would sit here and wait until the sun rose if that was what it took.

His wolf grumbled about a fur coat and how useful they were. Rolf brushed him off. Wrapping his arms around his chest, he settled himself against the wall and strained to catch a glimpse of his mate.

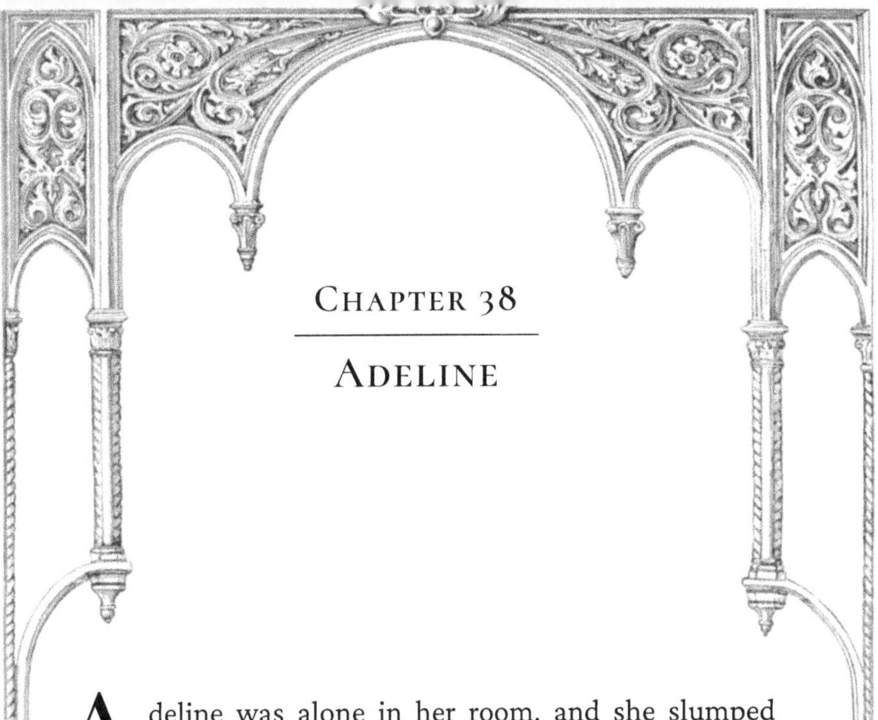

Chapter 38

Adeline

Adeline was alone in her room, and she slumped forward with relief, eager to rid herself of anything that Erik or Campbell had touched. The evening had been one big game of chess that she had navigated with less ease than she would have liked. The way Erik had responded to Campbell had thrown her off, and then, Erik's odd behavior was another. He was worried about something because every time Adeline looked at him, he was staring at the corners of the throne room. Each time someone came to talk to him, he was distracted and uninterested. Only when Adeline shifted in her seat would he focus on her movements with hawk-like precision.

Being unarmed the entire evening was unnerving, too. Though she had her wiles and wit, with Erik, there was never any telling what he could do. Or what he had planned. And she had expected him to be shocked at her wanting to move up the date, but he wasn't. He had smiled at her in such a way that it crawled underneath her skin and stuck there.

What was she going to do tomorrow night when she was expected to marry him? Without her usual cadre of weapons, Adeline would have to get creative.

She slipped out of her corset, laying it on her bed. The key to her chains dropped to the floor. She picked it up and placed it on the vanity, even though a tiny little voice told her to hold onto it. If Erik was already this tense, it would be easy enough to get under his skin at the ceremony, which, by her calculations from the moon outside her window, gave her a little over sixteen hours to prepare.

She knelt at the foot of the mattress, her hands sweeping underneath for the scissors. Panic flitted in her chest as she struggled to find them until, at last, her fingers touched metal. She slumped forward with an exhale, her forehead resting against the edge of the bed, and slid the scissors toward her so they would be easier for her to find again.

There was a knock on the door. Moving quickly, Adeline pushed off the mattress to stand. She eyed the hiding spot once more, ensuring that no part of the scissors was showing, and turned.

Juliette's muffled voice sounded from the other side of the door, and her key was already turning in the lock when Adeline called out, "Enter!"

She stepped over to her vanity right when Juliette entered Adeline's room with a large brown box. Her hands shook, and she looked as if she had seen a ghost.

"Everything all right, Jules?" Adeline wrapped the

ribbons around the corset and set it down on the chair near the vanity.

Juliette waved her off and set the box down on the bed. It was large and smelled of cedar wood and dust. Adeline wrinkled her nose. Whatever was in there was old.

"He insists you try it on before dawn so alterations can be made," Juliette explained as she opened the box.

Inside was a frilly monstrosity of yellowing lace, layers of tulle, and dull pearls. Juliette pulled the dress out, and as it unfolded, it somehow became even uglier.

"I can't wear this," Adeline said, staring at the white dress with disgust.

"Erik insisted," Juliette replied, cringing. "But it is rather hideous, isn't it?"

Adeline grimaced, tentatively reaching out to touch the fabric. "This is...the ugliest dress I have ever seen."

Juliette hummed in agreement.

"Alterations, you said?"

Juliette placed the dress on the bed and stood back, her eyes flicking over Adeline's chemise-clothed body. "Yes, we have a few fae seamstresses down in the laundry who are quite skilled."

"You mean the *prisoners*?"

Erik had always liked collecting valuable things, and before Adeline escaped the first time, he had run out of antiquities and treasures, so he had started collecting talent. When Juliette found out, she was distraught, so Adeline taught her how to glamour all the new prisoners to make their stay far less traumatic. But Adeline had thought it would be a passing fancy, that Erik would tire of them and return his conquests home.

How studiously ignorant I have been.

"Seamstresses?" Juliette cringed again, but then continued. "The dress isn't that bad. With some alterations, it might even look nice."

"Perhaps," Adeline mused. She picked up the hem of the dress, and the pearls glinted, refracting the light along with her silver cuffs. An idea began to form, but it would be a feat if she could pull it off. "The pearls look almost silver, do they not?"

Juliette stepped forward and rubbed some of the pearls between her fingers. "Yes, they match your cuffs. Erik insisted on this dress because of how unique it is. I believe it was worn by a queen at some point."

A hazy memory surfaced, and Adeline recalled that the queen who had worn this had been young, beautiful, and bright-eyed, full of hope for the future of her people. The new *Reine de la Terre* had donned the elaborate dress for her coronation—a white wedding dress to symbolize her commitment to the throne, silver pearls from the sacred waters of the lakes. She had said she was marrying her sovereignty, wanting to symbolize her commitment to ruling for her people. It was a beautiful ceremony and had moved everyone in attendance to tears.

Adeline had killed her several weeks later, and, wouldn't you know it, the next monarch was *much* more pliable under Erik's command.

Adeline swallowed a thick knot of guilt that tightened her throat. Her mouth felt too dry, and she ran her tongue along the top of it. The parallels were clear—wear the dress and comply, or meet the same fate. "I can't wear this—"

Juliette cut her off, saying, "It isn't *that* bad, but I need you to try this on so I can take it downstairs before the morning."

"How much time do the pri—seamstresses have to make this right?" Adeline asked.

"Until tomorrow night's ceremony, I suppose," Juliette said, brushing her hand over the top of the lace. "The dwarves and pixies are very talented, and I can alter their glamour to help."

"You're still glamouring them?" Hope bloomed in her chest. Adeline had been the one to insist on glamouring the servants so they would not remember their treatment. She didn't know that Juliette had taken up the mantle. She thought that maybe Campbell had been responsible—it would explain the myriad festering wounds and bite marks on the servants she had seen in the throne room.

Juliette gave her a confused look. "Of course. When you left, the glamour you had used didn't last long. But I cannot stop everything, Addy."

Guilt pinged in her chest again, another reminder that when Adeline left, she had abandoned the servants, too. She left the most helpless to deal with the fallout of her absence. Old Adeline, vampire assassin extraordinaire, didn't care. It was why she left the way she did. But after Rolf, after unraveling the threads of his story and how they wove into hers? It had woken something up within her. And, sure, he may be gone, but at least now she could set things right before she joined him in the Forever Night.

"I'm sorry, Jules, I know it hasn't been easy—living here, doing his bidding."

"No, it hasn't. But I can't let innocent fae suffer while I

still have Erik's favor." Juliette straightened and looked Adeline in the eyes. "I need you to know that I didn't want to bring you back here. Every part of me screamed not to follow his orders, but what if he found my mate, Addy? What if he—"

"Shush now," Adeline said, wrapping Jules in her arms. She knew what Erik could do, and Juliette was not made to withstand torture of any kind. "I understand. Besides, I promised I would get you out, didn't I?"

Juliette squeezed Adeline back and pulled away, sliding her hand down Adeline's arm to grab her hand. "You still haven't told me your plan."

"And I won't. I can't implicate you." Adeline couldn't meet Juliette's gaze. A sliver of doubt crept into her head because, for the most part, Adeline still didn't have a plan. She had concepts.

If only I could put all the pieces together...

The dress glinted on the bed, mocking her. Erik was always several steps ahead, so what was the purpose of making her wear this old thing?

I'll be the first and last *vampire queen...*

Adeline did *not* want to put it on. She didn't even want it anywhere near her body, knowing what it symbolized. But if she could request alterations, then maybe the prisoner seamstresses could add a few special touches.

She held out her hands so Juliette could unlock her cuffs. "All right, let's see what we have to work with."

Juliette left with the box tucked under her arms and a lengthy list of alterations. She had promised to come back in the evening with sustenance, but Adeline knew it wouldn't be fresh blood. Her stomach swirled at the thought of having to drink more of that gross liquid.

As the door shut, Adeline collapsed on the bed, exhaustion pulling her down into the blankets. She ran over her list of requests once more, hoping against hope that the seamstresses could at least take care of the most important changes she requested in such a short amount of time.

"I will not be a—" she began, but the sound of the lock turning made her sit up. The heartbeat outside was slow, measured. Hers was not. She called out, fake innocence weaving between her words, "Juliette? Did you forget something?"

Campbell slipped through.

The wards on her door shimmered, fighting to keep him from entering, but he somehow managed it. His eyes were blown wide, as if he had recently fed.

But his words slurred when he said, "Hello, cunt."

Adeline cursed internally. She did not have the patience or energy to deal with him again tonight. She propped herself up on her elbows, the chain of her cuffs pulled tight across her stomach. Juliette had forgotten to link them to a longer chain attached to the bed before she left, and Adeline thanked the gods that Juliette had been in a hurry to leave.

She tilted her head, becoming the picture of relaxed calm, deadly despite her body crying out for rest and fuel. "I thought Erik sent you to your room like a naughty boy?"

The door clicked shut behind him. The wards shimmered bright blue and then faded back into the wood. An alarm system that didn't work.

Great, she thought. *What use are wards if they don't work?*

She sighed with annoyance at having to deal with Campbell now, too.

"I thought you'd want company tonight," he crooned. He took a step in but stumbled. After righting himself, he leaned back awkwardly against the door.

"I hate to disappoint, Campbell, but the only company I planned on having was myself." She wiggled her fingers and slowly trailed her hands over her breasts and down her sides, letting them rest at the top of her thighs.

Males, she thought. All they ever wanted was one thing: power. Whether that came in the form of coercion or currency, their grubby little hands were always grasping at those whom they thought were weaker. As pathetic as it was, it did make them much easier to manipulate, and what better way to do so than with her body?

His eyes followed her movements, and he sluggishly licked his lips.

So easy to distract, she thought, dropping her hand to rest near the foot of her bed.

"Then I'll watch," he said and folded his arms over his chest.

Adeline sat up on the edge of the bed, refusing to give in to the fear that she was alone, weaker than she liked, and only had a pair of scissors at her disposal. She was an experienced assassin, and if Campbell was here in her room, then she'd just have to get creative.

"Campbell," Adeline whispered seductively. She leaned forward. Her hand slid down the edge of the bed. "Wouldn't you like a better view?"

He grinned, slimy and slick like the snake he was, and took a few steps forward.

"What would you do to me if I let you have your way?" she purred.

"All the things Erik would never let me do." Campbell chuckled, his eyes lazily taking her in as she bent forward, her chemise falling open.

How original.

She dragged her eyes down to his pants and raised an eyebrow.

"What, would you want me on my knees?" Adeline slid off the bed and knelt in front of Campbell.

He smirked down at her and shook his head. "I think you and I both know what I like."

It would take her two seconds to lean back and grab the scissors should he try anything. Her chained wrists didn't give her much freedom of movement, so she kept them close to her body. She tried to recall the last time she gutted someone in an intimate setting like this, and it had been a while, but—

His right hand was around her throat.

Move, Adeline!

He leered down at her, an expression that said he was hoping she would be pliant; instead, she wrapped her chain between her hands and blocked his advance, then threw his arm sideways. Off-balance, he stumbled, and Adeline dove low. She grabbed his right foot and yanked. His face slammed down onto the stone.

Dazed, he tried to get up, but she was on his back, her chain wrapped around his throat.

"I think you and I both know that this was *never* going to happen," she grunted in his ear.

Her shackles strained as she pulled, and pulled, and pulled. His skin tore, blood squirting where the chains cut into his flesh. She grunted as he tried to fling her off his back. Her thighs gripped his chest as she twisted the chain. She wasn't letting go until his head was severed.

"Fucking die already!" She pulled harder, still fighting to stay on top of him and keep the tension on the chains.

Finally, Campbell's neck crunched. The chains slipped, and Adeline tightened her grip. Her hands burned. Her wrists screamed in pain. She could do this. She'd done far worse and much weaker. Her fingers turned white from the tension.

The door flew open, and a familiar scent filled the room, battling with the cloying iron of Campbell's spilling blood.

Adeline's vision strained as she kept pulling.

Too weak.

Large hands grabbed Campbell's hair. The sound of flesh and muscle and bone separating filled her ears, drowning out her grunts and doubts. Her chains came free, and the pain immediately receded.

Her beast stood above her, Campbell's severed head in his left hand. Blood dripped down his right hand, a large dagger hanging limply from his fingers.

"Rolf?"

His beard was gone, and so was the long, shaggy hair.

It was like she was staring at a ghost. It was like she was looking at an older version of Colin.

His amber eyes were hard, but he stood there in all of his beastly beauty and asked, "Did you plan on killing all of the vampires in here with your own bare hands?"

Chapter 39

Rolf

Rolf's hands shook, and he dropped the head to the ground, kicking it several feet away from the body. Then he gathered his mate in his arms, picking her up off the ground until she was nowhere near the dead body of the vampire.

"Well, it's not like I knew you would be coming to my rescue," Adeline said, giving him a petulant pout. "I had it handled. Almost."

And then she crumpled against him and started crying.

"Shh, shh," he whispered. She gripped him tightly, as if she were afraid he would leave.

He wouldn't leave again. Whether they made it out of here alive or not, he was fully prepared to die fighting, just as long as he was by her side.

"I thought you were dead," she sniveled.

"I thought *you* were dead," he echoed.

"How?" she asked, and he knew the answer.

Does she think I would have left her?

"I came for you," was all he replied.

He wiped his bloody hand, as best as he could, on his pants and threaded his fingers in her hair. It was partially undone, perhaps from the scuffle from earlier, but he didn't mind. He pressed his nose against the side of her head, and the scent of petrichor and amber swirled around him when he inhaled. Other scents were wrapping around her, trying to stick to her skin—mainly death and disease and whatever else had been on that vampire. But he buried his nose deeper into her pinned hair and pushed the thoughts away. He didn't want to think of anyone else putting their hands on her body.

On what was *his*.

He inhaled again.

Home, he sighed.

Relief flooded him as he tipped her head back and consumed her mouth. She was soft and strong, her body firmly pressed against his, but melting in his arms at the same time.

"My darkness," he growled into her mouth.

Mine.

It was a plea, a promise, a claim.

She whimpered as he crushed her to his chest; he never wanted his hands to leave her body. He would wipe away all the scents of everyone else on her with his kisses, his touch, his love. Sparks erupted across his vision as she pressed against him, her nails digging into his chest with the same fervor.

His wolf yipped in his head, prancing around like an excited puppy who had finally found his person.

"My beast," she sighed, melting into his touch.

"Hmm," he hummed between fevered kisses. The taste of salt made him pull back. Her tears were on his tongue as he cradled her face in his hands. "I'm here, Adeline. I'm here. You're safe."

"I know." Adeline nodded, her normally bright blue eyes dim. "But if you didn't…if it had been another minute…if only I was stronger…"

He wrapped his arms around her shoulders, stroking her hair as she wept. Anger ricocheted inside him.

"My darkness," he whispered back, kissing her eyelids. He smirked into her hair, chuckling lightly. "But you told me you had it handled."

"I may have lied. What are you doing here?"

"I'm here to get you out," he said. "To take you home."

Adeline swayed.

She's weak, you need to carry her, his wolf barked.

Rolf scooped her up in his arms and headed for the door, but she stopped him with a hand on his heart.

"No, Rolf. Stop."

"No?" He stilled, but refused to put her down. He didn't want to let her go, not when he finally had her. Not when she was wearing chains, like a prisoner.

His wolf growled. *We need to leave. Now.*

"We need to dispose of Campbell," she said. She slid out of his arms with ease, landing delicately on the blood-soaked rug.

"What?" he asked, frantic.

"The body." She kicked Campbell's feet.

"You can't be serious?" He gestured to the door. "We need to go. Who cares about his body?"

The blood squished underneath her feet as she shifted her weight. She grimaced.

"Are you weak? Worried we won't make it?" Rolf looked at the early dawn light. He rolled up a sleeve and held his arm out to her. "Eat, take whatever you need. Then we go."

Adeline stood firm, but her eyes flicked to his veins. She leaned in slightly, but she didn't bite.

"It's not only that, Rolf. I promised Jules that I would help her get free." Her eyes pleaded with him, and her voice trembled.

"Fuck that," Rolf said, and he reached forward to scoop her up again. She slid out of his grasp effortlessly. Something jangled, and he looked down, then grabbed the chains of the cuffs around her wrists. His chest rumbled, and he ground out, "You're the one who's a prisoner."

"I also made a promise." Her nonchalance irritated the hell out of him.

"Yes, but it's time to leave." He turned to the door, tugging on her chains.

"No." Her voice was firm. She yanked her chains from his grasp.

Rolf looked back at her, his heart breaking. "We can come back for her, I promise, but we need to leave now."

Adeline shook her head and widened her stance. "I can't break this promise."

"Who is this Juliette? Is she a slave?" Rolf asked. He could understand Adeline needing to help some of the fae trapped below, but so help him if she was—

"A vampire," Adeline said, looking him right in the

eyes. She lifted her chin as if challenging him to question her.

"A vampire. You want to stay here and risk the window of time we have for another vampire?" Disbelief filled the spaces between his words.

She can't be serious! His wolf grumbled as it paced.

Adeline took his face in her hands. "When I left, right before I met you, when you were a human, I...I left this place and abandoned Juliette. I left her here to take my place, and I didn't even give her a second thought. And the guilt of that will always eat me up. This is my chance to make things right, Rolf. I have to make sure that she gets away, too."

"And how do you propose that, Adeline? The odds are already stacked against us, and time is running out." Rolf gestured to the window. Sunrise edged ever closer, and if he was going to set the castle on fire and free the prisoners, it had to be today.

His wolf growled in agreement. Neither of them liked hearing that Adeline didn't want to leave, not after they came all this way to free her and take her back home.

His wolf snarled, *Just throw her over your shoulder!*

Adeline grabbed his hands. "I have a few plans I'm working on, Rolf."

Rolf groaned and sat down on the edge of the bed. Her hand was so small in his, but he gripped it tightly, worried that if he broke contact with her, he would wake up and this would all be some kind of dream. And he didn't want to find out if that were true.

Adeline nudged his knees open and stood between his legs. She wrapped her arms around him, pressing his face against her stomach. Her hands stroked his back, her chains clinking together. If it weren't for the fact that they were trapped in a horrible predicament, he would have her naked and underneath him in two seconds. He had missed being this close to her. Smelling her, holding her, hearing her voice. His heart ached.

He hesitated to admit how he was feeling, but her obstinacy was annoying. He had plans, too! "I just..."

"You had your own plan," Adeline interrupted. She smiled down at him—with pity or understanding? He couldn't tell.

Is she making fun of us? His wolf asked.

"Well...yeah. I was going to come in here and whisk you away back home. And on our way out, I was going to burn the place down with all of the vampires in it."

"You wanted to be the assassin's hero?" She barked out a laugh, but quickly clamped her hand over her mouth when Rolf frowned. Her cheeks flushed, and she cupped his cheek. "That's the sweetest thing anyone has ever done for me."

She has a pretty laugh, his wolf said, smugly. *We've chosen well. Even if she is a bit stubborn.*

Quiet, you.

Rolf frowned.

"We will go home, I promise." She bent to kiss the tip of his nose.

His wolf instantly calmed and said, *Hear her out.*

Rolf groaned and rested his forehead against her stomach. "So what's your plan?"

She inhaled sharply. "I am going to marry Erik. Then I'll behead him."

"You'll what?" Rolf's heart stopped beating. He forgot how to breathe. His vision went black.

I changed my mind. Throw her over your shoulder now, his wolf huffed.

"You want to stay here and pretend to get married to the creature who tortured you for centuries?" Rolf was aghast. It was the most unhinged idea he had ever heard. They were trying to get *away* from Erik, not get *closer* to him.

Adeline cringed and tried to take a step back, but he grabbed onto her chains and yanked her closer. She fell into his lap and refused to meet his eyes. "I am getting married to Erik tonight."

No, no no no no. She couldn't marry Erik. She was *his* mate. His chest squeezed, and it was getting hard to breathe. Was he having a panic attack?

"No. Tonight? No. Absolutely not."

"It'll be fine, Rolf," Adeline said, stroking his back. "I have it all figured out."

"No, I—I can't risk losing you again." He almost told her that they were mates. He almost told her that there was nothing left for him if she went through with this. He almost told her that losing her *again* would be the death of him.

What else is there to live for?

He buried his head in the curve of her neck, and the temptation to claim her, to bite her neck, to mark her completely overwhelmed him so much that he started to shake. His wolf swelled with pride and egged him on, but he shut him down.

She pushed away from Rolf and forced his head up to

meet her gaze. Her fingers dug into the hair near his temples as she pulled, and he grunted. Her eyes were bright blue, refusing to let him look away.

A small part of his resolve crumbled.

Damnit.

"You have to trust me," Adeline insisted.

"You're infuriating," he sighed, but there was no malice in his voice.

She is, his wolf agreed and added, *but she is ours.*

"So I've been told," she said quietly.

"You want to marry Erik and save another vampire." Even saying it out loud made him want to rage. "I don't understand but..."

Then one look in her eyes, and he knew he had no say in the matter. He loved every part of her, despite how irritating she was, how infuriating, how stubborn. Still, he wanted to throw her over his shoulder and cart her out of here, kicking and screaming. Rolf sighed and dropped his head. Slowly, he stroked his hands up and down her legs, one hand inching closer and closer to the apex of her thighs where he wanted to sink himself.

Was all of this for nothing?

"You don't have to understand," Adeline said. She stepped out of his grasp and began pacing, her chains tinkling while her hands gestured. "Juliette isn't just any vampire, Rolf. She is the closest thing I have to a sister in this life. She took my place and has been caring for the servants and...I'm not asking you to dive into hundreds of years of history, but I don't think I would be able to live with myself if I didn't see this through. I can't abandon her again. All I need is for you to *trust* me."

"I trust you. I always will. What do you need me to do, my darkness?"

"First, we need to get rid of the body," Adeline grunted as she picked up the edge of the rug, rolling Campbell's body within it.

Rolf nodded and helped Adeline finish rolling the body into the blood-soaked rug. She stuck her head out the door and gestured that the hallway was clear. He hefted the rug onto his shoulder and took it to the balcony. With a grunt, he tossed the body over the baluster and watched as the carpet unrolled and the headless corpse was dashed to bits against the sea cliffs. He'd be lying to himself if he didn't admit how immensely satisfying it was seeing the limbs get smashed to smithereens before sinking into the sea below.

With a sigh and a lot of reproachful comments from his wolf, he went back inside for the head.

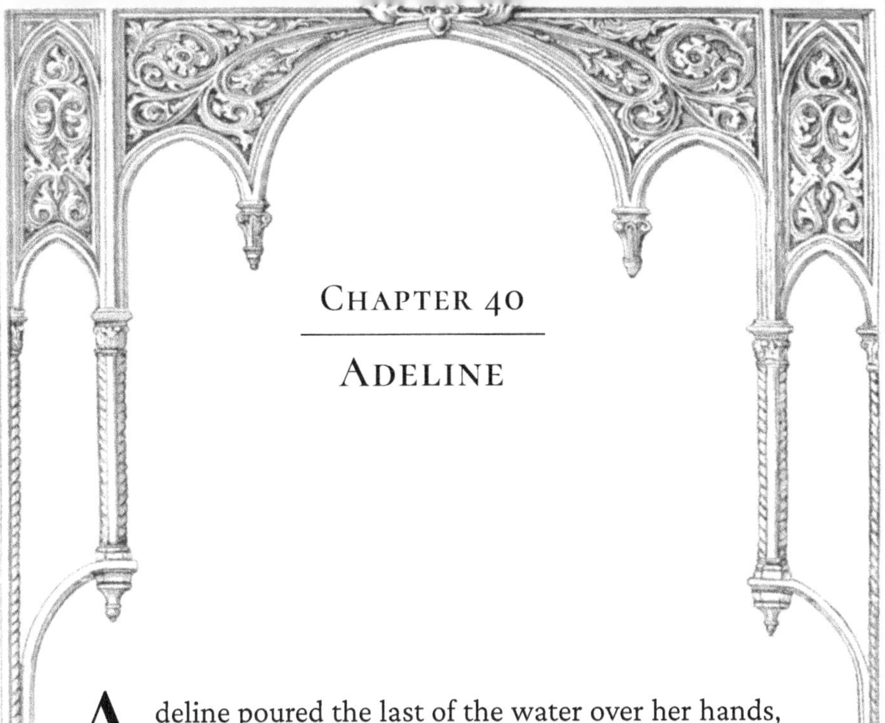

Chapter 40

Adeline

Adeline poured the last of the water over her hands, the liquid finally clear. As Campbell's head burned in the fireplace, skin and bones disintegrating into a pile of ashes upon contact, her mind whirled with all the different lies she might have to tell.

The best lies are simple and sprinkled with tiny truths. It had been one of the first things Erik had taught her. Looking back, she wondered how many times he had sprinkled small truths into the stories he told her.

She shook her head, trying to rid herself of those thoughts, and a few hairpins dropped to the floor.

Over her shoulder, she met Rolf's reflection in the mirror of her vanity. His shirt was unbuttoned down to his stomach, the tuft of his chest hair peeking through. He dried his hands on a towel, but his eyes never left her.

He strode over and bent down to pick up the pins, then began working his fingers through her hair. His deft movements had her tresses cascading down her back in seconds.

“Thank you,” she said and sat down at the vanity. She reached for the brush, but his hand covered hers.

“Let me.” His voice was gruff, but he stared at her with a heat in his gaze she hadn’t seen before. He took the brush from her and, working section by section, started brushing her hair.

She almost purred.

While he brushed, he asked, “Who was that vampire?”

“Campbell,” she said, not wanting to elaborate. There was no telling how jealous Rolf would get when he found out—

“He hurt you.”

No getting past him, is there?

Adeline looked down at her lap and fiddled with her fingers. She couldn’t hide anything from Rolf, so why try? “Yes, he was Erik’s second when I was away on my assignments. He wanted to be second-in-command regardless of whether or not I was home.”

Rolf grumbled, “He felt threatened.”

Adeline waved her hand. “Most males are when there are powerful women around.”

“It’s a wonder you haven’t killed them all yet,” he snarled, but continued to brush her hair with tenderness. His knuckles had turned white from gripping the brush so hard. It was a wonder he hadn’t snapped it in half yet.

“Truly,” she said bitterly. “Don’t think I didn’t try.”

And try, she had. Back when she was younger. But Erik had worked some kind of twisted magic on her mind. It wasn’t until recently that she wondered why it had taken her so long to break away from Erik's control. If Rolf had been able to so clearly see the treatment she had been given, why hadn't she?

Perhaps it had taken her falling for Rolf, back when he was Colin, to show her that she could be loved despite her misgivings. Or maybe it was because she realized that living an immortal life meant nothing unless you had some kind of purpose. And her purpose was never meant to be Erik's killing machine. It could also have been that the conditions of her servitude to Erik had gotten so bad that she had finally snapped. Or maybe it was everything, the perfect combination of circumstances that finally let her wake up and realize her self-worth. Whatever the reason, she was glad it had happened. She was tired of the smoke and mirrors, the deception, the push-pull between wanting to appease her abuser while still resisting his control.

Rolf seethed behind her. "We have to burn this place to the ground. With every vampire in it."

"We will," Adeline said. The fire cracked and popped, and some of the ashes landed on the floor.

And then Adeline was struck with an ingenious idea. But she needed Rolf to think clearly before she told him anything else—he was too emotional right now to deal with logic. Men were like that—too emotional and prone to reacting poorly under pressure. Women, on the other hand, never asked what to do when the world burned. They acted with calm, with precision, with grace. It was why she had admired so many women rulers over the years. And it was also why she hated killing them.

She took the brush from his hand and stood to face him.

Adeline pulled him closer and deepened the kiss, knowing exactly what she had to do to get him calm. She needed the rest of her slapdash plan to come together. His hands roamed, traveling down to her backside. His tongue fought with hers, his scruff burning her face, and her stomach clenched with desire when he moaned into her. Just as quickly as she had begun, she pulled away, leaving him staring at her adoringly, gasping for air.

Adeline wiped her hands on her blood-drenched chemise and smiled. He had ripped Campbell's head off with such ease—it was, quite frankly, the biggest turn-on. Then, when he spat on the dead vampire's face before shoving it into the fire, she melted.

What a silly, licentious bloodsucker you are, Adeline. She was not used to her former lovers helping her murder her enemies.

"Can you help me get rid of this?" she asked, all innocence, gesturing to her bloodied chemise. She even added an extra pout and held up her hands. "I think you might need to...cut it off me..."

Rolf exhaled, a soft growl rumbling through his chest as he came up behind her.

"With pleasure," he whispered, and he leaned down, grabbing one of his blades.

Carefully, he moved her hair out of the way. With two quick movements, he sliced the shoulder ties, and the gown pooled in a flurry of silk at her feet. She kicked it into the fireplace, and it flared as the fabric singed.

His arms wrapped around her, and she arched into

him, feeling a tiny thrill when his hardness pressed against her stomach. She slid her arms up over his head and pulled him back down into a kiss. His chest hair rubbed against the hardening peaks of her nipples, and she sighed, needing to feel more of him.

He pressed his face into the side of her head and inhaled. "You smell more like you now."

"And what do I smell like, Rolf?"

Rolf nudged her with his nose and sighed. "You smell like rain on cobblestones after a hot summer day. You smell like slow evenings in the forest after the first frost. You smell like the sun on fresh-cut pine. You smell like a late afternoon curled up on the chaise in the library of my childhood home. You smell like a fresh summer garden. You smell soft, you smell like *home*."

Her throat tightened, and tears threatened. Never in her life had she been compared to anything soft. Never had she imagined she would evoke such tenderness as to be associated with the idea of home.

"I need you," she said, her voice thick with lust.

"It'd be my pleasure," he replied. "But first, we need to figure out how to get you out of these damned things. I don't like seeing you restrained by anyone else but me." His hands slid from her backside up her back, and she shivered when his fingers wound in the hair at the base of her head and pulled.

"They're dwarven," she said.

"I may have something that could work," Rolf said, smiling. From his pants pocket, he withdrew a ring of keys.

"Where did you get those?"

"I found them," he replied, shrugging.

Adeline raised an eyebrow.

"I lifted them, but they were sticking out of a door downstairs, and no one was around." He mumbled the last bit as if knowing she would admonish him for something so foolish.

He flipped through the keys, testing each one to see if it would fit. After a few moments, they both realized that none of the keys would work. "Gods damn them all! I thought since these were dwarven keys, they must be a match. After all, one worked for your door."

"It's okay." Adeline tried not to deflate in front of him as her chest tightened. What if these chains were unbreakable? What if she couldn't get Juliette out like she had promised, and now Rolf was here and everything was fucked and it was all her fault?

She grabbed the keys from his hand and put them back into his pocket. When she withdrew, she brushed her fingers over the outside of his pants, lingering a little longer on the tip of his hardened shaft.

She murmured against his lips, "We can get creative."

It didn't matter how little time they had together. Consequences be damned—she'd take whatever stolen moments with him she could since she was still unsure if any of her half-conceived plans would work.

Her hand wrapped around the shape of him, and she squeezed. Her heart yearned to feel his body against hers, as if his touch alone could wipe away the caresses from Erik and Campbell that lingered in her memory.

I have to marry Erik later. Bile rose in her throat. *It's okay, I can do whatever I need to get through. Rolf is here. Make a list.*

So she did.

Tonight, marry Erik. Sow more seeds of discontent. Cause a scene so Juliette can escape?

No. That won't work. The scissors! Stash those in my corset, and then when Erik tries to mate with me, stab him in the...

"Adeline?" Rolf asked, cupping her face in his hands. "Where did you go?"

"Sorry, I...I'm here." She shoved her scattered thoughts down and smiled at him.

One would assume that after centuries of killing countless creatures, she would still be good at planning, at getting out of tight spots, at being able to think on her feet in a moment's notice.

What changed?

Rolf. He had cracked her wide open.

Centuries of training were wiped away, all because of the hope and peace she felt around him. A part of her realized how badly she needed to feel that again. The yearning for a future, the desire to have someone to share her life with, the intense feeling of comfort. Things she had long forgotten since Erik turned her.

A life of immortality is wasted without a future, without a partner to share it with.

And her future was right in front of her, worshipping her with his deep brown eyes. And his luscious mouth. And his rough hands.

He pulled her closer to the bed and sat down on the edge. She stood between his knees and ran her fingers through his thick hair. He nipped her underneath the curve of her breast.

Rolf stood and in one swift motion, scooped her up in his arms and tossed her on her back onto the bed. He climbed on top of her, grabbed the chain, and held her hands above her head. Then he withdrew the knife once more from its holster in his boot and stabbed it into the headboard, pinning her hands.

"Will that do?" He grabbed his shirt and pulled it off, smiling down at her devilishly. He was waiting. For what?

Oh. He was distracting.

"Yes." She nodded emphatically, her eyes roaming over his body.

Chest hair swirled around his muscular chest, and a dark swirling path trailed down to his abs, dipping below the waistband of his pants. She tongued her fangs.

He slid from the bed and kicked off his boots, bending to remove his socks. When he stood, his stomach muscles rippled, and the candlelight caught on the spiderweb scar on his shoulder. She tilted her head, trying to see the hardened outline of him against his trousers. His fingers tapped on his buttons, and she peeled her eyes away, meeting his gaze.

His brows lifted.

"What're you looking for, Adeline?" His voice was husky.

She licked her lips, tongue lingering on her fangs, because she refused to answer, worried she would sound too desperate. His hands hovered around the buttons, and then he stroked himself through the tight fabric. He was toying with her, and she loved playing along.

Her stomach fluttered with anticipation.

He chuckled darkly as he slowly unbuttoned his trousers.

Suddenly, he was naked, kneeling on the bed between her legs, her ankles in his hands. She stared, awestruck. He was *large,* and though she had been with him as Colin, she swore that *this* part of him had also been enhanced when his magic came in. She craned her head to see if he had the rumored knot that were-shifters supposedly had.

Nothing. She couldn't help but feel a little deflated. She had always wondered if that was another rumor were-shifters had started to ward off other species. Still, the thought of finally being with him thrilled her.

Can he tell how aroused I am?

Heat pooled low in her belly. She clenched her legs together, but he grabbed her knees and held her open. His pupils dilated, and a low groan reverberated through his chest. The sound zipped down the length of her spine, and gooseflesh erupted across her skin.

He slid his hands down her thighs and stared lovingly at the most intimate part of her on display before him. It was the same look he gave her in the cabin—one of complete adoration.

She doubted she would ever get used to it.

"You're perfect," he breathed. "Never forget how perfect you are."

How could her scarred body and her damaged mind be perfect for him? It would never be what it once was. But her thoughts went blank as he slid a finger through her folds.

"Perfect," he said again. "And so wet."

He settled between her legs, holding her open with two fingers. Slowly, painfully, he licked up her center. A guttural moan escaped her lips so loudly she shocked herself, but he continued feasting on her. Her head swam with desire so thick that she could barely make out that he had said something about her and forbidden fruit, and how delicious it was.

"Rolf?" Tears lined her eyes with imminent release.

"Yes, my darkness?" He lifted himself, but his fingers slid inside her, and she bucked against his hand. Hers pulled against her restraints.

"I need you." Her legs trembled as she tried to hold off. The tension wound tighter, building with each twitch of his fingers inside her. "I'm going to..."

"No, you aren't," Rolf said and sat back on his heels. He stroked himself with one hand, while his fingers slowed but never withdrew.

I'm going to kill him, she said as the spool of tension began to unwind. She was at his mercy. "You're a beast."

"Trying to hurt my feelings?" He smiled smugly. "I've been called worse."

He squeezed his cock and, just when she thought she was going to lose all control, he slid his fingers out. He began kissing his way up her body, paying extra attention to all of the scars that peppered her skin.

She inhaled sharply when his mouth found her breast. He pulled one of her nipples between his teeth and bit down. Her back arched into him, and he wrapped one of his arms around her as he settled between her legs, his tip brushing against her entrance.

She shuddered.

"How're your hands?" he asked as he busied himself with biting the curve of her neck.

"My hands?" She had forgotten he had pinned them above her head.

"Can you stay like that a little longer?"

She nodded, her body twisting as it begged to be full of him.

"I need to hear you say it, Adeline," Rolf said.

"Yes, I can stay like this."

"Good," Rolf growled. "Because I never got to finish what I started."

His head dipped and he took one of her nipples into his mouth and sucked. She sighed when he moved to the next and then sucked on her breast. He dragged his tip through her folds, slicking himself with her wetness, teasing her open with his swollen head.

"You're enjoying this a little too much," Adeline ground out, desperation covering her with a fine sheen of sweat. He chuckled against her nipple, rolling it between his teeth. Then his fingers again found her entrance. It didn't take long for her to start aching for release again. It was unbearable. She panted, "You're taking too long. Someone could hear us."

"My wolf would let us know." Rolf framed her in his arms, then looked over his shoulder at the small window, sunlight streaming in. "Besides, the sun is up. We have time."

She was speechless when his bright amber gaze met hers, and she melted, head over heels in love with a were-shifter she had twice thought was dead.

But here he was, alive again. How? How did he survive

the vampires in the caves? She had heard his howling as the sun came up, and she thought for sure he had been killed. How did he find her here? And how did he get past the dozens of vampires and the enchantments that Erik had placed all over the castle? That Rolf had made it through was a feat of great strength. And determination.

Does he love me, too?

There was so much she should say, but she didn't want to ruin the moment. She didn't want to tell him that she loved him. She didn't want to tell him she was tired of losing him over and over again. She didn't want to admit that she didn't have a plan beyond tonight. And she did not want to tell him that she was worried this was all a dream.

But when Rolf looked at her with so much hope, she let herself give in. At least, while the castle slept, they had time together. The sunlight never affected Adeline as much as the other vampires, and it was a small bit of mercy—she wasn't about to waste this time.

The sun would go down, and *then* she would kill Erik and be free of him once and for all. She just needed to figure out how she was going to do it.

Chapter 41

Rolf

He couldn't stop staring at his mate and how she reacted to even the smallest movements his fingers made. She trembled underneath him, and when she cried out, he couldn't stop marveling at how sexy she was with her fangs out.

"You're perfect," he whispered into the curve of her neck.

"You keep saying that," she gasped.

"Because it's true." He added another finger, and she bucked against his hand when he nipped her skin. She clenched as his three fingers stretched her. He knew he was large, so he wanted her ready before he—

Claim her already! his wolf barked. He had been noticeably quiet until now.

Soon, Rolf snapped. He didn't want to claim her unaware, though. His wolf may be a controlling, possessive asshole but he was trying his best not to give in. *Now shut up and stay alert.*

His wolf huffed and went quiet again. Rolf hoped he would stay quiet for the rest of the day. It was still odd, knowing there was a part of him that was a wolf. Would the incessant inner thoughts drive him mad, eventually?

Rolf's thumb quickened, and Adeline purred, her legs trying to close against the rising tide of pleasure.

"Rolf, *please,*" she whined. "I *need* you."

He loved it when she begged.

"With pleasure." He smiled down at her, withdrew his fingers, and situated himself above her.

"Tell me, my darkness," he said, placing a kiss on her forehead. "Should I release you?"

"If you don't, I—"

Rolf grabbed the hilt and pulled the knife out. Adeline's hands fell free, and she tugged him down into a fervent embrace. Everywhere she touched, every part of him she kissed, ignited a fire deep within him. His cock throbbed and he stroked it a few times. He trembled against the impulse to claim her, rough and hard and wild, like his wolf wanted him to do.

No. He would take his time.

His darkness deserved to be worshipped. If they made it out of here alive, then he would replace the prayers he used to say to the gods with murmurations of her name.

Adeline, Adeline, Adeline.

Pausing between kisses, she panted, "If you don't fuck me, right now, I am going to bite you."

He flashed her a devious smile. He *wanted* her to bite him, like she had in the cabin, wanted her to sink her teeth into his skin, wanted to feel the insane pleasure that had coursed through his veins, wanted to see her cheeks fill with color. Wanted to come together, feel her clench around him as he spilled his seed into her, wanted to see her glistening with his release as he withdrew.

Mine, mine, mine. "Patience, my darkness."

She huffed and wrapped her arms around his neck, pulling up to whisper in his ear, "Fine, but I will make sure it hurts."

He silenced her with a kiss, her soft mouth meeting his. His tongue parted her pliant lips, and he flicked it against her fangs. A sharp prick on the end of his tongue and some of his blood filled her mouth. She moaned and he finally let go of his cock.

"I told you, back in the cabin, I was going to take my time with you." He placed kisses where the pink flesh knitted together at the base of her throat. He wanted to kill the vampire who did it. And he would. But first things first and all that. He dragged his teeth up her neck, nipping, wanting so badly to mark her. "And I plan on following through on that."

She inhaled sharply and settled back into the bed. Her hair fanned out behind her head, the thick black waves framing her face and the scar along the curve of her throat glistening pink and wet where his tongue had traced the line. Her blue eyes, contrasted by her dark lashes, shone with longing, but then he noticed the dark circles under her eyes, the sallowness of her skin.

"Bite me," he said, positioning himself at her entrance, rubbing his head up and down her slick, wet heat. She moaned, shifting her hips. "You need to feed."

She cupped his face lovingly. "Only if you fu—Oh, *gods.*"

He cut off her words with a kiss while he pushed inside her. Her eyes widened, her back arched, and she cried out. He was only a few inches deep, wanting to take his time as he stretched her. She was slick and hot and wet and better than his wildest imaginings.

But when she wrapped her legs around his waist so he could go even deeper, he had to clench his fists to keep from spilling his seed too soon. He withdrew, slowly, pulling a guttural moan from deep within her as he angled himself and thrust deeper, settling himself inside her. She smelled of amber and fresh rain, scents he had missed for decades. His cock throbbed as he remembered what it had been like to make her scream his name all those years ago. He shouldn't be so surprised, but this time was different.

But it was never like this.

This was new, this was glorious.

He thrust again, loving how she stretched around him.

"Adeline," he rasped. "You're so tight, so perfect."

She clutched his shoulders, sharp nails digging in harder. Each time he drove deeper into her and hit her wall, she moaned into his ear. He shivered, so close to losing control.

"My beast," she purred.

He withdrew slowly, pulling a groan from her when he sank again into her tight core. The more she moaned, the harder she gripped his shoulders, the longer he wanted to do this to her. It was all he lived for to hear his name on her lips, slowly watch her dissolve as he stretched her, watch her writhe under him as her climax climbed higher and higher.

He slid a hand between them, his thumb finding her bundle of nerves. She jolted, legs shaking, sheath tightening around him, until he, too, trembled with the beginnings of an orgasm.

Then her mouth was on the tender flesh of his chest, and there was no pain as she drank and drank and drank. He grew lightheaded but didn't stop thrusting, didn't stop playing with her clit. His mind went blank—a brief moment where both he and his wolf sighed in contentment before the fires of pleasure roared to life. He picked up the pace, she sucked harder. There was only bliss. His entire body was zipping with pleasure each time she pulled deeply from the bite near his heart. Everywhere she touched, he shivered. It was too much. It was world-ending.

It was...

Home.

He tilted his head, once, and ground out her name: "Adeline."

She continued to feed, but her eyes found his, her pupils blown wide, a trickle of blood trailing from her mouth. Her eyebrows knotted together in confusion. He couldn't hold on any longer but he needed to ask right now or he would lose all of his courage.

"Can I—" The pleasure was so intense that he lost his train of thought.

Her hands dragged down his stomach, her nails catching on the tangle of his chest hair, down the ridges of his muscles, to the tightness of his belly and the orgasm that threatened. She gripped the bottom of his shaft, and the world swam into focus once more.

He grunted out while he thrust, "Can I...bite you...?"

Finally, she let go. She licked the bite marks, sealing him up.

"Yes," she said, her eyes the clearest he had ever seen them. "Mark me."

"I want to do more than mark you," he said, his voice low, steady. He wanted her to know that what he was asking was serious. That what he wanted from her was a promise of forever.

"You want to mate?"

He nodded and slowed his movements, and she whined as he slid out of her.

One of her hands found his length, slick from her, and she stroked him as she asked, "Can we? As a vampire and were-shifter?"

Her hand twisted and stroked. He would come soon if she didn't stop.

How would her breasts look covered in my cum?

Like she's ours, the wolf answered, with a metaphorical wag of his tail.

He really needed to figure out a way to shut that animal up.

Rolf shook his head and shrugged. "My wolf seems to think so."

He didn't add that his wolf also thought they were already considered mated. Or that his wolf wanted to cover her in his cum.

"Then bite me," she said, her voice clear and steady. "I want to mate with you before I have to *marry* Erik."

He pushed a rumble of fury back down into his chest. As soon as he could, he would tear that bastard limb from limb. But for now...

"I don't want to think or speak of him. This," he said, leaning down to kiss her gently. "This is just us. This moment, this mating mark, is *only* for us. Do I have to fuck you again to make you forget?"

A mischievous smile tugged at her lips. "Oh dear, Rolf, I would hate for that to happen. It would be such a pity to have you inside me again."

"Flip over, mate."

She obeyed, pushing her hips back against him. "Like this?"

"What a good girl," he growled and positioned himself at her entrance. He ran his hand over her luscious curves and grabbed her waist. He slid his cock against her entrance. "Still wet, still perfect."

Adeline stretched forward, pressing her chest into the bed, and angled her backside up even higher. With his freehand, he reached around her front, grazing her softer stomach, before his finger parted her flesh and found her clit. She gasped and he slid the tip of his cock into her waiting heat and then withdrew.

"More," she begged into the mattress. She wiggled and arched her back.

"Not yet, Darkness." He stroked her clit and slid a little farther inside.

"Rolf," she groaned.

"Adeline," he retorted, stretching her more. "Taking my time, remember?"

He marveled at the way his cock slipped in and out of

her, glistening with her dew. With each slow thrust, she bucked up against him, pressing back into him as if to hurry him along. But he gripped her hips, forcing her to take him slow and deep, forcing her to feel each and every inch of his thickness, until finally her backside was flush against his stomach. His tip swelled each time he bottomed out inside her, and she groaned.

He was close. He shuddered and gritted his teeth, but it was no use. She felt too good, too tight, too wet, too...

Perfect.

"Fuck, Adeline," he moaned as he picked up the pace. She bucked against him, matching his rhythm, the curve of her ass smacking against the top of his thighs. "Grab the headboard."

She did as she was told and braced herself against his thrusting. He bent over her back and brought his lips to the sensitive flesh near the curve of her left breast. His wolf howled as he bit down, drawing blood. She cried his name, squeezing around him. He let go and roared her name, crazed with the need to have his seed fill her.

Everything felt right, finally, for the first time in a century. It was as if the very act of joining together sealed their fate. She was crying and gasping and moaning, and he was trembling with pleasure, and she was begging him for more as they came down together and collapsed on the bed.

His flesh throbbed where she had bit him, and his chest bloomed as the mating thread snapped into place. It reverberated down to his toes and filled his head with a harmonious sound, until he realized it was his wolf howling and yipping with glee. He smiled, wondering if she felt it, too. Then he looked down at the skin underneath her breast. A few puncture marks glistened with fresh blood. He adjusted on top of her so he could wipe them away with his thumb, but her hand wrapped around his, stopping him.

"Leave it," she whispered. Her pupils were blown wide, searching his face. "I want to remember all of this."

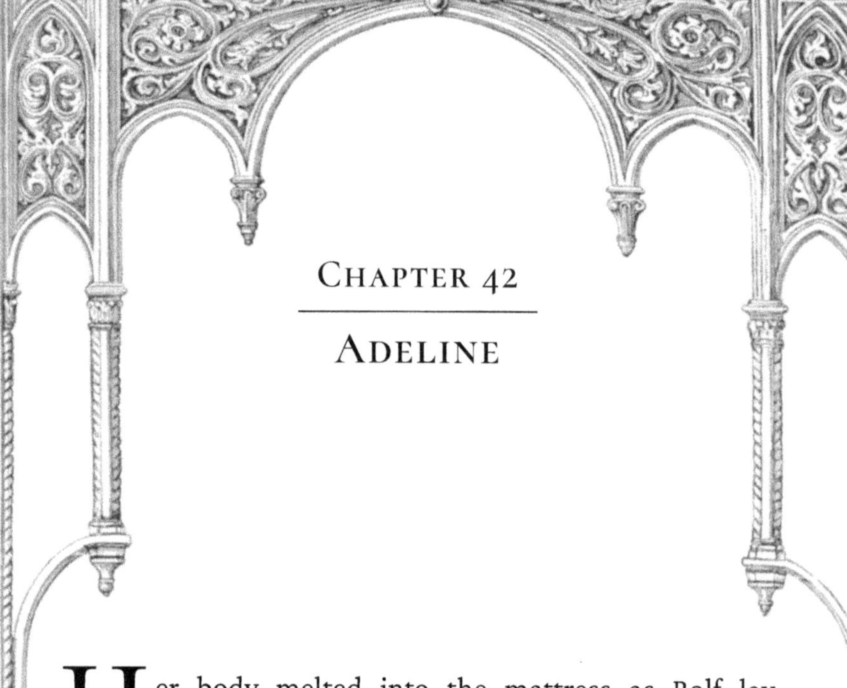

Chapter 42

Adeline

Her body melted into the mattress as Rolf lay panting on top of her, a comforting weight while he softened inside her. He withdrew slowly, leaving a trail of his cum against her leg. His hand cupped her backside, stroking the sensitive skin where her curve met her leg, then he dragged his finger through his seed, up to where his cock had just filled her.

"I want to fill you with my cum until it pours out of you," he whispered in her ear. He slipped his finger inside her, pushing his cum farther into her. She groaned as he wound her up again, and for the first time in ages, she didn't want to wipe herself clean.

She *wanted* his cum to spill out of her, to dry on her skin. She wanted to be covered in it. To be marked by him. To smell like him. To belong to him.

Her left breast throbbed where he had bitten her, the center of her chest pulsed with heat—an aching, blissful feeling that swam just underneath her skin.

"Adeline," he whispered. His fingers brushed her temples as he tucked a stray strand from her forehead. "Can you feel it?"

She turned slightly, rubbing the center of her chest where the slow heat had started to build. She closed her eyes, the new sensation tingling down to the tips of her fingers. "Yes."

He smiled and kissed her forehead. "It's like a fire inside that flares every time I think of you."

Rolf, she whispered.

Adeline. Her head whipped around to meet his gaze. His lips were closed, but she heard it again, clearer this time. *Adeline.*

Her chest pulsed, like someone tugged on an invisible string. Puzzled, she dipped her head to look between her breasts, then rubbed her sternum where the fire pulsed stronger. There was nothing noticeable on the outside but, yes, the fire he spoke of roared inside her.

"Is this—" She could barely form a thought.

"I think so," he replied. His voice was low, gravely, husky as he added: "Mate."

He wrapped his arms around her, pulling her against his chest. Thick and muscular and steady, his body scooped around hers. His heart thumped rapidly through his chest, against her back, and she snuggled into him.

They lay like that for a few minutes, passing thoughts back and forth until Rolf's breathing evened out, his arm got heavier, and his grip relaxed. She snuck a look back at him and saw that he had fallen asleep. As gingerly as she could, she turned in his arms. She stared at his sleeping figure, and deep contentment pooled low in her belly as she memorized his features.

I do much prefer the beard, she thought as she lightly traced the scruff that lined his jaw. He had a few scars that she hadn't noticed before. Some were small nicks, but there was one on the left side of his face, near his ear, that caught her attention. Two marks, equally spaced, but not deep enough or wide enough to be a bite mark. Her fingers touched one of them gently, her nails elongated to fine points, and as she traced it, she realized that someone must have tried to grab his neck with claws of a similar shape.

Erik? Or someone else?

Adeline filed it away to ask him about later and dragged the tip of her nail down his neck, featherlight, until she reached the spiderweb scar on his shoulder. She rested her hand against his skin, wondering why it had remained while the rest of him had transformed when his shifter magic was activated in the stones.

Rolf snored and Adeline suppressed a giggle as she burrowed her head into his chest. She inhaled his woodsy scent, the shifter musk, the smell of sweat and sex that danced across his skin and in his chest hair. She splayed her hands against him, his heartbeat strong under her fingertips, and within moments, she let herself rest.

ADELINE STRETCHED, AND HER LEGS STUCK WHERE SOME OF Rolf's seed had dried. She opened her eyes slowly—the late-afternoon sunlight streamed through the small window in her room. She had forgotten how bright the sun got as it changed course in the autumn sky. An orange glow set the gilded accents in the room ablaze.

Her hands brushed away an itch on her neck. She had fully healed and she could think clearly, the constant gnawing of hunger had abated, and though she craved more from Rolf, she knew that she could last a little while longer on what she had taken from him.

She closed her eyes for a few moments, and when she did, it was as if the entire room had come alive. She listened: the flicker of the candles next to her bed, the soft inhale of Rolf next to her, the beating of his heart, the silent hallway outside her door—all were easier for her to hear.

Air prickled her skin. The fire had long gone out, but Rolf was still sticky-hot beside her. His arm kept her pinned to the bed, and his thumb stroked beneath the curve of her breast. The swish of his skin as it brushed hers lit gooseflesh up and down her arms. Even her skin felt like it was alive.

She opened her eyes. The light had shifted, and the gilded accents dulled as the sun slipped out of view of the window. Opaque shadows curled at the edges of the room, forming distantly familiar shapes on the walls as the candles flickered. Adeline blinked a few times, but the shadows never changed. She swiped her hands in front of her, but when she lifted them, the silver around her wrists glowed with a halo of light. When she touched the wards, a jolt of energy traveled down her arm.

"Do—do you see this?" Adeline asked, turning her head to Rolf and lifting her arms to show him the chains.

His eyes were still closed, but he mumbled against the side of her head, "Hmm, you smell delightful."

"Rolf, I've never experienced this before," she said, shaking the bed to wake him. "The lights, the colors?"

The shadows?

"What do you mean?" he asked, propping himself up on his arm. He ran his hand over his face and yawned.

Adeline turned and braced against his chest. She gestured to the chains. "Are they glowing to you?"

"No." He shook his head, frowning. "They're shiny, but they aren't glowing."

She settled back into the bed, something gnawing at the edges of her memory. It was an odd sensation, seeing colors this rich, hearing sounds so clearly, watching shadows move on their own. As a vampire, her every sense was heightened, but nothing to the degree she felt now.

Mate, Rolf's voice tugged on the bond. "Where did you go, Adeline?"

"I—" She stopped. Was she going crazy or was this the reason why Erik wanted to mate with her? But now that she was mated to Rolf… "I know what we have to do."

A devilish smile curled at the corner of Rolf's lips. "What does my darkness have in mind?"

His darkness. Warmth bloomed in the center of her chest, and Rolf rubbed her back, trailing slow circles with his fingers between her shoulder blades.

"Mating gave us the advantage we need." She pushed off his chest and sat up, tucking a stray piece of hair behind her ear. Rolf's hand slipped from her back and rested on her leg, his thumb grazing the sensitive skin on her inner thigh. She shivered and placed her hand over his to still the distracting touch. She could see her plan laid out clearly.

Adeline looked to the window; the sun would set in an hour, and the vampires would become more active soon. "We have to act like Erik knows you're alive and coming to get me. He has contingencies upon contingencies. You mentioned you wanted to set this place on fire..."

"Burn the whole thing to the ground with the vampires trapped inside, yes."

"Then we do it."

Rolf smiled; his eyes flicked to the candles on her vanity. "Now?"

"Erik is eager to marry me," she said. "And—"

Rolf growled, cutting her off.

"Stop that. Just listen—we are running out of time and I have it all worked out."

Rolf held up his hands and sat up, facing her. "I can't help but get protective, Adeline."

Adeline cocked an eyebrow. "Yes, but I can't have you acting like a fool. Erik doesn't know you're alive or that you're even here, right?"

"As far as I know. It was just the enchantments down below, but I kept out of sight, and any of the servants I did see were all glamoured."

Adeline closed her eyes, trying to remember how long it had been when Erik glamoured the castle the first time. The two of them had stumbled upon the ruined shell of this place centuries ago. He had hired several local workers to restore it so he could make it a safe haven for his progeny. After the restoration was finished, Erik and Adeline drank the workers dry so no one could spread rumors. One night, she had been restless, wandering the halls, only to hear strange chanting coming from the throne room. Through a crack in the door, she found Erik covered in blood. He had painted symbols across his skin and the floor and he was mumbling incantations while his eyes glowed red.

Afterward, the castle was enchanted, and they had lived there in peace since. She didn't know if Rolf had triggered an alert, but she had to assume that Erik would know.

His eyes had been red... Something nagged at the back of her mind and she could almost recall why that now felt so familiar. *A fairy story?*

"If the castle knows there is an intruder, we have even less time than I thought. Hopefully, Erik doesn't know it's you, but again, let's assume he does. He's eager to marry me, he wants to mate, he wants me as his for eternity. When I suggested moving up the wedding date, he didn't hesitate. In fact, he said it was a good idea."

The list in her head kept going and she could feel her chest getting tight with anticipation, so she took a few measured breaths. There was no telling what Erik was going to do tonight, but the fact that he had been so eager to see her acquiesce meant that there were sure to be a few surprises. Erik was, after all, twenty steps ahead. "You need to dress as a servant. Blend in."

Rolf rubbed his jaw. "Then cause a distraction."

"Exactly," she said.

"I need to free the other fae first," Rolf added.

"Then you need to get down there, now. Wait until it is dark and then set fire to the lower levels."

"Flush them out, you mean?"

Adeline agreed. "If they aren't in the ballroom, where I think Erik will have us get married, then we need them in there. But you have to leave before the sun sets."

Rolf went deadly still, his mouth parted as if he was going to say something. Alarm reverberated down their shared thread. Adeline closed her eyes. His blood still thrummed inside her, fueling her, strengthening her as she listened to the sounds in the hall.

Voices. The message thrummed through their bond.

Juliette and one other...a voice she couldn't recognize.

"Rolf," she whispered, her eyes wide.

But he was already off the bed and grabbing his clothes. She forgot how quickly he could move as a wolf shifter, but even now, he had a grace to his movements he hadn't before. The bond pulsed between them, and they moved in sync, anticipating each others' movements seconds before they acted. It was like a dance. Rolf dressed, Adeline dressed.

Don't kill. Not yet. Adeline sent her thoughts down to Rolf. They couldn't risk their plan being foiled, not yet. Rolf needed to get down to the servants before anything else happened. He looked as if he wanted to object, but then his thread shimmered with agreement.

She was mated now. Despite the chance that they'd be discovered and their entire plan would be ruined, this was the calmest she had felt in ages. As if everything had slotted into place after centuries of loneliness. She'd never wanted to belong to any man, but having a companion? With Rolf, it seemed possible. How long had it been since she'd felt this connected to anyone else other than her mother and sister?

Too long. And she was ready to hold on to this with everything she had.

Erik wasn't going to take Rolf away from her again. Erik wasn't going to win.

My darkness, Rolf sent through the thread, snapping her back into the present.

She rubbed her sternum and met Rolf's gaze. He held up his fingers, signaling that the voices neared her room. She tightened the laces on her corset and looked around. They needed a distraction, something to get Rolf out of there safely.

Chapter 43

Rolf

Rolf bent over to retrieve the knife from the floor, and instead of putting it into his boot, he handed it to Adeline. He still had three more, but when he was getting dressed, he realized that Adeline didn't have a single blade in this entire room. He didn't doubt, however, that she could make a weapon out of anything. In fact, he was almost surprised she hadn't tried to use the candelabras or the mirror. Then again, she had looked awfully weak and malnourished when he first saw her.

She looks healthy now, his wolf noted.

She looked better than healthy now. She was immensely attractive when she was planning on killing her coven back in the cabins, but here, she was divine. Her skin glowed, her hair had turned glossy and so dark it was almost black, her eyes were deep blue like the night sky, her cheeks were ever-so-slightly flushed, and her lips plumped as she worried the bottom one between her teeth.

Gorgeous, he sent her through their bond. Her eyes flashed to him, and she sent him back the insatiable feeling of lust.

Rolf suppressed a groan, not wanting to give in to *those* feelings quite yet as it would prove difficult for him to fight when he was hard.

His wolf snorted.

Quiet, he snapped back.

"I am going to set the bed on fire," she whispered, casually holding his blade. It looked ten times more deadly in her small hand. She played with the weight of it, then slipped it in the gap behind her dresser, away from the door.

The voices closed in.

He guessed they were probably ten paces away since he couldn't quite make out what they were saying. His head whipped around the room. There weren't many places to go except under the bed (*Absolutely not*, his wolf growled) or behind the curtains (*Out of the question,* he scoffed). Rolf spun to the corner of the room where the door would open. He slipped into the shadows, another knife in his palm, and pressed his ear against the frame.

Adeline's eyes gleamed with delight as she took the candles and set the side of the bed on fire. Then she placed the candelabra on the nightstand and knocked it to the ground. Several of the candles caught the bed skirt on fire. Next, she tossed the sweat- and sex-stained sheets into the flames.

The room filled with smoke.

Adeline ran to the door and started banging. Rolf watched with a mixture of awe and pride as her body morphed into a façade of distress, the mask covering her from her face to her toes. This was an assassin—calm, calculated, deadly. She was a force to be reckoned with, and he was so glad that she had fed from him. Everything about her screamed to his basest instincts to run away.

He took a few deep breaths, keeping his heart rate low.

The door opened and Rolf's view was cut off.

"Juliette!" Adeline cried out.

"Adeline!" It was the same blond vampire from earlier.

There was some scuffling.

"Grab this!" Juliette cried. Two grunts and then his bond flared in his chest.

Run!

Rolf didn't need to be told twice. The smoke filled his entire view, so he felt his way around the door. Smoke billowed out into the hallway. His eyes burned. He suppressed a cough.

No one in the hall, his wolf replied. *But four feet running up the main stairs.*

What had happened to the other voice?

He didn't have time to find out. Rolf turned to his left toward the servants' doors and tripped on a large box. The lid flew off, revealing an intricate mask and white fabric, lined with pearls, that shimmered silver.

His heart stopped, his throat tightened, the room seemed to tilt underneath him. He stooped to take the items but at the last minute decided to leave them. Rolf reached for the handle of the servants' door; it turned before he could grab it. He sidestepped to the nearest window and slipped behind a pillar near a large fireplace, sinking into the shadows. A glamoured servant stepped into the hallway from the door he had almost opened. They walked with a measured pace to Adeline's room, completely unbothered by the smoke.

From his darkened hideout, he watched as two servants ran up the stairs with buckets. Juliette rushed out of the room and opened the balcony windows on either side of the hall. Fresh air poured in, and the smoke leaving Adeline's room slowed to almost a stop.

The hallway was abuzz with the comings and goings of the servants and their buckets. Juliette picked up the wedding dress and brought it back to Adeline's room. All the servants filed out and the door closed behind her. Soon, the hallway was quiet, as if the fire had never happened. But his wolf was still on high alert, so he stayed in the shadows.

Down by his feet was a set of spiderweb-covered fireplace instruments. A poker, a brush, a shovel, all propped up together. His hand wrapped around the poker and he pulled it out, careful not to let it clank against the other metal objects. He slid it behind his back, relieved he had found a weapon.

A lock clicked, the door to Adeline's room opened, and Juliette stepped out. She grabbed the box left by the door and walked down the hall. Right to Rolf's hiding place.

He stepped out from the shadows, stopping her in her tracks. He held his hands behind his back, keeping the poker hidden.

Her back straightened and she sniffed the air, eyes narrowing for half a second, and he wondered if she was trying to place his scent.

"The were-shifter," she whispered, eyes wide as she looked him up and down quickly.

He cocked his head to the side but said nothing. Sweat cascaded down his back, but his wolf kept his heart rate in check. They were hunters facing off. Neither of them could show fear.

"I'm Juliette, I'm—"

"The vampire who slit Adeline's throat," he growled. A threat if she tried anything.

She held up a hand. "It's not what you think..."

"And you think you're going to convince me otherwise?"

Juliette's act of innocence may have fooled Adeline, but Rolf wasn't buying it for a second. He didn't trust her, he had no reason to. As far as he was concerned, this was the vampire who was second-most responsible for why Adeline was in this horrific position to begin with. She'd slit Adeline's throat, weakened her enough to bring her back here, and was acting as...what? Adeline's chum all of a sudden?

Juliette said, "I didn't have a choice."

Her shoulders slumped forward, and she sighed. Alarms went off in his head; his wolf snarled at the change. Rolf looked down his nose at her petite figure. She was small, but he knew how deceiving looks were when it came to these creatures.

"Ah, so this is where I get lectured on how you have no free will under your maker," he scoffed.

Rolf didn't understand Juliette being on their side. He knew not to trust anything a vampire said—it didn't matter that Adeline had promised to help her get free.

How long had it taken Adeline to break out of Erik's clutches? A hundred years? Juliette, on the other hand, was still here, acting as his puppet, but then all of a sudden wanted to get free?

No, something wasn't adding up.

Distrust, his wolf snarled. *Eat her up.*

"Consider me impatient," Rolf said. What angle he played from here on out depended entirely on whether or not Juliette knew everywhere he had been. The keys weighed heavily in his pocket. The mate bond thrummed to life between them. He only hoped that the stench down in the servants' cells and the smoke from the fire had covered up his scent. He figured he might as well act as if he hadn't even been in Adeline's room yet. He took a step forward, almost bumping against the box in Juliette's arms. "Where is she?"

"I—I can't tell you that. Not right now, it would ruin everything," Juliette whispered and shook her head. Her eyes darted everywhere and finally settled on his face. She adjusted the box on her hip, and the silvery mask slipped from the top of the dress. Layers of lace were gathered underneath a silk-covered corset. Fine beading lined the boning of the bodice, and the delicate crystals glinted with elaborate silver thread.

"Is that a wedding dress?" Rolf cocked his head and raised an eyebrow. He knew the answer, but something told him Juliette wouldn't give him one.

Instead, Juliette gave him a pained expression and shifted the box away from him. "You weren't supposed to see this; you aren't supposed to be here."

"Why?" Rolf asked, stepping closer. "Hiding something?"

"No, the timing, it's not—"

"Fuck your timing," Rolf said, again stepping closer, reaching for the dress. "If this dress is meant for Adeline—"

"Wait!" Juliette whispered, taking a step backward. "I—"

Anger rumbled beneath his skin, his wolf threatening to dismember anyone who got in the way. If Juliette ran, there was no doubt in his mind that his wolf would give chase.

Liar. She's a liar. His wolf hadn't been wrong yet, and she needed to pay for what she was doing to Adeline. There was no way Juliette was an innocent bystander in all of this.

But before Rolf could do anything, laughter echoed from the main stairs, down to where they stood. Fear gripped him, and suddenly, it was as if Rolf acted outside of himself. He watched, detached, as one of his hands snatched the dress out of the box. Slowly, he backed his way toward the servants' door.

A small group of vampires ascended the stairs, and the eyes of one of them locked onto Juliette, who had the decency to pretend to be shocked. Then the vampire's eyes shifted to Rolf, and his face split into an evil smile. He was tall, with long black hair, and those eyes seemed to look right through him. A terror shuddered through Rolf.

I'm his next meal, he thought. *Fuck that.*

With his other hand, Rolf swung the fire poker out to

his side, knocking a candelabra to the ground between him and Juliette. She took a hasty step backward as the flames licked at the carpet, creating a wall between him and the vampires. He held the train of the dress over the fire.

"No!" Juliette screamed, diving to get the dress before the flames consumed it.

Rolf dropped the dress just out of reach of the fire. She snarled, pointing at him as the vampires dashed down the hall. He turned and ran. He didn't look back, didn't dare.

He ripped the door open, slamming it shut behind him, and slid the fire poker through the door handle to barricade it. He took the stairs two at a time, not bothering to see if he was being pursued.

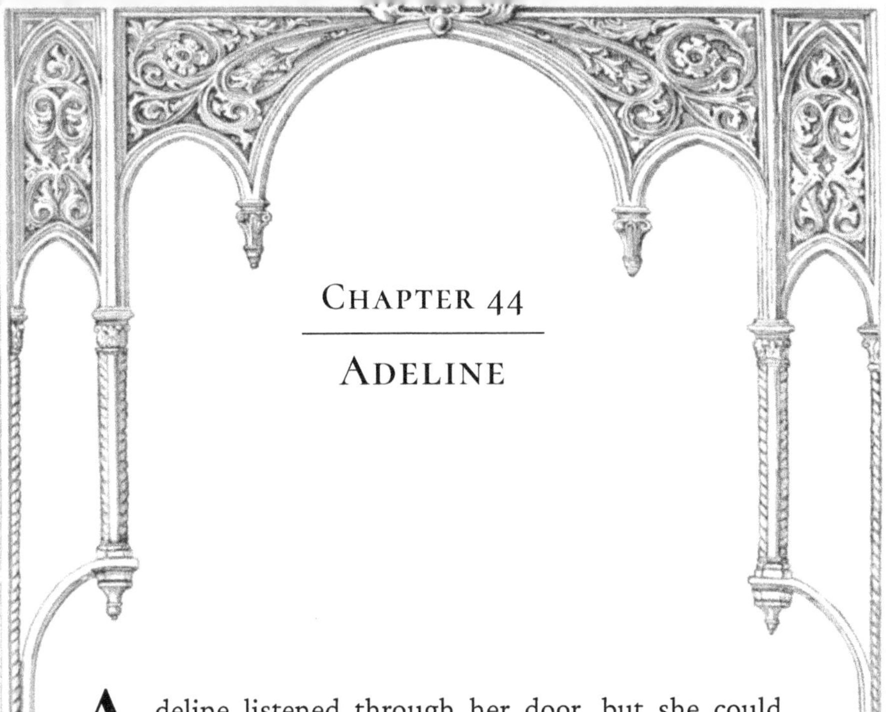

Chapter 44

Adeline

Adeline listened through her door, but she could barely make out the muffled sounds of Rolf and Juliette talking down the hall.

Juliette had known something was up the second she ran into the room. It was a rookie move, setting things on fire, knowing that the other vampires feared the flame, but it had worked. Except now Rolf was exchanging words with her?

Distrust, her mate sent down their bond. The sensation was so thick that Adeline took a step back. Distrust? Juliette? She closed her eyes and recounted the conversations they'd had. Juliette wouldn't try anything, would she? She needed help getting out. She had a mate on the outside.

"No!" Juliette screamed.

And then there was a stampede of footsteps rushing down the hall. Adeline's heart dropped.

Her nails turned to claws, and she clacked them together. She could leave her room and go find Rolf. His blood had given her enough sustenance; she was stronger now and could hold her own. She tried the handle. It clicked open.

Juliette hadn't locked her in this time. It would be so easy for her to kill everyone out there. Her fingers wrapped around the knob. If she left and went to Rolf's rescue, their entire plan would be exposed, and she would lose the tiniest upper hand she had.

Erik would know...

She dropped her hand and paced back and forth, clacking her nails together again as her mind whirled.

Assume you still have the upper hand. Don't get involved. Not yet. Rolf can hold his own.

The handle clicked open. Juliette stepped inside, her face ashen and her movements jerky. She held a box on her hip, and she slipped into the room clumsily. Smoke stained her cheeks, and some of her clothes and her hair had been pulled from her tight bun.

She quipped, "Adeline."

"Juliette," Adeline replied, matching the tone.

Juliette closed and locked the door, then spun around. "Rolf is alive."

The word bounced in her head—distrust, distrust, distrust.

"I know," Adeline said.

"I wondered what the scent was and why it was so familiar," Juliette continued, placing the box on the bed. She tried to smooth her skirts down and walked over to the vanity. Juliette began to clean her face. She spoke quickly. "And then I remembered where I had first smelled him. The cabin. And, curiously enough, once more down in the servants' quarters. The scent was so different back in the cabin, less musk. But in the servants' quarters, I swore he had been right next to me. I assumed it was just the castle playing tricks, but...then my keys went missing, and your room caught on fire only to have him step out from the shadows and confront me? It made him so much easier to scent this time, since he was right in front of me."

Juliette's nose wrinkled at each mention of his scent, almost as if she was disgusted to be close enough to smell him. Would Juliette smell Rolf in here? On her? Adeline was covered in so much soot and smoke that she doubted it. But still, there was a gnawing feeling that they would be discovered before their plan took place.

Distrust, the thread echoed again. But this time, it was Adeline sending it through.

"Wait... he's here?" Adeline asked, hoping she sounded eager enough.

"Yes, but you knew that already, didn't you?" Juliette looked at Adeline through the mirror.

"Which is why you're not fighting against your enclosure to get out and find him."

Adeline gave Juliette a tight smile. "I heard your voices outside the door."

"He tried to set fire to your dress."

Foolhardy popinjay. Adeline stifled a smile and the feeling of hope that blossomed in her chest. "Was he successful?"

"No, thankfully." Juliette looked down at the box. Adeline suppressed a pout. Juliette continued, "And... currently, he's being chased down by three of us."

Us. Us. Us. *That's an interesting choice of words.*

Rolf's feeling of distrust lingered. *He* was the only one she could trust, and she was glad she hadn't told Juliette any of her plans yet. A small mercy that she was a naturally secretive creature. And Juliette was still considering other vampires to be her kin.

She's too entrenched. Rolf is right, I cannot trust her.

"And then what?" Adeline asked, even though she didn't want to know. She could guess, given Erik's propensity for extravagance and taste for torture, that once Rolf was caught, he would be put on display.

Her heart plunged.

Run, run, run, she sent down the thread.

All she got back was a growl.

Stubborn beast.

Juliette shrugged. "Your guess is as good as mine."

Either Juliette genuinely had no idea, or she was being purposefully kept in the dark. Best to operate as if Juliette was working both sides, on purpose. Adeline would find a way to break her, though. After all, she had made a promise and planned to keep it. Whether Juliette would walk free would not be up to Adeline to decide.

Juliette must choose it herself. The best Adeline could do would be to show her the way.

Adeline softened, knowing how hard it had been for her to break Erik's spell. She would need to approach this carefully, but quickly, since their time alone was limited.

"Is the dress in there?" Adeline gestured to the box.

Juliette straightened, tucking her hair back into place, smoothing the stray pieces, and took a deep breath. "Your dress. And your mask."

"Mask?" Adeline's chest tightened.

"For the reception," Juliette explained. "Erik is hosting a masquerade before the festivities this evening."

Adeline went quiet. The last human queen, the one she had killed, whose dress Erik wanted her to wear, had thrown a masquerade as part of her coronation celebrations. It had been a week since she was crowned. Two days after the queen had denied an allegiance with Erik. And it was the night Adeline was ordered to kill her.

I was right.

It was another not-so-subtle hint. It was meant to scare her. Terrify her into compliance. Show her that he was still in charge.

He won't win. Not this time.

"A masquerade?" Adeline asked as Juliette pulled gloves on. "Will you be participating?"

With her gloved hands, Juliette reached into the box and withdrew the dress. It shimmered with silver thread. "We are all required to make an appearance, Addy. You know how these things are."

She did.

Erik loved the spotlight. If he were planning something, he would want to do it in front of everyone. The wedding was her fate, signed, sealed, and delivered in a pretty package. And the masquerade was a front.

Juliette laid the dress down on the chaise, carefully spreading out the layers with her gloved hands. She must have seen Adeline staring because she held up some of the trim and said, "There's real silver thread in here. Erik was worried about another vampire touching you like Campbell did. So he had the dwarves use pure silver thread as a warning."

"A cage," Adeline sighed.

What would happen if Erik touched the silver thread? She tried to remember if he had ever touched anything silver in front of her before. She couldn't remember. Her shackles and chains that he'd kept her in while she was being "disciplined" had all been iron. She touched the silver chains on her wrists absently, the scars still faintly there, and wondered if it had always been dwarves enchanting the metals that she wore, for she never had an issue. It had always been iron that caused her skin to rupture. It would blister as if she had spent too long in the fields with her mother.

"You'll be fine," Juliette replied, stepping back. If she was unconcerned about Adeline being encased in silver, then the dwarves must have enchanted it specifically for her. She clapped her hands together and smiled at Adeline. "They did wonders on the alterations."

Adeline murmured in agreement. It was a gorgeous dress, and were it any other occasion, Adeline might be compelled to enjoy wearing it. What had once been a frilly, outdated monster of tulle, lace, and frills had turned into an elegant ball gown. But as it was, it would restrict too much movement, and the skirts would surely get in the way.

She bent down to look more closely at the work the dwarves had done in such a short amount of time. Energy zapped as soon as she made contact with the lace, a spark traveling between Adeline's fingers and the dress. Her chains clinked as she withdrew her hands, holding them close to her chest. Her eyes flicked to Juliette, but she had turned to grab something else from the box.

Adeline rubbed her hands together, hovering above the dress, wary about touching it again since the shock was still reverberating through her fingers. Delicate dwarven metalwork was woven into the dress, and it shimmered as energy thrummed underneath her hands.

Strong magic is woven into this fabric.

There was no telling what would happen should Adeline choose to put it on. Was the magic baneful or benevolent? Juliette seemed unbothered about Adeline wearing it, so she assumed that it would be fine, but her mother's voice echoed in her head with a warning.

"Exercise caution, Adeline, especially around magic you are unfamiliar with." Her mother had told her this often enough that it had become a mantra when she was a child, even though Adeline had always thought her mother's teachings were superfluous. The last thing on her mind was mastering the craft her mother so carefully practiced. She had been a surly young woman, navigating an isolated life at the edge of a village that shunned them.

They all feared us, Adeline thought bitterly. The villagers refused to let them into their society, but never hesitated when they needed something from their mother—whether it was an herbal remedy or a love spell. But the wards her mother had carved in the door never lied. They would shine when someone who wished them ill was near. One moment in particular had stuck with Adeline. But her memory was hazy, and the face of the man who threatened her mother that night blurred. If only she could see his face, she could—

"Well, Adeline?" Juliette asked, holding up the mask. "What do you think?"

The mask was a crescent moon, turned skyward, resembling the symbol of the goddess of old, and encrusted with tiny diamonds that caught the light every which way, twinkling and glittering like stars in the night. Adeline's breath caught in her throat. She had seen that symbol all over her house as a child growing up; her mother had carved it into every windowsill and doorway.

Her mother had a similar image burned into the skin underneath her left breast, but the crescent wasn't pointing upward. It was pointing down, and there was a star in the center. Adeline had seen it often when it was wash day, the scar puckered and pink, peeking out from her mother's chemise.

"I'm speechless," Adeline replied, through the fragments of the memory that tried to push to the surface. Her hand drifted to the top of her thigh, grazing the brand that Erik had placed there.

She had fallen asleep reading to her sister near the fireplace. Her mother had covered them both with thick blankets and furs as the fire died down and the house had gone cold. But upon hearing a knock at the door, Adeline stirred and rolled over, her eyes slightly parted in pretend sleep.

"I know of your kind," her mother said, refusing to take what the strange man at the door offered. He held out a sack in his hand, but her mother refused to touch it. The sigils on the door glimmered in the wood with defiance.

The stranger hissed, magic stinging his skin as he shoved his hand into their home, his finger pointing at her mother. Adeline almost leaped up, but something told her to stay hidden. "You have until the sun sets. I will return for her then."

A tar-black horse whinnied as the stranger mounted to

return to the protection of the trees, and both of them blended into the long shadows that formed before daylight struck.

"Come, Leena," her mother whispered. "We must talk."

Her mother had refused to sell either of her daughters to the stranger, and shortly after, Adeline had used the magic her mother had taught her and shoved her sister through a hole in the world into another place.

But what happened between saying goodbye to her sister and waking up covered in blood, screaming with hunger, while riding Erik in the middle of the woods?

She closed her eyes tightly, trying so hard to remember. The stranger's face was just out of reach—if only she could remember what he looked like and why those details were so muddy. If only she were alone so she could think, but Juliette was saying something, pulling her back into the present.

"Is everything all right?" Juliette asked, reaching for Adeline.

She swatted Juliette's hands away. "Leave me."

"I can't, I was under strict instructions to—"

Juliette's voice faded into the background as pressure built behind Adeline's eyes, the longer she stared at the shimmering gown. Her fingers tingled, and she flexed her hands. Her skin itched—she wanted to scratch it off. Her heart beat rapidly, and her breath was short.

Was she having a nervous break?

Adeline had never experienced such a thing as this. But after Rolf and the mating bond, she was in unknown territory. Shadows climbed the walls, swallowing the light from behind Juliette. Adeline watched, transfixed, as they pressed in. They weren't amorphous like she had previously thought.

No, the shadows moved like vines, climbing, clawing, clinging to the walls over Juliette's shoulders. Worry lined Juliette's features, but Adeline was entranced with the way the shadows turned when she moved her head.

Juliette rang a bell, and the shadows receded quickly, as did the itchiness of her skin and the pressure behind her eyes. Adeline blinked a few times, holding on to the post of her bed as she fought off a wave of dizziness.

The door opened, and fresh air blew the hair from Adeline's face. She inhaled deeply. Rolf's scent still lingered in the hallway outside.

Mate, she sent to Rolf, gratitude laced behind the word.

A beat, then two. And finally, a faint response from his end: *Mate.*

Several servants entered her room. They carried trays full of jewels and accessories, hair tools, and pins. A servant walked behind Adeline and reached for the ribbons of her corset. But Adeline sidestepped, remembering the knife Rolf had given her and the mark on the underside of her breast.

No one could see her naked.

"I'll dress myself tonight, Juliette." Adeline lifted her chin defiantly, daring Juliette to object.

"No, Erik—" Juliette frowned. "He wou—he can't..."

"Fuck, Erik."

Even through their glamour, the servants' hands stilled. The room got quiet.

Try me. Adeline gave Juliette a pointed look.

"You're excused," Juliette announced and rang a bell. The servants retreated, as silently as they had come. On their way out, they placed the trays of accessories and hair tools on the bed. When the door finally shut, Juliette turned on Adeline. "What do you think you're doing? Erik will think something is amiss!"

Adeline rolled her eyes. She was past the point of caring. It was time to plan. "Let him."

"What?" Juliette wrung her hands.

This two-faced act of hers is becoming tiresome.

"He expects me to be complicit. If he asks, just give him the message that I wanted to surprise him." Adeline tossed her hair over her shoulder with an air of nonchalance despite the pit in her stomach.

Adeline began untying the ribbons of her corset slowly so she could unsnap the hooks without dropping the blade. She wrapped her fingers around the hilt and pushed it underneath the lip of the corset, wrapping the knife inside. Then she placed the corset gingerly on the chaise next to the dress and slipped off her chemise, keeping her arms tight against her body and covering her breasts.

"You don't have to be shy in front of me, Addy," Juliette whispered. Her face turned soft. "I've seen you naked before."

"Yes, but a lot has changed between now and then," Adeline replied. "You have a mate now."

Juliette's shoulders sagged as she sighed and looked out the window. Her face had gone pale, and her eyes were withdrawn, as if she were recalling a memory. A few moments passed, and when Adeline cleared her throat, Juliette flinched and spun around, her eyes wide.

"I'm—sorry. I must have..." Juliette waved her hand in the air before pressing her palms to the side of her head.

Adeline nodded. She knew how it felt to walk on eggshells every second of your life as you sidestepped around a destructive, volatile force of nature. You remained vigilant, always looking for the next threat, unable to fully relax. Every door slam, every heavy foot, every raised voice was the preamble to destruction that you would bear witness to. And no matter how quiet, how perfect, how docile you tried to be, it would always be your fault. Eventually, your nerves wore down so much that not even sleep was a reprieve.

It was one of the reasons why Adeline had sought out Juliette as a companion. Her gentle nature had been a balm to Adeline's battered reality. With Juliette, Adeline had found someone who was unmarred by Erik's ruthlessness. And their time together had given Adeline the courage she needed to finally step away.

But that was when Erik had swooped in and poisoned Juliette against her. If Adeline was going to finally kill Erik, she needed Juliette to trust her.

"Yes, and we wouldn't want your new mate to question your faith in your relationship."

Juliette frowned. "My faith?"

"Yes," Adeline said again, the lie weaving itself seamlessly. "Before you mate, you have to be faithful to each other for at least one moon cycle. Everyone knows that."

"No," Juliette whispered, horror on her face. "No, that...that's never been true."

Tiny truths, she thought as her words blended with fabrication. She needed to plant the seeds of doubt deep within Juliette's mind so she would start to question everything Erik had ever told her.

"It is," Adeline insisted. "Otherwise, the mating bond won't snap into place. You have to be thinking solely of the other person you're mating with, or it won't work."

Adeline quickly slipped the chemise over her head while Juliette paced the room. Then she carefully grabbed the corset, her right hand holding the knife in place against her ribs.

"How do you know this?" Juliette asked, watching Adeline's fingers work to fasten the clasps.

"I found it in a book in an ancient library." Adeline shrugged, watching as the cracks in Juliette's resolve grew. "When I was researching the history of the were-shifters. I had to know when they would be weakest. I picked up several texts that mentioned the specifications for mating bonds for fae creatures. When the were-shifters are in rut, they tend to be more careless. Blinded by lust, if you will."

"But vampires are different...We're only considered fae because of our immortality," Juliette countered, but the slight frown on her forehead was enough for Adeline to keep pushing, to see if Juliette would crack.

"Ah, but we also have magic," Adeline countered. "Technically, only fae creatures have magic."

There had been many mentions of mating rituals between fae creatures. When fae mated, their power would get stronger, and their connection with each other would strengthen. But there was nothing written about mating between vampires. Let alone vampires mating with other fae. There was only hearsay, but the lore

Adeline knew only assumed that it was similar to a fae mating ritual.

Because vampires lived in covens, their choice to mate with a solitary partner was driven more out of a craving for control than for love. They weren't the type of creatures to settle down and choose a mate for eternity.

Her decision to mate with Rolf didn't feel that way. It had been instinctual, born out of a desire to *be* with him, purely out of love. There had been no desire for power beyond that of connection.

She rubbed her sternum through the corset, absently. The thread still tingled.

But Erik wants to mate with me...

Adeline could see it unraveling so clearly now. He thought he could finally force her hand and become even more powerful by completing a mating bond. Then, once it snapped into place and his magic was secured, he'd kill her in front of everyone as a warning.

But once he figured out that she was already mated, she was going to be killed regardless. Having Juliette act out of fear was only a small part of Adeline's plan, but she needed it to work. And a part of her hated herself for what she had to do next.

The lies poured out of Adeline. "There *is* little known of vampire mates. But in the text I read, the author had witnessed a mating bond between vampires and was very specific. Since vampires are immortal and our magic is so distinct, if you try to mate before the month is done, the bond could kill you."

"The bond would kill me?" Juliette's face turned white. "Why...why didn't anyone tell me?"

"Why would they? You've kept your mate a secret, have you not?" Adeline tied off her corset and walked over to Juliette. She grabbed her ex-lover's hands and squeezed. "Why do you think Erik hasn't been able to mate with me?"

"No," Juliette whispered.

"Yes, he's tried ever since I was turned." Adeline didn't know, now, if she was lying anymore. The more she thought about it, the more she was sure that Erik *had* tried to mate with her before but had never been successful. Was there some truth to the lies she was telling, and mating had to be consensual between two creatures? She knew that vampires had magic unlike that of the rest of the fae, and that mating bonds between fae creatures could enhance their natural magic. But...

"But..." Juliette trailed off, her eyes going distant again.

"I've been promiscuous on *purpose*," Adeline whispered. The lie was too easy. It wouldn't take long for Adeline to get the information she needed to bring Erik down. All Adeline had to do was land the final blow. "So long as I took a new lover frequently, the mating bonds would never be able to take hold. It was one of the reasons *I* sought *you* out."

"No." Juliette stepped back as if Adeline had slapped her. "I thought...You told me..."

Adeline shrugged, but inside, she hated warping her memories with Juliette into a farce. But if it got her what she wanted, then she hoped it would be worth the betrayal. "It was an easy way for me to avoid being mated to Erik. Every moment I spent with you helped me stay out of his grasp."

Juliette looked like Adeline had stabbed her through the heart. "You said you loved me. You said you were going to help me."

"And I am, because I did love you...Once," Adeline said. She looked at Juliette earnestly, punctuating her words carefully so Juliette knew she could still be trusted. "And I promised you I would help."

Juliette's shoulders sagged. Adeline stepped forward and cupped her ex-lover's cheek, dragging her thumb across it to wipe the newly formed tears away.

"Did what we had mean nothing to you, then?"

Adeline's tongue grew heavy. This lie would be the worst she would tell her former lover. "You were always just a means to an end."

"A means to an end?" Juliette's voice was a whisper.

Adeline swallowed, forcing her face to remain neutral and uncaring. If Juliette knew how much she had meant to Adeline, the game would be over.

The truth was that without Juliette, Adeline would have never found Colin. She would have never gotten the courage to leave. She would have never realized that she was capable of being loved. Juliette had shown her as much in their stolen time together. And, in a way, Adeline supposed she should feel more gratitude toward Jules. She had thought, especially with the strange way Juliette had acted back in the cabin when the hunting coven had shown up, that everything was the same between them.

How wrong Adeline had been. How weak. How easily fooled. That familiar weight of guilt settled on her shoulders once more. Would she ever forgive herself for leaving

Juliette to take up the mantle she had been so eager to get rid of?

No, doubt has no place here. You need Juliette for this to work. Don't muck this up.

"You can stop pretending now." Adeline turned, giving Juliette her back. The time was done for games. If Juliette couldn't own up to her deceit, then Adeline would force it out of her. Her nails started to grow, and she clicked them together at her side. She added, "You've always been a terrible actor."

"Fine."

Wait a minute. It was that easy?

Perhaps Juliette was tired of it all, too. Perhaps being under Erik's thumb was wearing her down too much. Curious, Adeline pivoted to face Juliette.

"Thank the gods we're done with pretense," Adeline said. "You have too many tells. I should never have left you alone with him."

"Why? Because you were his favorite?" Juliette sneered, but there was nothing malicious in her tone.

"Favorite? I was only his favorite when I could give him something. No, I should never have left you alone with him because you were too naive. Too pure, even as a vampire."

Juliette scoffed. "Well, that's ruined now, isn't it?"

"I suppose so." Adeline shrugged. "What did he promise you, Jules?"

Adeline let the unspoken name hang in the air between them.

Juliette pursed her lips. Her green eyes flared with defiance.

Adeline counted on her fingers as she asked, "Your own coven? The safety of your lover? Power? Money? Freedom?"

Juliette flinched at the last word.

Adeline chortled.

Freedom. Juliette wouldn't have figured it out until it was too late, but she had all but handed Erik the keys to her life.

"I have had almost a hundred years being on my own with him." Juliette's face was hard. Her eyes stared off into space as she added, "A hundred years to learn things you never thought to teach me. A hundred years to figure out how to handle him. A hundred years to not be so naive."

A chill swept down Adeline's spine. *What has he done to her?*

"But there's one thing you're not considering," Adeline said, leaning back against the poster of the bed. "You've given him all the power."

Juliette blanched. "No. That's not true. He has no idea—"

"About your mate?" Adeline ventured a guess, but the way Juliette's eyes flashed with fear told her she had hit a nerve. She mocked Erik as she asked, "Why would you want your freedom so badly, Juliette. What could be so awful about having a free place to stay? You have food, you have a bed, you have a free roof over your head. And all I ask in return is..."

"My loyalty." Juliette finished and clapped a hand over her mouth. Her eyes went wide when she realized what it all meant. "No."

"He knows, Jules."

"No." Her voice broke. "You're lying."

"Why would I lie?"

"Because...because Rolf is still alive and you're planning something. Because you hate me. You want to see me fail. Because Erik is going to kill you anyway and—" Juliette stopped.

Adeline nodded. "I know he is."

"But why aren't you fighting back? Rolf is still out there!" Juliette gestured erratically.

Good. Let her get upset. Let her question everything, even though this is breaking my heart.

Adeline shrugged, a perfect mask of indifference on her face. "You sent your vampires after him. He doesn't have anywhere else he can go. The chances of him getting free from this place are not in his favor. Or mine." Adeline grabbed the dress. "Help me dress for my death."

Juliette said nothing as the tears slipped silently down her cheeks.

She looked so pathetic, and it annoyed Adeline to no end. But funnily enough, she didn't feel vengeful toward Juliette. Instead, Juliette's sadness only increased Adeline's hatred toward Erik. She was tired of him playing with others' emotions and lives like toys to be discarded.

It ended with her. No one else would be subject to his brutality ever again.

Tonight will be my wedding and his death.

Chapter 45

Rolf

Rolf opened a random door midway down the stairs —one that hadn't been there before. The castle's layout must have changed, because he could not figure out his way back to the servants' quarters. The door opened onto a darkened hallway, and he slipped inside. He kept to the shadows, quiet like the ancient specters that surely roamed these halls. Time was running out, and the longer it took him to get down to the enslaved fae, the less time he had to start the fires in the lower levels.

He crept down the hall, checking every window, but they were either nailed shut from the inside or they opened out to the sea cliffs. At the last window, he stopped, cursing his luck as he looked at the sea below. Waves crashed into the cliffs, battering into the rocks below. Then he glanced skyward.

Two hours left.

The moon rose higher, casting an eerie glow on the sea as it lingered on the rocks below. His breathing was labored, and he was running out of energy when a guard called out at the far end of the endless hall.

Gods damnit!

He hung his head one last time, dredging up the last burst of energy he had, and then made his way to another door. It didn't creak, and he blessed the stars above as he shut it quietly behind him. He held his breath, hoping he had slipped inside in time. There was no lock, so he took an unlit torch from the wall and shoved the end underneath the door.

A dark room yawned before him, only lit by the moon outside. The stagnant scent of dust and decay filled his nose. But he had to keep going despite the quietness behind him. He knew vampires loved a hunt, and right now, he was the only prey. A small servants' door was in the corner, and he crept over to open it. Behind was a simple wooden landing, covered in cobwebs, that led to rickety wooden servants' stairs.

The stairs hadn't been used in what looked like decades, and they wound several stories down. He hoped they would lead him back to the servants' quarters.

A faint pulsing threaded through his chest. *Mate.*

Mate, he sent back and rubbed his sternum.

Gratitude for the tether to Adeline eased his worries a little. He stepped gingerly onto the wooden platform at the top of the stairs, testing its durability. It creaked under his weight but held.

He sighed with relief. While he made his way down, he kept checking to see if his wolf was with him. It would snarl and then go back to listening.

As long as he's still here, I know I'm not back in one of those illusions.

The stairwell was punctuated by thin windows, some of the glass broken and in disrepair. The wind had carried moisture from the sea inside, and it coated the walls and stairs with a sheen of mildew. He slipped a few times on the moss-covered wood.

On every landing, he would stop and press his ears against the door, waiting to see if his exit lay beyond. But neither he nor his wolf could hear anything. And the handles wouldn't budge. He didn't possess anything he could use to pick a lock.

The air turned warmer with each level he dropped, and he figured that, eventually, he would find a way back to the servants' quarters.

When he reached the bottom of the stairs, three doors stood before him. The landing was well-kept and had been oiled recently, a sure sign that at least this juncture was used frequently.

One of these doors would be his way out.

Rolf leaned against the middle one; he heard raucous laughter and immediately shirked away. The one on the left was quiet and cold but smelled of barley and hops, and most likely led to the pantry the servants used. It would be a dead end, and he'd have to find his way out through a more public area.

He took a deep breath and opted for the door on the far right. It was quiet and slightly warm, indicating that there had been a fire behind it recently. Hopefully, the fire had gone out, and the space beyond was vacant. He prayed to the gods that the hinges had been oiled recently as his hand gripped the handle, and it turned.

Thankfully, the door opened without a sound, and he peered through the crack.

The whir of pedals filled the room.

Five spinning wheels lined the wall, and at each sat a hunched-over dwarf, their feet pressing the pedals, their gnarled hands spinning gold and silver nuggets into fine thread. Candlelight flickered in the room, catching on the mounds of silver and gold.

"Hello, wolf," one of the dwarves said. They didn't turn to face him, just kept spinning. "Are you here to rescue us?"

Rolf stepped forward, unsure which one to acknowledge. He squared his shoulders, knowing that what he told them might be a lie. "Yes."

Dwarves were not ancient mysteries, then, but well and truly alive.

Trapped, his wolf snarled.

Imprisoned, he agreed.

Rolf closed the door quietly behind him. He watched as the dwarves worked in such low light that he had to strain to see the finished product on the spool.

How could they do this in these conditions?

It was unacceptable. First was the enslaved fae under a glamour. And now ancient magical fae kept in this filth and expected to work until...when? Until they dropped dead?

Deplorable, his wolf growled.

There would be no way for them to recover quickly enough for him to get them all free. He was sure they were well on their way to the Forever Night. Besides, there was no telling if they were under a glamour or—

"Come," the dwarf said, not even bothering to gesture.

Rolf stepped forward to the front of the room where the spinning wheels were located. He faced the dwarves, trying his best to keep the shock to himself.

His jaw dropped. Each dwarf was gnarled, skin and bones sticking out against their burlap clothing. Ratty, sparse hair covered their scalps, and they barely had enough hair to braid into what was left of their beards. Their eyes were clouded over with white.

"You're all blind," Rolf whispered.

"But not unseeing," the same dwarf said. This time, Rolf noticed it was the dwarf in the center who spoke.

Another one spoke up, never once missing the rhythm of the wheel as they spun. "You smell like the Northern Mountains."

All the dwarves hummed in agreement.

"Yes," said one.

"Home," said two others in agreement.

"Mother," said a meek voice at the end.

Rolf was gripped with sadness. He wanted to gather them all up in his arms and carry them back home. His wolf raged underneath the surface, wanting to tear the spinning wheels and the vampires apart.

"You will not save all of us," the first dwarf said.

The rest of them hummed in agreement.

"But—" Rolf began, and then he realized what the dwarf said was true. They were all so weak that there was no way they would be able to get out before he started the fires to burn the castle down.

"You must choose who you wish to help," the dwarf said. "Because for those who cannot go, you must finish the job before the vampires can feed off our magical blood."

His heart dropped. The vampires fed off their magical blood?

Rolf was no stranger to the unfairness of death, but he had done his time.

In his previous life, the military offered no shortage of death. Countless times, he would have to choose who deserved to get medical care. And those who could not make it, Rolf stayed with them. He would hold the soldiers' hands as death was ushered in, telling them that their mother was proud of who they were and that they would soon find relief. If they had no hands, he would stroke their foreheads, trying to remember how his mother had swept the hair from his brow as a child at bedtime. He figured that if they had been willing to sign up and fight the senseless battles of those in charge, the least he could do was make sure their deaths were not in vain.

Rolf withdrew the keys from his pocket and the knife from his boot.

He would do the same for these dwarves. They no more deserved their fate than the young men he had fought beside.

"Which among you is the youngest?" he asked, his voice tight with sorrow.

They all raised their hands and pointed to the dwarf at the end, the one with the meek voice.

"What is your name, dwarf?" Rolf asked gently as he

walked over to the fae. The keys jangled in his hand. One of them glowed a soft blue as he knelt next to the ankle restraints.

"Arlo."

"Arlo, let's get you out of here." He slid the key into the lock and turned it, and the cuff clicked open. But Arlo continued to spin.

"Arlo," Rolf said, his large hand swallowing the dwarf's shoulder. "It's time to get you home."

The dwarf's feet finally stopped pedaling. His hands dropped. He tilted his head up to the ceiling and sighed. "No."

"You don't have a choice in this," the first dwarf said. "This is the way it is supposed to be."

Rolf scooped the dwarf up in his arms, and Arlo didn't even bother to fight back. He sank into Rolf's chest and wept silently, shoulders heaving, but no tears came.

Rolf opened the door he'd come through and set Arlo on the stairs, propping his back up against the railing. Thankfully, it was warmer in here than it was in the spinning-wheel room. Arlo's white eyes stared straight ahead. He said nothing; he knew what Rolf was going to do.

"I—" Rolf began, but then he snapped his mouth shut and walked back into the room.

He closed the door behind him. The wheels had stopped spinning, and the dwarves all held hands.

"Be quick, pup," the dwarf said. "We need time to bleed before they come back."

Rolf fought back a sob as his heart broke. He inhaled, searing the image before him into his head. If he were to do them justice, then the least he could do was remember the cruelty they faced. He would be the one to carry their memories, he would be the one to help them meet a peaceful end. The swiftness of his training came back, and he moved down the line, grabbing each one by the forehead, whispering a prayer to the gods before he slit their throats.

Their warm blood spewed all over the silver-and-gold thread, the walls, and the spinning wheels before them. It poured down their malnourished bodies. They didn't make a sound when he did it, and when they stopped twitching, Rolf gently folded them over their wheels and wiped his knife on his pants.

He sent a final prayer to the gods above, doubting they were even listening, and shoved the overwhelming feeling of anguish deep, deep down into his heart.

Arlo was curled up on the stairs, shivering and asleep. Rolf gathered him into his arms and rubbed his back. He spoke over and over, in soothing tones, "I'm here. It's going to be okay."

Arlo whimpered in reply.

Rolf's wolf rumbled underneath his skin, eager to get out and do some damage, to protect the creatures who were part of his fae family. But the full moon power was long gone, so Rolf would have to be the one to avenge all of them. He hadn't been able to save the countless lives that he had led into battle decades ago, but he could try his best to save these creatures now.

He turned to the remaining two doors and pushed open the middle one.

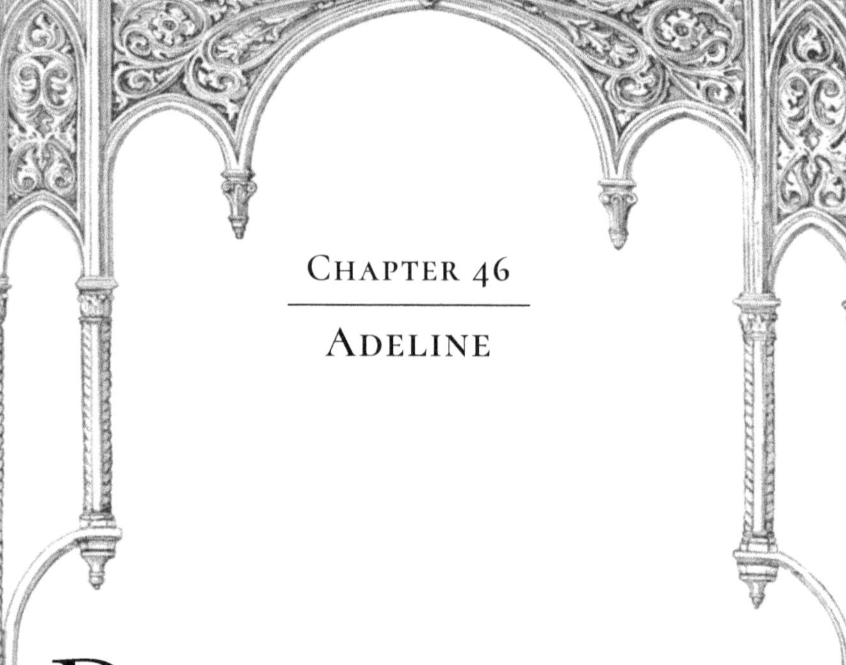

Chapter 46

Adeline

Dozens of vampires swarmed the ballroom, twirling and spinning, their masks glinting under the chandeliers that blazed above. Glamoured fae musicians sat in the corner, their eyes glazed over, staring vacantly as their fingers moved magically along their instruments.

Adeline sat on a throne next to Erik as the guest of honor. She didn't miss the irony that he had chosen these seats tonight and placed them together on a dais, overlooking the crowd below. The arch above looked eerily similar to the standing stones that had been near her home.

The ones she had played beneath as a child. The ones she had used to send Leda to another world.

He's trying to throw you off. It's just an illusion.

Decorations spanned the entire room, and large columns were magicked to look like stones covered in vines. Adeline forced herself to look as the shadows beneath the vines moved, seemingly on their own, stretching and unfurling, completely separate from the illusion magic Erik had placed on the room. She blinked a few times and then looked away.

The layers of the dress swathed her in itchy fabric, and sweat trickled down her back. The mask stuck to her face, and the veil kept her breath hot and trapped beneath the gauze. Her neck had healed after she drank from Rolf, so she had chosen the gaudiest necklace she could find to hide the lack of scarring. It spanned up her neck like a collar and cascaded around her décolletage with a spiderweb array of diamonds and pearls. It matched the detailing on her dress almost perfectly, but now it felt like a heavy hand gripping her throat, trying to strangle the last breath of life from her.

Erik was sending her a particular message about the entire evening. In the past, she would have either fought back or gone along with everything. It all depended on how Erik had treated her upon her return: Was she welcomed, or was she admonished?

But she was in uncharted territory and had no map, save for treasure at the end—the feel of Erik's blood as it splattered on her face.

Don't think about how good it will feel.

Erik could read her like a book, so she shoved everything down. Any emotion, any thought had to be locked away so tightly that he would be unable to read her.

She had decided, while Juliette helped her with getting dressed and the finishing touches, that she would be apathetic to every single thing that happened tonight. If he hit her, she wouldn't react. If he broke her bones, he wouldn't get so much as a peep. In the past, when she had shut down, he would send Campbell into the cell to do his bidding. But that was only after Erik had lost his temper.

Tonight, she would do the same; become numb to whatever he threw at her. Drive him mad. He would make a mistake then, and she could strike.

Erik's nasally voice snapped her back to reality. It had a way of slicing right under her skin.

"Drink," Erik chided, gesturing to the cup in Adeline's hand.

Not this again. She hid her disdain by bringing the cup to her lips, opening them enough to let the tiniest amount in. The sickly sludge coated her mouth as she pretended to drink until Erik grunted with satisfaction.

Her stomach swirled from the sip as the liquid slunk down her throat.

Erik stared at her as if he was unsatisfied with how much she had drunk, so she lifted her cup again and took another sip. And then another. Finally pleased, Erik looked away.

Everything inside her screamed to purge, but the theatrics would only spoil her plans. She glanced at the tall windows to her right, willing her stomach to keep the drink down. The waning moon climbed higher in the night sky, its ascent painfully slow.

Two hours left. She could manage anything for two hours. Rolf still needed time to free the fae servants below.

Outside, a thick layer of fog swirled at the cliff's edge, the sea spray mixing with the cooler air. Large sycamore and elm trees drooped over each other, their branches entwined like craggy limbs. She used to hate how twisted they looked, their sharp bends like a warning for anyone trying to leave. But tonight, they looked like they were reaching for her, trying to draw her out of the infested nest. It almost looked like they were beckoning her home.

How pretty the castle will be from those trees as it goes up in flames, she thought.

Erik kept glancing at her out of the corner of his eye, and it made her want to lunge at his throat and tear him limb from limb. But she couldn't act out of anger. She couldn't let her emotions get the better of her. Because then she would fuck everything up, and Rolf needed time and Erik needed to believe that they were going to mate. Besides, his desire to be the center of attention, to have all the control, to be the most powerful wherever he went, dictated that if he was going to do something, then he would do it here. In front of all of his spawn.

She just needed to last until midnight.

"I've asked Juliette to join us later," Erik said. He watched Adeline closely for a reaction.

He knows. Adeline feigned interest. "Oh?"

"When I requested her presence, she was noticeably distraught."

"Was she?" Adeline looked around the room. *What is he playing at?*

"Yes," Erik said, drawing out the word as he dragged a finger down Adeline's bare arm. She shivered involuntarily but forced herself not to flinch. "What did you say to her, Little Killer?"

What *hadn't* she said? Adeline waved her hand dismissively. "Only the truth about mating between vampires."

Erik stiffened and withdrew his hand.

What does he know that I don't? What she told Juliette

was a lie, a convenient, manipulative lie. She had never found any literature on the subject of vampire mates. In all honesty, for all she knew, vampires could have multiple mates, since the practice was so unheard of. She hated being out of the loop; it made her blood boil.

Blood. Her fangs threatened to come in, and she tongued the sharp ends. Yes, she would relish the way Erik's blood would coat her face as she tore his heart from his chest with her claws.

"Let's dance." Erik's nasally voice cut through her thoughts. He stood and turned to her, holding out his hand. He smiled, and she couldn't help but think how enjoyable it would be to break his teeth.

She kept her voice flat and placed her hand in his. "As you will it."

Impatience rumbled under Adeline's skin as they walked down the red carpet to the center of the ballroom. She stumbled a bit down the stairs, her head slowly starting to pound with a mounting pressure behind her eyes.

A headache? When was the last time she had one of those? She closed her eyes, trying to think of the last time her head felt so affected. Newly minted into the life of a vampire, Adeline had found an injured fae asleep in an alleyway, shivering and close to death, and sank her teeth into its flesh, drinking it dry. The result was several days' worth of illness on her end—a raging headache, an upset stomach, and full-body shivers. When she had asked Erik about it, he told her that perhaps the fae creature had taken some kind of *medicine* that disagreed with her system. The feeling passed less than a week later, but it was the beginning of her realization that she should never drink from fae. Especially without their consent. The effects were too risky.

When she opened her eyes again, the brightness of the room was blinding. She focused on the nearest thing to her, which, unfortunately for her, was Erik. Through her mask, she saw his eyes meet hers, and he flashed her a smug smile; nothing in his expression emanated anything kind. But why would it? He was here for one thing and one thing only.

A chill walked down her spine, its long, cold fingers landing firmly between her shoulder blades. She wondered, briefly, if this is what it felt like moments before her countless victims all met their ends at her hands. Or teeth.

This was a dance to her imminent death.

Not mine, his. His, she reminded herself.

The knife she had slipped into her corset dug into her ribs, a reminder that she wasn't unarmed as Erik's arm wrapped around her waist and pulled her close. His hand tightened on hers, and the chains forced her to keep her left palm plastered on his chest.

If only this were Rolf instead.

Erik's rank breath filled the space between them, reeking of staleness and putrefaction—the skin and blood of his victims left uncleaned between his teeth. She turned her head, trying not to gag at the scent, and stared off into the distance, fighting the sensation of dizziness that threatened to overwhelm her.

"Bored already, Little Killer?" Erik asked. His hand tightened around hers.

Adeline didn't answer for fear the drink had loosened her tongue. Feigning apathy was going to be harder than she thought.

"I have been looking for Campbell all evening," Erik said, his eyes boring a hole into the side of her head. "Funnily enough, he seems to have gone missing."

"That would be because I killed him."

Damnit. The drink *had* loosened her tongue, for that was one secret she shouldn't have revealed.

He said nothing in return. The only way she knew she had caught him off guard was when his fingers spasmed against her hand.

Before she could register whether that was out of shock or annoyance, he spun her around, whipping her about like she was a rag doll. She let him. The chains clinked, and her left hand pulled across her chest awkwardly. His hand tightened around hers so hard she felt some of its bones break. Her hand throbbed, but he didn't let go.

Small price to pay. She could withstand anything tonight, resisting everything until the time was just right.

Her mask slipped a few times with the vigor of his movements. But Erik would adjust it for her, letting his fingers linger along the curve of her earlobe. She had to suppress a full-body shiver each time and refrain from the desire to bite off one of his fingers.

They danced in silence for what felt like hours. So long that her feet started to ache. And then, not only did they ache, but they also started to blister. She paid them no mind because each time they took a turn about the floor, Adeline saw shadows coming to life around her. Tendrils curled toward her across the ballroom floor, trying to grab at the hem of her dress, only to recoil when she focused on them.

Erik twirled her about, spinning her around until the room swirled with her. If he was hoping to shake her up, it would take far more than a few broken bones in her hand, the ache in her feet, and the constant spinning on the dance floor.

The musicians played on. Never stopping. The vampires around them faded into the background. She felt herself slipping into a trance, disconnecting from the stench of Erik's breath, the pain in her broken hand, the blistering of her feet.

"I tire of this," Erik said. He dropped her hand, turned, and headed back up to the dais, leaving her in the middle of the dance floor.

Adeline said nothing. Felt everything. Another vampire in a black mask grabbed her hands and spun her around. Then he passed her to another, and still another, until the room swirled and blurred. Each time she tried to leave the dance floor, another vampire would swoop in and spin her.

The musicians played on. Her shoes began to fill with blood as the blisters rubbed off and the sensitive skin underneath split open.

Vampires swirled around her. Dizziness threatened to consume her, so she tilted her head back, focusing on the chandeliers. Candlelight flickered above her, and strange shadows crawled along the rafters like vines. Their long fingers stretched down, trying to reach her, and she wasn't entirely convinced this wasn't another illusion from Erik.

He had always been powerful, but if he was able to illusion the castle *and* get the shadows to move like this, what else was he capable of? No vampire she knew had magic this expansive, this powerful.

Finally, the music slowed, and Erik clapped his hands. The vampires all followed suit, their monotonous clapping filling the room with thunderous applause. She took that break as her chance to finally slip away. With a deep inhale, she steeled herself against the searing pain in her feet, grabbed her skirts, and headed over to the table of food by the tall windows. Carafes of red liquid were surrounded by dozens upon dozens of fresh pastries. Stacks of plates sat at the far end, as if Erik wanted to pretend everyone here was still human, but they were left untouched.

She thought it odd that the other vampires never enjoyed eating the food of humans after they had been turned. Sure, blood was the only thing that sustained them, but Adeline still delighted in the occasional dessert. Who wouldn't, when they were filled with rich cream and sugared berries, and dusted with powdered sugar—all decadent things she'd never had as a girl.

Erik demanded fresh food to be put on display every day. But no one would eat it, and it would be sent below. Oftentimes, it would be stale and moldy by the time it reached the enslaved fae servants. It disgusted her, and it was one of the many reasons she hated living in this place when she was done with her assignments.

She opened her mouth to take a bite out of a pastry when, out of the corner of her eye, she saw a blond blur push through the crowd on the dance floor. Adeline pivoted slightly, the pastry forgotten in her hand. Her feet screamed when she shifted her weight, trying to watch sidelong as Juliette rushed up to Erik.

Erik's face fell when Juliette bent down and whispered something in his ear. A mask of calm lethality replaced his mask of mild indifference. His eyes scanned the crowd, and before he could meet her gaze, Adeline turned back to the table.

He knows.

Every part of her screamed to kill him now. Be done with it. Slash his throat. Feel his blood on her face as she ripped him to shreds. She braced her hands against the boning of her corset. The knife was still there. It would be easy for her to slide it out from between her breasts once she got Erik alone. She still had enough strength left from drinking Rolf's blood—it would last her well into the early morning hours. But her heart raced, and she realized at that moment that she was terrified. The stakes were so high tonight, and what would happen should she fail? Who would suffer this time?

These were questions she wasn't used to answering. Even when she was killing the were-shifters, trying to free herself from Erik's iron-fisted grip, she never once considered the ramifications of her kills.

But now? Something had changed her.

Not something, but some*one.*

Rolf.

Acting impulsively wouldn't only affect *her* if she failed this time. No, it would be the servants and Rolf. Even Juliette—as much as she didn't want to believe her ex-lover had ill intentions, she still would never be able to reconcile with her conscience should she leave Juliette in Erik's clutches, again. They were all at risk should she act out of turn. She couldn't risk any of that. And if she failed, she would never be free again—that she knew for a fact. She *had* to be successful tonight, she had to time things perfectly. Because if she were unsuccessful in killing Erik, he would, in turn, kill anyone who tried to help her. Then he would lock Adeline up and torture her for the rest of her eternal life.

Shadows swirled around her ankles, caressing her skin as they slid toward the table. Where did they come from? She blinked a few times, trying to clear her vision, but each time she did, the table changed from being laden with pastries to holding dismembered and discolored body parts. She blinked a few more times before realizing she was witnessing one of Erik's illusions. Which one was real? The body parts or the pastries?

The shadows crept up the table, covering the pastries, and when they did, it was like the fabric of the world came undone beneath her. She reached her hand forward, grabbed the pastry she had picked up earlier, and passed it underneath one of the shadowy vines. As she did so, the pastry in the shadows turned into the rotting big toe of some fae creature. On the other side of the shadow, it returned to a pastry, but Adeline's hand remained the same—whether she was passing through the shadow vine or not.

Her stomach lurched.

No wonder no one else is eating...

Disgust filled her bones, and she gathered up her skirts, determined to finally end Erik's sick sense of control now. He was a disease that needed to be stamped out before his power got stronger, and Adeline would rather go down fighting to get free than see him get stronger. She took a deep breath and turned back to face the dance floor. She had to find Erik before the feeding she had from Rolf wore off. Already, she could feel the sludgy drink in her stomach trying to flood out what was left of her mate's blood. But when she spun to face the dais where Erik had been, everything looked different.

The dais was gone, and so were the thrones. The ballroom was devoid of wedding decorations. The vampires, still masked and dancing, didn't seem to notice that the chandeliers hung lower, or the columns that had been standing stones were now back to their original façade of gold-veined marble. She took a step forward, eager to find her maker in the sea of dancing bodies and plunge a knife into his heart.

A hand clamped down on her shoulder, claws digging into the delicate skin at her shoulder. Hot breath brushed against her neck. "Where do you think you're going?"

Chapter 47

Rolf

Rolf's mouth dropped open, and he had to bite back the bile that crept up his throat. He clutched Arlo to him, but even that couldn't stop the shaking that wracked his entire body at what he saw.

Two tables sat in the center of the room, and thick leather straps held two emaciated fae creatures onto them. The lower half of the table was elevated so their feet were slightly higher than their heads, and their arms were stretched out above them, a slow stream of blood dripping from their wrists into buckets on the floor.

Rolf's heart lurched. He set Arlo down in the only clean corner.

And then he walked over to one of the buckets and vomited.

What he witnessed was nothing he had ever thought possible.

The fae moaned, both of them twitching in agony. One was a small shifter fae, but what kind, Rolf couldn't tell.

He assumed maybe some sort of forest creature, but she was so far gone that she was merely skin and bones now. The other fae was a gnome, built for running through the forest and caring for the wild creatures who roamed in sacred groves. He had never seen a gnome out in the wild, but he knew they existed.

Forest protectors, his wolf said.

How do you know? Rolf asked, but was met with silence. *Fine, be ornery. But at least let me know how much time we have.*

His wolf snorted. *We have time.*

His mind raced. He had to get these fae out of here. They were too close to death to move on their own, though. And if they were all caught in here? It would be a slow, painful death for all of them. There was a door on the other side of the room, and he needed to secure it before he tried to get them upright. But there was nothing besides the tables and the buckets.

These fae were so weak, and he had no idea how long they had been left here to drain. As he leaned over the first one, her eyes focused briefly enough to show shock at who stood above them.

"You're going to be okay," Rolf whispered, brushing some stringy hair from her face.

The fae shook her head and tried to speak, but all that came out was a rasp. Rolf looked around for water but could find nothing.

"Please," she croaked. "Save him. Let me go."

She no more deserved her fate than the dwarves in the adjacent room had. He reached for her hand. She could barely grab onto him, her arm shaking with effort.

She met his gaze, her eyes pleading for mercy, for release. And it was the only permission Rolf needed. In one motion, he snapped the fae's neck.

He swiped his fingers over her lids, closing them so it looked like she rested peacefully. He only hoped in that final moment he had been able to bring her some peace. No fae deserved to be treated as such. No creature should be drained slowly, over and over, for the amusement and nourishment of those in power.

He walked over to the gnome, who was shaking from shock.

Rolf spoke in a soothing tone, "I'm here to help. It's okay. I'm like you."

The gnome's eyes shut tightly, and he whimpered.

"I promise, I am going to get you and everyone else out of here." He was surprised at the determination in his voice. It was clear that these helpless creatures were not equipped to go up against the vampires. They needed his help, but how many more were imprisoned, being drained for their blood?

The leather straps were easy enough to undo, their buckles coming undone within seconds. Gingerly, he helped the gnome sit up. The cuts on his wrist weren't too deep, which meant that he would heal soon. Rolf looked around for something to bind the wounds, but the room was sparse.

They would have to leave anyway, but going back through that other door was not an option.

Rolf lifted the tiny creature in his arms, undoing the buttons of his servant's coat, and tucked the gnome inside. He clung tightly to Rolf's shirt, and his cold body soon warmed and went lax. Rolf looked down and was relieved to see that the gnome appeared to be sleeping; he held his hand underneath the tiny fae's body to keep him from slipping out. Then he walked over to Arlo, whose wide eyes told Rolf that he had seen everything, and picked him up, too.

Rolf crept to the main door and pressed his ear to the crack—no sounds emanated from beyond it, so he turned the handle slowly. Through the crack, he could make out a dimly lit hallway; the dampness of the sea seeped up from the floor. He pressed his body against the wall and opened the door fully.

Beyond, in the dimly lit hallway, were doors that looked familiar. He had, unknowingly, entered the servants' quarters from before. Each door was padlocked, save for the one where the deceased woodland fae had been housed.

His shoulders sagged with relief. But it was fleeting because within seconds of closing the door behind him, voices echoed from beyond the door he had hidden behind when he first arrived.

His wolf growled, *We have company.*

"Fuck," Rolf exhaled.

He scanned the doors until he found the woodland fae's room. The padlock hung on a hook by the handle. The keys were still in Rolf's pocket. He took a step forward.

"No," Arlo whispered, his grip tightening on Rolf's shirt. "Don't leave us here."

"I have to. If we have any chance of getting out of here alive..." Rolf hesitated, unsure if he should finish what he was going to say. He knew what he was about to attempt would be ludicrous and might even backfire. But his wolf was itching under his skin, and he had to warn Arlo of the danger. “Do not, for any reason, open this door until you hear *my* voice.”

The voices down the hall grew louder. Rolf slipped inside the room. He set down Arlo on the driest part of the floor and placed the sleeping gnome on his lap. Arlo stroked the gnome’s back absently, and the tiny body unfurled slightly. Rolf grabbed the keys and placed them in Arlo’s free hand.

“I do not need these,” Arlo said, his foggy eyes flitting back and forth as if trying to focus on something unseen. “My magic is returning. So, too, should my eyesight. I will be able to open any warded locks within these walls.”

“Good. You are surrounded by glamoured fae. Fae who need to get out.” Rolf ran his hand through his hair. He had planned on freeing all of them, but should he not return, the dwarf would need to find his way out.

Arlo dipped his chin but said nothing in response, just held the keys out for Rolf, who took them and placed them in his pocket.

He grabbed the dwarf’s hand one last time and added, “I’ll be back. But if I’m not, and if your eyesight does not return, follow the wall on your right, out of this hall. Several yards down, there is a stairwell. It will lead you through two rooms to a door that will lead to a tunnel to the cliff’s edge. When you are well—”

Quiet, his wolf snapped. Rolf snapped his mouth shut.

A few pairs of footsteps padded down the hallway. A door opened and shut. The hallway went quiet once more.

Rolf released a breath. “Should I not return, find the

doorway. The tunnel is stone and leads to the outside cliff."

Rolf debated sharing more about his plans, but the fewer who knew, the better. Instead, he punctuated each sentence by squeezing the blind dwarf's hand as he said, "Stairwell on the right. Go through two rooms. Then the door to the tunnel outside."

"All will be well, pup," Arlo said.

For a moment, Rolf thought the dwarf was going to prophesize like his elder had, but then the silence stretched on. So he dropped the dwarf's hand, hesitating a moment before standing. Was he doing the right thing? He hoped that both the dwarf and the gnome would heal quickly and get out. But without knowing what they needed to heal, he felt hopeless that would be the case.

Rolf kept to the shadows and peeked through the crack in the door.

The servants' quarters were empty, so he pushed the door open as quietly as he could.

Juliette stood in the hallway, watching him emerge from the cell. She looked vicious, staring him down with disdain in her eyes. There was fresh blood spatter on her face, and some had even made it onto her clothes. Her arms were crossed, and she tapped the fingers on her hand against her forearm.

His hackles rose, and the hair on his neck stood on end.

"I know what you did," she said, her voice unreadable.

"Which part?" Rolf almost laughed but decided against provoking her if he didn't have to.

"The dwarves. The fae changeling."

Rolf nodded, but said nothing.

They waited, standing there sizing each other up, when Juliette took a step forward. Rolf held his ground again, refusing to show her any weakness.

"I didn't know he had been draining the fae." Her voice wavered.

Was she going to cry?

Doubtful. Rolf's wolf snorted and paced in his chest. His skin tingled. His teeth ached with how badly he wanted to snap her neck from her body.

Rolf still said nothing in reply.

Juliette stepped forward again, her words frantic. "Tell me what you need me to do to get them free. We have limited time, and Adeline said—"

"Adeline, huh?" Rolf stepped closer. He doubted very much, that was the case. Adeline had sent him the feeling of distrust after he had parted ways with Juliette in the hallway earlier in the evening.

Juliette nodded. "Adeline gave me instructions to find you and do whatever it took to get you and the fae free. She's going to marry Erik to give you all time to get away and—"

He stepped closer still, subtly sniffing the air between them, picking up on hints of excrement from the cells and the vampire blood on Juliette's face. But nothing of the scent Juliette had when he first identified her.

Interesting.

"Whose blood is on your person? It is vampiric in origin."

"One of the guards." She waved her hand dismissively.

Liar.

"The guards?" he asked. Everything she said was tainted with lies so transparent that he would be able to tell she was lying with his eyes closed. None of this made any sense. Adeline hadn't even shared that many details with *him,* and they were bonded. So why would she share her plans with Juliette?

Juliette kept talking, but Rolf had completely tuned her out. The one thing he didn't understand was how Juliette could lose her scent. All the creatures had such a distinct scent, and the disappearance of Juliette's could only mean one thing.

Rolf leaned against the wall, his head close to a sconce holding a torch. "Tell me, Juliette. In the cabin, what was the first thing you smelled?"

Juliette's mouth snapped shut. "You."

"It wasn't blood?" Because there had been, purposefully, so much blood splattered around his home.

Juliette blanched.

"As I thought," Rolf said and grabbed the torch from the wall. He swung it wildly in the air before him, the flames catching on some of Juliette's clothing, and she shrieked as the blazing cloth singed her skin. He lunged, tackling the burning vampire. The image of Juliette shattered as he knocked her to the ground. In her place was another vampire, their eyes blown wide and bloodshot, neck lined with bite marks, thin black hair plastered to their face. They gnashed their jaw, but they had no fangs. Instead, their gums were bloody, as if someone had pulled their teeth out.

The vampire snapped at the air between them, desperate to feed from him.

"Warm blood," they growled, thrashing against his hold. But they were too weak and easy for Rolf to keep at bay. "I *need* it."

"Not today, I'm afraid," Rolf said and palmed a knife. He drove it straight into the thing's eye socket and twisted. The vampire convulsed but still fought, their fingers desperate to grab hold of him. Rolf withdrew the knife and, in one swift motion, jammed it into their neck and pulled, ripping their throat out. The vampire gargled, choking on their blood.

Rolf stood and watched as the life quickly drained from the vampire. Then he picked up the torch and lit the body on fire. With their throat torn out, their screams were muffled blabbers, and their hands tried desperately to staunch the flow of blood. Until, finally, the fire consumed the vampire and turned it into ash.

He swiped at his sweaty forehead with the back of his hand and gripped the flaming torch harder. The vampire had been illusioned to look and sound like Juliette. If it hadn't been for his keen sense of smell, would he have even noticed the change?

Probably not, his wolf snorted.

Thank you for the help, Rolf bit back.

It was my *nose that noticed,* his wolf sneered.

Well, let's hope you help in more than one way next time, Rolf said and shut his wolf down.

He would need all the weapons he could get if any more illusions came his way.

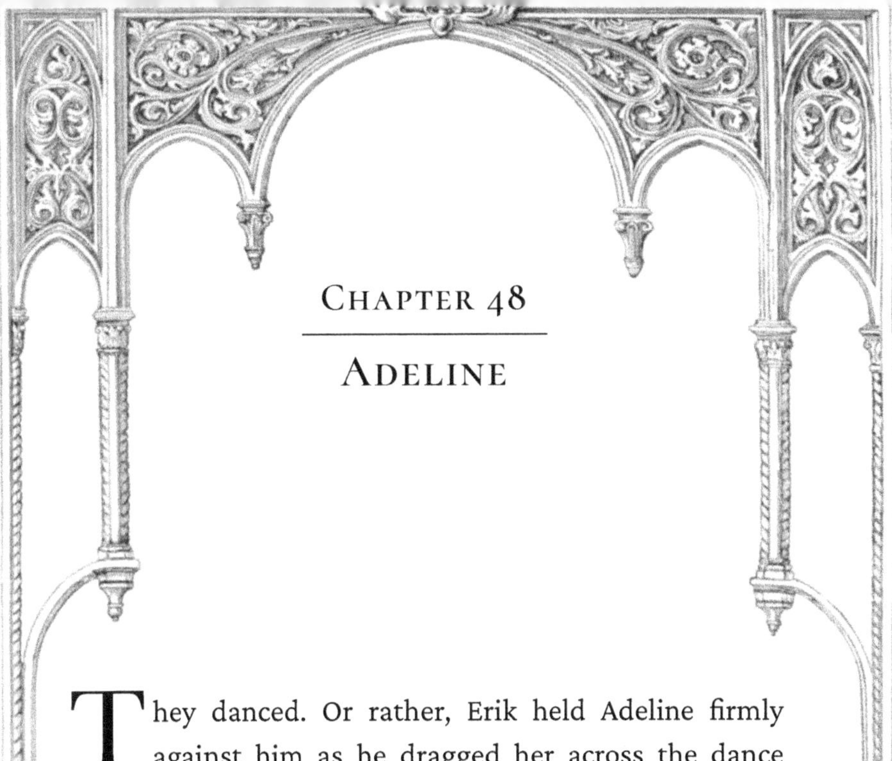

Chapter 48

Adeline

They danced. Or rather, Erik held Adeline firmly against him as he dragged her across the dance floor. Her feet were leaden, not quite healed from the spinning earlier, so she let him pull her around while she thought about how to get out of this and what the fuck Erik had up his sleeve. There was nothing delicate about the way he held her, either. His hand grasped her lower back, but he dug his fingers and claws into her side. She was grateful for the protection her corset provided; otherwise, she was sure his claws would have punctured her skin.

Erik spun her around and around. The music picked up the tempo, and so did their movements. The room spun with them, and soon she was too dizzy to make out who surrounded them.

The sludge she drank earlier swirled in her stomach, too, and it took everything she had to keep herself lucid.

"Adeline, keep up." Erik's voice was full of disdain.

She said nothing back. He continued to berate her over and over, and soon, she found herself agreeing with his words.

"I have always been so disappointed in you, Adeline. Time and again, you have let me down. Do you know how sad it makes me when you refuse to live up to your full potential? You have never let me drop your hand in this lifetime," Erik drawled. "Always needing me to hold you up, support you, take care of you. It displeases me that you have never been a true creature of the night."

A creature of the night. Those words were so familiar.

Erik whirled her again, and her shoes filled up with more blood. She stumbled a little, and Erik dropped his hands, throwing her out into a spin with disgust.

"Pathetic," he said before he pulled her back in. "If you had shown even an ounce of resolve, you could have been my queen. But now?"

She swayed loosely in his arms. *I would have been a queen.*

But once upon a time, when she was still a human, she had forsaken that decision. She had chosen to ride her horse back home to her mother and sister and forsake her life as a royal. It was a decision she never regretted. And she would make that choice again, without hesitation. She only wished that she could be back there, with Leda, listening to their mother's stories.

As Erik spun her, the room blurred, and the pain in her feet became unbearable, so she let her conscious mind go. And then it hit her: there was a memory lodged deep within her, one that she had kept hidden for so long, one that she finally released.

"Once upon a time, there was a lonely princess." Her mother's patient voice filled the quiet room. The scent of drying herbs and boiling dandelion tea floated in the air.

"Mama, I have heard this one already," Adeline whined. Leda nodded her head in agreement.

"Not like this, so listen," Aurélie said, staring into Adeline's eyes with a ferocity she had never seen before. Adeline sat up straighter but still doubted this story would be different from the other fairy stories her mother had told. Once the two girls were settled, Aurélie began again. "Once upon a time, there was a lonely princess. She wasn't just a princess but also a creature of the night. She could hold the darkness in one hand and the light in the other. Where she walked—"

"How is that even possible, Mama?" Adeline asked.

"Because it's a story, *Adeline," Leda said, gripping her rag doll tightly to her chest. Leda loved these stories and devoured them each time their mother told them.*

Aurélie nodded. "This lonely princess had the power of both light and dark. But she was forced to walk where the darkness would follow. Cursed to walk the earth alone, she was a creature caught in the twilight of the world between worlds. Until she met someone who was both the light and the dark, as well. She met the Moon."

"But the moon is in the night sky," Leda said.

Aurélie sipped the tea, her blue eyes flitting between both girls. She waited patiently until finally, Adeline spoke.

"The moon shines in the night sky, so it must be of both the light and the dark." Adeline looked at her mother expectantly.

Aurélie smiled and said—

"Adeline?" Rolf asked, his strong arms wrapping around her. He held her still in the center of the ballroom.

She shook her head, reality slowly filtering through the fading memory.

A creature of the light and dark.

Her moon was here. With her. Relief filled her body. Maybe it had all been a horrible nightmare after all. She tilted her chin to take him in, reaching up to remove his mask. But before she could, he turned his head and kissed the inside of her palm.

She sighed.

Rolf's amber eyes stripped her bare despite the layers she wore. She was exposed to him to do whatever he wanted to her. And she wanted him to do whatever he wanted to her, just like back in her bed.

She looked around then, trying to find a place for them to go. Somewhere discreet. Somewhere, Erik wouldn't find them. But the ballroom was empty. The lights were still low, but the vampires were gone, and the musicians were gone, their instruments resting on their chairs. Only a solitary chandelier cast light—the rest of the room was full of shadows.

She grabbed his hand and led him into a dark alcove.

"Rolf." She beckoned him into the shadows of the ballroom. She didn't care who looked; she just wanted to be with him again. And here he was, in all of his wild glory.

He followed her diligently and then, at the last minute, spun her around, pinning her against a column. Anticipation and desire wrapped around her, tightening inside her chest. His arms framed her in, and his broad shoulders filled her vision. He leaned down to kiss her.

His lips tasted like wine and something else sweet, and his tongue tentatively explored the seal of her lips, teasing her mouth open. He held her tight, half supporting her in his strong arms, which was a relief since her feet hurt for some strange reason, and she didn't want to put all of her weight on them. The soles of her shoes felt wet, as if she had stepped in a puddle.

"I crave you, Adeline," Rolf slurred into her mouth. Or maybe it was her head swimming with delirium that made everything sound mushed together.

"You crave me?" Adeline whispered as he planted sloppy kisses on her jaw.

"I do, I always have," Rolf said. He held up a key and slipped it into the lock on her cuff.

The chains fell away and she gasped. She was finally free! Her hands moved without restriction, and it felt so good that she wrapped her arms around his neck and pulled him close again. He pressed his nose to the side of her head. She melted against his wide chest.

"You smell like him," Rolf growled.

"Smell like who?"

"Your *maker*," Rolf practically spat. He consumed her exposed skin with his mouth like a man starved, and she felt her entire body melt into the support behind her. Her legs grew weak, her stomach tightened with anticipation. She didn't care if anyone else was around; she needed him like she needed air. He started untying the ribbons that kept her dressed.

"What is this?" He hissed, pulling away his hands with a grimace.

Her head swam with desire, but she blinked and focused on his fingertips, which looked burned. "I don't understand?"

"No matter," he growled and leaned forward. "I need you."

His lips trailed up her neck, and she heard the laces being sliced. The ties fell away as Rolf let the outer garments slide into a puddle at her feet. She stepped out of them willingly. Then he bent down on his knees and untied her shoes. They made a suctioning sound as he pulled them off carefully. His hands trailed up her legs to her upper thighs, his fingertips grazing her hot center. She moaned loudly as he grabbed the tops of her stockings and unrolled them, peeling them off her wet feet.

Then he stood and stared at her. His eyes raked over her chest as it rose and fell with labored breath. She was flushed, and the look in his eyes told her he knew that she wanted him. They crashed together again, lips meeting lips as her hands wove into his hair and his fingers undid the laces of her corset.

"No," Adeline panted. "Leave it."

Why can't he undo my corset? She knew there was a reason, but she had forgotten what it was.

His hands stilled, but he had loosened the corset enough that an object slipped through. Something clattered to the ground between them, but before she had a chance to look, he grabbed her chin and devoured her once more. Their teeth knocked together, and Adeline slipped her tongue inside Rolf's mouth, playing with him, teasing him.

But then her tongue grazed something sharp. She pulled away.

"What—" She couldn't finish her question because Rolf ripped the necklace from her throat.

"No scar," Rolf said, almost in awe. "How is that possible? Unless...?"

Her head swam, but she reached up to her neck and tried to trace where Juliette's knife had sliced her open. It wasn't there because of Rolf.

But Rolf had seen her neck heal with his own eyes.

He would know she had no scar.

"I need more, Rolf," Adeline said. "I fear I am still not well."

"Take it," he said, his voice low and sincere. He held open his collar with his right hand.

Adeline blinked a few times, but the spiderweb scar wasn't there. She frowned but leaned in, her fangs elongating as she opened her mouth and pressed against his skin.

But she couldn't bite. The lack of scarring tickled something in the back of her head.

She pulled back.

"Take what you need, Adeline," Rolf said.

"I—can't," she replied.

"Can't? Or won't?" And before she could answer, Rolf had her pinned against the column again. One of his hands held her up by the throat and the other held her shoulder down. "Then I will."

She thrashed against his hold, squeezing her eyes shut, knowing deep down that something wasn't right.

Adeline had shared more with Rolf than she had with anyone for hundreds of years. He was like a hammer—all it took was a simple tap from him for the outer shells of her protective barrier to shatter into a million pieces. Fate had led her to his doorstep, even in whiteout conditions.

Her soul had known she was safe with him from the moment she opened his door. Her heart had called out to his for a hundred years, if not more, and finally, they were together. And nothing would take that away from her.

We are mates.

The blurriness cleared for a moment as a voice screamed inside her head: *Rolf wouldn't do this!*

Her eyes flew open.

He wouldn't, because he wasn't Rolf. Not-Rolf's hand tightened on her neck and her claws grew to sharp points. She scratched and clawed and kicked, but he held on tight. He shook her and growled, her head tossing from side to side. He opened his mouth, fangs sharpened to a fine point, and time slowed as he leaned forward to bite her neck.

This isn't how I die. Not tonight. Not ever.

Adeline held her breath, but the bite never came. She watched, in awe, as thick, shadowy vines laced with thorns writhed and climbed down from the ceiling and up from the floor. A humming filled her head. Her chest tightened. Her fingers tingled. It felt like a hundred years of pain vibrated through her.

I can hold the darkness in one hand and light in the other.

Summoning the last of the strength she could find, she wrapped her left hand in Not-Rolf's hair and yanked his head back. He screamed as shadowy tendrils snatched him backward. Free from his grip, Adeline slid to the floor, her bloody feet unable to hold her upright.

Chapter 49

Rolf

Rolf ran through the castle, armed to the teeth with knives he had stolen from the kitchens. He was going to find that bitch of a vampire if it was the last thing he did. But she was nowhere to be found. And neither, it would seem, were all of the other vampires.

Odd.

Fear pulsed through him the closer he got to the main floors, and he tried his best to shut it down—there was no use worrying about Adeline if he couldn't even finish his part of their plan.

But still...

He couldn't help but worry that he wasn't there to help her, that she was in really big trouble, especially since he couldn't feel anything through their bond. And that made him stop.

Don't worry, I'm here, his wolf snorted.

Oh, thank the gods, he said back. *Not an illusion.*

No, but we don't have time for this.

Too right, he said and continued up a stairwell. Rolf pushed open a small door midway up that opened onto a main hallway. The sound of music filtered down from a large pair of closed doors at the end.

Don't! His wolf shouted, but before he could stop himself, he stepped into the hallway. Too late, he saw the dozens of vampires lurking in the shadowy recesses.

"Fuck," he sighed and palmed two knives.

Slowly the vampires slid from their hiding places. A blond vampire stood at the far end, near the doors where the music came from.

"Don't let him in!" Juliette shouted, and then it was chaos.

Rolf felt fierce pressure in his chest; he vibrated with an intensity he hadn't felt during any shift. His wolf roared in his ears. His hands turned into claws.

The vampires swarmed around him even as he shifted into his wolf form.

Thick fur, sharp teeth, deadly claws, his movements became mechanical—swipe, gnash, roar, twist, leap, swipe, gnash, roar. One by one, the closest vampires fell, their heads separated from their bodies, their mouths locked in eternal shock.

He was blinded with rage and the desire to decimate the creatures who held his mate captive. But soon, he was surrounded; the vampires pressed closer, and his range of motion became smaller. A vampire sliced into his haunches, and he let out a ferocious roar. He whipped around and snapped the vampire's head off, bones crunching in his jaw.

Something flashed in his peripheral vision, and he

spun around. Was he going to get stabbed again? Two blades sliced through the crowd, and fountains of vampire blood shot into the sky. For a moment he thought it was his mate, but her scent didn't fill the room.

Rolf's wolf still swiped and gnashed, keeping a perimeter where the vampires dared not get close. But they crowded around him from a distance and backed him into a corner. He limped backward, his right flank bleeding from the stab wound, until his paws touched something metal.

A cage! he screamed at his wolf, but his animal was so distressed that he didn't hear and kept backing up.

A scream echoed down the hallway, the piercing, guttural noise cutting above the crowd. Rolf growled. The vampires paused briefly. The echo faded and soon, the scream was forgotten and the vampires pressed forward again.

There was another glint of metal, then more blood spurted, and a head launched into the crowd. A few vampires turned away from Rolf, trying to see what was happening to their brethren, when Rolf saw Juliette. Her face was drenched in blood, but she wore a snarl as she sliced and sliced and sliced her way through the vampires.

"Come on, wolf!" she yelled, panting only slightly when her blade met resistance. She yanked backward and withdrew her sword from the neck of a vampire. Blood sprayed across her face. "Kill them!"

His wolf hesitated. Was she tricking them? But then she sliced into another vampire, and Rolf urged him to move, begged him to get free of the cage. His wolf leaned back on his hind legs and with one giant push, he launched into the air, landing on the other side of the vampires, right next to Juliette.

Together, they fought side by side, until the hallway was covered in vampire blood and bodies.

His wolf panted. Juliette wiped some of the blood from her face. Her eyes were hard, her face set in a sneer as she looked over the vampires she had killed.

She began to speak, but he growled. He didn't want to hear her excuses. Her reasons. Sure, he should give her the chance to say her piece, but why? He got stabbed. Adeline was still in Erik's presence. The fae downstairs were all still glamoured.

"Listen," she started, trying to put a hand on his fur.

He snarled and backed away.

Juliette held up her hands. "I know what this looks like."

He huffed hot air in her face. She didn't blink.

"Just let me speak," Juliette whispered. "It will make sense. I promise."

He bared his teeth and walked a limping circle around her, but didn't snarl again. The fae in this place were still glamoured and he needed to get them out. Time was short, even shorter now that he had been ambushed, so he would give her a few seconds to make her case, but then her head would be in his mouth if he wasn't satisfied.

"Erik had this planned. I had to tell him everything I knew. Which"—Juliette shrugged—"wasn't much. But now he plans to drink from Adeline and absorb her power by forcing her to mate and if I had to venture a guess..."

He snapped at the air between them so she'd hurry up.

"I think you two are already mated, yes?"

That stopped him. He tilted his head and stared at her, the question hanging in the air between them.

How does she know?

"It isn't the full moon, and yet here you are in a shifted wolf form." Juliette arched an eyebrow. "And if that's right, then Adeline is a dead woman once Erik finds out."

Another guttural scream ripped through the air, shattering the silence around them. Juliette's eyes flashed to Rolf's.

"Go," she said, gesturing to the doors at the end of the hallway.

But he was already leaping over dead and dismembered vampires and throwing himself against the barricaded doors.

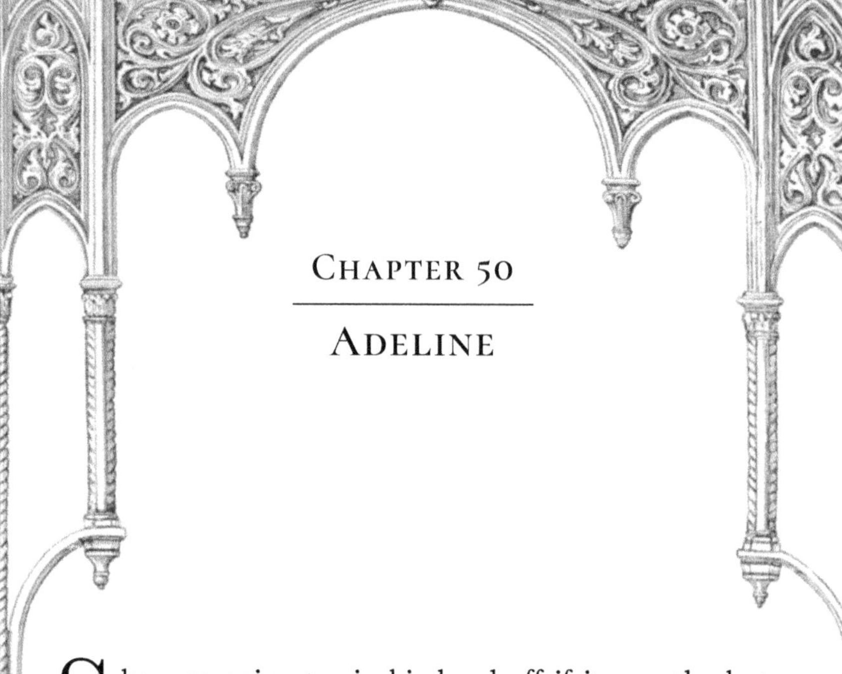

Chapter 50

Adeline

She was going to rip his head off if it was the last thing she did.

Her shadow magic had torn Erik from her and whipped him across the room, the vines slamming him into the opposite wall. She stared, surprised and delighted that shadows swirled around her, trailed from her hands, swarmed her feet. The vines wrapped around Erik, holding his arms out at his sides. His head was concussed, and blood dripped from a split above his ear.

The vines around her hands were softer and thinner, and she held them up, turning her palms outward. The vines that held Erik twisted with her movements.

Interesting.

She tightened her grip and yanked with her right hand. Erik screamed again as one of his arms tore off. Blood spurted from his torso and she smiled, watching it paint the floor red. His eyes watched her wildly, an emotion in them she had never seen there before.

Fear. She reveled in it, looking at him with a wide smile. Then she pushed herself to stand and limped across the room. With a twist of her fingers, the vines tightened on his other arm. The illusions he had placed on the room dwindled, reality setting in. The walls were covered in mold, there were no candles, and the gilded details were dulled and chipping.

He screamed, "Wait, wait! I'll do whatever you want!"

"Oh, dear sire," Adeline crooned. "I think it is far too late for that, don't you?"

Her breathing was labored, sweat lined her brow, and her hands shook. But when she twisted her left hand, the vines dissipated. The power rushed out of her with a *whoosh.*

No, no, no, no, no. Adeline's heart dropped as Erik slid to the ground. She held her hands out, trying to call to the shadows, begging for their help. But nothing came. Exhaustion threatened to swallow her whole, and she knew that if she was going to kill Erik now, she had to do it without the use of her magic. His wound was slowly stitching together, staunching the flow of blood. She had known that his magic was strong, that his ability to heal was faster than hers, but she had never seen him get critically injured before.

His feet landed in the pool of his blood, and he stared at her as if he had just discovered the biggest treasure in the entire world.

"Adeline, my little killer," he said, reaching toward her with his only hand. "Come. Come with me. Help me. We could rule the world together."

Adeline backed away. She flicked a hand out to her side. Nothing happened.

Fuck. She was royally fucked.

Erik kept advancing, his eyes blown wide. "Adeline, Adeline. Listen to me. Your power is unique. I have never, in all of my life, in all of these worlds, seen a power like yours."

Worlds? What did he mean, worlds?

Fear clenched her throat closed. She had been scared before, but she had never felt fear quite like this. Her feet tangled in her skirts and she tripped, her back slamming into the column. She threw her hand out to catch herself, her palm landing near a hard object.

The knife! Now she remembered. Her corset had been loosened by *Erik*—not Rolf—and the knife had slipped out and landed between them. It was sheer luck that Erik had been so possessed by the desire to claim her that it hadn't been discovered yet.

She palmed it quickly, hiding her hands in the folds of her discarded gown. Erik neared; his arm was still outstretched toward her. The closer he got, the less he looked like a man. His eyes had turned red, his black hair was dull and scraggly, as if losing that much blood had sucked the literal life out of him. It struck Adeline as odd, that he should look this ill despite his ability to heal so quickly.

He looks like a victim of the blight.

It had been centuries, but she would know that look of death anywhere.

"How?" she heard herself say.

"How?" Erik asked back, almost mocking. He stopped

walking toward her and then cackled. "In the simplest way possible."

"You survived the sickness," she said, still trying to wrap her head around the fact.

Erik smiled down at her. "Yes, my little killer. I did. You see, I wasn't born in your world. I followed someone here. She slipped from my grasp and leaped into this place." He gestured wildly with his only arm. "It took me years to figure out how she did it, and only then did it require a massive sacrifice."

"A sacrifice," Adeline repeated, almost numb to the realizations she kept having. It was as if she could see clearly for the first time, or maybe it was because the illusions Erik had woven around himself for centuries had finally ceased to work, but Adeline remembered where she had seen his face before.

The man at the door. The one who promised money for my sister's life.

Her blood ran cold. This was the one her mother had warned her about.

The Ominous One. She had been one of his victims after all.

"Yes, as always with magic, a sacrifice is needed. So tell me, Adeline, who did you sacrifice to get your magic?"

A blood sacrifice. She had sacrificed a lot when she sent Leda through the rip in the world. Her mother, Aurélie, and her own life. Two lives for one. She had always felt it was a justifiable payment. Leda, after all, was the one who deserved to live. Her head spun. She tightened her grip on the knife's handle and slowly adjusted herself to sitting, slipping the knife behind her.

Erik looked out over the room. Adeline didn't dare follow his gaze; she kept her focus solely on her maker. She didn't need to look around to know that the illusions he had once placed on the room were gone, and she wondered if the rest of the castle was also falling prey to Erik's weakening magic.

He's weak, you numpty! Get up and finish the job!

"My sacrifice?" Adeline asked again. This time, she stood. Her feet were tender but she didn't care. She leaned against the column seductively, the knife still in her hand behind her back. "I don't know what you mean."

Erik's eyes flitted to her chest but settled, finally, on her neck. "Where is your scar?"

She tilted her head, angling it enough to draw him even closer to inspect her neck. "I sacrificed my own life, as well as that of my mother's."

"Your scar is gone, little killer." Erik reached up, his finger hovering above her collarbone.

"Call me your little killer one more time," she growled and grabbed his arm, pulling him in close. He gurgled with shock as she plunged her knife into his neck and yanked, tearing a slice down his chin to his collarbone.

Could have been cleaner, damnit! But this would have to do.

Blood seeped from the wound, thick and black like tar. She recoiled in horror and gasped when his hand clasped her left arm. His claws grew rapidly, sinking into her flesh. She stifled a scream, unwilling to give him the satisfaction of hearing her in pain.

His eyes glowed red, and he sank his teeth into her shoulder. He drank deeply from her as she tried to shake him off. She jerked backward, and he finally let go. "So powerful."

"Not. Yours. To have," she said through gritted teeth, trying to shove him back, but he held her fast.

"Stubborn *and* powerful," he sneered. "Just like your mother."

"Don't speak of my mother. She is dead," Adeline said, and ripped the knife out of his throat. She shoved him back with all of her might. "No thanks to you."

Erik's claws shredded her left arm, and she cried out. He stumbled backward and fell into the cold pool of his spilled blood. He landed with a grunt and struggled to right himself as his throat bled. "You could be so much more. Your mother was so powerful. You are a De la Fôret. I only wanted—"

With a bloodcurdling scream, Adeline cut off his words. If she let him talk, she was convinced that he'd talk her out of killing him, that it was a bad idea. She dove after her maker, pinning him under her legs. Her left arm was useless, hanging there limply as she drove her knee into his forearm.

"You spoke of sacrifice. Do you want to know what I sacrificed?" Her voice was low as she fought back tears. She drove the knife into one of his blood-red eyes. He grunted and gasped, thrashing beneath her. "I'll tell you about sacrifice. It started with a girl, desperate to make sure her mother and sister were taken care of. I sacrificed my freedom so they would live in luxury." She withdrew the knife, and his eyeball came with it. With a flick, she sent it flying. It smacked into the far wall. Then she plunged the knife into his shoulder. He screamed, but it was garbled. "But I was lied to and kept in a tower."

She withdrew the knife and plunged it into his other shoulder. He writhed beneath her, grunting as he bled out. She kept talking, "Then I sacrificed my life—and my mother's—to get my sick sister out of this world and somewhere she would be safer. Because of *you.*"

He gurgled. "I could *help* you."

"I don't want your help," she snarled and twisted the knife one more time and let go. The knife trembled with each ragged breath he took.

"What do you *want*, Adeline de la Fôret?" he sputtered, blood trailing out of his mouth. "I can give you anything."

His voice grew weaker with each word, and Adeline knew he was close to the blessed end.

"I don't want *anything* from you. You're a monster who made me in your image. And I will live the rest of my life trying to forget the despicable hell you ever put me through."

Her nails grew into sharp claws, and she clacked them together.

His eyes fluttered closed. The doors behind her rattled—someone was trying to gain entry. They shook again as something heavy launched itself against the threshold.

"Look at me," she said, grabbing his chin and squeezing—mimicking the same tone he used when he would force her to watch as he pulled out her fingernails. "I want you to know what death looks like as you stare her in the eyes."

And then she pulled her arm away from his face and sank her claws into his chest. Her fingers took hold of his slow-beating heart. In one swift motion, she clamped her claws around it, twisted, and yanked her hand back through the cavity in his chest. He stared at her, aghast, as she squeezed his heart in her hand. Thick black blood trailed down her arm. And then she threw the heart against the wall in disgust.

"I will never kill again!" she screamed over and over again, as she hacked away at Erik's neck with the knife.

The doors behind her slammed open.

Chapter 51

Rolf

Rolf shifted back into his human form seconds after he entered the room and assessed the threat level. Now, he watched Adeline finish decapitating her maker with the small blade he had given her. She was pure fire and vengeance as she roared at the limp carcass beneath her.

Fury personified.

The head had long been severed, but judging from the amount of damage her maker had incurred, she had been taking jabs at him for a while. He knew at this moment that he would never be more proud of her than he was right now. He crossed his arms, staring down at his ferocious beauty with such awe that he forgot his leg was injured and he was standing in the room naked.

The scent of smoke filled his nose, and as much as he wanted her to beat Erik's body into a bloody pulp, they needed to get the hell out of this place before it went up in flames.

"He's gone, my darkness," Rolf said, staying a healthy distance away.

As if she had been in a trance, she finally came to a stop. Her shoulders dropped and that's when he saw her left arm hanging limply at her side, the muscle torn clean from the bone.

"My Darkness, please let me help." He trembled with anger. His hands wrapped around hers. One by one, he pried her fingers from the knife. He set it down in the pool of blood that swirled around her knees, then he grabbed her face in his hands and turned her to him. Her eyes were hard, unfeeling, and he wiped some blood off her face as he said, "He's gone, my darkness."

She shook her head and then eyed him up and down. Her right hand held her injured arm and she struggled to stand. He supported her as he pulled her away from the mess beneath her.

"Why are you naked?" she asked, heaving with breath.

"I shifted," he said, stretching his neck out near her mouth. "You need to heal."

"I'll be fine. It's already healing," she said dismissively, but then she slipped in some blood and almost took them both down. "Okay, maybe a taste."

She licked his neck and he didn't even feel her puncture his skin. He grew lightheaded as she drank deeply, but he would give her anything—anything she wanted—just so long as they both got out of there in one piece. Finally, she pulled away and licked the punctures.

"Better?" he rasped.

"Yes," she said and dropped her shoulders. He watched her look around the room, her blue eyes hard and calculating. They landed on the mangled, bloody pulp of her maker. A smile spread across her face and she laughed.

"I did it," she said between manic chuckles. Tears spilled from her eyes and her whole body relaxed into his. "I really did it."

"Yes, my darkness, you did," Rolf said, eyeing her bloody arm. He looked around the room and found her discarded dress. It was soaked in blood and soiled from the dirty floor, but he grabbed her knife from the pool of blood and tore off several strips of fabric from the skirt.

"We need to support your arm until it heals," he said, holding up the strips of cloth. Adeline nodded, still staring blissfully at the mangled corpse behind him. He fashioned a makeshift sling out of some tulle, tying it off behind her neck. He tucked a stray hair behind her ear as he finished and gingerly kissed her temple. She sucked in a breath and finally tore her eyes from Erik's body, meeting Rolf's gaze with an intensity he had never seen in her gaze before.

"I'm free," she said.

He nodded.

"He's gone." Her voice was a whisper this time.

"You killed him," Rolf added, reverently. Would she ever know the depths of his love and admiration for her? Probably not, because even he did not know. It felt fathomless, eternal. All-consuming. And he had almost, very nearly, lost her. He took her in once more—her bloodied face, her fangs, her ocean-blue eyes, the tendrils of hair that clung to her forehead. She was his and he was hers. For eternity.

He shook his head, unbelieving that this glorious creature was his mate.

Fire! his wolf snarled. *Did you forget?*

Right. Rolf inhaled; the scent of smoke was thicker now. He had already pushed their limits too far. He opened his mouth to tell her it was time to leave when she reached up and cupped his cheek.

"You came back for me," Adeline said, stroking his lip with her thumb.

"Of course I did. But I knew you had it handled."

Adeline quirked a smile. "You knew I had it handled?"

"I knew nothing was going to stop you. You are fierce and determined, compassionate and brave. And once you set your heart to something, there is nothing that can stop you. I wish I had half as much grit as you. You inspire me, my darkness. In so many ways. So yes, I knew you had it handled. I just wish I had gotten here earlier to see you land the killing blow."

Adeline beamed up at him this time, snuggling into his side and nuzzling her nose against his ribs. "My mate."

She turned to lead the way but took one step forward and winced. He caught her as she swayed. Was it her leg? Her foot? He looked her up and down frantically, unable to see if she had more injuries from all of the blood that covered her.

"Do you need more blood?" he asked, his heart rate ratcheting up.

Was she bleeding out? Dying?

"No, it is only my feet." Her voice was calm and measured, but that did nothing to ease his worries. "I am well enough to walk out of here."

The sound of crackling flames licking the farthest corners of the room they were in reached their ears, and smoke crept its way into his lungs. If they didn't leave soon, the walls would crumble around them, and then they would be joining Campbell in the sea.

"Then, my mate, let's get the hell out of here."

Rolf half dragged, half carried her out the doors and down the hall. He limped, his injured leg unable to take his full weight, and Adeline stumbled. The air filled with smoke, and for a damp, mold-infested castle-by-the-sea, it was catching fire quite quickly. His energy was fading fast and his leg throbbed each time he took a step. Adeline hobbled next to him, her left arm cradled in her right. His wolf, exhausted and quiet, was no help, and several times he growled out of frustration.

"Where are you going, you idiot?" Juliette yelled from behind them.

Rolf froze in place and half turned. Juliette's silhouette loomed through the smoke but then in a flash, she was on the other side of Adeline, grabbing her around the waist. Rolf hesitated to let her help, but Juliette snapped, "Get over yourself, I'm *quite obviously* helping."

"Fine, but you have a lot to answer for once we're out of here," he growled, relenting his hold. Juliette's arm wrapped around Adeline's back and linked with his.

"Yes, fine, whatever you want. Hurry up, I don't want to burn to death," Juliette said.

"That's one of us," Rolf retorted, not wanting to let Juliette anywhere near Adeline.

Even though she *had* dismembered those vampires and she had urged him to go save Adeline, he felt a pang of guilt over all of the fae still trapped below. How was he going to get the fae out of there if the whole castle was going up in flames? He looked over his shoulder, unable to see the room they had exited for the flames and smoke that smothered his vision. The guilt was going to swallow him whole.

"After you," Juliette said, pinching his arm.

"Ladies first," Rolf snarled before he could stop himself.

"Have we finally stopped posturing?" Adeline asked drily. "Great, then let's get the hell out of here."

With a grunt, Rolf hoisted Adeline up under her good arm and all three of them made their way down the final hallway. Soot covered them from head to toe, and the heat from the fire pressed against their backs. Wood crackled, and each time the embers popped in the damp wood, Juliette jumped. His leg was slow to heal, and the lack of fresh air clogged his lungs. By the time they got to the front gates, he was wheezing and coughing, taking in deep lungfuls of the sea breeze.

Adeline slipped out of his grasp, standing strong on her healed feet. She patted his back as he struggled to clear his lungs.

"You're still naked," she whispered. Adeline pulled away, and he glanced down at her.

He shivered involuntarily and stared into her soot-black face. "Ah, so I am."

Adeline laughed and shuffled toward the trees. The fire roared to life behind them and the castle was soon lost to the flames. Plumes of black smoke rose into the night, blotting out the stars in the sky. A solitary falcon soared above, screeching once and then flying off into the trees beyond.

Rolf's shoulders dropped at the thought of all the fae still locked in their cells below. Perhaps they would be okay in the stone foundation? No. That was wishful, delusional thinking, at best. He hung his head and followed his mate, dragging his injured leg behind him. Adeline stopped short and he almost bumped into her.

"Wha—" he began, but then he followed her gaze to the edge of the woods. He stopped in his tracks, too, and his jaw dropped.

There stood Arlo, leaning against the trunk of a large oak tree, clutching a tiny gnome to his chest.

"Arlo?" Rolf's voice cracked. He fell to his knees before the ancient fae. "Is it you?"

"Wolf?" Arlo asked, his eyes not as cloudy as before.

"I am so glad you made it out safely," he said, choking up.

"I am, too, pup. I am, too." Arlo patted his head, the gnome silently watching the entire exchange.

Then Rolf finally saw that the forest was full of fae, some of them malnourished, all of them free of their glamour and huddling together in the shadows. "Are... are they all here?"

"There used to be so much more," Adeline said, her voice trembling.

"I got out all of the ones I could," Juliette whispered. "Some were too far gone to help, so I had to—"

Rolf had no words. He stared at Juliette as she bent over and scooped up a tiny winged fae. It took him a few moments, but then he finally found his voice and asked, "You did this? You got them out?"

Juliette shrugged, tears lining her eyes. "I had to."

"How?" Rolf counted at least thirty fae altogether that he could see. His eyes filled with tears. "I had hoped to go back for them."

"I couldn't leave them in the castle to burn, not after what Erik did to them." Juliette's voice wavered.

So she, too, knew what had occurred in the depths of that castle.

"What did Erik do to them?" Adeline asked. Juliette opened her mouth to respond but Adeline stopped her, holding up her hand. "No, don't tell me. I don't want to know, and certainly they don't need to relive anything."

Rolf met Juliette's eyes over the top of Adeline's head. He gave her a sullen nod and took a deep breath. "Well," Rolf said. "It seems we have quite a few fae who now need a home."

Adeline turned to Rolf, her eyes wide. "Can we take them home? Do we have a home left?"

"We do, barely. But I think we can make room," Rolf replied, leaning down to press a kiss to her soot-stained forehead.

"The cabin will need to be expanded, and the tunnels will need to be cleaned out, and then, if you have a garden, we will need to double its size. How many fae are here?" Adeline spouted off question after question.

All Rolf could do was stare.

This paradoxical creature was *his* and his alone. He wrapped his arm around her shoulders, and she stopped mid-sentence. "What?" she asked.

"I love you so much," he said, full of pride and hope for the first time in *days*. The thought sent him reeling. How had it been only a mere week since everything had happened?

Adeline gave him a strange look and smiled coyly. "I love you, too."

"No, my darkness, when I say I love you, I mean that I love you into the darkest depths of the night. And I will continue to love you until the moon stops shining and the stars all shimmer out of existence. When I say I love you, I mean that I love every broken, shattered, sharp edge of you, as well as the tenderness and the softness you carry. My heart belongs to you in every lifetime, Adeline. I wish I had never forgotten you."

"Rolf," she whispered, her eyes full of tears. "I was always going to find you. And if not in this lifetime, then in the next."

He wrapped her up in his arms, kissing her as if he were breathing his last on earth. Her hands encircled his neck, and he pulled her to him, relishing the feel of her pressed against him. She was all luscious curves to his hard angles, and he would never tire of the way she molded to him, as if they were made perfectly for each other.

"In this lifetime and the next," he promised. He would be forever grateful that she had found him—the vampire huntress stuck with the hermit in the cabin in the woods.

And so it was that the princess saved herself, got her knight in shining armor, and lived happily ever after.

Epilogue

It is a tale often told that travelers disappear should they enter the ancient woods in the Northern Mountains.

Rumors abound about a home on chicken legs that moves through the woods only on the darkest nights. Sometimes, it is a home with candied walls and a furnace that burns bright all day long. A wayward soul once claimed he came upon a gigantic castle, with spires that reached for the heavens, a ghastly beast that kept a beautiful woman as a prisoner, and plants that moved as if by magic.

But those are just fairy stories.

Or so we're told...

The bony, burnt skeletal remains of the castle still clung to the side of the cliff. It looked softer, though, covered in slick moss and sea spray. Adeline stared at the charred remains of wood and stone and smiled. It was fitting, for the place that once held the memories of cruelty and torture, that it was now returning to the wilds. It had been years since that night, and now and again, she felt compelled to make the trek down from the Northern Mountains and visit.

Had it all been a dream? Would Erik still be there waiting for her?

No.

Erik was well and truly gone. Thank the gods. No matter how many times her brain tried to trick her into thinking that she was still under his glamour, her visits here confirmed what she had overcome.

Her life with Rolf was one of ease and peace. She had her mate, they had their home in the mountains full of fae, and she was learning the gift of her magic. It took Rolf and Adeline some time to build out the cabin and clean the tunnels from the fire she set, but with the help of Arlo and some woodland fae, their home was now a multi-story home covered in magical fae flora that blended into the ancient forest around them. She used her knowledge of wards from her mother and wove her shadow magic into her spells to create an illusion that would keep them safe forever.

Their house had become a haven for all wayward fae creatures, and she was determined to keep it that way.

And now, as she stood looking at the castle ruins, she let herself feel awash with gratitude.

"Thank you for coming with me," Adeline said, turning to Juliette.

Juliette sighed, a frown creasing her brow. "I can't say that I'm happy to be here, Addy."

Adeline tensed. Was this a mistake?

"But," Juliette continued, and Adeline's shoulder dropped with relief. Juliette gestured to the charred wood. "It helps that it's just *this.* But I still can't look at it for too long. It's too much."

With a huff, Juliette walked away, stooping now and then to pick up some wildflowers.

Adeline knew exactly what Juliette meant. Bringing her here wasn't a mistake, but it wasn't easy, either.

Visiting this place was Adeline's way of overcoming *everything.* It helped her to see that the castle no longer loomed threateningly like it did in her nightmares. It also helped her uncover the layers of lies Erik had told throughout the centuries. The castle had been infused with his glamour magic, and it had suppressed her memories of all his horrific abuses. Which was why, when she was hunting the were-shifters, she had been able to unravel the hold he had on her. She hoped that it would help Juliette, too.

Juliette walked back to where Adeline stood and slipped her hand into the crook of Adeline's elbow. She handed Adeline the small collection of wildflowers. Their eyes met, and she gave Juliette a soft smile. They hadn't quite made up yet, their friendship was still tenuous at best, but Adeline never stopped making an effort to repair the bridges she burned. The guilt lessened, year by year, but Adeline was impatient.

That was something she was trying to work on. One

would think that after being alive for hundreds of years that patience would come naturally. It didn't.

"You're tense," Rolf whispered in Adeline's ear. Rolf never let her go down here alone. Every time she felt the urge to leave their home, their bond reverberated, and he dropped whatever it was he was doing to join her.

Adeline was now sandwiched between the two creatures she held most dear. It made her heart swell.

"It's still hard," Adeline said.

Juliette hummed in agreement. "Hard, brutal."

"I think this will be my last time here," Adeline said. "For centuries, I never knew how much of a hold Erik's magic had on me or this place. I used to be able to feel it, pulsing quietly. But it's grown so faint and now I can't even detect it."

She held out her hand, soft grey shadows twirled between her fingers. Her magic used to tremble in response to the leftover energy. And though her magic was still new, after suppressing it since being turned, she knew enough that what she felt was true. She still had years left to learn how to master her particular kind of magic. But it had gotten easier after she found her mother's grimoire in the willow tree.

Adeline had sought out answers to what her magic meant after Erik told her that her mother, Aurélie, had been powerful. So, Adeline and Rolf had travelled for days, back to the villages on the plains in the south where the Old Mill, her childhood home, once stood. But, it was as she had feared, after centuries of farming and growth, disease and famine, there was nothing left. Only a few hectares of ancient trees stood where the endless woods of her youth had been. Gone was the sacred stone circle on the mound where Adeline had sent Leda away. Now it was a flat meadow nestled in the forest. The tiniest parts of the monolithic stones peeked out of the dirt in a haphazard semi-circle formation.

She had walked around and around, as if she were lost, until her feet took her down a path she had long since forgotten existed. Through the dense forest, each twig that snapped sent a shiver down her spine. She fought against the fear that Erik's ghost was lingering behind her. It wasn't until she came to a small cluster of willow trees that she realized she was in the same place where she had met *her* Angel of Death.

The large willow in the center stood just as it had when she had sought refuge under its boughs.

"Strange," Adeline had said to no one in particular.

How could the same willow be here centuries later? She walked around the trunk, images flashing before her eyes of the night she almost died.

Her skin erupted with gooseflesh when she stood in the same root formation that had cradled her broken body.

Rolf showed up moments later but stopped when he saw Adeline sitting curled up on the ground.

"My Darkness," he whispered.

Adeline couldn't look at him, the tears in her eyes blurring the world around her. "This is where it happened."

Rolf said nothing but sat down next to her and pulled

her into his side. She nestled against him, his warmth radiating into her bones. As she adjusted herself against him, her hand brushed the root. But it was no root. It was soft to the touch.

Adeline balked.

"What is it?" Rolf asked.

But Adeline didn't answer. Her hands were already digging around in the earth to uncover what she had touched.

After a few moments, she was brushing off the dirt from her mother's grimoire. It shone with wards, both protective and illusionary, but at the touch of Adeline's fingers, her mother's script appeared.

"Adeline," Rolf started. "What is this?"

She struggled to find the words.

This isn't real. It can't be.

But it was. She brushed the cover a few times, trying to get the last of the dirt off before she opened it. "It's my mother's grimoire."

"Her what?"

"Book of spells, some of her history. My family story. My life." The tears fell freely now, slipping down Adeline's cheeks.

Rolf reached up and brushed them away. "How?"

She shook her head. "I don't know. I don't know how it got here or why it's been here for so long."

Adeline looked around, a part of her hoping she'd see her mother or even her sister through the boughs of the tree. But it was merely a gentle breeze that rustled the leaves. They were both gone, and the grimoire was the only thing left of them that she had. She cradled it against her chest. Relief didn't even begin to cover what she felt at having found the book. It would take decades for her to master the spells in here, to see if her vampire magic would help or hinder the craft her mother had tried to teach her.

IT WAS JUST THE TWO OF THEM, ROLF AND ADELINE, WHO watched the clouds turn from soft grey to light blue to a blush pink as the sun rose along the horizon. Juliette had wandered off to go find Elizabeth, her mate, before the sun's rays forced her back into the carriage for the day.

He slid behind Adeline, wrapped his arms around her, and pressed her against his chest. He rested his chin on the top of her head. They stood in silence, words unnecessary, as their mating bond pulsed with feelings of peace.

The roar of the waves crashing against the cliffs lulled Adeline into a trance. It was in these moments, when she could let herself relax, let her guard down, that she could feel the vibration of the earth and the magic it held. She was right - this place held no more evil magic, and she would only be keeping that memory alive should she continue to come back here. It was best that she leave it well enough alone.

Under her feet, the earth beat with a rhythm of its own. Magic moved just under the surface, into the roots of the trees, with the water as the tide ebbed. Everything was alive, and the magic filled her up, breathing into her core.

She wondered if this thrum of vitality was something mothers felt when carrying their children. If Adeline had been able to get pregnant, she would have had no hesitation in carrying Rolf's children. She often wondered if he wanted children of his own and if he was saying he didn't just to appease her.

"Stop that," Rolf whispered. "I told you I don't need children with you to feel complete."

"How did you—?" Adeline pulled to the side and stared up at him.

He gave her a sly smile, and his hand spread out against the center of her chest.

Adeline rolled her eyes. "That damned bond. Is nothing sacred?"

Rolf barked out a laugh. "Come, my darkness. You know you have become awful at keeping secrets. Some days, it's hard to believe that you were a ruthless killer."

"And you think you're so funny," she mocked, playfully shoving him backward.

"Funny, eh? I'll show you *funny*." Rolf scooped her up and threw her over his shoulder.

Adeline squealed and beat his back with her fists. "Release me, you ogre! Gertrude, save me! Gertrude!"

"I don't know anyone by the name of Gertrude," Rolf growled.

He carried her up the hill, heading back to the carriage that would take them all home. As he crested, he tripped and sent them tumbling into the grass. They rolled to a stop at the bottom, Adeline sprawled out with Rolf beneath her.

"Gertrude?" Rolf asked between bouts of laughter.

Adeline grabbed his wrists and pinned them above his

head. She nudged his nose with hers. "You said I could call you anything."

"So I did, my darkness." Rolf's laughter quieted, and the way he stared at her now was the same look he gave her when they had walked out of the castle, covered in soot, bloody, and triumphant.

Her bond pulsed with a flood of emotions. She gasped.

"I feel all of that and more," he said. "I hope you know that my love for you is boundless, my darkness. Each day it grows more intense, more far-reaching than I ever thought possible."

"I do know." She peppered his face with kisses. "Because my love grows for you the same."

Afterword

This story was one of the hardest ones for me to write to date. Adeline became a character so close to my heart that it prevented me from pushing her. I wanted to protect her, keep her from harm. It wasn't until I realized that she could embody all of my disdain for the patriarchy and all of the shit we go through as a result of oppressive systems (from misogynists, homophobics, and just assholes in general) that I was able to push through. Once I let her embody all of my rage, I could play with her in the way that felt right for the story.

As a character, Adeline has faults. She's *supposed* to. Characters wouldn't be believable if they were perfect, especially when it comes to being blinded by their actions. Does she grow? Yes. By the end of the story, is she perfect? Far from it. Does she get her revenge? Yes. So many of us don't get the chance to kill our abusers by beating them into a bloody pulp and ripping their hearts out like they did ours. Adeline does. And that's what I love about her. I wanted her to live out the revenge I always wanted to seek out myself. Erik embodies a lot of my trauma, and I hope that his ending has healed some part of you like it has for me.

I like my characters to be realistic. I want their bodies to be hairy and wrinkly and curvy and scarred. I want them to love who they love which is why I write queer normative worlds. I want them to have biases that they can overcome. I want them to make mistakes and atone as best as they can. I want them to realize that they did bad things and do good things to make up for their faults. I want them to doubt their abilities, their thoughts, and then learn to trust their gut.

I like imperfections because if everything were perfect, it would make for quite a boring story.

This book was heavy, but Adeline's story needed to be told. For me. For all of us. Especially for those who have gone through hell and back.

May your glimmers outshine the triggers. ✨

Acknowledgements

So many people made this story what it was, and I would be remiss if I didn't take the opportunity to share my gratitude.

To my readers, first and foremost, you make this writing journey worth it. I wouldn't be writing and sharing these worlds if it weren't for you. I hope you have enjoyed this story as much as I have enjoyed (and struggled) with writing it.

To my children - I AM SO SORRY I AM SUCH A CRANKY ASSHOLE AROUND DEADLINES. I promise to be better. I love you so much. You make every moment on this earth worth fighting for. I just hope that you get to grow up in a world that prioritizes peace, equity, and justice for all creatures great and small.

To my husband, my Rolf. I love you. Thank you for believing in me. Thank you for being my ride or die. Thank you for putting up with me and all of the late-night ramblings about this story and these characters. The past ten years have been wild, and I can't wait to see what the next ten years hold for us.

To my mom, if you made it here - HAHA I got you to read a vampire story! 😈 I just hope that you had fun. It wasn't that bad, right?

To my alphas, betas, and author friends - thank you. Words cannot describe how grateful I am for your reading this mess of a story. Thank you for putting up with my awful impostor syndrome. Thank you for putting up with my frenzied messages at all hours of the day. Thank you for everything.

To my editors, Shawna and Jo, holy shit. Thank you. So much. For your kindness, your feedback, your gentleness. I am a tender little pile of mush, but both of you made this process so much easier. Please stay with me forever?

XO

OWL

Also by Ophelia Wells Langley

Published Works

The Stone Circle Series:

Of Smoke and Shadows, a prequel novella

The Borderlands Princess

The Stone Circle Queen

Novellas

The Lure of Shadows, Leda and Athena's story: a companion novella for the Gydenverse* Stories

When The Forest Enchanted The Fire, a novella featuring Adeline's mother.

Upcoming Releases

Of Feathers & Stone, a companion novella to The Stone Circle Series, forthcoming

Of Salt & Sky, a companion novella to The Stone Circle Series, forthcoming

Become a member of OWL's Patreon for Juliette and Elizabeth's upcoming bonus scene, for exclusive spicy scenes, artwork, and more!

For more information on works-in-progress, you can follow her socials and keep up with giveaways, signings, and more below:

*Gydenverse - a portal crossover with River Bennet

About Ophelia

Ophelia Wells Langley is the pen name of a mother of two boys. She loves reading, writing, and knitting, and you can almost always find her chasing after her high-energy children, pretending to be a dragon or a dinosaur.

She loves writing whimsical fantasy romance stories with spice, colorful, older characters with inclusive bodies, different ethnicities, as well as varying gender identities and sexual orientations.

Join OWL's Newsletter by signing up at her website: www.opheliawlangley.com

www.ingramcontent.com/pod-product-compliance
Ingram Content Group UK Ltd.
Pitfield, Milton Keynes, MK11 3LW, UK
UKHW012214060625
459388UK00002B/18

9 798986 297385